A SPLINTER OF RED GLASS . . .

He picked it up carefully, painfully between thumb and index finger. Lifted it up a foot or so. And then, with alarming suddenness, he plunged it into his left wrist.

"Good God!"

"Mr. Tiffany!"

We were both on our feet. Rushed to his side. It took a moment for it to register that he was smiling. Was in no discernible pain. We stopped in our tracks. The glass was thrust through his wrist; it protruded from the other side. But there was no blood. He was in no pain. Slowly, carefully he extracted it. Handed it to me to examine.

There was no blood on it, not a drop.

"Michael Paine is a startlingly good writer. Read him!"
—Charles L. Grant

Charter Books by Michael Paine

CITIES OF THE DEAD
OWL LIGHT
THE COLORS OF HELL

THE COLORS OF HELL

MICHAEL PAINE

CHARTER BOOKS, NEW YORK

THE COLORS OF HELL

A Charter Book / published by arrangement with
the author

PRINTING HISTORY
Charter edition / May 1990

ISBN: 1-55773-349-X

Charter Books are published by The Berkley Publishing Group,
200 Madison Avenue, New York, New York 10016.
The name "CHARTER" and the "C" logo
are trademarks belonging to Charter Communications, Inc.

PRINTED IN THE UNITED STATES OF AMERICA

10 9 8 7 6 5 4 3 2 1

for
Bill Roadman

PART ONE

In the Anti-Atlas
1958

Cerberus, devourer of flesh, the
brass-throated guardian of Hell,
a strong, relentless beast with
fifty heads.

           –Hesiod, *Theogony*

1

The hotel faced west, across the European quarter of Marrakesh. The sun hung low, just above the reach of desert sand; in half an hour it would be gone. The sky was a golden orange, and so was the sand. The hotel's whitewashed facade took on the glow, the color. Across the city, in the soaring tower of the Mosque of the Scribes, the muezzin began his chant, calling the faithful to evening prayer. One by one the callers from the other mosques joined him, made a counterpoint song for the sunset.

There was a breeze off the desert. It swept gently into Robert Semnarek's room, woke him from his siesta. He rubbed his eyes, sat up on the bed. Stared, blinking, into the bloodred face of the sun, which shone dully through the French doors that led to his balcony. Listened to the last falling notes of the Moslems' toccata. Looked at his watch. He had slept far longer than he'd wanted to.

"Front desk." The French-style telephone felt odd in his hand, not balanced properly. "This is Mr. Semnarek in Room 211. Is Mrs. Alderson in her room?" The breeze kicked up, gusted, died. Suddenly the room was hot. "I see. What about *Mr.* Alderson? Oh. Thank you."

There was a knock at the door. "Yes?"

From the other side of the door a boy's voice said, "A message for you, monsieur."

"Just a moment." He climbed quickly into his shorts, his trousers; pulled a polo shirt over his head.

The boy held the note on a salver that had been gilded once but was peeling, faded. He was dressed in threadbare livery; brass buttons turned green, frayed braid; when it was new it had been very ornate. His black Moroccan face wore a huge, ingratiating smile. It got him his tip.

3

Robert [read the note],

   We're in the what-do-they-call-it, the large marketplace. A snake charmer is following us around and trying, for some strange reason, to sell his cobras to Mother. Maybe he thinks she looks like them. At any rate, she's hysterical. Come and join us, and enjoy the show.

Steve

He crumpled the note up, put it in his pocket. Strolled out onto the balcony. The sun was enormous. Its lower rim just grazed the horizon. It sat there like a balloon; then, with astonishing speed, it sank below the world's edge. Robert stared at the spot where it had been. There was a ghost of it in his eyes, hovering ethereally above the now bloodred sand.

The city was lighting up for the night. In the Moslem quarter, lanterns hung in the minarets of the mosques, strings of electric lights lit up the booths in the marketplace, lamps shone in the windows of red stone buildings. In the European city, where the hotel sat, whitewashed buildings were bathed in dazzling light. Without warning a bank of floodlights came on, washed the facade of the hotel with blinding illumination. Robert covered his eyes and rushed inside. Switched on a low reading lamp and waited for his eyes to adjust, for the pain to go away. Then he finished dressing, socks, loafers, a tweed sports jacket. He had missed dinner.

The lobby was scattered with people, mostly Europeans from the look of them, and most of them in evening clothes. A palm court orchestra played Strauss waltzes. The decor was Art Nouveau; it must have been elegant in its day, but it had gone badly to seed. Above the main entrance and above the entrance to the hotel's restaurant were matching semicircular windows of stained glass, fifteen feet or so wide, in elaborate Victorian designs, all curves and fleurets. Robert scanned the crowd for a familiar face, but there was no one. He went straight to the restaurant.

"Good evening, Monsieur Semnarek."

"Good evening, Ahmed."

The maître d', like most of his clientele, was dressed formally. He glanced at Robert's casual clothes, registered for a discreet moment his disapproval, then resumed his professional manners. "A table for three, monsieur?"

"No. I'll be dining alone this evening. The Aldersons are off exploring."

"Yes, monsieur." Ahmed let him to a table, seated him. "Is there a likelihood that young Mr. Alderson will discover something?"

"I doubt it very much, Ahmed. He never has." He took the menu, scanned it.

"I see. How wise of him. Ibrahim will be with you directly."

Out in the lobby the orchestra switched to a sanitized sort of Cole Porter. When the waiter came Robert ordered fish and wine, then settled back to watch the other diners. Tourists, mostly European, a few American; no one who was immediately identifiable as a Moslem. The Americans, predictably, had gathered together in one corner of the restaurant. They watched Robert pointedly, said things about him. He smiled at them, nodded his head in their direction, but when they waved to him an invitation to join them he pretended not to see; studied the tablecloth.

Not long after his salad came, Charlotte Alderson appeared at the restaurant's entrance. She was dressed in safari clothes, complete with pith helmet. Breezed past the protesting Ahmed to Robert's table, pulled out a chair and seated herself. Rested her helmet on the table's edge. Her grey hair was pulled straight back, tied in a ponytail; she wore no makeup. Put on a huge smile. "Hello, Robert. I—"

"Madame Alderson!" Ahmed had followed her; was flustered by her entrance. The Americans across the room stared at the three of them. "Please, madame! There is such a thing as propriety!"

Her smile turned to a scowl. She stared at him icily. "Have someone bring me some tea. Mint tea."

"Madame, I—"

"Did you hear me?"

He withered. "Yes, madame." Departed.

"I wish I could do that the way you do." Robert grinned at her.

"Robert, I just wish you'd gone out with us." Her smile was back. "You missed the most marvelous entertainment."

"At the moment"—he gestured casually at their staring countrymen—"we are the entertainment."

"Oh." She did not look; kept her eyes on Robert, on the last of his salad.

"Have you had your dinner?"

"Yes. From stands in the marketplace. Delicious things." A waiter appeared with her tea; she poured it, stirred it. "Are they still watching us?"

"Like vultures."

She laughed. "Did you know that Mark Twain once suggested that the vulture should replace the eagle as America's national bird?"

Robert finished his salad, put the plate aside; sipped his wine. "Mm, this is good. Will you have a glass?"

"Thanks, no. Anyway, three of them"—she indicated the watching Americans with a nod of her head—"set upon us in the lobby this afternoon. Two of them were traveling salesmen and one called himself a self-exiled writer, whatever that means. They're aching to find out what we're doing here. We're the sensation of the local gossips."

"I've always known I'd make a sensation before I die."

"Do you still think it important that we not tell anyone why we're here?"

"Are you serious? Take a look around us. Just look at them. They look like the extras in an old Humphrey Bogart movie. If they found out we're here after nine million dollars, they'd be on us like . . . like . . ."

"Vultures?" She was wry.

The waiter came with Robert's main course. "And will Madame be dining this evening?" The question was directed at Robert.

But Charlotte answered it. "Madame requires nothing, thank you, Ibrahim."

Ibrahim, duly affronted at the boldness of this Western woman, withdrew.

"Have you heard the news from home, by the way?"

Robert cut into his fish. "No. I only woke up half an hour ago."

"What shocking sloth. President Eisenhower is ill. His heart. So Richard Nixon is, at least nominally, running the country, and he seems likely to succeed sometime soon. It was all the salesmen could talk about, in between their prying questions. As if it made any difference who the president is."

"It does." Robert sipped his wine. "When was the last time"—he made a sour face—"we had a president who wasn't a millionaire? Or who didn't become one? These deals Nixon keeps getting caught in . . ."

"You surprise me, Robert. I've never heard a lawyer sneer at money before."

He sat back in his chair. "I believe you were saying something about entertainment."

"Yes. In the marketplace. The Djemaâ-el-Fna." She said it slowly, let the long vowels roll.

"You seem to savor that name the way I savor my wine."

"I do." Charlotte put on a wicked grin. "Steve can't seem to pronounce it, so I say it every chance I get, to annoy him."

"A mother's love."

She ignored this. "The Djemaâ-el-Fna"—she lingered over its sounds even longer this time—"is a marvel. There are jugglers, acrobats, all the usual sort of marketplace performers. But this one has magicians, too. Wonder workers."

"The best magician I've ever seen is Orson Welles."

"These are better. And it's not just Indian rope tricks and that sort of cliché. These are real wonders."

He leaned forward, rested his elbows on the table. "North Africa is changing you, Charlotte. They say it changes everyone, but I thought you'd be invulnerable to it."

"I know what I saw."

Robert's eyes twinkled. "And were there any snake charmers?"

She turned suspicious; her eyes narrowed. "Why do you ask?"

He pulled the crumpled note from his pocket, handed it to her.

Uncertainly she smoothed the wrinkles out of it; read. Looked at Robert with a displeased smirk on her face. "My son the quarterback."

"Halfback."

"Whatever. He was more frightened of the snakes than I was." She drank some mint tea. "You and he are the same age. How can you have turned out so well, when he never grew past the mental age of a freshman?"

"You flatter me. I didn't know you thought I'd turned out so well."

She took a long drink of her tea. "I'm going back out to the," she let the words ripple, "Djemaâ-el-Fna. I want you to come with me. I want you to see the magic."

"You're turning romantic in your old age."

"I could fire you, Robert, and hire a Moroccan lawyer."

"When I've turned out so well?" They both laughed. "Come on. I'll settle my bill. Then I want to stop upstairs and get my wallet and things. Are we bringing Steve?"

"We most certainly are not."

The great marketplace, the Djemaâ-el-Fna as Charlotte kept repeating, was full of people. Torches blazed, lanterns burned brightly; strings of Christmas tree lights adorned booths. People strolled, haggled, drove hard bargains, purchased things. Robert and Charlotte walked for hours, took it all in; bought leather and silver for themselves. Every here and there a performer drew his crowd. A young boy, hardly more than fourteen, juggled an impossible number of balls in the air. Acrobats made living towers. Fakirs worked their age-old tricks, pushed skewers through their hands, flirted dangerously with asps and cobras, did impossible things with fire; one of them, to Charlotte's horror, poured boiling water into his eyes.

She turned her head, looked away.

"Are you all right?" Robert could not take his eyes off the wonder worker.

"Yes. What he did just caught me off guard, that's all."

"You wanted to see the magic, remember?"

"Yes. But not that. It's horrible."

"Well, he's finished now. You can look."

The fakir stood there, his face glistening with moisture, smiling a huge smile at Charlotte, staring directly into her face. He extended his hand for baksheesh. Unsteadily, uncertainly, Charlotte handed him a ten-franc note. Then they walked on.

"I suppose there's always the danger, when you go out after magic, that you'll find more than you wanted." Robert was amused.

"Fortunately"—Charlotte made her voice cold—"we are not in Morocco after magic, but after cold hard cash. And enough of it to make this worthwhile." She gestured at the press of people, at the fire everywhere. "I don't know, maybe it's just because it's dark now, but this pace, the Djemaâ-el-Fna, seems alien to me. Disturbing."

"We're in Africa, Charlotte. Did you expect it to be like Johnstown?"

"No, but . . ." She wrapped her arms around herself.

"Are you cold? Would you like my jacket?"

"Thanks, no. It's just that, I don't know, the strangeness of the country didn't hit me until just now. Tangier was . . . well, Mediterranean. There were Moslems all over the place, but it was still familiar somehow. And Casablanca was downright European. All those broad avenues radiating off the Place de France. But now . . . I mean, take a look around. Look at the grotesque things these people live with."

"What do you think they'd make of the War Memorial on a hockey night?"

"I'm serious, Robert. I mean, if it's like this here in Marrakesh, what are we going to find when we get out into the mountains?"

"Nothing more grotesque than the Johnstown Jets, that's for sure."

"There's no sense needling me. Steve did it all afternoon, and I'm all needled out. If simple conversation is beyond you tonight . . ."

"I'm not needling you. I'm just trying to put a bit of perspective on it all."

"Come on. Let's get back to the hotel."

They pushed into the crowd. Walked silently among the noises of the market.

"Charlotte, I think we're going the wrong way."

She stopped, looked around; was startled. "Are we?"

"The desk clerk did warn us against adventuring in the city without guides."

"Don't moralize. All the streets look alike."

"I know it."

They stood back to back, scanning the cityscape for familiar landmarks. Found none. Robert sighed deeply; lost all his energy. "In the movies, whenever American tourists are lost, a small native boy shows up and offers to guide them for an outrageous fee."

"Just our luck we're not in the movies. Let's try this way."

He looked doubtfully up the alley. "Why?"

"Why not?"

They walked. More booths, more people, more performers, more noise. They made conversation to cover the tension. "All the buildings are made of this red stone." She rubbed her fingers lightly across the front of a small house, felt its roughness. "Do you have any idea what it is? Steve kept insisting it was granite all afternoon."

Robert laughed. "It's what they call *tabiya* and it's not stone. It's a kind of rammed concrete made out of the local red earth. I remember you commenting on the train down here how red the desert is."

"Concrete."

"It's not very strong. That's why none of the buildings are more than two stories tall."

They rounded a corner. There were dervishes dancing, spinning, a dozen of them turning without cease, turning like the planets. Their robes were deep crimson, lit by blazing torchlight; the music was discordant and monotonous. Charlotte watched them for only a moment before the motion made her dizzy. She looked away. "It's terrible."

"It is prayer," said Robert softly. She could barely hear him above the music. "They spin, they turn, they gyrate, they weave a spell for themselves. They become one with the Lord, and they pray. Look at them, Charlotte."

Hesitantly she looked. "Good God, how do they do it?"

"I think you've answered your own question."

She blinked. "What do you mean?"

"Good," he said slowly and precisely, "God."

She stared doubtfully at the spellbound men. "They're Moslems."

"Exactly my point."

"Next you'll be telling me . . . Well, never mind."

"You're the one who wanted magic."

"Madame Alderson!" The high, thin voice came from nowhere. They looked around, could see no one familiar.

"Madame Alderson!"

A beggar, wrapped in rags, stepped out from among the spinning dancers. His djellabah, his turban were filthy. Under his arms he carried a covered basket. He made straight for them.

"Good God!" Charlotte started; without realizing it she took hold of Robert's arm.

"What's wrong?" He looked from the approaching beggar to Charlotte. "Do you know him?"

"It's the one from this afternoon. The snake charmer. He has his cobras in that basket." Her voice had a tense edge.

The beggar was upon them. "Mrs. Alderson. Please. You fled me this afternoon. You need my counsel, you need my snakes. Please, Mrs. Alderson."

Both of them kept their eyes on the basket, not on the man. Robert stepped between him and Charlotte. "What do you want with Mrs. Alderson?"

"I must talk with her. She is in danger."

Robert turned to Charlotte. Whispered. "This is absurd. It's like something out of an old horror movie. Next he'll be telling us we're under a curse."

The basket under the man's arm trembled; the snakes shifted inside. Charlotte forced herself to look at it. "No. Not us, Robert. Me. It's me he's addressing."

"How does he know who you are?"

"I don't know."

"Did Steve tell him?"

"No. I told you, Steve was more frightened than I was."

He turned back to the beggar. "Listen, you have no business with us. Go away, leave us alone or we'll call the police."

The beggar ignored him. "Mrs. Alderson." His voice became deeply melancholy. "Please, Mrs. Alderson. I know why you are here. Your heart and your mind are in peril."

For the first time Robert looked at the man's face. It was wrinkled, furrowed. Most of the teeth were missing. And there were no eyes in the sockets. The eyelids hung like flaps of cloth; behind them, red showed.

Charlotte moved to her right a few steps. The beggar's gaze followed her. "My snakes can help you. You need them. You . . . you are going into the mountains. You will find madness there, and death."

A cobra pushed its head out of the basket; spread wide its hood; hissed.

"My snakes. They can save you. When a snake whispers in the ear of a woman, it gives her the gift of second sight. She knows then what is coming, and she can avert it. You need that gift. Your sister is in the mountains, waiting for you. She lives there in company with death."

The crowd continued to move around them, the traffic surged, flowed. But it was silent. There was no sound in the world but the voice of the beggar, the hiss of the serpent. Charlotte's stare moved from the basket upward, slowly, to his face. The man smiled. The empty eye sockets gaped. His smile was . . . no other description was possible: it was kindly, it was benevolent. For a moment she thought to herself, against all sense, this man loves me, this man cares about me a great deal. She looked mutely at Robert, who was staring at the man's face.

The snake inched upward, coiled around the top of the basket. Raised its head to its master's cheek, licked it with its forked tongue. "You see? This is all. As gentle and simple as this. It can be like Eve and her serpent. Eve suffered. Eve got pain. But Eve *knew*. The snakes can give you that gift." The snake hissed.

She tightened her grip on Robert's arm. "Please, make him take it away."

"He's blind, Charlotte."

"I know that. I can see it."

"How did he find us? How did he knew where to come, who to speak to?"

"Robert, please, let's get away from this place." She let go his arm, took a step back.

"Charlotte, I think you have found your magic. I think maybe you should let the snake touch you."

For the first time there was real fear in her face. She looked, horrified, from the snake charmer to the lawyer. Stepped back still farther from them.

"Charlotte, I think you should do it."

"Madame Alderson, listen to your young friend," said the beggar's sad voice. "Your sister is death." He reached up and took hold of her sleeve; the two of them were linked, one to the other.

She wanted to cry, How do you know these things? Who sent you after me? But the situation was too disturbing, too . . . She looked around wildly. Fought the urge to scream out. She tried to pull away from him, but he held on. Took her wrist, lifted her hand to his face. Her fingers rested over the holes where his eyes should have been. Charlotte froze. "I can see without eyes, Mrs. Alderson. My snakes have given me the gift. Here"—he exerted mild pressure on her wrist—"push your fingers into the empty sockets. I can see without eyes. I can give you this gift, my cobras can." The snake began to slither along his arm, toward hers.

Charlotte screamed, pulled violently free of him. Pushed into the crowd. In an instant she vanished from sight.

"Good Lord." Robert watched her go; turned anxiously to the beggar. "Come to our hotel later. I have to talk to with you." He reached into his pocket, pulled out a fistful of franc notes, pushed them into the beggar's hand. Then he followed Charlotte into the throng.

Half a block later he caught up with her. She was at an intersection, had found a policeman, was asking for directions. "Charlotte, thank God I found you."

She glared at him. "Stay away from me." Pushed into the crowd again, with Robert, lamely, following.

In the lobby when she stopped to get her key, he tried again. "Please, Charlotte. Be reasonable. There was something about that man. He didn't have eyes, but he could see us. See you. How can you not want to know about that?"

"Get away from me. Leave me alone." She stepped into the elevator and the doors closed.

Robert looked around; the lobby was nearly empty. The orchestra had finished for the night. The lights were turned down, and there was a soft gloom in the corners. He found his way to the bar, bought a large double gin, settled down on a plush sofa to see if the snake charmer would actually come. Before the drink was half finished he fell asleep; dreamed disturbing things about snakes, about blindness.

Then he woke groggily and looked around; there was no one but the old night porter. He looked at his watch. It was well after midnight. He walked across the lobby to the porter's desk. "Did anyone come here looking for me?"

"I beg your pardon, monsieur. It is after midnight." The man smiled an inscrutable Moslem smile, left Robert wondering how to take what he had said.

"There was someone I asked to come here. A . . . uh, a snake charmer." He tried not to sound embarrassed about it; failed.

"Monsieur! This is L'Hôtel Grand." The man's indignation was mixed with amusement at this eccentric American.

Robert resented it. "I asked the man to come here," he said irritably. "I had a reason."

The porter smiled sardonically.

"Was he here? A blind snake charmer. Did he come here?"

"I am certain no one like that could ever be found in the lobby of L'Hôtel Grand, monsieur."

There was no point pressing it. If the man had come at all, he was long gone. Robert cursed himself for falling asleep.

He walked to the steps, began to climb them. Hesitated; found his eye drawn to the two huge stained glass windows. There was not much light for them, but they glowed faintly; the colors had a deep, faded quality that seemed to reflect L'Hôtel Grand and its city perfectly.

"Excuse me again. I don't think I know your name."

"Hassim, monsieur."

"Hassim. Have you worked here long?"

"Since the hotel opened its doors. Thirty-seven years ago."

"It is a beautiful building."

"Yes, monsieur."

"Those stained glass windows. They're quite striking works."

Hassim smiled with obvious pleasure. "They are from the famous Tiffany Studios. We have always been quite proud of them."

"Tell me, do you remember when they were installed?"

"Oh, yes. Very clearly."

"Who did the work?"

Hassim's eyes turned suspicious. "I have just told you, monsieur. The Tiffany Studios."

"Yes, but who actually supervised the work? Do you remember?"

"Yes. I do." Hassim turned to stone.

"Oh." Robert reached into his pocket, found appropriate baksheesh, laid it casually on the desk. "Who supervised the installation, Hassim?"

He eyed the folded franc notes on the desk in front of him. Plainly wanted to count them, but that vulgar display would be beneath him. He looked suspiciously at the money, then at Robert. "There were two of them."

"A man and a woman?" He had sounded too eager. A mistake.

"I do not remember, Monsieur Semnarek."

More money on the desk. "Try and think, now, Hassim. There were two of them. What were they like?"

Gradually, encouraged by his baksheesh, Hassim remembered; told Robert the story.

"And where did they go when they were finished with the work here? Do you remember where they said they were going?"

Hassim remembered.

Robert walked the steps to the second floor, knocked softly at Charlotte's door. "Charlotte?"

She opened it a crack. Looked drawn, exhausted. Stared at him blearily. "I'm sorry about before. That man and his snakes. I was upset, it was so awful. I—"

"Charlotte, they were here."

She blinked at him. "Clare and her friend?"

"Yes. Thirty years ago. They were here. Clare and what was his name, Kampinski. This isn't a wild goose chase. They were here."

She yawned. "We'll have to talk in the morning. I took a tranquilizer. I can't concentrate."

"Charlotte, they went off into the mountains. They installed the two windows downstairs, then they disappeared into the Anti-Atlas."

"The—?"

"Where the snake charmer told you you'd be going." He stared at her.

"Look, Robert, I can't think. I'll meet you for breakfast. All right?"

Robert walked down the hall, opened the door to his room. It seemed small, confining; like a tomb. He did not want to go in. Left the door open behind him; stripped off his shirt, his trousers, walked out onto the balcony. There was a moon. He watched the ghostly red of the moonlit sands and the jagged line of mountains to the south. There was a gentle breeze. He lit a cigarette, watched the smoke ascend into the moonbeams. The city was asleep. Aside from random night noises, he was alone, undisturbed.

❦

2

Prayer. The whispered voices of nuns at prayer. They echoed, hushed, along the corridors of the convent, carried to Mother Joseph as she progressed solitary on her way. Stone door after stone door, stone hall after hall. She turned into a small room. There was an open furnace, and a bellows. She took it in her hands, pumped.

Fire. Brilliant, blinding fire lit the stone chamber. There were sparks, shafts of incandescence. Smoke, fumes vanished upward into a chimney in the stone ceiling. Out of it all came a glowing mass, orange, red, yellow, pulsing with light in long slow rhythms.

Mother Joseph, her sleeves rolled up above the elbows, her arms covered in long asbestos gloves, held the glowing mass at arm's length on the end of its blowpipe; inspected it. Held the other end of the pipe to her lips and blew gently, firmly. The mass grew, cooled, made itself into a lopsided bubble. Then she slapped it, with surprising violence, onto a square stone table; rolled it flat. It glowed a dull red-orange.

"What is it this time?" One of the other nuns, dressed, like her, in plain grey homespun, stood behind her; watched with detached amusement.

Mother Joseph turned in alarm; saw the sister standing there, leaning casually against the stone doorpost. "Peter." She relaxed, looked down at the sheet she had made. Exhaled deeply. "It's going to be red. If I got the mix right, it will be the brightest red I've ever accomplished."

Sister Peter stepped into the chamber. "You've reglazed every window in the convent a dozen times over." She reached out a hand as if to touch the sheet.

16

"Stop! You'll burn your fingers off."

Sister Peter pulled back. Looked from the sheet to her companion. "Really, Joseph, you shouldn't be playing with things as dangerous as this."

"Producing beauty for the glory of the Lord," said Mother Joseph coldly, "can hardly be called playing. And stained glass is the only art I've ever mastered. Besides, I like doing it too much to give it up." She smiled a schoolgirl smile.

"It isn't that you don't do lovely work." Sister Peter watched the sheet warily, as if she thought it might get up and attack her. "Don't get me wrong. Your designs keep getting more and more elaborate, more and more beautiful. But really, Joseph, a convent can take only so much stained glass."

"That sounds mildly blasphemous to me." She frowned.

"It's nothing of the sort. It's concern for a friend and sister. Where will the convent be if its mother abbess burns herself up?"

"The convent has continued for a long time." She shrugged. "There'd be a new abbess to replace this deranged, driven one, and you'd all be better off."

"Deranged is certainly the word." She tried to make a joke of it.

But Mother Joseph responded irritably. "Look. I feel compelled to do this. Maybe it's self-indulgent of me. Maybe it's sinful. But I believe that to make this kind of beauty is a good thing. I wish you'd leave me to it."

Sister Peter clearly found the situation exasperating. She sighed a long-suffering sigh. "It's nearly time for breakfast. Shall I walk you to the refectory?"

"I'll come in a moment."

"No, you won't. Not while you've got glass to work on. But your presence is needed there."

It was a standoff. Mother Joseph shrugged. "This won't be cool enough to work with for hours yet, anyway. Let's go."

It was nearly sunset, nearly time for vespers. Soon the nuns would gather, chant, sing the glory of the Lord. In the meantime, there was worldly music, sweet secular music on the air. Schubert, the gentle adagio from the *Octet*. The strings played rich chords, the woodwinds—clarinet, oboe, bassoon, horn—wove their melody above and around them. The music carried along the corridors of the convent, echoed, reverberated, made warm the cold stone.

Mother Joseph was in her cell, listening to the music, working. On a huge stone table in front of her rested her sheet of red glass. She took carefully in hand a glass cutter, scored a soft curve into one side of the sheet, broke it. It broke neatly, precisely along the line she had drawn with the cutter. But the cutter's steel wheel made a shrill scream as it crossed the glass; shattered for a brief moment the musicians' harmonies. She stared at the glass, then at the open door of her cell through which the music was coming; wondered which she should prefer, her work or their beauty.

The adagio came to its quiet end, and after a moment's pause they began the minuet. The lilting waltz figure, the clarinet's whispering counterpoint. She found herself humming along. Took her cutter and made another score on the glass. Her voice covered the cry of the steel.

Minutes passed; she worked, sang, worked. Then a short scream interrupted the music.

She put down her tool, walked to the door. There was no one in sight. The players resumed. She listened at the door for voices, for anything to indicate what had happened. There was nothing. The music swelled, came alive, and Mother Joseph went back to her work. In no time at all she was lost in it again.

"Joseph."

She looked up. Sister Peter was standing there. She braced herself for more needling, more banter. But the nun's face was too sober. "What's wrong?"

"It's Martin again. And this time it's very bad. I'm worried about her."

"Where is she?"

"In the chapel. She was preparing it for vespers."

Mother Joseph exhaled wearily. She set down her glass cutter. "Let's go."

The corridors were lit by fire, by torches. Thick black smoke rose from them, stained the ceiling. The two nuns rushed along them, made a long winding path that led past room after room. The refectory, with banks of stone benches, tables. Nuns' cells, each framed with a granite lintel, faced with a heavy cedar door. The chapter hall where the eight musicians, dressed like Mother

Joseph and Sister Peter in homespun, played their piece. Then finally the chapel.

It was a cavernous room. Rows and rows of stone pews, more than the nuns could ever need. A massive altar carved from basalt, adorned with gold and silver. On it rested an elaborate monstrance in platinum and rock crystal; the Host in its compartment showed brilliant white in the firelight. Rich purple velvet was draped on the walls, fell in hundreds of folds, and there were ancient tapestries showing the stations of the cross. Golden threads were woven into them, to make halos around the Savior's head.

On the floor at the foot of the altar lay Sister Martin. She was in her early thirties, dressed in grey. Her body was rigid with seizure, her limbs twitched, her mouth was white with foam. Her breath, frenzied inhaling and exhaling, hissed through clenched teeth. Sisters Joseph and Peter rushed to her side. Her eyes were rolled up into her head; only the whites showed.

Sister Peter looked at her face, then looked quickly away. "I tried to force a hymnal into her mouth. I didn't want her to swallow her tongue. But it wouldn't go in." She extended her right hand. "Look. She bit me."

There was blood, a steady trickle of it. Mother Joseph looked back the way they had come; there was a trail of drops on the floor. "Find something to bandage it with." Turned back to the nun on the floor. "How long ago did it start?"

"I don't know. A few minutes. I came straight to your cell."

"Did she say anything?"

"No. She sighed, then she fell."

Sister Martin hissed. More and more white foam came from her mouth, ran down the side of her face, stained her wimple. Her arms flailed. One of them struck the abbess on the side of the head. She touched gently Sister Martin's temple, stroked it, caressed it. Said softly, "There, there, Martin. I'm here."

Sister Martin gasped. "Mother?" Her eyes were still rolled into her head. "Mother Joseph?" She hissed; spat.

The abbess stroked her temple. "I'm here, Martin. I'm right here."

"My head is on fire. My head is filled with flame. And light."

"There, there." She caressed the girl's head.

"I am burning with the light. I see things that are beautiful and frightening." Her arms, her legs flailed.

"What can you see?"

"A great flash of light from heaven is piercing my brain. It makes my heart and my whole being glow without burning them, the way the sun warms the object it envelops with its rays. The light shows me nature's secret causes." She hissed, groaned; rolled on the cold stone of the floor.

"What can you see, Martin? What does the light show you?" She spoke softly, she whispered, she asked the spellbound woman for her secrets.

"The Lord is dancing," hissed Sister Martin, "and all his creation is dancing with him." Her limbs were hard as rock. They slapped, pounded against the floor with alarming force.

Mother Joseph tried to stop them, tried to make them be still, but the force of them was too strong. She pressed her lips to the girl's temple, kissed it. Put her arms around her, held her. But with a violent thrust, Sister Martin broke free.

"I cannot dance, O Lord, unless thou lead me [she intoned].
If thou wilt that I leap joyfully
Then must thou thyself first dance and sing!
Then will I leap for love
From love to knowledge,
From knowledge to fruition,
From fruition beyond all human sense.
There will I remain and circle evermore."

Her limbs stopped moving, her breathing eased, and she was still. She was asleep in Mother Joseph's arms. The abbess kissed her again.

Sister Peter's hand was still bleeding. The abbess looked at it. Frowned. "I told you to bandage that. Here." She laid Sister Martin gently on the floor and stood up. Ripped a strip of cloth from the bottom of her habit. Bound the bleeding wound with it.

There was a hiss. Sister Martin reentered her seizure. Her eyes were wide open, but they were blind, they were white.

"The heavenly spheres [she chanted] make music for us;
The Holy Twelve dance with us;
All things join in the dance!
You who dance not, know not what we are knowing."

Then she was still again; then she was at peace.

The two older nuns watched her. A look of tranquillity softened her features, which had been a hard mask. They lifted her gently onto one of the pews; then they knelt and prayed.

From elsewhere in the convent, down the stone corridors, came the sound of the musicians. Neither Mother Joseph nor Sister Peter had heard it, had been conscious of it. The last, agitated allegro of the Schubert *Octet*. Then there was silence. In only moments the convent would sing vespers over the sleeping form of their sister.

In the morning, after Mass, Sister Martin requested an audience with her abbess. Mother Joseph sat behind an ancient cedar desk. The windows in the room were filled with vibrant stained glass; the morning sun made colored fire with them.

"Good morning, Martin. How do you feel?"

The nun was shamefaced. "My head aches, Mother. It always does, afterward."

"Do you remember any of it this time?"

"Not very much."

"Would you like to hear what you said?"

"Peter already told me. After vespers she went to the scriptorium and copied it all down."

Mother Joseph shifted her weight uneasily. "I came here and wrote it out, too. There is beautiful poetry in you. The poetry of the Lord."

She looked away, at the windows, at their color. "Is it in me, or does it simply pass through me?"

"I can't see that it makes much difference."

"I wish it would stop. These headaches . . . I hate it when this happens."

"I can imagine."

"The last time it ached for days. A constant, throbbing pain. I . . . I . . ."

"I wish I had some way of helping you." The abbess made her voice soft, gentle. "I wish you were not . . . gifted in this way. I love you; you know how much. I wish I had it in my power to give you the gift of plainness."

There was a silence between them. Then there was music, a solo violin playing one of the Bach partitas. Mother Joseph inclined her head to one side, listened, watched the nun in front of her. "If I . . . if I could . . . Listen, the morning's getting on. You should go and tend to your chores."

"There's something else, Mother. This time, I do remember one thing that I saw."

Mother Joseph stiffened; stood up. "What is it?"

Sister Martin stood, too. Took a few steps toward her. "I . . . There are people coming here. Not the usual kind of accidental visitors. These ones are looking for something, or for someone. And they are bringing madness with them."

"Someone knows what we guard here?" Her voice became icy.

"I don't know that. I only know they are coming with a purpose."

"You're sure these are not simply new sisters for the order?"

"No, only one of them is a woman."

"I see. Go and tend to your chores."

Sister Martin left, and the abbess sank into her chair; thought; prayed. After a while she rose and walked slowly to her room. The red glass was still there, waiting to be cut to its final shape. She picked up the cutter, scored the glass's surface; but the cry of the steel was too harsh. She went to the chapel, prayed for a long time; did not realize till she was finished that she still had the glass cutter in her hand.

3

"Well, good morning at last, Mr. Semnarek. I was just on my way up to see what had happened to you."

The lobby of L'Hôtel Grand was still full of gloom despite the brilliant sunshine outside. Lamps burned dimly; a taped recording of *The Art of the Fugue*, played much too slowly, replaced the orchestra. Robert walked slowly down the steps, rubbed his eyes. Charlotte was waiting for him, dressed again in her safari outfit, clearly full of energy. Robert yawned; he wished she weren't quite such an enthusiastic morning person. "There's no sense taking that chipper tone with me. I'm as grumpy this morning as I am every morning."

"Grump away, Robert dear, but do it out in the jeep. We've got to get moving."

He looked longingly at the hotel restaurant. "Isn't there time for a good strong cup of coffee?"

Charlotte sighed; took him by the arm. "All right, come on."

They seated themselves, looked around impatiently for a waiter. There was none in sight. Charlotte walked to the station where the coffeepot bubbled, poured two large cups, took them back to the table. "Steve's out there seeing that everything's packed properly. Should I go and get him?"

Robert yawned again. "Let him work. Your son's even livelier in the morning than you are. Your whole family is unnatural. Is the guide here yet?"

"Yes. His name's Aoud. Steve can't pronounce it." She grinned. "He's beginning to suspect that the whole Moslem world is conspiring to make him look stupid."

Robert took a long sip of his coffee. "Your son is on the verge

23

of self-awareness." He put on a doubtful look. "Of a kind, at least."

Suddenly there was a waiter. He saw the coffee cups, put on a disapproving frown. "And will you be having breakfast?"

"Charlotte?" Robert deferred.

"Steve and I ate an hour and a half ago."

"Oh." He was demoralized. Looked at the waiter. "Can you just make me a quick omelet?" He looked back, sheepishly, at Charlotte. "I'll eat fast."

"Please do."

"What is Aoud like?"

"It's difficult to say. He's not very talkative. He did look over all our equipment, for what that's worth, and he seemed to think we have everything we'll need. He's been very businesslike."

"That's probably a good thing."

"I suppose so." She wasn't at all convinced of it. "But still, you'd think he'd make some slight effort to socialize with the people he'll be spending—how long?—with."

"There's a certain native reticence. I'm sure it'll pass. I wouldn't be surprised if by this afternoon he was talking to us like we're old friends of his. You did make sure he speaks Moghrebi?"

"Yes. He spoke a few lines to reassure me. But then, for all I know, it could have been Turkish."

"Charlotte." He finished his coffee; wanted more; looked around for the waiter. He was nowhere in sight. "Are you sure you want to go through with this? I mean, this is your last chance to change your mind about it."

"You sound like the voice of doom." She was amused. "I've camped in the high Rockies in Montana and in Canada. The Atlas Mountains will be nothing." She snapped her fingers. "Besides, I want the senator's money."

Robert's omelet came. He ordered more coffee. "Well, I hope you get it, if only so I can charge you a properly outrageous fee for all this."

She turned serious. "We've found four people in the last three days who remember them passing through here, heading for the mountains to the south of the city. We're on the right trail."

"Yes, thirty years ago." He was uncertain whether to go on; decided to make her morning a bit less bright. "You know, as many times as we've discussed this . . . expedition, I've only heard you talk about the money. You've never said a thing about wanting to find your sister."

She shrugged. "As you said, it's been thirty years. And we were never close." He expected her to say more but she stopped talking, drank her coffee.

"Oh."

Robert left money on the table and they walked outside. "Is the hotel bill settled?"

"Yes, dear."

Blinding sunlight. Robert had to cover his eyes, let them slowly adjust. There was a hot wind off the desert, steady, driving. It carried sand, grit. He had to protect his eyes from the blowing sand as well as the sun. But Charlotte walked right out into it as if it were nothing. Steve was there, bundling things onto the rented jeep; fastening them in place. The guide Aoud, dressed in a faded blue djellabah, watched without helping. Charlotte strode out and gave her son a playful slap on the backside. Aoud worked to conceal his shock and embarrassment.

"We're just about ready to go." Steve was tall, golden, muscular. He checked the ropes holding the folded tents. "Did you find Semnarek?" He looked around, saw Robert standing at the hotel entrance, shading his eyes. "Bob!" His tone was much too hearty for Robert's mood.

"Morning, Steve."

"You're late."

He yawned. "Yes."

Charlotte walked around the jeep, inspected her son's work, seemed pleased with it. "Come and get in, Robert darling. You can sleep more on the way."

Robert turned to Aoud. Spoke to him in French. "Are you ready to leave?"

"Yes, monsieur. The young Apollo has already loaded my things for me." They both glanced at Steve.

Who was instantly self-conscious. Turned to his mother. "What did he say about me?"

"Nothing much. He's just captivated by your beauty, that's all."

Steve looked suspiciously at the man, narrowed his eyes as if to suggest that he knew the score about all Arabs everywhere, and this one had better not try anything funny. "We should have hired that French guide in Tangier."

Robert sighed. "I've explained to you a dozen times why that wouldn't have done. The language where we're going is Moghrebi. The people in the mountains don't speak much else. We need someone like Aoud here, who can translate for us." He looked to Aoud, translated briefly what he had said, then looked back to Steve. "Besides, you must not have noticed how that Frenchman was looking at you."

Steve turned a bright shade of red. "Well, this one can ride in back, with Mother."

Charlotte watched her son blush, stepped lightly into the jeep. "You should wear a pith helmet like me, Steve. You're beginning to sunburn."

Steve glanced at Robert, daring him to laugh. Robert laughed. Told Aoud, in French, to get into the jeep beside Madame. Then Robert and Steve took their places.

The wind picked up, gusted. Sand blew, filled the air, cut down visibility; the mountains to the south vanished behind it. Steve started the jeep. "If I'd known there was going to be a sandstorm I'd have wanted to wait until tomorrow."

"I don't think this exactly qualifies as one." Robert pulled up his collar to keep the driving sand out. "This isn't much more than a minor blow."

"There's sand inside my clothes, even down my boots. I feel filthy."

"As long as we can see the road, we'll be okay. In a real sandstorm, visibility wouldn't even be that good."

The wind died a bit, and the air cleared. But the mountains were still hidden. They drove off. For a few minutes nobody said anything. Then Charlotte leaned close to Aoud and whispered, without any discernible pleasure or anticipation in her voice, "This is going to be quite a trip."

"*Oui, madame.*"

She reached over impulsively and squeezed his hand in what she hoped was a friendly way, but he pulled it away from her; watched the landscape, not his companions.

4

There was wind, there was snow. Steve drove the jeep slowly through the mountain pass. The wheels skidded, spun. He struggled to keep control. Finally the wheels found traction, and the drive went on.

Charlotte sat in the back seat, wrapped herself in a second sweater to keep warm. Shouted above the wind. "This isn't exactly what I expected."

Robert looked back over his shoulder. "An experienced mountaineer like you? Besides, this is nothing compared to a Johnstown winter."

"I just wasn't prepared, that's all. I mean, Morocco's a desert country, isn't it?"

The wheels spun again. Steve pounded the steering wheel with his fist. "Damn! This is worse than the Alleghenies in January."

"Aoud and I can push, if you like." Robert smiled; was enjoying their discomfiture. He himself had brought a heavy coat and gloves, and was feeling warm and toasty.

"No thanks. I'll get us through."

"Spoken like a real man."

Steve scowled at him, floored the gas pedal.

In the back seat, next to Charlotte, Aoud sat impassively. Like Robert, he had brought appropriate clothing; had changed his djellabah for woollen trousers, a jacket and a fur cap. Charlotte moved a bit closer to him, for warmth; he was like stone, made no response at all. She might as well not have been there.

The wheels were still spinning. Angrily Steve switched off the motor. Jumped out and kicked the side of the jeep. "Damn it!"

Charlotte watched him, amused. "My son the quarterback. If it won't do what you want it to do, hit it."

Robert got out, walked around the front of the jeep to join
Steve. "Look, why don't you let us push?"

"This shouldn't be." Steve ignored him. "Yesterday afternoon
we were in a blazing desert. This shouldn't be." He kicked the
nearest tire.

"Steve." Robert made his tone firm; Steve snapped to something like attention. "Listen. It's freezing up here. We've got to
get through these mountains. Look at your mother. She's shivering like crazy. Let us push."

Steve's blond hair was thick with snowflakes. He reached up a
hand, brushed them away. "You're right. All three of us can push,
and Mother can drive."

The wheels spun, smoked. The smell of burning rubber came to
them briefly, then vanished in the wind. The jeep bucked forward.
Charlotte looked pleased with herself. "Well, what do you know.
I'm a driver."

"Right." Robert made a sour face at her. "It was all your doing.
You'll be driving in the Indy next year."

She giggled, ignored his sarcasm. "Now step on it, Steve. I'm
freezing."

Another few hours and they were halfway down the far side of
the range. The air was warm and dry, and there was sunshine.
Steve parked in a clearing not far from the pass, and they got out
to stretch their legs. Charlotte peeled off her sweaters; was in a
breezy mood. "If you boys have any more trouble, just call on
me."

"Right." Steve stared at the jeep with a puzzled expression on
his face, as if he couldn't fathom why it had betrayed him.

"I'm going to take a little walk. My limbs still have ice and
snow in them." Robert had had enough of mother and son, needed
a break from them. He headed off into a patch of forest, small pine
trees and a few scrub poplars. In a few minutes the jeep and his
companions were out of sight. To his surprise, there was a brook
bubbling through the copse. He got down on his knees and drank.
It was wonderful; cool, clean, fresh. He drank again, deeply.
Looked around; the setting and his solitude were wonderful. There
was an inviting spot between two roots of a pine tree; he sat, rested
his back against the trunk, sighed in sylvan contentment.

Below him was another reach of the desert, dark red sand
unbroken for miles. Then, beyond it, the second mountain range,

the Anti-Atlas. Black, jagged, spiky peaks. He watched them; there were storms raging there, too. He tried to guess how far away they were, how long it would take to reach them. After a few moments he closed his eyes, nodded off.

"Monsieur Semnarek."

He opened his eyes with a start, rubbed them, looked around groggily. Aoud was standing there; he had changed back into his djellabah. "Excuse me, Monsieur Semnarek. I didn't realize you were asleep."

"No, it's all right." He grinned. "Everybody always tells me I sleep too much."

"The Aldersons are bickering about something. I'm not certain what."

"You should be glad you don't speak English."

"For me, French is alien enough. But until we expelled our former masters, one spoke French or one did not advance."

Robert yawned, stretched. "Are things really better here since the . . ." He groped for the right word; knew that the Moroccans disliked having their war of independence called a revolution.

Aoud waved a hand. "Things are terrible. The government is even more corrupt now than it was when the French were here, impossible as that sounds. The money isn't worth anything, there is crime in the streets." He put on a grin. "It is all quite wonderful."

"Why do all Moslems have such a perverse view of things?"

Aoud smiled; decided to ignore it. "You know Morocco." It was a statement, not a question.

"I know parts of it. When I was young my father brought me. He had fought here in the war and wanted to recapture his memories. We were here for nearly a year before he realized that everything had changed, or simply vanished."

"War means a great deal to Americans."

Robert yawned again, stood up, stretched. "Not necessarily."

"War's spoils, then."

"Americans are hardly unique in that."

"No." He scratched his stomach.

"I've heard that we almost got Morocco after the war, when the powers-that-were were dividing the world among themselves. But the French were a bit too anxious to give it away, and Roosevelt turned cautious."

Aoud shrugged. "What the French regarded as troublemaking, we regard as life. Or at least as a good part of it. We can't see things as simply as Westerners seem to."

"Do I detect a note of arrogance, Aoud?" Robert smiled.

"Young Master Alderson makes arrogance difficult to avoid."

He laughed. "Ten years ago, when we were in college, he was considered a hero."

"And now you are his servant." The guide was stoic.

"No." It rankled. "I am his—and his mother's—attorney."

"It comes to the same thing."

Robert found it more and more annoying. "It most certainly does not."

"There is no disgrace in serving, Monsieur Semnarek. Far from it. I will survive this journey. I and my beliefs, my worldview, my *Weltanschauung*, as the Germans call it, will survive it."

"In the short time I was here before, Aoud"—Robert made his voice hard—"I learned to see through that native trick of speaking cryptic nonsense. You do it to impress outsiders. But it's only a trick."

"I'm certain that is what Master Steven would say."

It was exasperating. Robert decided to drop it. "We should get back to the jeep. Steve wants to be down in the valley before nightfall."

"Everything I have said to you, Monsieur Semnarek, was intended as a compliment. I am sorry you haven't taken it that way." He turned; left.

"As a . . . ?" He said it to Aoud's retreating back. Robert followed him, feeling completely irritable. So Aoud viewed Robert and himself as fellow servants, as different from the Aldersons.

At the clearing, Charlotte was questioning Aoud about what they could expect when they crossed the Anti-Atlas. The guide shrugged. "More of the same."

They adjusted themselves in the jeep. This time Robert drove.

5

Sister Martin slept peacefully on the pallet in her cell. And she dreamed.

There was a man, tall, blond, muscular, handsome. He was naked and covered with sweat. His body radiated heat, radiated energy. He walked to the bed. Kissed her, held her, made love to her. When they were through, he said softly, "Don't tell anyone I was here."

"I couldn't tell them, Steven. They couldn't understand."

Then he was gone. She rolled over on her side, smiled sweetly in her sleep, knowing confidently the truth of all her dreams.

6

"Back when we were in school together—Jesus, it was more than ten years ago—we went to the movies one day. I can still remember it. It was nearly Christmas, and it was snowing like hell. Steve wanted to go skiing, but it was so bad there was no transportation. So it was the movies."

They were in the vast valley between the two mountain ranges. It was midafternoon, and the sun was overpowering. The jeep had overheated, was cooling off slowly. Steve tended anxiously to it; regarded it as his own. The others took their rest on blankets thrown over the hot sand. There was no shade anywhere.

Robert leaned back and rested his head on a rock; looked up into the desert sky. "We went to *The Bishop's Wife*, a Christmas movie with Cary Grant and Loretta Young. It wasn't something Steve wanted to see, and he griped about it all the way. And I guess it wasn't really his kind of picture at all."

He paused, looked at Charlotte, who was sitting on a backpack and listening attentively. "Yes, I think I remember seeing it myself. It was a sort of bittersweet comedy, wasn't it?"

"Yes, that's the one." His face turned pink; he looked away from her. "At the end of the movie, I cried. Not out and out blubbering, mind you, but I got a few tears in my eyes. And Steve couldn't stop laughing at me. I don't think I've ever felt worse."

Charlotte was amused; tried to hide it. "Why should you care what Steve thinks? I mean, he's not exactly a keen observer of human nature, is he?"

"You can afford to laugh at him. You're his mother."

"So can you. You're his lawyer." She stood up, dusted off her safari trousers. Smiled, walked over to him, stood looking down

32

at him. "If Steve doesn't admire you, it's because he hasn't got the brains to realize there's something admirable. I've tried for years to convince myself he got that from my husband's side."

"He's a good son to you." He sat up impatiently. "Isn't he? And he's always been a good, loyal friend. I just wish he wouldn't laugh at us all the time. Or at least, I wish he wouldn't do it with such plain contempt."

"Quarterbacks, Robert, have contempt for everyone in the world who isn't a quarterback. You have a first-rate mind." She walked off to the jeep, started rummaging through her packs for something.

Robert looked to the south, to the mountains of the Anti-Atlas. There was a bank of heavy clouds hanging over them. In one place the clouds glowed a deep red-orange, reflecting something below them. "Aoud."

"Yes, monsieur?" He was basking like Robert on the sand, some ten yards farther out from the jeep.

"Are there volcanoes in those mountains?"

"Volcanoes? No. Why would you ask that?"

"Look."

Aoud looked. The clouds were red; they pulsed with a rhythmic rising and falling of light.

"What is that? What causes it?"

"It is nothing."

"Aoud, what is it?"

He stood up, dusted off his djellabah, shaded his eyes. "I don't know. It looks like there might be a fire there."

Robert got up irritably and walked back to join the Aldersons. "Take a look out there." He pointed at the burning clouds. "It looks like Mount Sinai in *The Ten Commandments*."

"Or like Atlanta in *Gone with the Wind*." Charlotte stared, fascinated, at the glow in the sky.

Robert walked pointedly to Steve. "What do you think it is?"

"Who knows?" Steve shrugged; saw no point in wondering. "We'll see when we get there."

This distraction past, Aoud went to sleep on the sand. But the others were too awake now. Steve stared at the engine, as if he wanted to make sure it knew how impatient he was. Robert leaned on the jeep beside him, watched him. Charlotte took a walk, and Robert, impulsively, followed her.

He found himself picking up on their previous conversation. "I've remembered it for years, Charlotte. It stung me that badly. And then the next time we went to the movies it was something he wanted to see. John Wayne and Montgomery Clift in *Red River*. Now, that was his kind of movie. But it bored the hell out of me. And after it was over I saw him laughing at me again. That was it: he was tall, powerful John Wayne and I was the weak one, I was Monty Clift, I was . . ." He looked away from her. "I've always admired the hell out of Steve, and I've never known why. He's the one I've always wanted to be like."

"Is there some particular reason you're telling me this, Robert?"

"No." He looked at the desert in front of them, not at her. "I don't guess there is. It doesn't make any sense, does it? I don't even know what brought it to mind."

"Steve mesmerizes everybody. Beauty does that. Do you believe that beauty and truth are the same thing?"

He stopped walking, astonished at the question. "What do you mean?"

"Steve was three and a half before he spoke his first word." She looked back at him. For a brief instant she seemed about to smile, but then it vanished. "I didn't want to admit that I'd mothered a dim child, but it was there facing me every day. Do you know how long it took him to learn his letters? And yet even then, everyone adored him. Not for his mind, not for his personality, for his beauty. Do you have any idea what it feels like to know that people love your child for something you know you didn't give it, and that you have none of yourself?"

"I've never heard you talk like this before." He lowered his voice. "You're being too hard on yourself."

"It sounds as if you and I have doses of the same ailment, doesn't it?"

They were half a mile from the car. The sun was halfway down the western sky. From behind them they heard the sound of the jeep's engine. Charlotte looked back at it, at Steve; Robert avoided the temptation. Kept his eyes on her. "He'll be wanting us back."

"Yes." She sighed. "Women as old as me don't often get to talk alone with handsome young lawyers. And when they do, their sons nearly always break it up. Let's go."

"Look on the bright side, Charlotte."

"Hm? What do you mean?"

"Women your age are the only ones lawyers my age trust themselves with."

She took a few steps, spoke back over her shoulder. "If that's supposed to be a compliment, dear, I'm afraid I don't get it."

Aoud and Steve were already in the jeep. To Robert's surprise they were seated side by side. Steve grinned at them as they approached. "I've been teaching Aoud a bit of English. He's a quick learner. What have you been talking about?"

Charlotte waved a hand in the air, became Auntie Mame. "This vast expanse, darling, has made us expansive." She and Robert exchanged glances, smiled; climbed into the jeep's backseat. The exhaust stirred up a cloud of red sand, the wheels dug into it, and they were off. In the distance, directly ahead of them, the reddened clouds shimmered, glowed, pulsed, billowed.

After a few minutes they started chatting again. "It isn't that I really disliked *Red River*," Robert said. His tone was almost apologetic. "It's just that I . . . I . . . Well, never mind."

7

The mountains were lit with moonlight. A huge bonfire was banked at the center of the village. People came from all around, took places beside it, sat and waited. There was music, harsh and discordant to the ears of the visiting Westerners. But Aoud took it all in with a proprietary pride. This was his home village.

More musicians joined the impromptu band, and more. Shrill flutes, whining strings, throbbing drums and tambours. Food was cooked on the fire, succulent meat, rice; there were dates and figs. Aoud introduced his companions to the village elders, then vanished among his people. Steve took it in, apparently interested in everything; his mother and Robert were more aloof, more careful.

"Have you talked to Aoud?" Robert unbuttoned his shirt; the bonfire heated the air, the people, everything.

"No. I had the impression he wanted to be with his own tonight, not with us."

"He does. But he asked the elders about Clare and her friend Kampinski. Asked them if they remember the pair of them passing through here."

Charlotte had a handful of figs, inspected them. "And he got the same story we've gotten in every other village?"

"Exactly. Not only Clare. Lots of young women. An endless line of them. They pass through the Anti-Atlas, they go to the northern rim of the desert, and they never return."

The music swelled. Charlotte frowned at it. "They want their baksheesh. They'll tell us anything we want to hear. And if one woman going through here is worth something, lots of women must be worth more."

36

"You're probably right. It just seems odd to me that we keep getting that same strange story everywhere we stop." He put on a contemplative look. "But it couldn't be true. It's too . . ." There was a blare of horns, flutes. It covered his voice, saved him the trouble of finding the right word.

"It sounds like the music those dervishes danced to in Marrakesh." Charlotte made no attempt to disguise her distaste for it. Bit into a fig. "These are too sweet."

"Is it possible for figs to be too sweet?" Robert listened to the music, found himself tapping a foot to the drums' beat.

"Evidently, yes." She looked around. "What do I smell on the air?"

"Other than the fire and the food?"

"Yes. There's something bitter. Pungent."

He inhaled. Smiled. "It's *kif*."

"Am I supposed to know what that means?" She was annoyed.

"Hashish."

"Oh." She scanned the crowd again, this time with a bit of wonder in her face. "You mean drugs."

"One drug, yes. I'm surprised you haven't smelled it before. It's common here. I noticed it not long after we landed at Tangier."

She took a step back, looked him up and down. "Is there a side to you I don't know anything about? A double life? A criminal past?"

"I smoked the stuff in school. Everybody did. Didn't you know that laws don't apply to lawyers?"

"Somehow, Robert dear, I never guessed you were a closet beatnik."

"Don't be square, mama. Let's get some eats." He walked off in the direction of the fire, snapping his fingers to the music. Looked back over his shoulder. "This is cool, baby, cool."

Charlotte scowled at him, and he went and ate. She was not enjoying anything about the village, the night; wished they'd pressed on through the mountains. She took another bite of her fig, made a face at it, tossed it outside the circle of firelight.

Steve had moved to a spot just beside the fire. He was naked to the waist, glistening with perspiration. Between his lips was a clay pipe from which a steady stream of smoke escaped. Charlotte walked over to him. "You'd better not be smoking what I think you're smoking."

He was staring, rapt, into the flames. Turned to look at her, a puzzled expression on his face. "Hm?"

"You're smoking hashish."

"Oh." He looked at the pipe. "Yes, I guess I am."

"How can you?"

"Don't be a mother, Mother."

"I mean it, Steven. How can you use that stuff?"

He held out the pipe to her. "Would you care to try it and find out?"

"Steve."

"I mean it, too. It'll do you a world of good."

She turned angrily; walked away. There were dancers now. With a dismayed shock, she realized that they were dervishes. A few of them were spinning already; others were praying, chanting, smoking their *kif*. The music got louder. She spotted Aoud in the thick of the crowd, clapping his hands eagerly to the drumbeat; there was a pipe in his mouth. She felt quite painfully alone. Walked over to join him, knowing it was not what she wanted. She gestured at the spinning men. "How do they keep from getting dizzy?"

Aoud looked from the fire to her, then back again. Did not stop his clapping. "I am told, Madame Alderson, that once they enter their trances, they are blind to everything but the Lord."

"Oh." It was dismaying. "Have you ever done that yourself?"

"No, madame, I have not been called in that way. But evidently your son is more blessed."

She looked. Steve was reeling among the whirling men, spinning like them. The firelight glistened on his sweating torso, made him into bronze.

It was the music. Charlotte told herself that. The music was too much. She walked off into the darkness, kept walking, found a place where the fire was only a distant glow. There was still the sound of the drums, but the other instruments were lost in the thin mountain air. There was a boulder; she sat, felt its coolness.

The moon overhead was brilliant white, nearly full. In its face she saw the figure of a woman, in profile, kissing a death's head. The drums pounded.

There was a sound, somewhere nearby her. Faint, rustling,

whispering. She looked around. Nothing. Looked again at the moon. There was the sound, hushed but definite. She wondered if perhaps she'd inhaled some of the hashish, was feeling its effects. What, she wondered, does hashish do to one's mind, to one's senses? She felt a fool for not knowing.

It was a snake. Slithering, circling her in the near-darkness. It coiled and uncoiled, it moved around her, slowly, slowly. She saw it; froze. It was a cobra. It reared its head up two feet in the air, spread wide its hood. "I am going to die here," Charlotte told herself. She froze, did not move, held her breath.

The cobra inched closer. Reared higher. Its black eyes caught the light from the far-off bonfire, gleamed faintly in the night. It hissed at her. Moved closer still.

Charlotte was petrified. What was the correct thing to do? Should she scream, or would that alarm the snake? If she held still long enough, would it leave? If it struck, would there be pain or simply a merciful losing of consciousness, of light, of life? The snake hissed. She remembered the blind fakir in the Djemaâ-el-Fna. Was this snake here, like his there, the offer of a painful gift? She looked at its shining eyes. It was watching her, its attention was focused on her, in a deliberate way that seemed perfectly unnatural. Or preternatural. Or . . . She leaned slightly forward, to see it better. "It can be like Eve," he had told her. "You can be like Eve." The cobra's eyes gleamed, its tongue shot in and out, it hissed at her.

She glanced back at the fire, at the village, at the crowd. The cobra lunged forward. She jumped, let out a small scream, and it stopped just at her feet. Looked up at her. It was swaying, moving slightly, dancing in time to the dervishes' music. Its eyes were on fire.

"Mother!" Steve's voice came from the village.

She looked; then looked back. And the snake was gone.

In the village there was minor commotion. Steve, Robert, Aoud and a handful of others had pulled themselves away from the feast and were running about, calling her name.

"Here! I'm out here!" She did not know whether to be relieved or disappointed. She looked up at the moon once again, and its whiteness was blinding.

They ran to her. Inquired anxiously whether she was all right. Aoud took charge of the interrogation. When he was satisfied of her safety he scolded her. "Really, madame, these mountains are dangerous. There are snakes, jackals, even lions."

Charlotte tried to sound aloof. "Lions? You're joking."

But they were not joking, and after a few moments their earnestness began to wear on her. "Come on," she said irritably. "Let's get back to the feast. I think I'm beginning to understand the music."

8

The nuns were at table in the refectory. A simple meal, bread, lentil soup, red wine for their spirits. One of them stood at a lectern and read passages from Scriptures as they ate. "And it shall come to pass after this, that I will pour out my spirit upon all flesh: and your sons and your daughters shall prophesy." The nuns ate silently, no prayers, no conversation. At the head table sat Mother Joseph and her functionaries. She watched her convent, watched them dine, listened to the invocation upon which, it was to be hoped, they were meditating.

There was a scream. Sister Martin stood with violent suddenness, threw her arms into the air, shrieked as if she were in horrible pain. Fell to the floor kicking, writhing. There was foam at her mouth, and this time it was mixed with blood. Her rigid limbs slapped the floor, struck the nuns on either side of her.

"Quickly!" Mother Joseph was on her feet. "Get something into her mouth. She's chewing her tongue!"

The nun beside Sister Martin pushed a spoon into her mouth. There was a grinding sound. She bit off the handle from the spoon and spit out the bowl. And she spoke:

"I saw the likeness of a woman having a complete human form within her womb.
And behold, by a secret disposition of the Most High Craftsman, a fiery sphere possessed the heart of that form,
and touched the brain and transfused itself through all the members."

The blood, the foam spread down across her face and chin, stained her habit. Mother Joseph watched, took a step toward her;

41

but it was too terrible. The abbess turned and rushed from the refectory. She swept through the convent halls to the stone chamber where she made her glass. The furnace was lit, burning. She pumped furiously the bellows, and the fire roared. It leapt out of the furnace, licked the chamber's ceiling. She pumped. There was smoke, thick black smoke; it made her cough, and it stung her eyes, but she pumped the fire, fed the fire the air it needed. The smoke, the flames were swept up through a chimney in the roof. Their roar was deafening.

"Joseph! For God's sake! Have you gone mad?" Sister Peter had followed her; she stood watching with horror in the doorway.

Mother Joseph fed the fire, threw coal into the furnace, pumped.

"Joseph! Stop it!"

The fire licked Mother Joseph's habit, and it started to smolder. Sister Peter rushed into the room, took hold of her shoulders and shook. "Joseph! For the love of God, stop this."

The abbess looked at her. "Let go of me. I have to make glass. I have to make beautiful glass for the Lord!" She struggled, pulled free of Sister Peter's grasp. "Color and light for the Lord." She took hold again of the bellows, pumped it furiously.

Then there was another nun. "Sister John, thank God you're here. Help me get her out of here."

The two of them caught their mother's arms, pulled her firmly, gently away from the flames. Led her to her cell and put her on the bed. She looked helplessly from one of them to the other. "Let me go back. I have a thing to do for the Lord."

"It will wait."

"No. My time is short. You heard what Martin said in her trance. I have my work to do."

"What Martin said had nothing to do with you."

"It did. The Lord made me her mother. And I made her what she is."

Sister Peter turned to her companion. "Go and get some wine. It will help her relax."

Sister John went. In the refectory everything, everyone had quieted down again. Sister Martin was asleep on the floor. A nun tended her; her other sisters had eaten and gone on to their prayers. Sister John took a bottle of claret and walked quickly, quietly back to the abbess's cell. In a short while Mother Joseph, like her prophetic daughter, was deep asleep.

The air was filled with smoke from the furnace. Sister Peter went back to the stone chamber to make certain there was no danger. The fire still burned bright and high; leapt out of the kiln and up its outer wall to the roof. There must have been a wind outside, because the flames rose energetically up the chimney.

And above, on the mountaintop, where the chimney vented, the fire danced with the driving wind.

9

Steve drove the jeep slowly, steadily. To their right the desert, the red of it, seemed to stretch on forever. The enormous ocean of sand was broken only here and there by scrub grass, by stone. Wind kicked up now and then, blew sand into the air, subsided. To their left were the mountains, the Anti-Atlas, black, jagged, more forbidding than the expanse of sand. Occasionally, small rocks would roll down off the hills, come to rest in the desert. That was the only movement; there was nothing else.

"There's something I don't understand." Steve drummed his fingers impatiently on the steering wheel.

"Yes?" Robert slumped in the front passenger seat, let the sun tan his face.

"Why aren't there any cactus plants?"

"Hm?"

"This is the desert. Why aren't there any cactus plants here?"

Robert sat up, took a quick glance across the landscape. "Cacti are native to the Americas."

"I thought they just . . . grew in deserts."

"Only in the American desert. Finding one here would be like . . . like finding a tiger in the Alleghenies."

"How can one mountain range be against another?"

"I beg your pardon?" Steve had completely baffled him.

"These are the Anti-Atlas Mountains, right? Well, that means they must be against the Atlas Mountains. It doesn't make sense."

"Oh." Robert looked around again. In the distance ahead of them the mountains looked even more bleak and desolate. They're black as sin, he told himself, black as death. "In Latin *anti* can mean either against or facing. This time it means facing. This range runs parallel to the Atlas. It faces it. You see?"

"I never heard that before. I thought it just meant against."

Robert turned, looked to the backseat. Both Charlotte and Aoud were sleeping soundly. Charlotte's pith helmet had slipped off and she was showing signs of sunburn. He reached back and shook her knee. "Wake up. You're burning."

"Hm?" She was groggy.

The disturbance woke Aoud. Unlike Charlotte he was instantly alert. Looked around to get his bearings. "What time is it?"

"After three."

"We should be there in another few hours."

Robert shifted his weight, looked directly at the guide. "You're sure we're headed the right way?"

"The elders said we should turn east when we left the mountains. There was nothing to the west but the desert."

"So far, that's all there's been in this direction."

"Relax, Robert dear." Charlotte was awake now. "There isn't much point to hiring a guide if you're not going to let him guide you."

They drove on. Steve kept their speed steady, kept his eyes straight in front of them, as if there were a road to watch. After a few minutes of the monotony, his three passengers were all asleep. The afternoon sun moved behind them; it cast a shadow in front of the jeep. As the time passed it got longer, narrower. Steve drove into the shadow. After a while he saw once again the red glow capping a distant mountain, watched it pulse, change, fade. He accelerated. "That's where we're going, isn't it?"

But everyone else was sleeping.

And then they were there. A broad valley, three miles wide, opened out of the mountains. It was filled with grass. There were sheep and goats grazing. And there was a village. People swathed in the black robes of desert dwellers; naked children. In the distance, at the head of the valley, a stream cascaded out of the black hills, out of the living rock. There were olive trees, and what looked to be citrus orchards. The valley walls were vertiginous cliffs. For a few moments Steve kept driving, till he reached the center of the valley's mouth. Then, abruptly, he stopped. "We're here."

It was the stop, not his words that stirred them. They wakened, each at his own pace. Saw the lush greenness spreading out to their left, reaching into the distance, into the mountains. The jagged peaks lining the distant horizon made it all the more striking.

Steve stepped out of the jeep. Looked up the valley at the water flowing out of the mountain stone. "And Moses struck the rock with his staff," he recited, "and the water flowed forth in abundance."

"Don't be absurd, darling." Charlotte turned to Aoud. "Are these people Bedouins?"

"Yes, madame." He took in the prospect; shaded his eyes to see better.

"You can talk to them, then? In Moghrebi?"

"Yes, of course."

"Good. Where are my binoculars?" She walked to the rear of the jeep, began to rummage through her bags.

Robert was still in the back seat. He watched his companions, not the landscape. Steve walked back and stood beside him. "It's beautiful. It's the most beautiful place I've ever seen."

Robert looked at him. Then out at the valley. "Compared to where we've traveled through, anyplace would be beautiful. I was starting to think good things about Johnstown, believe it or not."

Steve looked at him, plainly baffled at his insensitivity. "It's beautiful. 'And the Lord made a valley eastward in Eden.' "

Charlotte, still looking through her bags, looked up at him in surprise. "Since when have you been reading the Bible?"

"In Bible school"—he could not take his eyes off the green vale—"that mean old woman, what was her name, made us memorize it. I don't know what made me think of it now."

"Well, if you think this is paradise, your geography is probably off by a few thousand miles." She pulled out her binoculars; inspected the view. "Where does the stream go?"

Everyone looked at her.

And she looked back. "You can all see the stream coming out of the mountain up there, can't you? Well, we're here at the valley's mouth, and there's no sign of it. Where does it go?"

"The sand. The soil." Aoud was offhand. "We are in the desert, Madame Alderson. Despite appearances everything is dry, arid, sterile. The land soaks up the water as quickly as you would, if you were as thirsty as the Sahara."

"There was a river in Eden, too." Steve smiled. "Remember? In Genesis?"

The valley was lined on both sides by high mountains; the walls were nearly vertical. The westering sun lit them, turned the sandstone a deep orange. The cliff face was riddled with openings. Robert was the first to notice them. "It looks like there must have been prehistoric cliff dwellers here."

"Maybe the Bedouins still live in them." Charlotte turned her binoculars on them.

Steve took a few steps toward them, into the valley. "Maybe there are valuable paintings on the walls."

There was a sudden gleam. The sunlight struck one of the openings and reflected into their eyes. Charlotte, watching through her field glasses, was momentarily blinded.

"They must still be occupied." Robert ignored her discomfort. "Those are windows."

A string quartet played, softly, Mozart's Adagio and Fugue in C Minor. Mother Joseph sat at her desk, an enormous antique of cedar with brass fittings. In her hand was an ancient manuscript, a parchment. Her head was bowed; she was asleep.

"Mother."

She stirred, woke. The manuscript slipped through her fingers and fell heavily to the floor. Sister Martin had entered. The abbess looked groggily up; yawned. "I never used to fall asleep at my work. I'm getting old."

The windows of her office were of stained glass. Vibrant reds, blues, greens made a stylized crucifix; a figure of Christ, his right hand raised, blessed the viewer. Late afternoon sunlight poured through the windows, made the room vivid. A patch of green fell on Mother Joseph's face, dazzled her eyes. She held up a hand against it.

"Mother, they've come."

"They?" She was lost.

"I told you they were coming. Or rather, God told me."

"Oh." She tried to suppress another yawn; failed. Looked sleepily around the room, as if she expected to see them there. "Who are they? Where are they?"

"Down in the entrance to the valley. Come and look."

They left the office, went down the hall to a huge room whose windows were unglazed. In the largest of them stood a brass telescope on a tall wrought-iron stand. Mother Joseph walked to one of the smaller windows, looked down. An automobile. Four people. A party of Bedouins had gone out to meet them.

She went to the spyglass; looked. Two young men; an older woman; a Bedouin, presumably their guide, in Western clothing. They were dressed as if for a safari. The abbess smirked at them.

"I told you they would come."

"Yes." She did not move from the telescope's eyepiece. The Bedouins were talking to the strangers in a lively way; much waving, much gesticulating. One of the strangers was a blond man, extraordinarily handsome. She could not see the faces of the others.

"What are they here for?"

She turned to Martin. "You're the prophetess."

Sister Martin blushed. "I wish I weren't. I wish it were you."

"Thank you, love." She looked into the spyglass again.

"You're the mother superior. You should be the one."

More nuns entered the observatory. Asked impatiently who these visitors were.

Mother Joseph did not give up her place at the telescope. "We'll find out soon enough."

10

"You expect me to ride up there in that?"

They stood at the base of the cliff, looking up at the row of openings that were the convent's windows. Above the largest of them projected a massive wooden beam. From it hung a rope and a system of pulleys. A huge basket swung out from the window, and a team of Bedouins on the ground lowered it slowly.

Robert was dressed incongruously in a dark blue business suit; carried a briefcase. The rest of the party wore shorts, T-shirts. But the oddness of it did not faze him. He was a lawyer, here on a legal matter. He was sweating but did not seem to notice or mind it. He looked up at the precariously dangling basket. "Aoud, that thing can't be safe."

Aoud was stoic. "According to the men, they ride up and down in it all the time, taking provisions to the sisters."

Robert looked doubtfully at the men holding the rope. The basket bumped into the rock of the cliff, trembled, steadied itself, and the Bedouins continued lowering it. "Charlotte, you can't expect me to go up in that."

"Why not, love?" She was enjoying his nerves.

"It can't be safe."

"But, Robert." She shrugged an exaggerated shrug. "The men all say . . ."

He looked at them again. "Those ropes look hundreds of years old. They could break at any minute."

"Yes, of course, darling. They've been waiting for just this moment to disintegrate."

He looked at her, exasperated. "Couldn't you at least try to reassure me?"

"You should have come rock climbing with me all those times I asked you to." Steve was serious; seemed to be studying the cliff. "I've scaled harder rocks than these back home. This is nothing."

The basket was on the ground. Robert looked at it, did not move. "I feel absurd."

"It can't be more than two hundred feet." Steve walked over to the basket, took hold of one of its sides; shook it. "It feels solid enough."

"Stop that!" Robert rushed to his side. "Good God, there are holes in the damn thing."

Charlotte joined them, inspected the basket; poked a finger through one of the holes and wiggled it. "So there are. Listen, you keep reminding me how high your fee will be for this trip. I think it's time you earned it."

He stared at her; turned to stone. Aoud smiled at him as if to gloat, as if to say, You see, I was right, we are both their servants. Slowly, unsteadily, Robert climbed into the basket.

The men pulled the rope; the basket shifted; the floor of it gave slightly under his weight. In alarm he grasped one of the ropes, gripped it with all his strength. The basket bobbed up into the air, began its reascent of the cliff face.

"Whatever you do, Robert," Charlotte shouted gleefully, "don't look down."

He looked down. Panic struck. He grasped the rope with both hands, closed his eyes, prayed. The basket bobbed, swayed, bumped the stone of the cliff.

And then, after eternity, it was over. He felt the basket being pulled sideways, felt something solid underneath it. The heat of the sun went away. Still holding the ropes, he opened his eyes.

"Good afternoon, Mr. Semnarek. I'm Mother Joseph."

Without realizing it he had been holding his breath. He exhaled deeply; relaxed. "Good afternoon, Sister. It's a pleasure to meet you." He looked around. His basket was just inside the opening, perched on the edge of the vertical drop. "I think."

Mother Joseph laughed. Extended a hand to him. "Let me help you out of that thing."

Letting her take some of his weight, he stepped out onto the hard, reassuring stone. "I don't believe I made it. That thing can't be as safe as the Bedouins say."

"They told you it was safe? There are accidents all the time. We've tried to get a wooden car made, but the wood here just isn't strong enough for it."

This was the last thing he wanted to hear. He forced himself not to think about his descent. Took his briefcase out of the basket, brushed off his suit.

"Do you really have to dress like that? The sun outside must be sweltering."

He felt foolish. Looked at her heavy grey habit, but decided not to say anything. Looked around. "Is there somewhere we can sit and talk?"

"Certainly. Let's go to my office."

They walked through stone corridors. "How does there come to be a convent in these caves?"

"These aren't caves, Mr. Semnarek. All of these halls and chambers were cut out of the living rock."

He looked around again, with a bit of wonder in his face. "Why? I mean, why not just build something?"

"It was all done centuries ago. I'm afraid I've never been able to fathom their motives myself."

Torches burned, lit the corridors. Their path twisted, turned through the mountain; sometimes there were windows, filled with stained glass; sometimes the fires gave the only light.

"How many nuns live here?"

"There are fifty of us."

"That many? Where are they all? I mean, I haven't—"

"We're a cloistered order, Mr. Semnarek. I'm the only one permitted to deal with outsiders."

"I see."

They passed through the chapter hall, the chapel, passed chamber after chamber. Robert saw the glass kiln burning, glowing red in the half-darkness. In the chapter hall were musicians, a string quartet. Their music filled the corridors. Robert listened. It was Haydn, the *Lark*. "How beautiful."

"We love music here. It's one of the noblest ways we have to glorify the Lord that gave us minds."

They reached the office. The massive cedar desk; a few plush but timeworn chairs. An ancient clock made of brass and beveled glass. Just as they entered it chimed unmelodiously, two o'clock. The stained glass windows glared brilliantly with the sunlight.

Mother Joseph gestured Robert to a seat and took her place at the desk. "Would you care for some wine?"

"Yes, thank you. After that ride up here . . ."

Mother Joseph laughed and walked to a cabinet. The wine was a fine claret. She poured large goblets of it for each of them. Robert savored it, complimented it. "Isn't this unusual, though? Nuns drinking wine?"

"In the Middle Ages, it was the staple of most convents."

"The Middle Ages. But surely"—he looked doubtful—"since then the church has—"

"The church has changed a great deal since our order was founded, Mr. Semnarek. As near as I can tell from the records in our library, we have not." That was that. "Now, what exactly can I do for you?"

He took a long drink of claret and was instantly all business. Opened his briefcase, took out a handful of documents. "I am the attorney for Mrs. Charlotte Alderson, of Johnstown, Pennsylvania. Mrs. Alderson is the widow of Hubert Alderson, a manufacturer of tin cans, and the daughter of Senator William Markham, who represented his state in Washington for twenty-four years."

Her face was impassive. "Yes?"

"There is a question of a will."

"I see." She took a slow sip of the claret. "The husband's or the father's?"

"Well." He sipped his own wine. "Mrs. Alderson was not the only daughter of the senator. There was an older daughter, a Clare Markham, who disappeared in the late 1920s. We have managed to trace her to this region. The senator's estate, which is considerable, can't be settled until Clare is either found or proved dead. The money has been sitting there for several years now. It was only through a strange set of circumstances that we obtained any clues to her whereabouts."

"Surely the courts could simply declare her dead."

"No. The senator's will is quite specific. It demands proof. If none is found within ten years of his death, the money goes to charity."

She looked at the windows, at the colors. "Suppose I tell you that Clare Markham is dead?"

"I would need proof."

"Suppose there was none?"

"We would want to look for it."

"Not in this convent."

"Lawyers are trained to be persistent, Mother Joseph. Half of what we do involves making pests of ourselves until we get what our clients want."

She stared at him; fingered her goblet.

"Clare Markham was a designer with the Tiffany Studios." He ruffled through the documents in his hands. "Until her disappearance early in 1929 she was one of their best. The senator missed her so much, he bought up all the windows she designed—all that he could—and had them installed in his mansion." He looked pointedly at the windows in the office.

Mother Joseph started to stand up, thought better of it. "I was Clare Markham. I never knew that my father cared for me that much. Charlotte was the older daughter, by the way."

There was suddenly silence between them. Robert placed his papers neatly back into his case; looked uncertainly around the room; picked up his goblet, then put it down again. "I . . . we had expected that Clare—that you—had been here. All this stained glass. Even from the base of the cliff, what can be seen of it is quite striking. But . . ."

"Yes, Mr. Semnarek?"

"We expected to find you dead."

"Oh." She leaned back in her chair, swirled her wine in her goblet. Smiled. "Expected? Or hoped?"

Robert felt himself blushing. "Who could have thought there'd be a place like this here, and that Clare—you—would have . . . ?" He spread his hands in a noncommittal gesture. "I mean . . ."

"In a very real sense, Mr. Semnarek, I am dead. Dead to the secular world. This place is mine, now, and has been for most of my life." She smiled again, and he wondered if she was teasing him.

"I wish you'd call me Robert."

"Robert." She smiled even more widely. Left the ball in his court.

And he decided to be frank. "You're alive. That's a problem."

"Not for me. Not for the Lord or the convent."

"Would you be willing to . . . to sign a waiver, disclaiming your half of the inheritance?"

"Is that what my sister wants?"

"She doesn't know you're alive. She wants her money."

"I won't sign a waiver, Mr. Semnarek. Robert."

"Then you'll have to come back with us, to the States."

"That's what you think."

"Then . . . ?" He was lost.

"Which charities will get the money, after the ten years?"

"Oh." His face turned to stone. "There are quite a few of them. The Heart Fund, the March of Dimes, the Cancer Society. But half of them are crackpot things."

"Like . . . ?"

"The Flat Earth Society. A flying saucer research group. It would be a shame to see the money go to them."

"My father didn't think so."

"Your father's dead."

"Yes, but it's his will we're talking about, isn't it?"

"It was his will that you take the money."

Sister Martin entered. "Mother, I . . . Oh!" Robert's presence seemed to shock her. "Excuse me." She covered her face with her veil, exactly, Robert noticed, the way a proper Moslem woman would do. She turned to go.

"Sister Martin."

She turned back to look at them; kept her face covered. "Yes, Mother Joseph."

"Please ask the other sisters not to disturb us. I'll join them in the refectory for dinner."

"Yes, Mother." As she left, the brass clock chimed the half hour.

Robert looked at his watch. "We'll hardly be that long."

"I know it. I have other work to do." Her voice was like ice.

"Oh." He felt suddenly like an intruder, like a thief. "I see. Well, I wouldn't want to keep you from it. But there is the problem of this nine million dollars." He gestured broadly around them. "With your share of it, you could electrify the convent. Modernize it. There are all sorts of possibilities."

"The simplest of which is to stay as we are." She took a long drink, drained her goblet. Sighed. "Look, I don't mean to be difficult."

She paused; gave him his opening; but he kept silent.

"All right then, yes I do mean to be difficult. Nuns are supposed to be difficult. And we're supposed to be anachronisms. That's the whole point about us, isn't it?"

Robert drank his claret; listened.

"I never expected to hear from my family again. Especially not like this. I don't have happy memories of them. When I left home, Father was still a preacher, not a politician. My older sister and I . . . Well, let's just say that we weren't close. The past isn't something I'm anxious to remember. I wrote a memoir once; I thought it would exorcise the past, get it out of my system, get me over it all. But now here you are. You and . . ." She looked away from him. "I don't know what to think. You'll have to give me time. I'll have to confer with my functionaries."

"And with the local bishop?"

"There is none."

He was surprised. "The Vatican, then?"

"We haven't been in contact with them for centuries."

"Then . . . ?"

"We're quite autonomous. The Bedouins supply our needs. We . . . Dealing with outsiders—with lawyers and relatives—that isn't something we're used to."

He was tempted to ask about the Bedouins, about why they were here at all, much less here as servants. But he decided not to press. "Would you like to meet with Charlotte?"

"No." She spoke too quickly to sound convincing. "I don't know. Look . . . I'd like you to leave now. I have a lot to think about. Give me a day or two."

The Mozart piece ended. For a few moments there was silence in the air. Then there came the sound of women's voices singing a hymn. Robert recognized it as part of the Divine Office.

He looked around him. A convent cut out of a mountain; nuns answerable to no one, not even to Rome. He couldn't resist. "Perhaps the priests here, your confessors, perhaps they could help you decide. If I could meet with them . . . ?"

"There are no priests."

"But . . . but who says Mass for you? Who hears your confessions?"

"We tend to our own spiritual needs, Mr. Semnarek. Under a special dispensation from Pope Honorius I. Let me show you back to the lift."

That was it. The interview was over. She ushered him into the corridor, took a torch in hand, guided him back the way they had come. In the chapel were the nuns, singing their hymn. There were rich harmonies, counterpoints.

The basket was still perched there on the lip of the opening. Below, the Bedouins were waiting for him. He extended a hand. "Well, it's been a pleasure meeting you, Mother Joseph." He put on his most ingratiating professional smile. "A pleasure, and a bit of a puzzle."

She shook hands with him. "I've enjoyed meeting you, too. You remind me of someone I used to know."

He took a stab at it. "Marty Kampinski?"

Mother Joseph registered shock, and he knew that he had scored at least one point in their exchange.

"Oh, by the way, Robert."

"Yes?"

"Charlotte *was* the older sister, not I."

"Oh. Uh, yes."

He stepped into the basket, tried to cover his nervousness at the descent; took hold of one of the ropes and closed his eyes as he swung out into the air.

11

The water cascaded out of a vent in the mountain; roared, churned. The pool it formed was covered with white foam. Around it was lush growth, grass, shrubs, bushes, flowers. There were dozens of rosebushes and begonias growing. Steve got down on a knee, swirled a hand in the water,. "It's warm. I thought the water'd be cold, but it's warm."

Robert stood a few yards away; watched him. "I'd have expected the water to be cold, too. Maybe Aoud is wrong. Maybe these mountains are volcanic."

"Like Yellowstone?"

"Exactly."

"Let's go for a swim."

"No, that water's pretty rough. It might be dangerous."

Steve stripped off his shorts, his tank top. "Chicken." He jumped in. Stayed under for a long moment, then popped up; he shook the water out of his blond hair. "Come on. This is great."

Robert watched him. Could not take his eyes off him. The sun was ready to set; its light made everything orange. Steve seemed bronze in it. Slowly, halfheartedly Robert undressed. Jumped into the pool. "Jesus! This is freezing!"

"I know." Steve laughed at him.

"You told me it was warm, you bastard." He climbed quickly out, tried to dry himself with his clothes.

"You're too squeamish."

"You're too crazy. Come on out of there."

"No. I like it." He swam a few strokes. Tried to splash Robert, but the spray fell short.

"All right, stay in there, then. Die of pneumonia. Your mother'll have to find a new heir, and she might pick me."

Steve dove under the surface and stayed there for a long time. When he came up his face was red. He blew out a mouthful of water. "From what you say, she's not going to come away from here any richer than when she got here."

"There's still the money your dad left her."

"I already have my share of that."

"Well, go ahead and drown, then." He got into his damp things.

Steve climbed briskly out of the pool, stretched out on the grass. The cold water had turned his body bright red.

"Get dressed."

"I want the sun to dry me."

"The sun will be gone in another fifteen minutes."

"Then I'll stay wet." He turned his head to look at Robert; laughed at him.

"You're in one of your moods."

"Yeah."

"I think I'll go and find your mother. She needles me, too, but at least she doesn't laugh in my face."

"You'd rather have people laugh at you behind your back?"

Robert glared at him.

"Besides, she's so hung up on Aunt Clare actually being here, she can't talk about anything else. There goes the money. Or at least half of it."

The storm had passed. Steve had found a new topic. Robert sat down on the ground beside him, crossed his legs. "Doesn't it upset you, too?"

"No." Steve's face was blank. "Why should it?"

"It's your money, too. Or it would have been."

Steve grinned. "Minus lawyer's fees."

He decided to ignore this. Leaned back on his hands, looked around. "What do you make of all this? I can't figure out why the Bedouins, who are good Moslems, would stay here as servants to the nuns."

Steve adjusted himself on the ground, found a comfortable spot. "It's like that book, isn't it? *She-who-must-be-obeyed*. And all those lost races or whatever they were staying around to serve her."

"Why, Steve." Robert could hardly contain his astonishment. "You've actually read a novel."

"Yes, but I was young, and I didn't know any better. No jury would convict me."

The conversation was coming round to Robert and the law again; more needling. He decided not to let it happen. "I think I need to stretch my legs. Take my advice and get dressed, or you'll have pneumonia by morning." He got up and walked casually off down the valley. Steve watched him go; laughed; stood up and jumped into the pool again.

They had pitched three tents in the center of the valley. Robert and Steve shared one, Charlotte had a large one of her own, and there was a third, small one for Aoud. As it turned out, some of the Bedouins were distantly related to him, and he went off to stay with them; so they used the third tent for provisions.

Robert found Charlotte perched on the hood of the jeep, staring up the mountainside at the convent windows. A light breeze off the desert ruffled her hair. She glanced idly at Robert, then focused her attention on the convent again. "Where's Steve?"

"Swimming."

"Oh." The dying sun was reflected in one of the windows. It dazzled her eyes, and she covered them. "It's so odd to think of Clare living up there. And for all these years." He started to speak, but she cut him off. "And please don't make any of your usual jokes about Johnstown."

Robert laughed. "You know me too well."

"I've been wondering. Do you think it really is Clare up there?"

"The way she reacted when I mentioned Kampinski's name . . . I think she must really be your sister."

There was, ever so faintly, the sound of music coming down from the mountain. The nuns, singing vespers. The sound of it got quickly lost in the breeze and vanished.

"But I'd think"—Charlotte ran a hand through her hair—"she'd want to see me. To ask about Mother and Father. To . . ." She shrugged.

"She said something about a memoir she wrote once. To get the past out of her system, or something. Maybe that was enough remembering for her. You told me yourself there was no love lost between the two of you."

"Yes, but . . . I don't know. It just seems weird, that's all." She looked directly at Robert. "Clare was the older of us, by the way."

"Yes. Of course."

"You believe me, don't you?"

"A good lawyer always believes what his client tells him."

The sun vanished behind the western cliffs. The sky turned orange, then red, then grey. The brightest stars came out. From behind the eastern hills came the glow of the moon; it would be full. Then suddenly the air was cut by a horrible groaning noise. Robert and Charlotte looked in its direction, the mountain above the convent.

Robert shuddered; realized that his clothes were still wet.

The groan came again. Echoed through the valley. Charlotte climbed impulsively back onto the jeep, as if getting off the ground would protect her from whatever it was.

Aoud came rushing across the valley from the Bedouins' settlement. "I'd suggest that you both get inside your tents and stay there."

"Why, Aoud?" Charlotte wrapped her arms around herself. "What on earth is it?"

"There are lions in the hills, madame. Last week two of them came down into the valley and carried off a pregnant woman. And as you can hear, they are restless tonight."

"Lions."

"Yes, madame. Where is Monsieur Alderson?"

"Swimming in the pool up at the head of the valley."

"You should go and fetch him." He rushed off in the direction of the Bedouin camp.

"Lions." Charlotte looked at Robert; held herself even tighter. "How much protection do you think these tents will give us?"

"Not much." He frowned. "But at least they might cut off our scents, or something. I'll unpack the guns." He started going through the supplies. "I hope Steve packed plenty of ammunition."

"Gallons of it, darling. You've seen him during hunting season back home. When he finds out he may get to shoot at a lion, he'll probably break into a dance."

Steve lay on the grass and watched the sky darken. The valley below him was black. There were lanterns, torches. Up on the mountainside the convent windows glowed faintly.

The desert wind kicked up, and he felt a chill. He climbed into his shorts, shirt, boots. Ran a hand through the water. It felt icy now. He shivered.

The full moon inched above the mountain, gave the landscape a ghostly light. Around him the roses and begonias showed a shadowy pink. The groaning of the lions filled the air again. He couldn't think what it was; decided to ignore it.

There was movement, somewhere in the bushes near him. He became alert. Looked around; listened. Hushed voices. Whispers, giggles. There was someone nearby. Carefully, quietly he pushed his way through the shrubs to see who it was.

An old man, a Bedouin, leaned against a small tree. He was in his nineties, wrinkled, withered, bony, almost grotesque. He was naked. On her knees before him was a young girl, an adolescent. She was giving him oral sex. She worked feverishly, but the man was casual, relaxed, almost uninvolved. The sight of them excited Steve. It was not just the sex, it was the mingling of old, dry flesh with young flesh that excited him. He watched. Inched nearer.

And then, suddenly, they were aware of his presence. The girl stopped. Turned and looked at Steve with ferocious hatred. Hissed at him. Spat.

"I—"

She ran at him. Reached out her fingernails and scratched his cheek. Drew blood.

The old man leaned patiently against his tree; ignored what was happening.

Steve lurched back into the bushes; turned and walked quickly away. Reached up and felt the blood dripping from his face. He could not forget the venom in the girl's look.

There in front of him was the valley. Torches, lanterns; tents showing white in the moonlight. He could not go down while there was still fresh blood. He wouldn't be able to explain it. Later, when it dried, he could say he scratched it on a bush. The cliff was pale grey; the sound of the nuns' hymn came down from it. The stained glass windows glowed. Robert had made it all sound so odd. He had to see.

The sandstone of the cliff face was rough. There were lots of handholds, footholds. Slowly, carefully he climbed. The cool night breeze on his cheek stung; the scratch throbbed, pulsed like a deep cut. He wondered, Should I get something to put on it, should I have stitches? The glass above him showed warmly;

shimmered with light and color; invited him. He climbed. Halfway up, in a crevice in the stone, was a bird's nest; the bird pecked at his hand, drew blood. He nearly lost his grip and fell. The nuns' voices made sweet harmony in the air above him. He licked the blood from his hand and climbed.

The lift basket was perched at the edge of the landing. He had to climb, awkwardly, around it; there was not much footing. Then he was inside. Torches burned brilliantly; after the cool moonlight, they hurt his eyes, and he had to wait for a moment while they adjusted. The sound of the nuns' hymn was louder; it filled the air. Cautiously he stepped into the main corridor and looked around. There was no one in sight.

He walked. Found first the chapter hall. There were musical instruments piled everywhere, violins, lower strings, horns. In opposite corners were a piano and a harpsichord. He walked to the harpsichord, ran a finger down the keyboard. It tinkled loudly; the sound echoed, reverberated. He looked around in alarm, thinking someone must have heard it. But no one came.

It was a short way to the chapel. The nuns were gathered in pews; were absorbed in their singing. One of them sat at an ancient organ; an assistant pumped it furiously. There were candles everywhere, enclosed in stained glass shelters. Steve backed slowly away, went off exploring in the opposite direction.

He turned down a promising hallway. Door after door, some open, some not, one granite lintel after the next. The sisters' cells. Candles, again in glass shelters, provided them with light. He looked into each open room. On each lintel, just inside the entrance, was carved an abstract marking. He ran a finger along the outline of one of them, wondered what it was. Finally, after dozens of rooms, he found someone.

A young woman, about his own age, with soft blond hair and delicate features. She was asleep on the pallet in her cell. The door was wide open. She snored softly, just audibly above the continuing hymn. Steve found her beautiful. He watched her for a few minutes without moving. Then, hesitantly, he took a step into her cell.

She was quite fast asleep. He looked around, but there was not much to see. A spare habit hanging on a hook. A few books. He looked again at the girl. Thought for a moment of the couple he had seen in the orchard, the old man and the girl.

She awoke groggily. Looked at him. Recognized him from her dream. "Who are you?"

Steve grinned at her. "I'm the nephew of your abbess."

"What are you doing in my cell?" Without wanting to, she yawned.

"Looking for you. Who are you?"

"Sister Martin. Mother Joseph sent you for me?"

"Yes." He took a step toward her; stood over her, looking down. "She wanted us to meet."

"Why?" She yawned again.

Steve smiled a schoolboy smile. "Who knows? Maybe she just thought we'd like each other."

Sister Martin sat up. Her face was only inches from the front of his shorts. She moved awkwardly around him, got to her feet. "I should join the others. It's almost time for confession."

"Confession?"

"Yes. Didn't she tell you?"

"I'm afraid not." Another innocent grin.

She remembered Steve more and more vividly from her dream. "What exactly did she tell you about me?"

"Just that I should meet you." He knew the lie was transparent; smiled his most ingratiating smile and hoped for the best. "You're beautiful."

Her wimple and veil had been sitting at the foot of the cot. She reached for them, put them on. "I'll have to go."

"I said you were beautiful."

She stood still. Looked him up and down. "So are you. God gave us each that gift."

This was not going at all the way he'd hoped. He decided to switch to another tack. "That figure carved in the doorpost. What is it?"

She arranged the wimple; did not bother to look. "It's a fish."

"A what?"

"A fish. You know—the symbol of Christ."

"The . . . Oh." His bafflement was obvious. "Why aren't you with the others? Singing, I mean."

"I needed rest. I have . . . seizures. I always need to sleep afterward. I have to go."

"The guy who managed the team had epilepsy." He was desperate to keep her there.

"The team?"

"The football team. In school. You know? I was the star halfback."

"No, I'm afraid I don't know."

Steve was appalled. "Never heard of football?"

"No. Now, if you'll excuse me . . ."

"Can I come back and see you again?"

Sister Martin looked him up and down again. "Mother Joseph didn't send you here at all, did she?"

It showed in his face.

"How did you get here? How did you get up the cliff?"

"I climbed it." He was shamefaced. "Look, I meant what I said. You really are beautiful."

"Thank you. But you shouldn't try climbing that cliff. It's too steep and too high. Mother is always warning the Bedouins to keep their children away from it, but there are accidents all the time."

"I'm an experienced rock climber." He was proud of it. "You never answered my question."

She was at the door, ready to leave. "Really, confession will be starting anytime now. I should be there."

"Confession." He tried not to let his bruised ego show.

"Each night one of us confesses all of her sins to the convent. Begs her sisters for forgiveness. It's one of our most important rituals."

He took a step toward her. Reached out and touched her cheek tenderly. "What sins do you commit?"

And she touched him in return. Put her head flat on his chest. Rubbed it gently in a circle. "I know a lot more things than just the ones I've experienced. No one in the convent is aware of all the things I know."

"I don't follow you."

"Good." She ran her hand down the flat of his stomach. Kissed him, lightly, on the side of his neck. "I have to go now. You can come again tomorrow night, if you like. Late. After midnight, if you can. Everyone will be asleep by then." She kissed him again, on the lips this time. "O brave new world, that has such people in't."

"What?" He felt off balance; did not like it. "Listen, don't tell anyone I was here. All right?"

"I couldn't tell them. They wouldn't understand. Goodbye for now, Steven."

"Wait! How did you know my name?"

But she was gone. The nuns ended their hymn. He resisted the temptation to follow her. Found his way back to the cliff, climbed gingerly down. The lions were calling to each other across the valley, and the moonlight was cold and white. But Steve could not forget the warmth of her presence, the fire in her touch.

12

"Well, I'd like to know how you managed to find me here. I'd have sworn it was impossible."

Robert sat facing Mother Joseph, drinking wine. "It was all a fluke."

"Yes?"

"Yes." He was reluctant to talk about it; stared into his goblet. "Well. It all started about a year ago. When Louis Tiffany's mansion burned down."

"Laurelton Hall? Do you mean Laurelton Hall?" The news plainly upset her.

"I think that's what it was called. The one out on Long Island."

"Yes." She set her goblet on the desk. "Laurelton Hall, gone. And in flames, yet." Slowly she recovered herself. "Did you ever see it?"

"Only in ashes."

"It was beautiful. It was wonderful. It was magnificent. Mr. Tiffany put into it everything he had learned in a lifetime of making beautiful things. His design, his glasswork, his ceramics, all of them came together there."

"It must have been something."

"It was. I've never seen a place more lovely. Were the windows all destroyed?"

"I think a few of them were left, but not many. I don't really know much about stained glass. I'm afraid all it makes me think of is oldness."

"Mr. Tiffany was, in his minor way, in his minor art form, quite a genius."

The topic, and his ignorance of it, were making Robert

uncomfortable. He looked around. "Are all the windows here your work?"

"Yes. I reglaze them compulsively every few years. The convent bears new windows the way trees bear new leaves."

"Your designs are quite wonderful. If Mr. Tiffany taught you your craft, he must have been quite a master indeed."

"It is the only art form, you see, in which light is the essential element. If you accept the principle that God is light, then . . ." She made a vague gesture, left him to complete the thought for himself.

As always, there was music in the convent. Robert let himself get lost in it for a moment, hoping to find his way to another topic. "This is quite a beautiful quartet. What is it?"

"Schubert. *Death and the Maiden*. I've always loved it."

"It's a fine piece of music."

"Schubert is my favorite. Listen to that rich melody. You could listen to Brahms for a month without finding anything like a melody." She wrinkled her nose, made her face look sour. "You were telling me about Laurelton Hall."

"Yes." Back to business; he was relieved. "Among Mr. Tiffany's personal papers they found some letters from you and your friend Kampinski. From Rome, from Paris, Berlin, Istanbul. You were . . . looking for something? Something he sent you for?" He prompted her.

"Yes." But she was giving nothing away.

"Yes. Anyway, the letters stopped. In 1929. You vanished. Neither Mr. Tiffany nor anyone else heard of either of you again. But at the bottom of the last letter we found scrawled, in Mr. Tiffany's hand, the words *Marrakesh. L'Hôtel Grand. Two windows*. And in the same bundle as your letters was the hotel's order."

"There should have been a cablegram, too. We sent it from shipboard."

"There wasn't. Anyway, we added it up and came here on the chance that someone might remember your passing through. Or that we might find . . ."

"My grave? Evidence of my death?" She was amused; turned quickly serious. "I'm so sorry to learn about Laurelton Hall. All that beauty gone. It's no accident that the mystics always see fire in hell."

The abrupt transition left him off balance. But he decided to take advantage of the opening she'd given him. "You still have good memories of the world outside. Of your life before you came here."

"Yes. I suppose I do. We don't get much news from the world. Every now and then a caravan will pass with a newspaper from somewhere or other. Not much that we do hear is very pleasing. Cold wars instead of good healthy hot ones. Moons made of wire and sheet metal. The twentieth century is a disease, Robert."

There went the advantage. But he decided to try and press anyway. "Charlotte would like to see you."

"She wouldn't recognize me."

"You're her sister, for God's sake."

"Charlotte, as I recall her, was made for this modern world. I was not. I'd have been at home in the tenth century, not this one."

"You have a way of hiding your motives with mysticism." He smiled, drank some claret.

"That's part and parcel of being a nun, Robert. I don't want to see my sister, and that's that."

"I see. She'll be sorry to hear it." Mother Joseph's mood had turned dark. He knew there was no point to asking; but he had to ask. "And what about your father's money?"

"I haven't decided yet. I'm inclined to let the charities have it, crackpots and all."

"You mentioned a memoir once. It must be fascinating. Have you ever thought of publishing it? Perhaps . . ." He pressed on with his gamble. "Perhaps if you could let me see it. Perhaps then I could . . ."

"No one has ever read it, Robert. Not even my sisters. And no one ever will. Certainly not Charlotte, certainly not her lawyer. It is stored away safely in my cell, and it will remain there."

"If you really didn't want to see her, you'd just send us away."

The nun stood up. Sat down. A dozen conflicting emotions showed in her face. "I don't know. I can't tell you how deeply I wish you'd never come here. And that Laurelton Hall was still there, and all the lovely glass. And that . . ." It was getting to her. Robert took his leave, knowing that things were progressing according to his plan.

At the base of the cliff, Charlotte was waiting for him. "Well?"

He jumped out of the basket, steadied himself on a rock. "I

wish I thought I'd get used to that damned thing." Dusted off his suit. "But she's weakening. I think we'll get what we want. For that matter, I think she will, too."

Late; nearly midnight. A brilliant moon just past full. The lions had moved off somewhere else; their cries carried faintly on the night wind.

Steve lay on his cot in the tent; on top of it, not under the blanket. Across the tent Robert slept soundly; snored. The usual breeze off the desert shook gently the sides of the tent. Steve rolled over onto his stomach. Rolled back again. It was no good trying to think of anything but the girl. He climbed silently into his things. Decided not to wear a shirt; women liked his chest. Walked outside and looked at the cliff.

There were fires burning in the Bedouin camp. They must be celebrating something; they nearly always were. He wondered if they'd see him climbing and, if they did, what they'd do about it. Oh, what the hell.

The stone was lit more directly by the moon tonight. To climb was easy. He kept an eye out for angry birds. The climb seemed to take no time at all; then he was in the convent. Torches, candles. Open doors, closed doors. Sleeping nuns snored, muttered things in their cells. Steve wasted no time; he went to Sister Martin's cell.

She was awake. She sat cross-legged on her cot, a book in her hand; she was clearly waiting for him. When he reached the door of her room she looked up, smiled and held a finger to her lips. She jumped up. "Don't make any noise. I know where we can go."

"Hello." He tried to kiss her, but she avoided him.

She giggled. Reached out a finger and tickled his side. But when he laughed, she held up a hand and covered his mouth. "I said be quiet."

"That's not fair. You tickled me."

"Sh."

She was wearing her veil and wimple. Steve reached out a hand to pull them off. "Let me see your hair."

"No." She fought him off playfully.

"Please. Blond hair turns me on."

"Well . . . all right." She took them off, ran a finger through the hair that fell about her shoulders. Steve leaned down and kissed it. "Mm. It even *smells* beautiful."

"Stop it. Let's go. And be quiet." She walked briskly into the corridor, took a torch from a fixture in the wall. "This way."

It was a labyrinth. Dozens of halls branched, disappeared into darkness. Others were wide and brightly lit by torches. Occasionally there were rooms, widenings in the passage, some of them small, others so huge the light from Sister Martin's torch did not reach the walls. From time to time Steve thought he heard sounds in the dark. Rats? Snakes? Bats? He began to feel edgy. "Where are we going?"

"To a place no one ever visits."

"Where?"

"To the mausoleum."

"To the—?"

"Yes. No one goes there except for funerals and feasts of the dead. We'll be alone there."

"Yeah, just you and me and some dead nuns."

She stopped. Turned on him. "Don't be disrespectful. You're a guest in this convent."

Her vehemence startled him. "Uh, yes." He looked at the flame of her torch. "I'm sorry."

"Are you really?" She seemed to be having second thoughts about their liaison.

"Oh, yes. Honest. I didn't mean to . . . uh . . . I mean, it's just such an odd place for us to meet in."

"Come on, then." Her manner was still a bit stiff. "It isn't much farther along here."

There were fewer and fewer lights, there was more and more darkness. They passed through a cavernous room, and it was only from the sound of their footsteps echoing off the distant walls that Steve realized how huge the room was.

Steve was feeling on edge. He wanted to talk, to help calm himself. "What do you call this convent? Does it have a name?"

"The Bedouins call it the House of Fifty. None of us ever calls it anything but the convent."

"House of Fifty? Is that how many of you there are?"

"Yes. Exactly." The torch was close to her cheek. Her skin was golden.

"It's a dumb name."

"Oh?" She had not stopped walking.

"Yeah. What happens when some of you die? Or when new nuns come to join your order? What happens to the 'fifty' then?"

"It's never happened, Steve. When one of us dies, someone new arrives to take her place within a month or two. There are always fifty of us. At least there always have been, in my time here."

"Don't be silly."

"It's the truth. Honestly."

They rounded a corner, entered still another corridor. And there were faces in the wall. Rows and rows of them, hundreds of ghostly white faces stared out of the stone. Steve stopped in alarm. "Good God, what are they!"

"I told you." The nun was calm. "This is where we bury our dead."

"But . . . but I—"

The white faces stretched on down the corridor, as far as the torchlight and beyond. Blank likenesses of women, pale as chalk, expressionless as the stone around them. The nearest of them seemed to stare at him blankly, the empty eye sockets seemed to watch him as he moved. It was unnerving.

Martin kept walking, torch held up high. But Steve found it impossible to follow her. "Wait. I can't make love in a place like this."

"Make love?" She stopped. Looked back over her shoulder. "I thought we might talk first. You're the first man I've ever met. I want to get to know you."

"Uh, yes. But does it have to be here?"

"It's the only place in the convent where I'm sure no one will bother us. I told you, no one ever comes here."

He looked around himself, at the faces. "This is so weird. I've never seen anything like it."

"It's the way we've always done our burials. Look."

The faces were hung on the walls in vertical rows. Some of the rows were long, others had only one or two faces in them. Martin held her torch near the top of a long row; let Steve inspect the features. Then she lowered the light, slowly, face by face.

And he saw. "They're all the same woman. Older each time."

"Mm-hmm." She nodded. Got down on her knees. Steve followed the light downward; watched the anonymous woman age before him. At the bottom of the wall was a niche, cut into the stone, in which rested a heap of polished bones. Atop the pile was her skull. Its eye sockets, like those of the plaster faces above, seemed to mock Steve. "I don't like this. It's weird."

"You keep saying that. I think it all makes perfect sense. When a woman enters the convent, we make a life mask of her. And then every seven years we make another one. We keep making them until she dies and we place her bones here, beneath the visible record of her life. Every nun who ever served in this convent is buried here, under her masks. It is tangible history. We know what we have been."

Steve, still on his knees, looked down the corridor ahead of them. White masks, hundreds of them, thousands, stretched into the darkness. The thought of all those lives, of all those bones, unsettled him. "Who cleans the bones for burial?"

"Far down at the end of the corridor there's a cave full of beetles. We leave the bodies there, and when we come back all the flesh is gone. The processions back from the cave are quite beautiful and we say elaborate prayers over the bones when they're placed in the proper niche."

He looked again at the skull in front of him. In his mind he could hear it laughing. "I don't think I can make love in a place like this."

"That's not what we came here for."

He turned to her, startled. "I thought—"

"Believe me, Steve, we're going to copulate. I don't think there's much either of us can do about it. But not tonight, and not here. I want to get to know you first."

"You still haven't told me how you know my name."

"I know everything about you. Believe that. I even know what our lovemaking will be like, when it finally happens."

He found himself wondering if she might be crazy. "This isn't the way things are supposed to happen. The man is supposed to be in charge."

"You're in my world now, Steve, not yours." She got to her feet. "Come on."

They walked on down the dark gallery, flanked by unseeing faces. There was a draft, and the torchlight flickered. "Where are we going now?"

"There's something else I want you to see. To help you understand me."

"What is it?"

"Be quiet. You'll see."

The corridor stretched on and on. An unending series of blind eyes, mute lips on the walls. Steve tried to keep count of them, but there were too many. Hundreds of them. Eons of them. The monotony, the sameness, the unvarying rhythm of row after row, face after face. "How long has your convent been here?"

"No one knows. In the library we have a letter from Pope Honorius I. He reigned in the seventh century. From the tone of the letter, I gather we were old then."

They walked. White faces like ghosts. Wind fanning the torch. Their own voices, footsteps echoing softly. The hall branched. Martin took the right-hand branch. Finally there were no more faces on the walls. From ahead came the sound of running water.

"Is this where you keep those beetles?" The thought of them made his skin creep.

"No. They're in the other passage. Down here are my pets."

"Pets?"

"You'll see."

It was a cave. A huge cavern. Stalactites, stalagmites. The walls, what Steve could see of them in the torchlight, glistened with moisture. Down the center of it flowed a small stream. Then the stream widened, formed a pool. Martin got down on her knees beside it, rested her torch against a rock, swirled her fingers through the water. There was movement in it. "Come and look."

Cautiously Steve knelt beside her. There were fish in the pool, circling, moving in unison. "They're fish."

She looked at him, as if she were surprised at the obviousness of what he'd said. "Yes. Take a closer look at them."

Instead he looked around the cavern. "We must be in the heart of the mountain."

"Yes, we are." From a pocket of her habit she took a handful of bread crumbs, sprinkled them on the surface of the water. The fish ate greedily. "No one knows about this place but me." She looked into Steve's eyes. Reached out and rested her hand on his forearm.

He moved to kiss her, but she backed away. "No. Not yet. Not here. That's not the way I envisioned it."

"Women are so damn romantic."

"You haven't taken a good look at my fish yet."

"They're fish. What is there to see?"

"Look."

Steve looked. The fish were still eating, squabbling among themselves for the remaining bread. He moved close to the water. "Good God, they're blind."

"Yes."

"But . . . but they don't have any eyes."

"Yes."

"But . . . but how can they see? I mean, I saw them swimming in a school. Look. They know just where the breadcrumbs are. It isn't possible."

"It is quite possible," Martin said calmly. "They're doing it."

Steve put his hand into the water, and one of the eyeless fish swam into his palm. He lifted it out of the water. Where there should have been eyes, there was . . . nothing. Scales. Not even a trace of an eye socket. He let the fish fall gently back into the pool. "How do they see?"

"You keep asking me that same question, with variations."

He was totally lost. "Look, I don't like this. Let's go."

"You don't want to make love anymore?" She was quite sober.

"Not here. Not tonight. No."

"But, Steve . . ." She could not resist gentle teasing.

"Please, let's go now." His hand trailed through the pool; a fish rubbed against it. He pulled it out.

"I don't know what you're afraid of. They're really harmless."

"I don't like this place. I can't stand it. Nature meant this place never to be seen."

"But we've seen it."

He was more and more upset. "Please, let's go now."

Martin smiled, stood, picked up the torch, kissed Steve lightly on the forehead. "Come on, then."

Back up the burial gallery. The white faces in the wall, the polished bones. Steve forced himself to keep his eyes on the torch. How many generations of nuns, preserved in plaster, fed to greedy insects, displayed here like art in a museum? Row after row of them, face after face, endless records of the lives of unnumbered women. He watched the torch.

Suddenly Martin stopped. Screamed. An ear-piercing cry. "Oh my God!"

"Martin, what's wrong?"

"My eyes! My eyes are filled with fire!"

He caught hold of her shoulders, shook her. "Martin, what's wrong? I don't understand what's wrong."

"I cannot see for the fire!" she shrieked. Fell to the stone floor. Her mouth foamed, her limbs went rigid. She hissed, spat.

"Martin, for God's sake!" He slapped her, hoping to bring her out of it.

"I see the Lord as it were a burning sphere."

"Martin, stop it!" He cupped her face in his hands, shook her head.

She turned her face to one side and bit him. Drew blood. Moaned in agony as her body wrenched on the floor.

"Evil eyes! Evil eyes!
You shall not see me,
You shall not see my shame,
You shall not see my present crime.
Go dark,
Go blind eternally to what you ought never to have seen,
Go blind to the men my heart has ached to see."

He shook her again. Blood from his wounded hand smeared her hair. "Martin!"

She hissed at him. She spat.

Steve panicked. Her screams must have echoed through the halls, through the whole convent. They would be awake, they would be looking for her. He turned and ran. Looked back once at her lying helpless on the stone floor; then ran. There was still blood flowing from his hand. He held it to his lips, licked it up.

There was motion, activity in the convent. The nuns were up and about, were looking in alarm for Sister Martin. He hid. Made his way slowly from one nook to another. Finally made it to the entrance. There were heavy clouds in the sky now, and a hard cold wind blew down from the north, across the mountains.

13

Just before dawn there was rain. Not a long shower, but cold and heavy, with a chill edge that cut through the desert air. Then, with astonishing suddenness, the clouds broke and there was brilliant sunshine.

Within hours the desert was in bloom. From just outside the mouth of the valley the flowers stretched off to the horizon. Enormous yellow blooms like giant buttercups; vibrant red and purple blossoms like poppies; flowers of every color and shape.

The Bedouin children flocked into the desert to pick them; brought back basket after basket of them, covered their tents, their clothing, everything in the valley. Soon they were sending load after load of them up the cliff to the nuns.

Charlotte sat on the hood of the jeep, tried to concentrate on the novel she was reading. Then the children began to bring her flowers, to cover her with them. At first she found it annoying, then she just lay back and enjoyed it. The flowers' perfume washed over her. She closed her eyes and felt the softness of the petals, smelled the beautiful aroma.

Robert came out of his tent, dressed for business, briefcase in hand. "You look like you're about to be sacrificed to the volcano god or something."

She kept her eyes closed, her head back. "You never suspected I'm a virgin, did you?"

"It will come as news to your son."

She sat up, made a wry face. "Nearly everything does."

"He sleeps later every day. God only knows where he goes at night."

"Someplace foolish. Why worry about it? Let him sleep."

Robert shrugged. "It's hard not to be curious. What are you reading, by the way?"

"*Northanger Abbey*. Thank God I thought to bring my complete Jane Austen on this little trek. You spend every day up in the convent, and Steve's useless as company."

He looked self-conscious. "I'm off to visit your sister again right now."

"So I gathered. Would it kill you to dress like something other than a lawyer for once? The informality might charm her."

It was a new thought. He looked doubtful. "She's a fascinating woman. I enjoy talking with her every day. I just wish I could figure out what she's got in the back of her mind. If I could read her memoir . . . Besides, it might give me the leverage I need to move her."

"Maybe she doesn't know what she wants herself. She always did have a tendency to dither."

He shrugged again. "I'd like to get my hands on it. It would get us what we want, if anything can. I have to get going. See you later."

"*Au revoir*, Robert dear. If you want me, I shall be here, among my book." She lay back in her flowers, brushed them up so that they covered her completely.

The Bedouins were waiting to raise him up the mountain. He stepped into the cart. Then, to his annoyance, a crowd of children ran up and covered him with flowers. The basket bobbed into the air. He closed his eyes, gripped the ropes; uttered a short prayer.

"Relax, Robert darling. You're here." Mother Joseph pulled the basket onto the landing, extended a hand to help him out of it. "How are you today?"

"Quite fine, until I got into that thing."

She laughed. "I thought you might like to see more of the convent today." She looked at him questioningly.

"Yes." He seemed surprised at it. "But won't I be intruding on the cloister?"

"We'll survive. None of the others will speak to you, or even acknowledge your presence."

"Oh." He wasn't sure how he felt about it. "Well, it's hard not to be curious about the place."

They walked. Chatted. Robert commented again on the beauty of her stained glass work. In the kitchen there was a huge, elaborate window. A geometric design, very intricate, very Islamic. Patterns interweaving with patterns, geometries intersecting, lines vanishing behind other lines and then reappearing. "It's wonderful. And it's not at all like anything else I've seen here."

"No. I found the pattern in an Algerian rug. A caravan stopped here with it, and the driver let me copy it."

Robert walked up to it, began tracing the convoluted path of one line through the pattern.

"It's difficult to resist doing that, isn't it?" Mother Joseph watched him. "To make sense of the design, you have to follow its lines. But the minute you concentrate on one line, you lose sight of the design. There is a great deal about the Moslem worldview that makes more sense than the way Christians have always viewed things."

Robert stopped; looked at her. "You never stop surprising me, Mother Joseph."

"Why don't you just call me Joseph?"

"You're a woman."

"Nevertheless, it's my name."

It was disconcerting. "On the subject of Moslems—why do the Bedouins stay here and serve you? I mean, they are Moslems, aren't they? Not Christians?"

"They are perfectly good Moslems, yes. And they stay here for obvious reasons. This valley is fertile. There is water. It is a good place to live in. The alternative for them would be nomadic life in the Sahara. Which would you choose?"

"I see what you mean. But they seem to be so devoted to you. I mean, you're infidels."

"I think in their minds we're all madwomen. And therefore sacred to Allah. They've never actually said so, but . . ." She shrugged.

"How long have they been here?"

"For as long as we have records."

"But that goes back even before there was such a thing as Islam. What—"

She had had enough of the subject. Dismissed it. "Look, Robert, over here is where I make my glass."

The stone chamber, the kiln. The fire glowed, pulsed. As they walked in, she idly pumped the bellows, and flames sprang up.

"It reminds me of the fire that glows up on the mountain."

Robert was in a mood to probe. "What is that glow that we see up there?"

"A trick of the light, that's all."

"There." He pointed to the chimney. "Doesn't that vent the flames up onto the mountaintop?"

"There's nothing up there that would interest you." Her voice took on a hard edge, and he backed away from the subject.

"This—hobby?—of yours, this glassmaking. It seems so secular. So worldly. I'd have thought you'd have left it behind when you entered the order here."

"The need to create is the profoundest spiritual need I know, Robert. Come with me. Let me show you what I'm working on now."

The corridors were filled with the Bedouins' flowers. Vases, urns of brass, of terra-cotta overflowed with them. But in the convent torchlight they looked artificial, unnatural. Their scent mixed with the smoke; turned foul.

As they walked, they passed other nuns, all of whom kept their eyes demurely averted from Robert; kept silent and passed hurriedly. Robert was amused at them. "Did you tell me there are fifty of you here?"

"Yes."

"Where do you all come from?"

"From everywhere in the world. We even have a sister from China."

"And what brought you all here?"

"Our stories don't vary much. We all understand each other very well."

"That isn't an answer."

"Yes it is, darling."

"Do you have any idea how much like Charlotte you are?"

She stopped walking, turned back to look at him. "No. I don't."

"She can be maddeningly stubborn and evasive, too." He put on a wide grin.

"I am," Joseph said slowly, "neither of those."

"What brought you here? What did Mr. Tiffany send you to find? What did you write about in your memoir?"

"Here we are at my workroom. Come in." There was a large pattern laid out on the stone table, and pieces of glass were fitted into their spaces on it. "I'm doing a portrait of St. Lawrence. Of his torments. The Romans roasted him on a grid. We have a sister here from Canada who is especially devoted to St. Lawrence. This is to be installed in her cell."

Robert inspected her work. Only half of the pieces were cut and in place. The curves of the glass body suggested severe pain. "You are a true artist. It's a pity the world will never see your work."

"Pain isn't difficult. I simply find a line that reflects what I feel in these." She held out her hands. They were swollen, twisted with arthritis.

Robert had not noticed them before. "I'm sorry. I didn't realize. That you can do such exquisite work with them is . . ."

"Every year they get a bit worse. I used to say Mass for the convent, but my hands are so clumsy I drop the Host too often. Now I delegate Mass to Sister Peter."

"But you still work. You're a marvel of a woman."

"It's a compulsion with me. You're right. It's much too secular. I often think it must be sinful of me to indulge myself like this. But I can't resist. Mr. Tiffany was arthritic, too. Let me show you the chapel."

They walked again. Robert tried to find neutral conversation. "Fifty of you. I took a lot of Greek in school, and there are lots of parallels. Fifty was the usual number of women when there were colleges of priestesses. Especially of the moon. The Danaids. The Nereids."

Mother Joseph walked silently; listened to him.

"It's a funny thing. There's even a legend that when Poseidon was making love to one of the Danaids, he struck a nearby rock with his trident, and water poured forth from it. The Danaids murdered their husbands, you know."

"Yes, I remember that."

"Now that I think of it, there's even a legend that Cerberus—you know, the dog that guarded the entrance to hell—had fifty heads."

"Surely he had three."

"That's the usual myth, yes. But one of the earliest versions says fifty. The mythographers interpreted it as meaning that one of the mouths of hell was guarded by a college of fifty priestesses."

He had meant all of this lightly. But Joseph was clearly upset by the talk. She walked on ahead of him quickly; kept silent.

He rushed to catch up to her. "Listen, I seem to be saying the wrong thing. I keep meaning just to converse, but everything I say seems to put you off. I'm sorry."

They were in the chapel. It was ablaze with candles in colored glass shelters. Joseph sat down in one of the pews. "There's nothing to be sorry for. I have so many things I wish I could unremember. You just keep reminding me of them, that's all. It isn't your fault."

"But I don't understand how what I was talking about could . . . I mean, it was just chatter. Greek myths. Nonsense."

"Please, don't give it another thought."

He sat in the pew in front of her; turned around so he could face her. "Are you sure there's nothing we can talk about? I mean, something you need to . . . confess, I guess."

"I confess my sins before the whole sisterhood. It ought to be enough, but it isn't. That memoir that so interests you. I thought it would cleanse me somehow. Purge me. But it didn't." She looked into his eyes. "Look, I'm being a terrible hostess. Why don't you come back tomorrow? I'll be better then."

He stood, slowly. "You still have that memoir. I want to read it."

"You're Charlotte's lawyer." Her face was stone. "And her friend."

"Yours, too. I represent the estate."

"I burned the manuscript." The lie was transparent.

"Please, Joseph, I'd like to read it. I'd like to know."

"There is no possibility of it."

Robert sat down again. "Joseph, what did you come here to find? And what did you find instead? And"—he was uncertain whether to go on; decided to press—"what happened to Marty Kampinski?"

"Get out of here, God damn you!" She was suddenly on her feet; she was screaming irrationally. Picked up a candle shelter and threw it at his head. It struck him, drew blood. "It should have hit your eyes! It should have blinded you! God damn your soul, get out of here!"

A thick stream of blood flowed down the side of his head, stained his collar, his suit. He pressed his hand over the wound, ran from the chapel. Joseph sat in her pew, buried her face in her arms and cried uncontrollably.

Halfway down the corridor Robert met Sister Peter. "Mr. Semnarek! Good Lord, what happened?"

"An accident, that's all."

"Come with me. Let me bandage it for you."

He was still shaken, not so much by the cut as by Joseph's savagery. "You're not supposed to talk to me."

"I'll confess it tonight. The Lord will forgive me. Come with me. I can't leave you like that."

14

"I'm telling you she's beautiful, and I'm telling you I'm going to fuck her."

Charlotte was in her tent asleep. Robert and Steve talked over a low campfire.

Robert let his distaste show. "Nuns are never beautiful. I saw enough of them in grade school and high school. You're lucky to have been raised Protestant."

"She has the softest, blondest hair. Like mine."

"The nuns who ran my school were a German order. Their mother house was somewhere behind the Iron Curtain. I'm privately convinced that they only got into the school business after the bottom fell out of the market for Hitler Youth Camps."

"She keeps telling me she knows we're going to make it." Steve was in a reverie. "She says she's already envisioned it, she already knows what it's going to be like."

Robert abandoned his unpleasant reminiscence. "She's probably a lunatic. I'm starting to think that's what your Aunt Clare is." He reached up and touched the bandage on his head. "Nuns are all psychotic."

"I'll bet you never fucked one." Steve leered at him.

"Lunacy must run in your family."

Steve laughed; rubbed his crotch; whistled. "As long as I can share my padded cell with a woman who looks like that . . ." He leered again. "She even forgave me for running away when she had that seizure or whatever it was. She must love me. Women always do."

Robert decided to ignore him; lay back and watched the gibbous moon, the desert stars. There were, unusually, clouds tonight. The

night breeze was cool. "Climbing that cliff is crazy, even if
nothing else you do is. You'll break your damn fool neck. I can't
stand you when you show off."

"Yes, Mother."

"Stop it." He closed his eyes; wished Steve was someplace
else.

"I could get Aunt Clare's memoir for you."

He sat up. Stared directly at Steve.

"I could. It'd be easy. I've explored the whole place by now.
She's shown it all to me. And the nuns go to confession every
night after they're through singing. The place is abandoned."

"That would be theft." Despite himself, Robert was intrigued
by the idea.

"Yes." Steve grinned at his own bravado. "I could get into her
cell, find it and throw it down to you."

"You'd get caught."

"No one's caught me yet. You said she keeps it in her cell?"

"Your girlfriend will squeal on you."

"Not without admitting she's been seeing me."

Steve stripped off his shirt. Climbed the cliff face, slowly,
carefully; found handholds, toeholds; by now the surface was
familiar to him. Robert waited nervously below.

The stone corridors; the torches, the candles. Steve found his
way through the maze; stole quietly into Mother Joseph's cell.
Looked around. Where could it be? Under the bed? It was too
obvious. He got down on his knees, looked under. There were a
number of small parcels, each wrapped carefully in linen. They
were along the back wall. One was much larger than the others;
that would be it. Steve had to reach to get at them. Turned his face
away from the bed, stretched out his arm and groped. As he
moved his hand about, something dug into it. Something sharp
pierced his hand. He screamed, pulled out from under the pallet.
It was a piece of glass, red glass, long and slender, tapering to a
vicious point; as he pulled it out, its linen wrapper fell away. The
glass stuck through his hand, and there was a river of blood; the
pain was like nothing he had ever felt. "Good Jesus!" He looked
around; no one was there, no one could have heard. Slowly,
carefully he extracted the glass; picked up the swath of linen,
wrapped it around the wound. The pain was beyond description.
He felt tears welling in his eyes. "Good Jesus, why did this have

to happen?" He looked around again. Tried to decide what to do. Lay flat on the floor and pushed the piece of glass back under the bed.

He noted carefully the place where the largest of the bundles sat. Reached slowly, tentatively; felt its heaviness, brought it out. Unwrapped it. It was a box, of clear leaded glass. Inside it was a thick sheaf of papers. The heading read: *Memoirs of Sister Joseph, formerly known as Clare Markham Kampinski*. This was what he wanted. He put it back into its box, carried it to the entrance.

Robert was waiting below. Steve tossed the box to him. It hit the ground and the glass shattered to splinters. Robert looked at it. "Damned idiot. Send an ape to do a man's job." He took the manuscript carefully from among the debris, read what he could of the first page by moonlight; was surprised at its thickness, its heaviness; walked off, back to his tent.

Steve watched him go, then turned and hurried to Martin's cell. She was waiting for him. Kissed him. Kissed his chest. "Hello, darling."

And he kissed her, a long, slow kiss.

"What happened to your hand?"

"A sharp rock on the mountainside."

"You're so accident-prone."

"I love you." He kissed her again. "Let's make love."

She pressed herself against him, kissed his neck. "This is forbidden. It's so exciting."

"Surely you're not the first nun to do this." He lifted her hand to his lips, kissed each finger.

"But with a blood relation . . ." She was breathing hard.

But it stopped him. "What?" He pulled back away from her. "What did you say?"

"I thought you understood. Mother Joseph is—"

"Your mother superior, yes." He wanted it left at that.

"No. She's my mother. She gave birth to me. Here, in the convent. I thought you understood that."

"No. I . . . no."

"Yes." She stepped close to him, rubbed his chest.

"Stop that!" He pulled away.

"But Steve, you said you wanted—"

"That was before."

"Steve." She stepped up to him again, laid a hand on his thigh.

"We're going to make love. I've already seen it. I've already seen how it will be. Not quite yet, not tonight, but we are going to make the beast with two backs."

He felt her breasts against him; felt her warmth. Her hand moved slowly up his leg. "Please. Not now. I need to think."

"I love you, Steve."

Without wanting to, he said it. "I love you, too." Her hand reached his groin. And they kissed.

She put her arms around him. Dug her fingernails into his back. It excited him. "I want," she whispered softly into his ear, "to make love to you before you die." But he was so lost in his passion that the words never registered.

In the chapel the nuns finished their vesper hymn; began their nightly ritual of confession, unaware what their sister was doing in her cell. The Bedouins in their settlement danced, sang, ate, feasted. Charlotte sat in her tent communing with Jane Austen. Robert unrolled the thick manuscript that was Mother Joseph's memoir, turned up the flame in the lantern by his cot. He had to know this woman, had to know her secret. And he read.

PART TWO

The Glass Apostles

The mind is its own place, and in itself
Can make a Heaven of Hell, a Hell of Heaven.
—Paradise Lost

1

I can still remember with remarkable clarity [read Mother Joseph's manuscript] my first day of work at the Tiffany Studios. It was early spring, April 1926; there was sun, the air was filled with the scents of fresh-bloomed crocus and daffodil. I was up early, walked through Central Park, took in the lush greenness. Many of the houses along Fifth Avenue were planted in front with lilies, for Easter. It was such a beautiful day, I could have stayed there in the park. But underneath everything else I felt was the excitement of a new job; of the career I'd come to New York to make.

I walked for blocks without tiring. The beautiful day had brought people out in their hundreds. Elegant ladies in bright spring colors and new hats. Young gentlemen in boaters and fashionably tight suits. A pair of them whistled at me as I crossed Madison Avenue at Sixty-first Street.

More blocks, and more; and then I was there. There was nothing exceptional about the building. But on the plate-glass door elaborate Art Nouveau lettering announced: The Tiffany Studios. On display in the showcase windows were pieces of the studio's work. A beautiful blue and lavender wisteria lamp, designed, I knew, by Mr. Tiffany himself. A small window, illuminated from behind, showing a field of flame-red poppies against a mountainous background. A dragonfly lamp: a cone of mottled blue-green glass girded by a ring of dragonflies yellow as the sun. This lamp, I knew, had been designed by a woman, a Miss Clara Driscoll. I looked from the lamp to the door and back again. The circle of golden dragonflies seemed to promise me the career I'd always dreamed of. As I pulled open the heavy front door I remember thinking that the colors of nature looked poor and weak beside the palette of Louis Tiffany.

The showroom was ablaze. Lamps of every pattern and description burned there. Trumpet vines, flowering dogwoods, peacock feathers, shimmering rings of acorns and mushrooms. On the walls were hung backlit windows. Vibrant landscapes, exuberant floral scenes, visions of God. One in particular caught my eye: a delicate young Roman woman, seated casually in her villa, bent over to feed her pet flamingos. The pink of the birds, the pale tones of her flesh, the gold of a fish circling in a bowl suspended above her head, all of these glowed like nothing in the world. It was art painted with lightning.

A young woman in stylish business clothes approached me. "Good morning, ma'am. May I be of some service?"

I had not wanted the silence to be broken; wanted nothing ordinary to interrupt my mood. I looked around hesitantly. "I'm Clare Markham."

She smiled, tried to conceal her puzzlement; clearly had no idea who I was. "Yes?"

"I'm to begin working here today."

"Oh." Her smile disappeared. "In Sales? You'll have to see Mr. Steiner. Just a moment." She turned to go.

"No, not in Sales. I'm to work in the studios."

She stopped in midstep; looked back at me. Eyed me up and down. "The employees' entrance is around the side of the building."

"Oh." I looked around quickly again at the lamps, at the windows; at the flamingos. "Oh. I see. I'm sorry to have troubled you."

"It was no trouble at all." She smiled to show me that it had been a good deal of trouble.

I turned to go. On a table beside me was a wonderful cherry tree lamp, all green and red and pink. I reached out a finger toward it; wanted to feel the surface of the glass.

"Please don't touch the merchandise." She was smiling even more icily.

"Oh. I'm sorry."

The front door seemed even heavier than it had before. Then I was back on Madison Avenue, in the moving press of people. The sunlight blinded me for a moment, seemed hard and harsh after the windows and lampshades inside. I pushed through the crowd, found my way to the alley that ran alongside the building. Walked hesitantly into it. And was in another world. The traffic kept moving behind me but I scarcely seemed to hear it.

I was alone in the alley. It was littered with wastepaper. There were huge trash bins; empty chemical drums; four concrete steps leading up to a wooden platform and an iron door on which was painted "Staff." The place that I had always imagined was inside the front entrance: the lamps, the color, the light. Not this.

From behind me came the sound of footsteps. A young man, no older than I was—if that—walked up to me. He tipped his hat, smiled. I was too nervous to say anything. He watched me expectantly. "Uh, good morning."

"Good morning." My voice was soft; I was mortified at my own timidity.

The boy was still smiling. He had black hair and blue eyes and looked so much like the boy next door it was silly. "You work here?"

"Uh, yes." I felt myself relaxing a little. "I'm just starting today."

"Well, that's great!" He seemed genuinely delighted to hear it. I had no idea why; I certainly can't have made much of an impression. "Which department are you in?"

"I don't know yet." I felt foolish saying it. "I'm to report to Miss Agnes Northmon."

"Oh, she's in Windows. She's a hell of a designer. You'll like her." He hesitated a moment, then went on energetically. "I'm in the Window Department, too. In fact, I'm Mr. Tiffany's chairman there. So we'll be seeing a lot of each other."

"I—" He had me completely off balance.

"Look, it's nearly starting time. Let's go in. Wouldn't want to be late your first morning, would you?" He jumped up the steps two at a time; pulled open the door. "Come on."

I walked slowly up the steps, nervous beyond description. It was not just a new job; it was what I had always wanted. And now I felt like turning and running. I stopped at the top step. Looked at my young man. And suddenly found myself giggling. "I don't know what I expected. Art. Beauty. Glamour." I looked inside. It was like a cave; I could smell chemicals. "But this is a factory."

"Yep." He laughed too. "My name's Marty Kampinski."

I introduced myself and we shook hands.

We were still standing absurdly outside. Marty lost his smile. "Well go ahead in. It's not the gateway to hell, you know."

I stepped inside; Marty followed me and let the door swing shut. It was dark. No stained-glass windows, just plain old dirty window glass. No Tiffany lampshades, only bare light bulbs at the ends of wires. The air smelled more and more strongly of chemicals; my nostrils stung. And there were factory noises, hammers, hacksaws, the shrill singing of glass cutters.

Marty took off his jacket and hung it on a rack near the door. "So it's not what you thought it would be?"

"No, I guess it isn't." I looked around uncertainly. "I was expecting . . . I don't know, a Parisian garret, or the Sistine Chapel, or . . ." I laughed again.

"Stained glass manufacture," he said slowly and carefully, "is an *industrial* art."

From a room not far from us came a crashing sound, and I jumped.

"Somebody just dropped a sheet of glass. You'll get used to it. Anyway . . ." He looked directly into my eyes for the first time. "Anyway, don't let it all fool you. There's still room for creativity here. Lots of it, you'll see. And not just in the design stages, either. It just doesn't go on in a very romantic setting."

"I can see that." I made a sour face.

"No, I mean it." He took a work apron from a peg, put it on. "We make real beauty here. Miss Northmon's office is on the second floor. The stairs are over there. Anyone up there will show you the way. Will you meet me for lunch?"

"Yes." I said it without thinking.

"Great. I'll meet you here at noon." And he was gone, into a room mysteriously labeled "Foil."

The metal steps seemed not to have been dusted for a hundred years. Halfway up them was a landing and a bare light bulb. Then I was at the top.

A middle-aged woman rushed busily down the otherwise empty hallway. Her hair was greying and she wore thick eyeglasses. I called after her. "Ma'am?"

She kept going.

"Excuse me. Ma'am?"

Turned into a room.

There was no one else in sight; I followed her. Stenciled on the door of the office was the name *Agnes Northmon*. I knocked; looked in. "Excuse me. Miss Northmon?"

She had sat down at her desk and was rummaging through a stack of sketches. Looked up at me. "Yes?"

"I'm Clare Markham. I'm supposed to—"

"Come in. Sit down. I'll be with you in a moment." Her voice was low, raspy, impatient. The desk in front of her was littered with ashtrays, piles of paper, a heap of glass fragments, a telephone.

"Yes, ma'am." I took off my coat, sat, folded it in my lap. On three of the four walls were taped up enormous sketches for what I presumed would become stained glass windows. A field of tulips and lilies with a stream running down the center; a magnificent bird of paradise perched on a tree limb; Christ preaching to the children.

She looked up at me again. "Oh. You're the new girl."

"Yes. I—"

She had been tense, full of energy. Now she relaxed. Smiled at me. "Clare—?"

"Markham."

"Yes. Markham. Well. Welcome to the Tiffany Studios."

Hearing those words made me forget all the morning's disappointments. Miss Northmon's welcome sounded perfectly genuine, and warm. "I couldn't be happier to be here."

"Good." She opened a desk drawer, pulled out a bottle of Coca-Cola, opened it and took a long drink. "Would you like one?"

"No, thank you."

"A cigarette, then?" She took one herself, lit up.

"No thanks."

"If I couldn't get caffeine and nicotine, I don't know what I'd live on." She put on a sober face. "Don't spread it around, though. I've got everyone here convinced I smoke opium. There were some impressive things in your portfolio."

"Thank you." I blushed.

"I especially remember that still life of the irises. It was lovely."

I felt awkward. "Thank you."

"That's the one that got you the job. We do a lot of flowers around here."

I glanced at the sketches on the walls. "So I see. I was expecting more . . . more . . ."

"Jesus and the Apostles? That sort of thing?" She smiled. "That used to be our bread and butter. But somehow the prewar boom in religion never picked up again after the Armistice. Too much pain, too much disillusionment, I don't know. We still do a good sprinkling of church windows, but it's not the same anymore. Mostly we get private commissions." She took a long drag on her cigarette.

"I'm a preacher's kid. When I think of stained glass, I think of church."

"Really? This place will soon cure you of that." She drained the last of the soda. "When I think of stained glass I think of randy junior designers and rough-speaking artisans."

"I think I know what you mean. I've already met the chairman of the Window Department. He didn't lose much time moving in on me."

"The—?" She looked completely baffled.

"Isn't he a bit young for such an important job?"

She was staring at me blankly. "You did say chairman of the department . . . ?"

"Uh, yes." I was puzzled by her tone. "Marty Kampinski."

"Oh." She broke out laughing. "The chairman. Yes."

I was lost. "Do you mean—?"

"Never mind." She was still laughing. "Chairman." She stubbed out her cigarette in a tray full of butts. "Exactly how much do you know about stained glass manufacture?"

"Well . . ." I was suddenly self-conscious. "I've read what I could. But there aren't many books. At least not in my library."

"You have a library of your own?"

"I worked as a librarian back home."

Miss Northmon lit a cigarette. "Home."

"Zelienople, Pennsylvania." I felt myself blushing again. "It isn't really much of a library."

"You don't have to apologize for it. I came here from Gumbow, Illinois. Everyone in New York was born somewhere else, and no one wants to admit it. They wouldn't be sophisticates then." She stood up, brushed some cigarette ashes from her skirt. "Come on. I'll show you around. In a little while, Mr. Tiffany's going to inspect some windows we're constructing. He keeps check on everything we do. I want you to meet him."

The telephone on the desk rang. She picked it up impatiently. "Yes?" There was a long pause. "Are you ready now?" Pause. "Okay." She hung up; looked at me. "Have you ever seen glass being made?"

"No, ma'am."

"Stop calling me ma'am. Come on."

We walked into the hall. It was still empty of people but filled with the sounds of craftsmen at work. Hammering, sawing. Voices raised above the din. We quickly descended the steps, walked into the enormous studio where the windows were actually assembled. Miss Northmon talked all the way. "Most of our glass is made out in Camden, but we have some kilns here. Every now and then we have to make a special piece under the supervision of a designer, and it just isn't convenient for us to make trips out there all the time."

The studio was filled with glass "easels," huge backlit tables. Patterns were affixed to these easels, and the pieces of glass and lead were fitted precisely into place over them. I saw flowers, trees, rivers, birds being assembled piece by piece; the workmen handled the glass as if it were nothing, as if it were indestructible. Miss Northmon led me to an easel in the back corner of the room. "Here. This is what we're working on."

It was a figure of Christ. He was staring full-face at the viewer. And his chest was cut open. His heart was exposed, wrapped in a withe of briars. Blood seeped down onto his robes. "It's for a Catholic church in Ohio," she said. Her distaste was obvious. "Catholics choose the most disagreeable subjects."

I wasn't certain what to say to this. "Your design is quite . . . lovely."

"Thank you. Look here. This is the piece we'll be rolling now." She indicated the chest of the figure, just below the heart, where the blood streaked the folds of his clothing. "We could set in separate red pieces, but it would look odd. We can do better than that. Come on downstairs."

I followed her. At the opposite corner of the studio a flight of steps led downward. I'd expected the basement to be cool, damp. But there was blazing heat. A line of furnaces roared in the darkness, provided all the light. Everything was red, orange, yellow. Men, stripped naked to the waist and covered with sweat, tended them busily and methodically. The fires bellowed, hissed; the floor vibrated with their roar. A smell of strong chemicals stung my nose. For a moment I was overcome by it, lagged behind.

Miss Northmon turned back to look at me; shouted above the fire. "Are you all right?"

"No."

She walked back to me, put a hand on my arm to steady me. "I should have warned you. After a while you'll get used to it."

"I can't breathe. It's like hell. All we need is Satan."

She laughed. "No, he's up in his office. I told you, you'll meet him later."

I looked at her unsteadily. "I think I'll be all right now."

"Good. Come on."

Not far from the furnaces was a row of large iron tables. We walked to the rearmost of them. The heat was stifling; my eyes watered and I could feel myself starting to perspire.

Miss Northmon spoke to the workman tending the last of the furnaces; their words were lost in the roar. I noticed two long blowpipes protruding from the furnace. The workman nodded at whatever she had said; set to work. He took the larger of the two pipes in his gloved hands, extracted it from the flames. At the end of it was a brightly glowing mass of molten glass. It was almost white with fire. He inspected it, then rested the midpoint of the pipe on the edge of the nearest table, and he began to blow. The mass grew, distended. When it had become a large bubble he slapped it with surprising force onto the iron tabletop; rolled it flat.

Then, somewhat to my astonishment, Miss Northmon went to work. She pulled on a huge pair of asbestos gloves—long enough to reach nearly to her shoulders—and grasped the still-glowing sheet by one edge. She wrenched it from the tabletop, twisted, turned, pulled, massaged it until finally it met her satisfaction. I took a step nearer, to see what she had done: when the glass cooled, it would hang like drapery, like the folds of the Savior's robes.

But it did not end there. The workman pulled the second melt from the furnace. It was smaller, and it glowed a dull orange. He blew it, but only until it was a foot or so across. Then he slapped it onto the table so that it just touched the edge of the first sheet.

It was once more Miss Northmon's turn. On the wall behind her was a rack of tools. She selected one, a large steel hook. Without an instant's hesitation she walked to the table, stood on the side just opposite the new melt. Reached out her arm and plunged the hook into the center of it. There was a dull ringing sound. She drew the hook slowly toward her, through the first sheet; drew long strands of the second glass through it.

I realized now what was happening. The second glass would be red when it cooled, the red of blood. And there would be drops of it streaked through the drapery of the other glass. I looked at Miss Northmon with a bit of marvel.

But there was something else. There was a scream. When she plunged her hook into what would become the heart of Christ; when she drew out the blood from it; there was a scream. A shrill, high scream. I thought for a moment I must be imagining it. Or that it was coming from somewhere else, from one of the furnaces. Tried to tell myself it was the scrape of metal hook on metal tabletop. But it was not a metallic noise. It was organic, animal; human. When she plunged her hook into the blazing heart of the Lord, it screamed.

There was no warning. No fog, no ringing in my head. I simply passed out.

I had always tried to tell myself that I didn't take conventional religion too seriously. My father was a Unitarian minister and raised me—or tried to—to be open-minded, liberal. But he sent me to a Catholic girls' school. It was, quite simply, the best education to be had for me. The St. Jude School, operated by a sect of Russian nuns displaced by the revolution; I can still see its ancient brick facade, at number 2025 Forbes Avenue in Pittsburgh. The nuns got to me. Broad-minded and freethinking as I had always tried to be about religious matters, the nuns and their brutal mysticism had got under my skin. When I fainted on the job, it was their doing; they made me fearful and impressionable, though God knows those are things I'd never have chosen to be. No, it was not the heat from the furnaces, not the noise, not the suffocating lack of air.

I came to on a sofa in a lavishly decorated office. Two windows of cascading wisteria behind a large mahogany desk gave the room an ethereal glow. There was a desk lamp of leaded green glass in the shape of a nautilus shell. I looked around. Standing over me was Marty Kampinski.

He was smiling at me, almost laughing. "So our little hell overcame you, did it?"

I was too embarrassed to say anything; gaped at him.

"If it's any comfort, you're not the first."

It was no comfort. "Where are we?"

"Mr. Tiffany's office, at the top of the building. He's quite concerned. He seems to have taken a personal interest in you."

"Oh. I was hoping he wouldn't have to know about this."

"This is his place. Completely. I doubt if you can get a drink of water without him knowing about it. Like a spider at the center of its web."

"What a reassuring image." I tried to sit up, and the room turned foggy. "Speaking of water . . ."

"I'll get you a glass." He rushed out into the hall.

Very slowly, carefully, I sat up. The sofa I was on was made of heavy silver velvet. I pressed my fingers against it to feel the plushness.

"Here you are." Marty was back, with Miss Northmon behind him. I drank the water, smiled weakly at her. There was an awkward silence in the room.

"I think I'll be all right now. May I get back to work?"

Miss Northmon studied me the way she might one of her windows, to find the imperfections. "If you want to rest a bit longer, it's quite all right."

"No, I think I'll be fine now."

"Good." She broke into a smile. "I feel as if what happened was my fault. Once you're used to conditions downstairs, it's easy to forget how they can affect someone who isn't."

"No. No, it was my fault. I should have—"

"Nonsense. I just wasn't thinking. The heat and the close air down there could sap a heavyweight boxer."

"It—" I started to protest that the heat, the air, the noise had had nothing to do with it. But I thought better of it. I'd rather be suspected of weakness than of superstition. "It's all right now. Really. I'd like to get back to learning my job."

"Good. Then let's get downstairs to the Window Department. Mr. Tiffany should be starting his inspection soon."

I stood up; hoped I didn't look as unsteady as I felt. There was another awkward silence as each of us stood there, waiting for one of the others to go through the door first. Then at the same instant we all laughed.

Miss Northmon looked at Marty. "Shouldn't Mr. Tiffany's chairman be there at the beginning of the inspection?"

Marty looked puzzled for a moment. Then, quite to my delight, he blushed. A deep crimson.

She glanced at me from the corner of her eye, then looked back at Marty. "I wish I could get some glass made in that shade of red."

I had no idea why, but this whole exchange seemed to mortify Marty. He stammered at us. "Uh, I have to go." And he ran into the hall; vanished. We could hear him clattering down the metal stairs.

I looked at her, confused. "What got into him?"

But she ignored it. "Come on. We should get down there ourselves." And so we went downstairs.

And there, just inside the door of the studio, stood Louis Comfort Tiffany. A short man, only five feet six, yet he dominated the whole vast studio. He was past seventy, with grey hair and a grey beard, like steel. His eyes were animated; moved about the room taking in everything, everyone. He glanced at me and smiled.

Miss Northmon pulled me forward to him; I was as nervous as I've been in my life. Introduced me. Mr. Tiffany shook my hand, told me how impressed he'd been by my portfolio. "And by your background," he said mysteriously. "You have the perfect background. I hope you'll be happy here."

Then he turned to Miss Northmon. "How is your Sacred Heart of Jesus coming?"

"It is proceeding." She made a sour face to show her displeasure with the subject matter. "I rolled the last of the glass this morning."

"Yes, so I heard." He looked at me from the corner of his eye. I felt an inch tall. "Well, why don't we have a look at it?"

There was quite a crowd of people. Designers, assistants, glass cutters, solderers . . . With Mr. Tiffany at the lead, we all moved slowly through the studio to the back corner, to the easel where Christ was being assembled. Miss Northmon took hold of my arm, made certain I stayed near the front of it all. I watched

Mr. Tiffany watching his glassworks. He was, to my surprise, infirm physically. Walked unsteadily, had to balance himself against a table here, a workbench there. Then I noticed his hands. They were twisted, swollen, disfigured. He suffered from arthritis, crippling and painful. Still, he seemed to take in everything. Then, when we reached the back of the studio he simply . . . sat down. Stopped moving. His legs bent. And from nowhere a chair appeared out of the crowd, just at the right moment. He had not bothered to look back and see if it was there, just took it for granted. I can't tell you how much it impressed me. That, I said to myself, is wealth, that is power.

Then I realized who it was who had provided the chair for him. It was Marty Kampinski. "Chairman." Indeed. I glared at him, but all his attention was on his employer.

Mr. Tiffany studied the window—what there was of it at that point. Considered for a long time. "Yes. It's good." Then the entourage moved through the studio, stopping at one easel after another. At each stop Marty was there with the chair. Mr. Tiffany would sit, study. "No, I don't like that piece there. The treetop. Find one that's less mottled." "There's a small crack in that rosebud." "This sheet of glass here—you see the flaw in it? Use it horizontally and it will look like a ripple in the water." And on and on. I wondered what he would think of the bloodstained drapery Miss Northmon had made; it was still in the basement, cooling.

After the inspection tour we went back up to Miss Northmon's office. I told her how surprised I was at the sharpness of Mr. Tiffany's mind, in contrast with the weakness of his body.

"Don't judge him by his age. Or by his physical condition. He supervises everything in this building. Keeps every lamp, every window in his head. He's a complete wonder."

Marty appeared; grinned at me. "Ready for lunch?"

I stood to attention. "Mr. Chairman." I sounded as cold as I could manage. It wasn't easy; I wanted to laugh.

He blushed. "It's lunchtime. You said you'd eat with me."

"That was before I knew how important you are. You're way out of my league."

I teased him for another few minutes, then we went and ate. Over lunch he told me that he was an apprentice designer, like myself; he had only been working at Tiffany's for three weeks.

I let him take me to dinner and a movie that night. Lon Chaney in *The Phantom of the Opera*. It wasn't something I much wanted to see, but Marty was keen on it. "Chaney fascinates me," he explained eagerly. "The way he tortures himself for his art. For this role he had to insert metal clips into his nose and wear springs inside his mouth, to get the proper grimace. He suffers for us. Like Jesus."

"Don't be blasphemous."

"All artists are like that." He grinned like the boy he was. "They have to be. They suffer for their art, and for us."

2

For a year Marty and I dated. Dinners; movies; we often went dancing. I had seen no one else, and I don't believe he had, either. But I had managed to keep a bit of distance between us. His naïve earnestness, his happy boyishness . . . I had never quite been able to . . . It was no use. There were too many things still unknown between us, and I had a suspicion they were unknowable.

Then one afternoon I was sitting in the studio, cutting glass for a mountainscape. The cutter wheel was on the glass, I was in the middle of scoring it, and Marty came up behind me and put his hands over my eyes. "Guess who?"

"Stop it, Marty. I'll cut myself. You're such a little boy sometimes."

He smiled boyishly. "I thought that's what you love about me. You've been telling me so for months."

I laid the cutter carefully down on top of the glass. "I have told you that I love your boyish looks. That's not at all the same thing."

"It's close enough for me." He grinned.

"You look perfectly idiotic when you do that." I think I must have sensed what was coming, and it made me irritable.

"I know it." He smiled even more widely. "I don't want to seem threatening."

Then from out of nowhere Agnes Northmon appeared. "Exactly what are you two doing? Hugging on company time isn't kosher."

"I wasn't hugging him." I was still annoyed. "He was hugging me."

"Even so. The person hugging and the person being hugged are equally responsible. Why don't you hug him more at night, so he can concentrate on his work when he's here?" She put on a suggestive tone.

It was exasperating. I picked up my cutter, went back to work, and tried to ignore the pair of them.

But Marty was on the offensive. "Now tell me, Agnes, is that any way for her to behave to a man who came over here to say how much he loves her and to ask her to marry him?"

"To what?" I dropped the cutter on the glass and spun around to face him.

"Be careful, Clare. You'll chip the glass." Agnes leered at me.

"But . . . but . . ." I looked from one of them to the other.

"Go ahead, Clare. Tell him you accept his proposal. Or at least flutter your eyelashes and say something like, 'This is so sudden. I need time to think.'" She lit a cigarette, filled the air around us with smoke.

I didn't know which was more disconcerting, Marty's proposal out of the blue or Agnes's gentle mocking. I adopted the coldest tone I could manage. Glared at both of them. "But this is so sudden. I need time to think."

She laughed, dragged on her cigarette. "There's such a thing as thinking too much, you know."

Agnes was annoying me more and more. She was a spinster, after all. I looked at Marty. "Look, I do need time. You couldn't have caught me more off guard."

"Let me take you to dinner tonight. We can talk it over."

"Well . . . all right." Agnes smiled triumphantly; I kept my eyes on Marty. "But don't take anything for granted."

"I won't." For once his schoolboy smile was gone. "Your place at eight o'clock?"

"Fine."

"And how about a movie after we eat?"

"Fine, Marty."

"Good. I'll see you then." He pecked me on the cheek, ran off to his own corner of the studio.

"He's such a handsome boy." Agnes was enveloped in smoke, like a fire-breathing monster.

"You've put your finger on the problem. He's a boy."

"But a fine figure of one."

"Agnes, I don't think I'm ready to be married. And I'm positive he isn't."

"He loves you."

"I know it."

"And you love him."

I hesitated.

And, finally, she understood. "Oh." She stubbed her smoke out on the side of a table. "I sort of took it for granted . . ."

"Yes."

"You don't love him, then?"

"That's the problem. I don't know." I looked into her eyes; felt foolish saying it. "I don't even know if I know how to know."

"Oh." There were ashes down the front of her blouse. She tried to look nonchalant as she dusted them off.

"You should wear a work apron, like the rest of us."

"No. It'd make me feel like I was in a kitchen."

"Is that so horrible?"

"You don't seem to be in any hurry to become a homemaker. Why should I like it any more than you?"

"Homemaker." The word sounded alien. Ugly. "I don't want that. I want my career here. Mr. Tiffany says I'll be a journeyman designer before too much longer."

"With a husband like Marty you could have both."

I looked across the studio. Marty was fitting pieces into a wisteria window. There were hundreds of them, some of them no longer than a thumbnail. He sneezed, sent a handful of them clattering onto the floor. Agnes and I were both feeling uncomfortable; our relationship had been professional, not at all intimate. I wanted to tell her, I don't know what I want, and I don't think Marty has any real idea what he wants, either. So how could we . . . ? But the conversation had already reached too far into my privacy. "I'd better get back to work. There's a lot of cutting to do here yet."

Over dinner that night, he would talk of nothing but his proposal. He was hurt. He was passionate. "Don't you love me, Clare?"

How is it ever possible to answer that question? I hid behind my intellect. "It's a problem of definition, Marty."

"What do you mean?"

"I mean just that. What does love mean? If it has to be absolute and irresistible to be love, then no, I don't love you. But if it can be a relative thing, then I do. Very much." I looked at him.

"Oh." I don't think he had any idea what I was trying to say. He played with his dinner on the plate. "I always thought with women it was . . . Well, never mind, I guess." He perked up; took a long drink of coffee. "What movie shall we see? There's a new Lon Chaney. Something called *The Unholy Three*."

"No thanks. Nothing like that tonight."

"Oh. Well, what, then?"

I didn't much want to go to a movie. "There's a new Buster Keaton. How about that?"

"You're sure I can't talk you into Chaney?"

"Positive."

"All right then, Keaton it is."

So we went to see *The General*. A Civil War story about a boy and his train. And he has to master his train to win the girl in the end. Except that the train seemed much more important to him than the girl. She was a prop; he loved the machine. I can't say it helped my mood.

"I still remember your irises." Mr. Tiffany sat behind his desk; he was in a paternal mood.

"Thank you, sir." In the year since I had first met him, he had hardly aged at all. But the deformity in his hands had gotten worse. He could barely hold a teacup for himself. But he still supervised everything, still knew, understood, approved of all that we did in the studio.

"I'm thinking of adding a new wing to Laurelton Hall."

"Oh?" I wasn't following his train of thought at all.

"Yes. And it will need windows, of course."

"Yes?"

"Yes. I thought, if it was all right with you, that your irises would make a lovely one."

I could not have been taken more off guard. And I could not have been more flattered. "Yes, of course, I'd be so honored to have my work incorporated into Laurelton Hall. Yes, I'd love that." I was embarrassed to gush like this, but I couldn't help myself. "Only . . ."

My hesitancy puzzled him. "What's wrong, Clare?"

"I'm just not sure I'm good enough to do it, that's all."

"Oh." He turned sober. "Well, to be frank, you're not. I've asked Agnes to adapt the design."

My disappointment must have been plain.

"But you'll be working under her. As closely as ever. It'll be your work, too."

"Yes, sir." I couldn't hide what I was feeling. "I only wish I were good enough to do it all myself. For you."

"Thank you, Clare. I'm touched that you feel that way."

"It would mean so much to me to be able to—"

"I have more important things in store for you than just making me windows."

"I beg your pardon?"

"I told you when I hired you, you have the proper background for something I've had in mind for years."

"I'm afraid I don't follow." He had said this kind of thing to me before, and then had always left me mystified.

"Good."

"You're not being fair, Mr. Tiffany."

He rested his head on his hands; fell silent for a moment. "The nuns who educated you taught you Greek and Latin, drilled you in the classics."

"Yes." I was lost.

"And in church history. You studied the great medieval mystics."

"Yes. But I don't—"

"They washed you, as it were, in the Blood of the Lamb."

I stared at him. "I think I'll get back to work now, if you don't mind."

He became a mandarin. "Yes. Work. By all means. The important thing will come in time."

3

"There's a good deal about hell you don't understand. You're too young." Mr. Tiffany's tone was casual, offhand.

It was two years before I was permitted to design windows of my own. A long, difficult apprenticeship. I had learned how to make glass; could fold draperies, could draw blood through them like Miss Northmon herself. Fractures, mottles, textured cathedrals, I was expert with them all. I don't know how many times I burned my hands learning to use the soldering irons of the craft. My fingers became so scarred from it, I had to rely on other people to do all my cutting. But then, I was in training to be a designer, not a craftsman. It was in learning to oversee all of these—and more besides; learning to blend carefully all the elements, all the steps—it was there that the real challenge lay.

Then I was assigned my first window. A vision of God the Father on the Day of Judgment. I was so nervous. But I worked up a preliminary sketch which Mr. Tiffany approved almost at once. It was a simple thing. A rose window, eight feet in diameter. A stern figure of God the Father, facing the viewer; surrounded by flames, the flames of damnation, emanating from him like the petals of a flower. I used the most vibrant reds, yellows, oranges in our palette of glass. And the clients, a small Catholic church in Mill Creek, Pennsylvania, were duly pleased. Mill Creek is not far from Zelienople, where I grew up; which added to my pleasure at my first completed design.

It was the second one that led to my encounter with Mr. Tiffany. A Lutheran church in Vermont wanted a hell. Judgment Day again, but this time the tortures of the damned. I did a sketch in the manner of Bosch, twisted figures, agonized faces. Above them all, framing them all, was Satan, wings outspread, a gloating smile on his face; his body, like theirs, was bent in torment.

Mr. Tiffany called me to his office; had the sketch in his hand when I got there. He offered me a seat and smiled. "You have a penchant for these apocalyptic scenes."

I shrugged. "They're what Agnes assigns me. I'd really rather be doing floral windows."

"You will. But for the time being, you do these extremely well."

"Thank you, sir."

He sat back in his chair; avoided looking at me. "But—"

"There would be a but." We both laughed.

"But." For a moment he was silent. From time to time his arthritis gave him twinges of pain, which he covered with silence. I studied one of the wisteria windows behind him. Then he let out a long breath, seemed to relax. "But"—he smiled—"what you have here is a depiction of torture. Our client wants hell."

"I've given them Satan." I was totally lost.

"Satan is too conventional. This is the Tiffany Studios." He took up a pencil in his crooked fingers. "Watch." I walked round behind him. With the eraser he took out just a few of my Satan's lines. Sketched lightly a few new ones to replace them. And the Lord of Darkness became the Lord of Light; the devil, spiky wings spread wide, was transformed into Jesus Christ on his cross. The features were the same; the pain was the same.

I was a bit shocked. It struck me as blasphemous. "Christ in hell."

"Yes." He smiled; was pleased with himself.

"Surely you've gotten your Scripture wrong."

"The Lord Jesus Christ spent, I believe, precisely three days in hell."

I stared at him. "That's only in the Apocrypha."

"Even so. It makes sense."

His sketch, the more I studied it, seemed more and more distasteful to me. It must have shown in my face.

"Heaven and hell are the same place. It isn't possible to find one without discovering the other." He sounded weary.

"Perhaps so." I'm afraid I must still have sounded disapproving. "I've read my Milton. But this . . ."

He had been watching me; trying, I think, to guess what was

going through my mind. Then suddenly he was all business. "It's only a suggestion. Think about it for a few days. For a week. If you decide not to use it, I'll approve your original concept."

That night Marty proposed to me for the second time. We went to dinner. Italian; mountains of spaghetti, glaciers of Parmesan cheese. My mood was distracted; I couldn't get over what Mr. Tiffany had done to my sketch. It was so grotesque. Our client would never agree to it. But then . . . Mr. Tiffany seemed so certain it was right.

Unlike me, Marty was in fine spirits. "There's a new movie playing. About the undead."

I slurped up a long strand of pasta. "The what?"

"The undead." He smiled gleefully. "It's called *London After Midnight*. It's the new Lon Chaney."

"The undead." I stared at him.

"You know. Vampires. *Dracula*. That kind of thing." He looked around furtively, lowered his voice.

"You sound as if simply seeing the film would give you a share in its vice."

He grinned his boy-next-door grin. "They say that Chaney had to put loops of wire into his eye sockets to get the right look for this one."

"No thanks." I took another forkful of pasta. "Nothing like that tonight. Couldn't we just go dancing?"

"Aw, come on."

"Why do you always pick horror movies? There's a new Buster Keaton out that I'd love to see."

"Well . . ." He was sullen. I'd robbed him of his fun.

"Please, Marty, no horror tonight." And so we went to see *Steamboat Bill, Jr.*

And afterward Marty proposed. Right in the theater lobby. Most of the people were gone already, or I would have been embarrassed. "I love you, Clare. You know how much. Now that we're both designers, we can afford it." He actually got down on one knee and held his hat over his heart.

But in my mood that night . . . I bent over and kissed the top of his head. "No, Marty. I can't. Not now."

"Not now." He looked like a wounded schoolboy. "If not now, when?"

"I don't know. When I . . . when I know what I want. When

I know where I am. When I find something, anything to believe in."

"I thought you might believe in me. In us." He stood slowly up.

"I don't know."

He walked me home, kissed me good night at the door. He was such a sweet man. To this day I don't know if I loved him. To this day I feel guilty about giving in, finally, to his proposals; about marrying him. But then . . . but then, marriage was not the most awful sin I committed against him.

My sleep that night was filled with nightmares, with blood and fire. We might as well have gone to see the vampires, after all.

And the next morning, first thing, I went to see Mr. Tiffany. "Your vision of hell is the right one. I want to do the window that way."

I had expected him to look—or sound—pleased. But he was all business. "Fine, fine. Send the sketch on to the client for approval."

And so, duly taught by my master, I began work on my first important piece of art. I looked inside myself and found the truth, and I began preparations to turn that truth into a glowing wall of light. Mr. Tiffany gave me a detached kind of guidance, a correction here, a suggestion there. But all of the images, all of the hell came out of me, out of myself, and I have never in my life felt so alone.

4

Laurelton Hall.

Marty and I rode out to Long Island on the train one Saturday afternoon in early June. Our invitation was for the weekend; we brought evening clothes with us. There were to be other guests, we had no idea who; but Mr. Tiffany's salon was famous.

Conversation on the way out was difficult. Marty was still protesting his love, asking me to marry him. Or to make love to him, which was worse. I tried again and again to explain that without a certain distance between us, I would never be able to see the situation clearly; but he could not understand that. If I loved him at all, it was because of his direct earnestness.

Mr. Tiffany had a Rolls-Royce limousine waiting for us at the train depot and we rode, in greater luxury than either of us was used to, to Oyster Bay. It was late afternoon; everything was flooded with sunlight. The view of the bay was magnificent. It was easy to see why, of all places in the world, Mr. Tiffany had chosen to live there. The house itself was grand, but not at all overornate in the way of so many mansions of the time. Clean, simple proportions; no excessive ornamentation. It was surrounded by lush gardens; and the walls were covered with the wisteria vines Mr. Tiffany loved so much.

We rang; were admitted. An attendant took our evening clothes, showed us in. The atrium was a marvel of design. Water flowed in a gentle fountain from a large ceramic vase of Mr. Tiffany's own design. There were dozens of plants. And there were carved stone columns, with bright yellow glass daffodils set into their capitals.

After only a moment Mr. Tiffany appeared, pushed in his

111

wheelchair by one of his daughters. His legs were covered by a bright tartan blanket. "Clare. Marty. I'm so glad you were able to come."

"It's a delight to be here, sir." I gestured at the room around us. "I've always heard that this house was your greatest work of art, and that certainly seems to be so."

"The 'serious' artists dismiss me and what I do." He said it in a tone that clearly dismissed them, and their opinions. "Let's go into my study."

His daughter pushed him and we followed. Everywhere were splendid pieces of the glassmaker's art. Everywhere was tasteful furniture, elegant but not too lavish. In what I took to be the breakfast nook, a cone-shaped lamp of flowering dogwood blossoms hung over a small table. The rugs, also designed by Mr. Tiffany, complemented their rooms perfectly. It was an artist's heaven.

Just as we were about to enter his study, I caught a glimpse of a rather severe-looking woman walking at the far end of the hall, a drink in her hand. One of the other guests? She looked vaguely familiar, but I really didn't get a good enough look to be sure.

Then we were at his study, and I saw at once why he'd wanted to meet with us there. My irises. Or rather, his now. The most vibrant purple petals. And for the background, he had selected a gentle red-gold glass that made perfect contrast with the flowers. I had worked on the window's construction; had even seen it complete; but seeing it here, in its proper setting, flooded with Long Island's clear, crisp light . . . I had a mixture of feelings. It was beautiful; it was mine; and yet it was not mine. But the greatest feeling was the sense of its powerful beauty. "I can't tell you how lovely it is."

"It's your doing, Clare. The design, the composition, the lines—all of those are yours. Only the medium is mine."

I had no idea how to thank him for this generous statement.

Meanwhile Marty had been looking around at the other windows in the room. They were gorgeous. A series representing nature's transformations through the four seasons. A classic, almost Roman mural, but done in glass, of young women bathing in a stream. "I can't get over it." Marty kept looking around, like a dazzled boy. "I work with the stuff every day, but I never get tired of its beauties. And of its marvelous possibilities for artistic expression."

Mr. Tiffany gestured us to a pair of wing chairs. "Please, make yourselves comfortable. Can I offer you some wine?"

"Yes, please."

He rang, and in a moment a servant appeared with a decanter of chardonnay. We tasted it, complimented it; it was delicious; waited for him to take the lead in conversation.

"There is," he said in low, sad tones, "something I want to show you. I have wanted you, Clare, in particular, to see it."

He paused, let this have its due effect. Marty and I were silent.

"Marty, would you do me the favor of drawing all of the curtains?"

"Yes, sir. Of course." He went around the room, closed one set of drapes after another. There was still daylight coming in, but not much. The room was in its own twilight.

"Now look at this." From under the tartan blanket he drew a long, slender piece of glass. Red glass. The reddest I had ever seen. Redder than seemed possible. The color was so vibrant that it took me a moment to realize that there was something even more remarkable about it. "It looks like it's glowing."

"Yes."

So far Marty had said nothing. He stared at the fragment, spellbound. "We work our tails off trying to make glass that can glow like that with so little light to illuminate it. How did you make it? Where did you get it?"

Mr. Tiffany ignored him; turned to me. "What are the first recorded words of the Lord, Clare?"

The question was so unexpected, it took me a moment to think. "Why, he said, 'Let there be light.' "

"And why is that significant?"

The drift of our conversation eluded me completely. "Why . . . why . . . there are any number of possible explanations for it. The simplest is that God himself—his essence—*is* light."

Mr. Tiffany smiled. Evidently I was passing whatever sort of test he was giving me. I found myself thinking of all his cryptic references to my background. So it was to be theology, or mysticism, or something of the sort. He extended his hand, held out the glass to me. "Here. Examine it. Handle it carefully, though; it's quite sharp."

I took the fragment between two fingers. Felt the razorlike edges. And was astonished. It seemed to have no weight, none at all. It seemed that in my hand I held a shred of pure light. I let out a small gasp.

"Be careful!" Marty thought that I had cut myself.

But I showed him my hand, uncut. I passed the splinter to him. And his reaction to it, to its lightness, was the same as mine. "It isn't possible. This must be a quarter inch thick. But it weighs nothing at all."

Mr. Tiffany smiled; we had obviously taken the important point. Marty handed the glass back to him. But the old man's crippled hand could not grasp it properly. It fell. I was alarmed, afraid it would shatter before we could learn its secret; but the pile of the carpet was thick, and the fragment landed harmlessly. There was a look of pain on Mr. Tiffany's face; or of embarrassment at his uncontrolled clumsiness. I picked up the splinter, placed it firmly in his hand. "Thank you, Clare. I'm afraid I . . ." His discomfiture was plain. It occurred to me for the first time that we were seeing this man in his home, as his guests; the formality of the workplace was not quite in effect here. He looked suddenly ancient to me.

His daughter returned. Looked around the room, made certain everything was as it should be. Inquired briefly if we—if he—needed anything. Was discreetly gone.

"My girls love me." There was pain in his voice. From the arthritis? "They see to me constantly. Even the oldest of them, who is married now and has children of her own, returns here to tend to me. And I love them, much too deeply."

The room was still full of gloom. The crimson glass in his hand still glowed. Still held, despite Mr. Tiffany's self-revelation, my attention. I felt vaguely guilty.

Then suddenly his spirits brightened again. "We want light. The rest of this conversation will need light. Marty, would you . . . ?"

Marty was on his feet, making for the drapes.

"No. Not the windows. Turn on my lamps."

There were more than a dozen of them in the study. One by one they were lit. Dragonflies, daffodils, rose bowers, American

Indian patterns, flowering lotus. The room was ablaze with color and light. And in it, Mr. Tiffany looked old, pale. He held up again the glass splinter. "Look."

It was glowing, as brightly as the glass in the lampshades.

My curiosity got the better of me. I couldn't contain it. "Please, sir, tell us about that."

"You're not drinking your wine."

I raised my glass to my lips. "Neither are you."

He reached for his own glass. And it slipped through his fingers; splashed onto the carpet. Once again his embarrassment was clear; in the lamplight his face showed crimson. Marty rushed to soak up the spill with his handkerchief.

"No, leave it. It doesn't matter." He lowered his voice. "I can't tell you how much I hate myself for being like this. Every year there are fewer and fewer things I can do for myself. It is constant humiliation. It is not a way for a man to live."

We were silent.

"I don't want to be alive, Clare. I don't want the pain anymore."

"But surely, sir . . ." I had to say something to him, but I had no idea what. "But surely there are good things left. The love in this house. Surely that matters."

"Less and less as the pain increases. It is not possible to desire anything but that it should stop." He was barely whispering to us. "If I tell you something, will you promise not to be shocked?"

"Yes, of course." It was the only possible answer.

"The only thing that prevents me from taking my own life is that I know how much it would hurt my daughters. It is far better that I should suffer than they."

Marty shifted uneasily in his chair. I knew I had to get the talk onto another subject, or he would say something boyishly impulsive. Or worse, something embarrassing. For that moment, at least, I did not love him.

I waited a long silent moment. Spoke softly. "Mr. Tiffany, weren't you going to tell us about that red glass?"

"This glass." It got him out of his melancholy. "Yes. This splinter of red glass." He picked it up carefully, painfully, between thumb and index finger. Lifted it up a foot or so. And then, with alarming suddenness, he plunged it into his left wrist.

"Good God!"

"Mr. Tiffany!"

We were both on our feet. Rushed to his side. It took a moment for it to register that he was smiling. Was in no discernible pain. We stopped in our tracks. The glass was thrust through his wrist; it protruded from the other side. But there was no blood. He was in no pain. Slowly, carefully, he extracted it. Handed it to me to examine. There was no blood on it, not a drop.

I had no idea what to think, what to feel. I looked from Mr. Tiffany to Marty and back; looked around the room, at all the glowing glass. Marty looked stunned. Mr. Tiffany smiled faintly. "Sit down, both of you."

We sat. Watched him. We had both handled the glass, felt its sharp edges; had seen it project through his arm.

"I found this glass in a curiosity shop in Berlin six years ago. At first it was only its color, its glow that attracted my interest. The shopkeeper told me that he had had a great deal of it once, but that this was the last piece of it in his stock. It came, he told me, from a ruined cathedral at a small town called Obergurgl."

"Obergurgl?" Marty laughed.

"Yes, believe it or not, that is the name of the place. At any rate, I bought the glass. Wanted to have it analyzed, wanted to learn what gives it its astonishing color and lightness. Back in my hotel room, I accidentally cut myself with it. Or rather, *would* have cut myself, except for the phenomenon you just witnessed. What I had bought as a curiosity was beginning to look miraculous."

He handed me the glass again. I drew it, carefully, across the tip of a finger. It did not cut. It penetrated, I could feel it beneath the skin, but there was no cut, no blood. I offered the glass to Marty but he refused it.

"And so I made inquiries." Mr. Tiffany took back the fragment. "There was a local legend that the stained glass in that cathedral— the red glass, that is—had been made with the blood of St. Andrew the Apostle."

"Glass made with blood?" Marty scowled. "It isn't possible."

"Red glass is colored with iron." Tiffany was abrupt with him. "There is iron in blood. Who can say what is possible?" He drew the glass through his fingertip.

A servant came. Asked if we required more wine, or food perhaps. But we had barely touched what was already there.

"I have some medieval manuscripts. In church Latin. Can you read them, Clare?"

"Yes, sir." I looked at Marty, who was clearly lost.

"You will find in them references to the blood of the Apostles. Blood preserved miraculously. Blood made into glass, red glass, for certain churches. But it is all too vague to be useful. Will you read them?"

"Yes, of course." I was eager.

"I want you to go to Rome. To the Vatican Archives. I want you to learn where the other glass is, and to find it, and to bring it to me, if you can."

"You think it will cure your arthritis?" Marty was slow.

Tiffany glared at him. "I do not. I want it because it represents my art in an ultimate way. I believe in God. I believe that creation is the essence of divinity. And my whole life has been devoted to creation, to the creation of beauty. If it is possible for my art to bring me closer to the divine than it already has, then I want that. Surely you can fathom that."

It showed in Marty's face that he could not fathom it at all. But I understood Mr. Tiffany perfectly.

"You will even find references to a legend," he said softly, "that there is glass made from the blood of Christ himself. Perhaps you'll be able to track that myth to its roots."

For a moment I was speechless. But I wanted very much to do this for him. And for myself. I did not want to seem the least bit hesitant. "I'll go wherever I need to. I'll find it, if it is real."

He smiled. "I always said you had the right background. And the right temperament. I've already spoken to my friend Cardinal Hayes. He will give you letters of introduction to the proper authorities at the Vatican. You should have access to whatever you need." He turned to Marty. "And I want you to go with her. A woman can't function very well alone in a place like the Vatican. You're to be her guide and protector."

My heart sank. If it had been anyone but Marty . . . But Marty's face lit up. The prospect of a grand tour with me obviously delighted him. "I'd love to go with her, sir."

"Fine. Then it's settled." He reached up and switched off, with obvious pain, the lamp beside him; sat in relative shadow. "But of course you see the danger in all of this."

"A danger." Marty's voice was flat.

"Coming so close to the divinity also brings one perilously close to hell."

This disturbed me; but once again Marty seemed oblivious to it. I did not want him traveling with me. But there seemed no way to avoid it.

"Look at these hands of mine." He held them both out before us. They were twisted, bent, hideous. "Look at how grotesque they are. I have devoted them, all my life, to the divine act of creation; to beauty and to life. And yet now they bring forth only pain and ugliness. The same instrument produces both, and that instrument is man."

I avoided looking at Marty; could imagine the puzzlement I would see on his face.

Another one of Mr. Tiffany's daughters entered discreetly. "Excuse me, Father. It is less than an hour to dinner."

"Already?" He looked irritably at his wristwatch. Sighed. "We've been talking for a lot longer than I realized. Why don't the two of you go upstairs and get ready for dinner. I shall go and be gracious to my other guests. We'll have to talk about this more, Clare."

"Yes, sir. Of course."

A butler showed us to a pair of adjoining bedrooms. We shared a bathroom. Marty wanted to shower, so I let him have it first. In a moment there were clouds of steam coming out from it, and Marty sang, off-key, a song by Gershwin. I walked to the French window that opened onto my balcony, opened it, walked out. The daylight was dying; the sun was low and it lit brilliantly, deeply the waters of the bay. The trees, the bushes were just beginning to take on the colors of the evening; the air was heavy with the scents of early summer blooms.

I walked back inside, lay on the overstuffed mattress of my huge four-poster, closed my eyes, savored all the opulence around me. One day, Clare, I told myself, you will live like this. One day you will be recognized as the successor to Louis Tiffany. You will have wealth and fame and you will show the cold family you left behind what a woman they lost in you. After Mr. Tiffany dies . . . I stopped myself, shocked at the thought; I felt like a ghoul.

Marty was still in the shower. I glanced at my watch. We would be late for dinner. "Marty."

He could not hear me for the steam and the bad singing.

"Marty." I knocked on the bathroom door.

Still no response.

I opened it a crack. "Marty." He had just stepped out of the shower; was drying himself with a thick towel. His body was beautiful. In the two years we'd known each other, I'd never seen him in as little as a bathing suit. But his body was beautiful. And wet; dark hairs clinging to his skin, his body excited me. I stared for a moment; wanted to touch him, wanted to walk into the steam-filled room and touch his body; pulled the door quietly shut. Knocked. "Marty darling, we have to hurry. It's getting late and I still have to wash up."

He opened the door, wrapped in his towel. Smiled at me. "You called me darling!" He was grinning his patented grin. But I barely noticed. The hair on his chest was still matted, wet; I could not take my eyes off it. "We'll be late."

"Let's stay up here all night." He leered at me. "The others'll never miss us."

"Others?"

"Patrick Cardinal Hayes is coming to dinner. And Governor Smith. And somebody named Parker. I'm not sure who else. I overheard two of the servants talking about seating arrangements."

"The cardinal will be coming about our . . . mission."

"A wild goose chase." He winked at me.

"You saw the glass."

"Nonsense. Just tricks."

"But Marty . . ."

"The bathroom's all yours, Clare." He walked out past me, still dripping wet. Just as he entered his own bedroom he let the towel fall, and I saw once again his naked body. Lust was a new emotion for me; I was not certain I liked it. I went into the shower and washed up as quickly as I could.

Afterward, I climbed into a plush terry bathrobe, let it dry my body. I strolled back to my room, enjoying the feel of the cloth, the coolness of the early evening air. Stepped out onto the balcony again. The west had sunset colors. I studied them; thought, One day I shall have to duplicate that sky in glass.

From his room Marty called, "Ready yet, Clare?"

It shook me out of my reverie. "No, I've still got to dress."

"Well, get a move on. I think we're late already."

I stepped out of the robe, started dressing. "Dinner is at eight. What time is it now?"

"Five after."

"Oh my God. I'll be right with you."

I was just climbing into my underthings when I felt something odd. Looked at the connecting door. It was open a crack. Marty was there, watching me. I walked over and pushed the door violently shut; it struck his head and he cried out in pain.

"Jesus, Clare!"

"Let that be a lesson to you."

"Christ, I'm bleeding."

I half suspected a trick. Pulled open the door. It had struck the side of his head, just behind the eye. It was bruised, swollen; there was a trickle of blood. "I'll get one of the servants to bring bandages and disinfectant."

I rang. While the maid tended to Marty's injuries I finished dressing. And finally, fifteen minutes late, we entered the dining hall for our first dinner as Mr. Tiffany's guests.

As we expected, we were late. The servants were clearing away the soup, serving the fish. A butler poured wine. As we made our entrance, horribly self-conscious, Mr. Tiffany saw Marty's bandages. "Good Lord, what happened?"

Marty grinned. "Just an incident with the door." He looked at me and leered. "The bedroom door."

Mr. Tiffany stiffened. "Let me introduce you to my other guests. This is Patrick Cardinal Hayes."

The cardinal, dressed in a business suit, was distinguished, grey. He nodded at us; clearly disapproved of Marty's little joke.

"Governor Al Smith." Mr. Tiffany gestured at the governor, who of course we both recognized.

Seated next to the governor was the woman I had seen in the hall earlier. She ignored us, ignored everyone and everything, concentrated intently on the wine in her glass, which she swirled as if she were teasing it. This time I recognized her, from all the caricatures in *The New Yorker*. "This," our host announced, "is Miss Dorothy Parker."

Without looking up she said, "If you had any sense, dears, you'd still be up in that bedroom." She was tense; kept her gaze turned inward; drank.

"I've admired your writing for a long time, Miss Parker." I was a bit awed to meet her. "Your poems. And I think 'Big Blonde' is a wonderful story."

"A lover of fine art." Her face lit up, but she still watched only the wine; took a long drink. Her tension was spreading through the room; no one moved but her.

The fourth guest had a rather unexpected look about him. Large, burly, more like a longshoreman or a teamster than like someone who'd be dining with this company. He seemed ill at ease. Mr. Tiffany introduced him. It was Lon Chaney.

Marty's eyes widened. "Mr. Chaney! I'm your biggest fan!"

"I thought you were *her* biggest fan." Miss Parker actually looked at me.

But Marty seemed not to hear her. Spiritual power, political power, artistic power, even love or lust, all paled for him before this living icon, before this movie star. He groped for words. "I've never seen you before without makeup. You're actually one of us." He seemed to have no idea how this sounded.

"What did you think he was, Marty?" I couldn't resist goading him. "A man from Mars? It's a great pleasure to meet all of you. I'm so sorry we're late." We took our seats.

Mr. Chaney looked decidedly uncomfortable. I was seated next to him. Cut into my fish. "This is delicious." I hoped neutral conversation would put him at ease. "It's whitefish, isn't it?"

"I believe so, yes." His voice was strained. He seemed to be having trouble swallowing. "Have you tasted the wine?"

I sipped it. "Wonderful. Spicy. I don't think I recognize it."

"It's called gewürztraminer." He took a mouthful of fish; drank again. "It's from Alsace. Excuse me, I seem to have a bit of a sore throat."

From across the table Marty stared at us; at Mr. Chaney. Seemed unable to believe I was talking familiarly with the Phantom, the Hunchback, the Vampire. Cardinal Hayes said something to Marty; but Marty was lost in rapt contemplation of the movie star.

Miss Parker was drinking the wine rather freely, I thought. It was only the second course, and her speech was becoming slurred.

"Sore throat, Lonny? What's wrong, have you got the talkies stuck in it?"

"Dorothy." Governor Smith cleared his throat. "Just three glasses of wine and you're already getting a case of—what is it you call them?—the frankies. Lon isn't feeling well."

"Be careful, Al. You're not president yet."

"That," Cardinal Hayes intoned, "is a situation that will soon be remedied."

"I just want to know when Lonny's going to make a talkie, that's all. The time for mere dumbshow is past." She tried to sound kittenish; failed. Looked pointedly at Marty, who was directly across the table from her. "You'd like to know, wouldn't you, young man?"

Marty had not touched his fish. He looked, flustered, from his plate to Miss Parker to his screen idol, then back again. "My name's Marty, Miss Parker."

"Yes, Marty. You'd like to know, wouldn't you?" She was staring at him in what I thought a rather speculative way.

"I, uh, I'm afraid I don't like talking pictures. They don't seem right to me. I used to have a crush on Vilma Banky. Then I heard her voice. The talkies are too real."

"Yes, but then there's Clara Bow." The governor smiled broadly; I had the impression there was some private memory behind it. "Now *there* is a real lady."

"A lady, indeed." Miss Parker laughed, reached for the wine bottle and poured herself another glass. "Every inch a lady. Or at least, every other inch. Have you heard about her and that football team?"

"Miss Bow," the governor said heavily, "is a great beauty." He stared pointedly at Miss Parker, as if to emphasize her own lack of that quality.

It was getting out of hand. Mr. Tiffany looked around his table, obviously groping for something to say. Finally his gaze settled on the cardinal. "I think we should have started this meal with you saying grace, Patrick."

"Nonsense, Louis. This is an education for me." The cardinal was above it all. "I'm afraid I don't know much about the pictures."

I decided to dislike His Eminence; like Miss Parker I took a long drink of wine. "Surely you've seen at least *The King of Kings*, Cardinal Hayes."

"I'm afraid not." His voice was like ice. "Popular entertainments . . ." He shrugged, made a sour face. "Those of us with religious callings—especially those of us who lead—must observe all of the proprieties. Popular entertainments would hardly be suitable."

Servants appeared, cleared away the course; poor Marty had only just begun to eat.

There was steak, filet mignon. It was delicious, succulent. And there was a fine claret. For a few happy moments the diners all concentrated on their food and left off baiting one another. Mr. Chaney was having quite a difficult time of it; had to wash down each mouthful of steak with a swallow of wine. I was beginning to be concerned at his clear discomfort. There had been enough pain in the air that night. "Are you sure you're all right, Mr. Chaney?"

"It'll pass. I've had this on and off for the last three months. It comes and goes."

"What do the doctors say?"

"It's just a stubborn infection."

I watched him. Studied him. He moved as gracefully as a cat, as a dancer. Even his hands—even his head, when he moved it from side to side—had a grace, a fluidity about them. The kind of films he'd always made were not to my taste, but it was not hard for me to see, here, now, why so many people found him hypnotic to watch.

He cleared his throat; was in pain. I thought I could see the beginnings of tears in the corners of his eyes.

Miss Parker had grown bored with her steak. Her eyes roamed around the table, looking for someone to play with. Mr. Chaney was the most obvious target. "So, Lonny, you were saying."

"I was?"

"About when you're going to make your first talkie."

"No, I wasn't."

"Well, tell us now, then. I'm sure we're all anxious to know."

He sipped his wine. "I think I agree with Marty." He smiled, nodded at Marty, who was obviously dazzled at the recognition. "I don't like them. They're not movies, they're photographed stage plays."

Miss Parker was enjoying herself. "The public's clamoring for them. You and Charlie are the only holdouts against them. Did you know that more people go to the movies each week than to church? You're a god, Lonny, and you have a duty to the mortals who worship you."

The cardinal shifted his weight uneasily. Looked around the table, hoping someone would say the obvious thing for him.

Governor Smith spoke up. "Tell me, Dottie, if the people had wanted Michelangelo to draw comic strips rather than painting the Sistine Chapel, should he have done it? Should Dickens have written crossword puzzles instead of *Oliver Twist*?"

"W. H. Auden *does* compose crosswords, darling. He is obviously a truer democrat than you." She drained her wineglass, then filled it still again.

Suddenly, quite violently, Mr. Chaney coughed. Loudly enough to startle everyone in the room; loudly enough to hurt my ears. I thought he must have a piece of meat stuck in his windpipe. But then I looked at the napkin he was using to cover it, and there was blood. I stood up beside him, put an arm around him. "Quick! Call a doctor!"

He was coughing uncontrollably. There was more and more bleeding. And tears; he was crying like an infant. Mr. Tiffany rang urgently for the servants. Everyone else got up and rushed to Mr. Chaney's side. Everyone but Miss Parker, who I think was finally feeling—rather than just showing—the effects of all she had drunk.

The servants managed to get Mr. Chaney up to his room. By then the coughing had subsided. But the man was in pain; could not talk. He asked me, by gestures, to remain by his bed. After what seemed an age the doctor arrived. Ordered me out of the room while he did his examination. Came out into the hall, took Mr. Tiffany and me aside. "He has a cancer of the throat. I don't believe he knows."

"You didn't tell him, did you?" I was alarmed; that is the one disease that is too horrible to mention.

"No, I did not. Perhaps, in time, he will realize. But if God is merciful, he will not."

"What can we do for him, Doctor?"

"I have given him a drug. He will sleep the night. Here is another dose." He handed Mr. Tiffany a small vial, and Mr.

Tiffany handed it to me. "Give it to him in the morning if he needs it. He should be tended by his own physicians." He said this in a vaguely accusatory tone, as if the whole thing were Mr. Tiffany's fault for having Mr. Chaney as a houseguest.

Back at our rooms, Marty was eager for news.

"He's resting, Marty. He should be all right tomorrow." I lied with a blank face.

"Did he say anything about . . . what we were talking about?"

I stared at him. "What do you mean?"

"When will he make his first talkie?"

"I thought you said—"

"Did he tell you? When will it be?"

"Not soon." I went cold. "Every time he makes a new movie, you ply me with stories about the pain he underwent in making it. Don't you think he's given you enough of himself?"

"I can't wait till he makes one."

We were summoned back to the dining room, to finish our dinner. Miss Parker was by that time quite as indisposed as Mr. Chaney, though not for the same reason. At the table were the worldly prince, the churchly prince, the prince of art and the two of us. There was not much conversation.

The June night grew humid. It was difficult to sleep. I got up in the middle of the night, drew apart the curtains over my windows, hoped there might be some slight breeze to cool the room. But everything was still. My body was damp with perspiration. I stepped out onto the balcony.

There was a moon. Across the grounds the millions of flowers showed ghostly colors in its light. There were occasional night sounds, birds, cats; faintly, distantly, came the sound of the surf in the bay.

It had been such a . . . long day. Long. Not at all what I had expected. The wan colors of the moonlit blossoms made me think of my iris window. Art: more alive, more vivid than the real world. It was not a reassuring thought.

I went back inside; lay on the bed; tried to sleep. It was too hot. Or perhaps I slept awhile without realizing it. But it was light sleep, restive, not even remotely satisfying. I found myself staring at the connecting door, thinking of the room beyond it, thinking of

Marty. The impulse was impossible to resist. I pulled on my robe, walked to the door, opened it as silently as possible; and went in.

His windows, like mine, were opened against the humid night. The moon lit the room. Lit Marty. He was sleeping, facedown, on top of the bed, on top of the covers, and he was naked. Sweat covered his body. He was breathing heavily. I walked slowly, carefully up beside the bed. Wanted to touch him, wanted to kiss him; it seemed the only thing that might relieve the day's tensions, the night's heat.

He rolled over. Snorted in his sleep. His arm fell over the side of the bed at an awkward angle; it would be stiff in the morning. He was dreaming. I wanted, more strongly than before, to touch him, to feel his body. Held out my hand. Reached, slowly, tentatively for the firm muscles of his stomach. Wanted to slide my fingers along them.

I could not do the thing. I could not do it. Suddenly, insensibly, there came into my mind's eye the picture of Mr. Chaney coughing up blood. The man was in pain, the man was dying, and here was I, yielding to my lust. Marty wanted me; I wanted him. But I wanted only his flesh, his touch, not the man himself. The pain in Mr. Chaney's room seemed vastly more real to me than the thing I was feeling. I pulled my hand back, turned, and left Marty's bedroom. For the rest of the night I felt tainted, and I hardly slept at all.

Neither Miss Parker nor Mr. Chaney appeared for breakfast. Again we did not talk much among ourselves. The cardinal and the governor exchanged whispered comments; the air was conspiratorial. Mr. Tiffany seemed slower, older than he had the previous day. Marty wore only sandals and a pair of loose-fitting shorts; was his usual self.

Later in the morning there were refreshments in the garden. Everywhere was lush growth. Flowers billowed, flowed, overwhelmed one. The air was heavy with their scents, and there was blinding sunshine, so bright the blooms seemed almost animated. We were served tea and lemonade on a patio of flagstones. Chatted about the day, the weather, the beauty of it all. Mr. Tiffany's two youngest daughters played croquet on the lawn. Midway through the morning Miss Parker came down, wearing a sundress in bright blues and greens. She glared at us all, enjoying the morning, as if she thought us mad. "The fact that I woke up this morning, dears, is, I assure you, contrary to my every wish." She held the sides of her head; closed her eyes against the sunlight.

All morning we had avoided the subject of Mr. Chaney; of his condition. No one seemed to want to broach it. But finally, unexpectedly, he too came down to join us.

He was pale; drawn; looked almost emaciated. Sipped tea; did not eat. Despite his obvious weakness he went off for a walk, alone, through the grounds. "I need flowers this morning," he told us. "I need living things."

"Well, don't look at me, Lonny." Miss Parker took a long swallow of strong black tea.

I watched him as he went off, solitary, across the manicured lawn, past the playing girls; he disappeared into an orchard of ornamental fruit trees.

"Lonny's sweet. I just wish he weren't so naive." Miss Parker was looking restless already. Locked her eyes onto Marty, who was half asleep in a lawn chair. She plainly liked the look of him in his shorts. "Young man."

He stirred and looked up at her.

"How'd you like to hear the story of my life?" She took him by the arm and, like Mr. Chaney, they disappeared off into the gardens.

Watching them go made me feel uncomfortable. I tried to tell myself it wasn't jealousy I was feeling; but of course that is exactly what it was. How could she be so forthright? Last night I could have touched him, could have had him, but I had no resolve; and here he was with her.

Governor Smith crossed the patio and sat down beside me. "How did you sleep?"

"Not at all well." My eyes were still on the retreating couple. I turned uncertainly to the governor. "It was much too warm."

"From the look of things, today will be warmer still. At least for some of us. Dottie's a bit of a shark."

It was the last thing I wanted to hear. "They say you haven't got a chance of beating Hoover."

"They say all sorts of things." He scowled. "Herb should have stayed down in his damned mines."

"For the country's sake, or for yours?" Miss Parker's style was catching, I'm afraid. But it was dangerous of me; he was a man of national importance; I retreated from it. "I'm sorry, Governor. As I told you, I didn't sleep well."

He was stiff. "Of course."

"The Klan is opposing you quite actively, I hear."

"Bigots. Lunatics. They don't count for a thing."

"They vote."

"So do Catholics. And there are more of us. Religion can't be stopped, Miss Markham. It's in all of us, it's in our blood. There's no way to escape it. That's what will make me president."

I stared at him. He was talking like a man drunk. Drunk with . . . what? "Do you mean that, Governor? I mean, religion is one thing. Roman Catholicism is something else. If you see what I mean."

"Louis gave me the impression you're Catholic." He looked puzzled, as if he were unsure whether he'd been indiscreet.

"I went to a school run by nuns. But my family are Unitarians. My father's a minister, in fact."

His eyes widened. He had said too much.

"*Political* Unitarians," I added quickly. "My father is, I hear, running for mayor of Zelienople, Pennsylvania. As I said, he's a man of the cloth. I think he's counting on that to get him votes. So I understand perfectly what you're talking about."

I had let him off the hook. He seemed relieved. He actually sighed. "You know what I mean, then."

"Yes, I suppose I do."

Then there was a silence between us. We sipped our drinks, watched the landscape.

"This place of Tiffany's is such a haven. An idyllic thing." The governor turned wistful. "I can't say I'm looking forward to going back."

"Back to Albany?"

He was letting his guard down again; frowned. "Back to the Secret Service. You can't imagine what pests they make of themselves."

But my mind was still on our earlier topic. "I can't say I think my father would make a good mayor. He's too ambitious. He'd ignore the town and work on his next step up the ladder. But then, we've never been very close."

"Politics is a career like any other, Miss Markham." He stood rather stiffly up and went back to Mr. Tiffany.

The morning passed slowly. I drank too much lemonade and began to feel bloated. Kept staring off at the orchard; kept thinking of Marty there embracing Dorothy Parker. The cardinal and the governor had brief, private exchanges between them, broke off whenever anyone got too near. Mr. Tiffany kept trying to get the cardinal's ear, but His Eminence was focusing all his attention on his worldly counterpart. Finally, after what seemed an eternity, the amorous couple returned. Both of them were covered with perspiration; both of them wore imbecilic smiles. Miss Parker went straight into the house. Marty took a chair beside me. "Did you know that she's some kind of writer?"

I could not believe I was hearing it. I answered him icily. "I had heard rumors about it, yes."

"She's not all brains, that's for sure."

Without saying anything more I stood up; headed across the lawn to the spot where I'd seen Mr. Chaney disappear.

"Hey!" He called after me, but I pretended not to hear.

Among the trees it was cool and shady. There were birds singing and the air smelled wonderfully of dogwood. It was another universe. I strolled, hummed to myself, tried to forget the society I had just left behind. Wished it were earlier in the year, wished it were spring so I could see all the trees in blossom. There was a spot at the foot of a cherry tree that was too inviting. I sat; lost in myself in my thoughts. Every now and then I found myself wondering: Where had they done it? Was it under this tree? Did they stand or lie on the ground? The sun through the trees made everything green; I forced myself to think of my work in glass.

Then Mr. Chaney was there. He stood over me. There were—I could see them quite clearly even in the shade—tears in the corners of his eyes. "Miss Markham."

"Clare."

"Clare, then." He smiled. "Can I join you?"

"Please."

"I thought I wanted to be alone today. But I find I need company." He sat down between the roots of the next tree.

"How are you feeling?"

"Better, I suppose. Not well. How are you? Are you withstanding Dottie's little barbs?"

"Just barely."

"They were in the next clearing. I could hear them."

I said nothing.

"Are you in love with the boy?"

"How can I know that now?"

"Louis tells me you're quite an artist."

"I'm learning, I think."

"He showed me your iris window yesterday. It's marvelous There is a bit of genius in you."

"Thank you, Mr. Chaney."

"You can't call me Mister while I'm calling you Clare."

I smiled. "Lon. Or do you prefer Lonny?"

"Dottie's unbearable. Why don't you marry him and ask her to the wedding?"

"I'm afraid she'd invite herself on the honeymoon."

Lon laughed. Then winced. His throat.

"Are you sure you're feeling all right?"

He shrugged. "I'm used to it."

"You're . . ." I was unsure whether to say it. Decided to be bold in my new friendship. "It looks like you're crying."

He reached up, astonished, and touched his eyes. "There are always tears, these days. I did a picture last year. About a vampire. I wanted my eyes to bulge for the role. So I made two loops of wire and put them in the sockets, and it gave me the effect I wanted. But an infection set in and won't go away, so my eyes water all the time. I think it must be that infection that spread to my throat."

I wanted to tell him the truth about himself. "It seems like a lot to go through for a movie."

"For art. My characters live in pain. Acting—dumbshow, as Dottie calls it—is all the art I have. I'd do anything for it. Undergo any pain, myself, to get the truth about my people onto the film."

I had no idea what to say to this. I watched him. The tears were flowing freely now.

He reached up a finger and touched them. "It was worth it. But you're the same, aren't you, Clare? You have to be the same. Suppose you needed a deep red glass for one of your windows. Suppose the only way you could get the red right was to make it with your own blood. You'd do it, wouldn't you? Give a bit of your blood to make your glass be true?"

"You're getting too close to theology, Lon."

"Exactly."

I looked at him again, bathed in the orchard's green light. Green, the nuns had taught me, is the color of hope; of spring. I thought once again of his cancer; it was impossible to tell him about it. The sides of his face were washed with flowing tears. Slowly I stood, crossed to him, bent over him, kissed the tears on his face; kissed his lips.

5

"The cardinal is working on your credentials. It will be some while before you and Marty sail for Europe."

I was in his office. Here he was alive; here he flourished in a way that he did not at home. It had been less than a week since our visit to Laurelton Hall. "I don't understand. How long can it take him to write a letter of introduction?"

"It appears it isn't that simple. Anyone wanting access to the closed collections of the Vatican libraries must have permission in advance. Patrick has written to Rome for us. For you. But you know how slow the transatlantic mails can be."

"Yes." I was disappointed. Wanted to be off, find the stuff and get back; wanted, simply, to create more glass. "Yes, I suppose I do."

"He's rushing it, Clare. He's doing what he can. In the meantime there are several commissions I'd like you to handle for the studios."

I brightened up. "Yes, sir."

"You didn't think I'd let your talent go to waste, did you? Agnes will go over the commissions with you."

In the hall on my way to her office I met Marty. "Clare. Sweetheart. I haven't seen you all week."

"I've been busy."

"Dottie invited me to a party this Saturday night. I was hoping you'd want to go along."

"I'm afraid I have other plans."

He looked quite unbelieving. "What are you doing?"

"Minding my own business." I pushed past him.

"Are you going to see him?"

132

"Why not?" I kept walking. "You're going to see her."

"I asked you to come along, didn't I?"

"You think that makes it better?" I turned; shouted. "That makes it worse."

"But . . . but . . ."

Agnes was not in her office. I walked to my own. Taped up on the wall was the cartoon for my hell, for the hell I was constructing. I sat at my desk, studied it. Studied the death's-head grin on the face of the Lord, the rictus. Looked at the twisted figures in torment below him.

It was not enough. There was not pain enough. Like Lon—like Mr. Chaney—I had to find more of it inside myself. I took a pencil and began to resketch.

6

The summer passed. There were more commissions, and more. Floral windows, landscapes. My reputation as a designer was growing; people asked for windows specifically created by me. More jobs than I could handle. I was assigned an apprentice designer of my own. His name was Bill and he had blond hair and green eyes; I found myself, inevitably, trying to capture the green in glass. He was an attractive man, taller and more muscular than Marty. Somewhat to my relief—even to my pleasure, though I am a bit ashamed to admit it—he fainted the first time he went down into the basement. Dorothy Parker commissioned a duplicate of my iris window, but I refused to work on it. Agnes gave the job to Marty.

The church architect who commissioned my hell wrote. The building plans had changed. Could we please make the window three feet wider? Fortunately work had not proceeded much past the design stage. I went back to my sketchbook.

Something about the design had never satisfied me. Christ in hell. Christ presiding over the torments of the damned. It was right; Mr. Tiffany had shown me how right it was. And yet there was something missing. Day after day I sat in my little office staring at the cartoon, wondering what more—or less—it needed.

One hot afternoon Marty knocked timidly at the door. "Can I come in?"

"No. Go away."

"I want to make peace, Clare. I've brought the pipe."

"I'm busy."

"Will you go to the movies with me tonight? There's . . . there's a new Lon Chaney opening. Something called *West of Zanzibar*."

134

"No thank you."

"Mr. Tiffany says the cardinal's letters should be arriving from the Vatican anytime now. We'll be sailing. We have to live with each other, Clare."

"Living with each other and dating each other are two different things."

"Can't we at least have lunch and try to talk things out?"

Lon Chaney. It struck me then. I remembered his tears. I knew what I needed. "Do you believe in God, Marty?"

"What?"

"Do you believe in God?"

He stared at me. Seemed not to know what to say. "Look, I really meant what I said. I want to make things up between us. You don't have to make fun of me."

"I'm not. I'll have lunch with you later in the week. All right?" I was already preoccupied with what I had to do.

"You don't sound all that enthusiastic."

"I've just figured something out. I'll see you tomorrow."

Tears. God presiding over the torture of his creatures. How could he not feel pain? How could he not regret the necessity? My window, my Christ needed tears.

I spent the afternoon sketching, resketching. Nothing looked right. There was no way to add tears to the design. They had to be deeper. They had to be in the glass.

I went straight to the basement. Had the workman fire a kiln for me. "What color glass, Miss Markham?"

"Flesh tone. I'll be streaking a darker flesh color through it. You have the right mixes here?"

"Yes, ma'am."

The furnace roared, bellowed. The fires danced out of the grated door; the fires from which my hell would emerge.

My apprentice Bill found me. "Clare, what's going on?"

"I'm making the Lord weep."

"The—?" He was lost.

"My window. The inferno."

"The— Oh." He looked around the fiery basement. Seemed not to want to be there.

"Will you be all right?"

"Yes." He was lying.

"If it's too much for you, you can go upstairs and work on those sketches."

"No. I want to stay." He was perspiring heavily.

Soon the first melt, the lighter flesh, was ready. The workman rolled it. Then came the darker flesh, the contrasting flesh. I pulled on the asbestos gloves, took up the hook, drew glass through glass. Listened to the shriek of metal on metal, an old familiar sound by now, a sound that seemed right. But when the glass cooled, it looked wrong. Streaked, but not with tears; it looked merely odd.

Again. The fire, the melt, the hook. Time after time, day after day, again and again I forged a face for the Lord, tried to give him proper tears; time and again it did not work, did not look the way I wanted it to.

Agnes Northmon came to talk to me. "Clare, you're pushing too hard. The design looks fine without tears. It's close to brilliant."

"The design—the essence of it—is Mr. Tiffany's. The tears are mine. I want there to be tears flowing from God's eyes."

"You've tried everything possible. There's no way to get it."

"I'll get it."

"Clare, you'll suffocate down here. You've got Bill scared half out of his wits. He thinks you've gone mad."

"I have. I want those tears."

"Mr. Tiffany's worried. He wants you to stop this."

"Mr. Tiffany understands. Or he should. Tell him to look at his hands."

"Clare."

"There has to be some other way. Not just one color streaked through another. There has to be."

It was days before I found it. In one corner of the studio was a pile of splinters, sweepings, glass dust; they should have been thrown out. I stared at them. Watched the light play on them. They were what I needed. I took handfuls, glovefuls of them down to the furnace. Had more glass melted. Set the splinters at one side of the melt and pulled them through. Long, crystalline streaks. When the glass cooled I held the sheet up to the light from the fire. The streaks shimmered. Looked like tears flowing, looked like the tears I wanted. Bill was at my side. I hugged him, kissed him without thinking. Carried the glass upstairs into the studio and looked at it again, backlit on one of the easels. Yes. It was correct. The tears I wanted were there. I took up a grease pencil, sketched on the glass. "Now here. This is the area you're to cut for the face. When you paint the features on it the tears will be placed correctly. Bill, we've got it."

"Congratulations, Clare."

"I feel like he must have, coming out of his tomb."

"He?"

I touched a fingertip to the glass.

"Oh." He looked at it, and at me, with plain doubt on his face. "Orpheus coming back from the underworld might be a more appropriate metaphor."

"Doesn't that mean I've left my love behind, in hell?"

He smiled a wry smile. "Not necessarily."

I kissed him again. "Thanks for that."

The next afternoon I was ready to face Marty. We had lunch together. I had an enormous appetite, and the good aromas in the restaurant sharpened it.

"Everyone's talking about what you did with that glass. It's quite brilliant of you."

"I needed to find a way to do it."

"Yes."

"I've never felt driven like that before, Marty. It's both awful and exhilarating at the same time."

"I can imagine."

"I feel like I've finally mastered my craft."

"Our craft, Clare."

"Uh, yes." The waiter was slow bringing our orders. I looked around for him.

"Mr. Tiffany told me this morning he got the letters from the cardinal. We'll be leaving soon."

"Not till I finish my window."

"It's all routine now. Bill can handle it. If he needs help, there's Agnes."

"I want to see it complete."

"When we get back."

Our meals finally came. I ate; did not want to talk.

"Clare, I still love you. Don't you think you've punished me enough?"

"I'm not punishing you. I'm doing what I have to do, that's all. There's no choice."

"There are no liners sailing for the next few weeks. Mr. Tiffany has booked us on a steamer."

"It doesn't make any difference."

"I thought we'd be crossing the ocean in style."

I ate.

"I thought . . . I thought it might be a honeymoon cruise for us."

"Stop it, Marty."

"I love you. I think you love me. You just don't know it. Or you don't know what to do about it. Why else would you have been so jealous?"

"I was not—" I broke off. Did not want to discuss it. It went too near the bone.

"Our steamer is called the *Clara Thornhill.* I find myself wondering who she is."

I looked around the restaurant; looked at the other diners.

"Or was." He smiled. Needed approval. Needed something positive from me. The boy next door. Handsome. Beautiful.

But I could not think of anything to say. Small talk eluded me.

The silence between us got longer; more uncomfortable. I could see the emotions crossing his face as he looked for the right words.

Finally, "I'm sorry, Clare. I'll try not to make too much of a pest of myself on the trip."

I wanted to tell him, I'm sorry, too, Marty, part of me does love you. But I cannot give you what you want.

7

The *Clara Thornhill* sailed early on the evening of the first of September. It was a cool night; there were clouds. The air smelled of autumn. Longshoremen worked busily filling the holds; other passengers, crew boarded the ship. Marty and I waited impatiently on the dock. Mr. Tiffany was to come and see us off, and he was late. We were afraid he might miss us.

Marty studied the ship. "I've never been to sea before. I wonder if I'll be sick."

"I wouldn't worry. The rails look good and strong."

"I've always had a queasy stomach."

"You'll be fine."

I watched the crowd. The last of the cargo was being loaded on board. Then finally I saw Mr. Tiffany. His new chairman, my blond assistant Bill, was pushing him quickly through the crowd. Next to his young aide, he looked impossibly old. His skin was grey, almost white. He was wrapped in heavy blankets against the evening's coolness.

Marty was still watching the ship, the workers. "Do you think we'll see any icebergs?"

"Marty, Mr. Tiffany is here."

"Clare, Marty, how good to see you. I was afraid we wouldn't get here in time."

"Good evening, sir. Hi, Bill." I kissed Bill on the cheek.

We all said our hellos; Mr. Tiffany inspected our ship, seemed pleased. "The *Clara Thornhill* looks like quite a lady."

"Marty's worried she'll have the same fate as the *Titanic*."

"It's too early in the season for icebergs."

Marty was plainly relieved.

The ship's whistle blew. It was time for us to board.

"Bill, will you leave us alone for a moment?" Mr. Tiffany was suddenly businesslike.

"Of course, sir." He walked off to a far corner of the dock; watched pointedly the workers, not the three of us.

"Here. I want you to take this with you." He reached under his blanket, just as he had done four months earlier at Laurelton Hall. Produced the red glass. Brilliant red. I had not seen it since that day at the mansion. And I was startled once more at the vibrancy of it.

Neither of us spoke.

"Here. Take it." He held it out unsteadily.

"It's so precious." I could not take my eyes off it. "I wouldn't want the responsibility."

"I want you to take it. I want you to have it with you. I want you to keep it in mind; keep in mind what you're after. There's more like this. Find it for me." He held the splinter out at arm's length.

Uncertainly, not really wanting to, I took it. Tried to hand it to Marty, but he backed off a step. Neither of us wanted possession of the thing. I looked back to Mr. Tiffany hoping he'd relent and keep it. He was smiling. "What are you feeling?"

As he had done, I held the glass out the length of my arm.

He watched me; smiled, but I was not certain it was a smile of pleasure. "Imagine the power those windows must have had when they were entire."

The glass was so red.

"Find more of it for me, Clare. I want all of it that exists."

"I . . . Yes, sir."

The steamer's whistle blew a second time. We had to leave. Marty climbed the gangway to the ship. Impulsively I hugged Mr. Tiffany. Waved to Bill, to signal him to come back. In a moment he was with us again. I put my arms around him, gave him a goodbye kiss; told him I'd be anxious to see him again. Started for the gangway. But Mr. Tiffany caught hold of my hand; would not let go. Pulled me down and whispered in my ear. "Glass is the most human substance for an artist to work in, Clare. Like us, it shatters easily."

I thought he was simply warning me to take good care of his fragment. "Don't worry, sir. I'll bring it back to you intact."

He said nothing. I had missed his meaning. After a moment's silence he said, "Hurry. You'll miss the boat."

I walked quickly up the gangplank; got on deck just as they pulled it away. Marty was already there; had watched my goodbye to Bill. "Why did you kiss him like that?"

"I like him. And I'm going to miss him. We work well together."

"Work, and what else?"

"Marty."

There was a lurch; the tugboats pulled us out into the harbor.

Our crossing was to take ten days. For most of the first week Marty was seasick. I was glad of it. It kept him from, as he had put it, making a pest of himself.

The captain was Dutch. Captain van Boeven. A genial man, young, thin and blue-eyed and very blond. He could have been Bill's older brother. We dined at his table every evening and he was quite gracious to us. He could not have been more appealing. I found myself trying to imagine him in the shower, the way I had seen Marty.

The other passengers were all European; spoke no English. I tried talking to a few of them in my schoolgirl French, but it was no use. Except for the captain and each other, we had a lonely voyage.

One day, off to the north, there was a brilliant glow. Sharp, almost blinding. I climbed casually up to the bridge; asked the captain what it was.

"There are ice fields to the north, Miss Markham. When the sun is at the right angle, they reflect it to us."

"Ice fields?" I was alarmed.

But van Boeven laughed. "It's quite common. There's nothing to worry about."

"But—"

"What happened to the *Titanic* was a fluke. The ice won't hurt us."

I watched it. The whole horizon was aglow with it. "It looks like the edge of the world is on fire."

"Fire and ice."

I looked at him. He was smiling at me. Was he finding me as

attractive as I found him? I did not like what he had said. "There's been too much talk of hell in my life lately. I need a bit of heaven." I was shocked at my own boldness.

"Seek, and ye shall find it, Miss Markham."

"Clare."

"Clare, then. Will you call me Michael?"

"Wouldn't that be a violation of ship's protocol?"

"*Clara* won't mind." He reached over and touched my hand. I took his in mine and gave it a squeeze.

Marty saw what was happening between me and Michael. Did not like it. Was jealous. Brooded. Scowled at me. Withdrew. I found the situation enormously uncomfortable. And I tried to talk to him about it. But he was impossible. "First with that monster, and now with a goddamned sailor! Everybody but the man who loves you. Clare, how can you do this to me?"

"I am not doing anything to you."

"That isn't funny."

"It wasn't meant to be. Lon is not a monster. Until you actually met him, you admired him."

"As a monster, yes."

"You seem to be forgetting a certain lady writer."

"Nothing happened between us."

"Lon was in the next grove. He heard it all."

"A goddamned monster! A snake!"

I backed off. Was ashamed of myself for getting involved in such a scene. "Every Eden has its snake, Marty."

"What's that supposed to mean?"

"Never mind." I walked away, left him standing there. There was no other way to cope with it.

The eighth night of our crossing. There was a huge moon. I stood at the rail watching its reflections on the waves. The stars, the planets were brilliant.

There were dolphins. One of them rode our bow wave. Others swam along beside us, dove in the *Thornhill*'s spray, raced with us. Just barely, beneath the ship's noises and the ocean's noises, I could hear them chuckling, talking to one another.

I had the red glass with me, the blood glass. It pulsed with the moonlight and the ship's motion. I could feel it; it was not cold like glass, it was warm like blood.

"Some people never understand why other people love the sea." Michael had come quietly on deck; stood beside me.

I slid the glass quietly into my pocket. Looked at the sea, not at the sailor. "It's beautiful. It's alive, not at all tranquil, yet it gives me such a feeling of peace."

"Clare." He reached out, touched my hand.

I said nothing, did nothing; did not resist.

Michael moved his hand slowly up my arm, rested it on my shoulder. I tilted my head, touched my cheek to his hand. Then we kissed. Michael took me in his arms and we kissed again and again. I could still hear the dolphins, the sea; slid my free hand into my pocket and felt the warm blood glass there, pulsing. It was wonderful.

Then I opened my eyes. Standing at the far end of the deck, cloaked in shadow, watching us, was Marty. Despite the shadows there I knew his form. I went cold. "Michael, stop."

He kissed me again.

"Michael, we're not alone."

He let go of me; looked around. "Your young man."

"He is not mine. He only thinks he is."

"Right now, that comes to the same thing."

I took his hand. "Kiss me again."

"Not here. Not with him watching."

"In my cabin, then."

He hesitated. Looked down the deck at Marty, then back at me. Squeezed my hand. "All right."

We went quickly. Dimmed the light; were in each other's arms again. I took the glass splinter from my pocket and rested it on the night table.

Later; very late in the night. Moonlight poured in through the portholes, made the room a pale grey. Michael was still beside me. One arm was still around me. His body was impossibly warm; he pressed me against the cabin wall. I whispered, "Michael."

He was sound asleep.

I tried to shift my weight without disturbing him. On the table beside us I could see the fragment of glass glowing deep red. It was no use, he was too heavy against me; I could not move. "Michael."

He stirred. Put his other arm around me. Kissed me in his sleep. I touched him. Pushed. "Michael, wake up."

He kissed me again. Tightened his arms around me. "Clare."

"Wake up, Michael."

"Clare, I love you." He kissed me on the throat. I was tempted to kiss him back, I wanted to do it. Found myself thinking of Lon, and of my blond apprentice Bill.

"Michael, I need room. Move over." I pushed him playfully.

Half asleep, he rolled over, away from me. I gave him another light shove, moved him another inch or so. Then suddenly he screamed. "Good Jesus!"

I sat up in alarm. "What's wrong?"

"Oh, good Jesus!"

"Michael!" I crawled over him; switched on the light.

His right wrist was bleeding. And the fragment of glass was stuck through it. The blood was flowing onto the bed, the floor; Michael himself was covered in it. He pulled the glass out, threw it into a corner.

"Good God, Michael!"

I ran to the door. Screamed.

In a moment there were people. One of the sailors tore a strip of cloth from the bloody sheet, made a tourniquet for Michael's arm. The ship's doctor arrived. Stitched the cut; dressed it. A deckhand did a hasty cleanup. Then everything calmed down. We were alone again. I found the glass in the corner where he had thrown it. Took it to the washbasin and began to clean it of Michael's blood. He watched me. He was pale. "Why would you have a thing like that lying around?"

"I'm sorry."

"It's dangerous. A piece of glass like that, just sitting on the table."

"I'm sorry. I didn't think it would hurt anyone."

"Look at it. It's jagged as anything."

"It's . . . it's special glass. It's a . . . ." There was no way to explain.

"I could have bled to death."

"I'm sorry, Michael. It was all my fault." I left the splinter on the washstand, crossed to the bed. Sat next to him. Kissed him. But he turned away; I kissed only his cheek. "Please, Michael. I've said I'm sorry."

He looked uncomfortable. "I should go back to my own cabin. I'll rest better there."

"Yes. Of course." I wanted to throw myself off the ship. "Let me walk you there."

"No. I'll be all right." He got unsteadily to his feet; crossed to the door. Stopped there. "Good night, Clare."

I touched him; tried to kiss him again. But once more he turned away. "Good night, Michael." And he was gone.

The glass was still on the washstand. I finished cleaning it. Switched off the light. The red glass glowed. What had happened? I took it up carefully. Touched its sharp tip to my wrist. Pressed. It went below the skin but did not cut. It should not have cut Michael, and yet his blood had been everywhere. The corners of the floor were still moist with it.

Sleep was impossible. I walked back out onto the deck. The moon was low in the sky now. The dolphins were gone; were playing somewhere else. In the shadows on the deck I could see Marty's form, waiting, watching me. I wanted Europe. I wanted to be there; told myself that, even with Marty at my side, it would be a release. A change. Perhaps a chance to find myself, at last. I went back to my cabin, locked the door; but did not sleep. The blood glass glowed.

8

The *Thornhill* docked at Plymouth. Michael said a civil goodbye to me; no more than that. I could understand him being upset about the accident. But his distance from me personally, as if it were my fault . . . that I could not fathom.

Our things were transferred to another steamer, a smaller one, called the *Alma*. It left port in a few hours. I was grateful for the rapid sailing; was suddenly impatient to do what had to be done and get home again. The *Alma* stopped at Calais, then passed through the Pillars of Hercules and touched at Marseilles. We coasted along the Riviera, and it was beautiful. Bright, sunny, not at all like early autumn, or at least not like the autumns I knew. At each port we docked, let off cargo, took on more.

From Marseilles we headed to Genoa and beyond. I watched the coast anxiously; wanted landfall. I had not unwrapped the blood glass since that night on board the *Thornhill*.

Marty joined me on deck one hot afternoon. "Look, there's an island off to the west. Is it Sicily?" He had, thankfully, been keeping his distance. No more brooding watchfulness.

"No, Sicily's way to the south. That's Elba."

"Elba?" It took him a moment. "As in 'Able was I . . .'?"

"Yes. A place of exile. Of isolation."

"You're in another of your moods."

"You know me too well."

I had given him an uncomfortable opening, but he let it pass; was silent.

"Marty, what do you know about the Vatican libraries?"

"Not much, I guess."

"I find myself wondering what kind of shape they're in."

He stared at Elba. "What do you mean?"

"How they're catalogued. How they're organized." There were two dolphins swimming along with us. I did not want them to be there. "I mean, these collections must go back hundreds of years. Maybe two thousand or more; they might have ancient manuscripts the world knows nothing about."

He turned his back to the island; leaned against the rail. "So you think we might make some fantastic discovery?"

"No. I just wonder . . . I mean, suppose the books have just been . . . accumulating. Piling up randomly. It could take forever to find what we want. It could take the rest of our lives."

"Mr. Tiffany doesn't expect us to take that long."

"Mr. Tiffany isn't a librarian."

He fell silent again.

There were more dolphins. Like Marty, I turned my back on the sea. "I want to be back in New York, working."

"Isn't this work?"

"Not creative work, no, it isn't."

Then we were at Rome. We checked into the Venezia Palace Hotel and became tourists. Saw St. Peter's and the Sistine Chapel. The Vatican was intimidating. There were priests everywhere, cloaked in black, in crimson. And nuns. Seeing them, I lost myself; became again the little girl at the Catholic boarding school. Working here—finding what we'd come for—would almost certainly require asserting myself. How could I do it? The city was suffocatingly hot.

The second morning, clouds began to accumulate and by afternoon there was rain. We watched glumly from the windows of my hotel room; the line between grey sky and grey city was blurred. We bought two large black umbrellas and went on with our sight-seeing. Water cascaded down the tiers of the Colosseum, poured in rivers from the roof of the Pantheon. The Forum became a miniature lake.

The third morning we dug the cardinal's letter out of our luggage and set off, apprehensively, for the Vatican, not as tourists this time but on Mr. Tiffany's business. I was terrified. The rain was even heavier than it had been the day before; made worse my mood.

One of the Swiss Guard inspected our letters, asked us to wait in a small room. The ceiling was disproportionally high, the windows were tall and narrow, streaked by the rain; a room out of *Alice in Wonderland*. Everything was overornate, Baroque. The heat in the room was stifling and the sound of the rain beating on the roof made me even more nervous.

We waited nearly an hour. Marty was impatient. "They have to let us know how unimportant we are."

I looked around. "And Mussolini thinks *he* runs Italy."

Then from nowhere, from out of the wall, appeared an impossibly old, impossibly thin man in black robes bordered with scarlet. Attending him was a young man wearing a plain black cassock; he did not look much older than eighteen or so. He had green eyes and black hair, and his cheeks were the red of his master's regalia. The old man looked us up and down. Addressed Marty. "Signore Kampinski?"

"Yes. Uh, *si*."

"I am Monsignor Pontecorvo. Pius welcomes you."

We looked around, bewildered. After a puzzling moment I realized he was speaking for the pope. "Oh." I whispered an explanation to Marty. "Please tell His Holiness we are grateful."

The monsignor held out his hand. Marty started to take it in his own, to shake it. I nudged him; whispered. "He wants you to kiss his ring."

"His . . . ? You're kidding."

"Don't be such a Protestant. Bend over and kiss it."

Glumly, obviously bewildered, he pressed his lips to the old man's hand. The monsignor was pleased; turned and offered his ring to me. I took it, kissed. His hand was like parchment; it was like the paper in the books we would soon be searching through. My kiss did not seem to please him as much as Marty's had. He looked from one of us to the other. "So, our old friend Cardinal Hayes wishes you to have access to the libraries here."

"Yes, sir." Marty was completely out of his element.

"And how exactly can we assist you? What is it that you are looking for?"

"We . . ." Marty turned to me. "Signorina Markham is the librarian. Perhaps she should explain."

The monsignor looked at me disapprovingly. "Signorina. Such a beautiful young woman. You should be married and producing children."

My eyes widened; I could not conceal my shock at the man's rudeness. "I'm not familiar enough with your collections here to know precisely what we need. Information about relics of the Apostles. And details of the building of the great cathedrals around the Continent, the places where such relics might be found."

"You are treasure hunters." His voice creaked like a rusted hinge.

"No, sir. As I think the letter explains—"

"Louis Comfort Tiffany. Yes. You are his treasure hunters."

Marty spoke up. "Surely His Eminence Cardinal Hayes would not have given our mission his blessing if—"

"Cardinal Hayes is an American cardinal."

There was not much we could say to this. Just a moment before, Cardinal Hayes had been "our old friend." We were both of us nonplussed by the monsignor. The knowledge that that was probably what he wanted was not much comfort. Our little room was growing hotter and hotter.

"Excuse me." For the first time the monsignor's young companion spoke. We all turned to him. "If you will permit me, Monsignor, I know the collections here as well as anyone. Perhaps I could help our guests find what they need so that you will be free for more pressing duties."

"I was going," said the monsignor ponderously, "to have one of the nuns assist them."

"I know the libraries better than any of the nuns." The boy grinned.

"Yes, I suppose you do."

"No one's introduced me." His grin grew even wider. "I am Giovanni Pinello." He shook hands with us; had nothing for us to kiss.

I liked him; smiled as warmly as I could manage in the hot room. "It's a pleasure to meet you."

"Thank you, Signorina Markham. But the pleasure is mine entirely."

Monsignor Pontecorvo had taken in this exchange; seemed even more disapproving of us than he had before. "Giovanni has important work to do."

"Oh?" I pretended to be curious.

"He is doing research into certain . . . confidential documents from the ancient world." This was supposed to impress us.

But Marty ignored it completely. "Well, Giovanni, when can we get to work?"

"Why," asked Monsignor Pontecorvo, "are Americans always so rash?"

"They have a job to do, and they want to do it." Giovanni smiled as he stood up to his master. Shrugged an exaggerated shrug. "Why make more of it than that?"

The monsignor did not know whether to be angry at having his manners corrected in this way. His face turned for a moment to stone. Then thawed. "Yes. Of course. It is no more than that. Well, you must give them quick assistance, then, so they can be on their way." He extended his ring hand once again, let us kiss it, turned wordlessly and left, vanished through the door in the wall.

"Alarming, isn't he?" Giovanni smiled at me again; his eyes twinkled.

"That's one adjective for him, yes."

"I could give you the whole catalogue of them, if you like."

"No thanks. How is it that you know the collections here? I mean, how long have you been here?"

"My parents sent me here to study for the priesthood when I was fourteen."

"And when will you be ordained?"

"I received holy orders four years ago, signorina." He looked away from me; was shy.

"Four years ago? But—"

"I'm older than I look, signorina. I'll be thirty next year."

"Oh. I thought . . . Well. I didn't mean any offense."

"I didn't take any, signorina. I'm used to it."

"Please, call me Clare. And this is Marty."

Giovanni smiled from one of us to the other. Looked us up and down. Seemed to like what he saw. "Come, let me show you the stacks."

We opened our umbrellas, followed him in the driving rain across the great piazza, through the basilica and outside again. Heavy sheets of water struck the roof of St. Peter's, poured noisily to the pavement below. Behind the basilica there was a cluster of stone buildings, like everything else in Rome too ornate for my taste. "Those are the museums." He gestured vaguely at them.

'Collections of everything from Egyptian antiquities to modern art. Pius has a particular taste for the Cubists. Don't ask me why."

Marty had been silent for the longest time. Watching our host, studying him. "It's difficult to imagine modern art in the middle of all this. People dressed in medieval costumes fancying Picasso. It doesn't fit."

He ignored Marty's ill-chosen words. "The Vatican is a more worldly place than most people think. It is a center of government, after all." He led us into the rearmost of the buildings. Even after the grey gloom outside, the rooms were dark; the air was thick with dust. It took a moment for our eyes to adjust to the dimness.

"Goverment?" Marty looked around the museum. Ancient Sumerian gods and goddesses, men and women beaked and winged like birds, stared at us as we passed among them. "Surely it's a religious center."

"A—?" Giovanni made straight for the rear of the gallery. "Oh. Yes. That too."

Creatures frozen in stone were everywhere around us. Monsters; grotesquely bearded kings and nobles; lions wounded, bloody and dying after the hunt. I took it all in. "I expected only Christian art."

At the back of the room was a descending staircase. We stopped at the top of it. Giovanni's smile disappeared. "Do you have any idea what exists in these rooms? What things from the ancient world? Manuscripts and artifacts the rest of the world has long forgotten. The secrets of the ancient priesthoods. The hidden rites of the mystery cults. There are handwritten memoirs of the Apostles, earlier books than any of the Gospels; earlier and more revealing. All that knowledge, and more. We have it."

"And you don't share it with the world." I looked straight into his eyes.

"No, we don't." He stared right back at me; did not flinch at my accusation. "It's difficult enough for us to maintain our own orthodoxy in the face of all of it. How could we expect laymen to?"

"You are afraid of the truth. Even the truth about your own faith."

"Faith and truth don't have much to do with one another." His smile was back. His manner was offhand. "One of my predecessors here—a German—let himself get carried away with it all, oh, some thirty years ago. He ended badly."

"A German? I thought you Italians had the Vatican pretty much sewn up for yourselves."

"Every once in a while"—Giovanni stared at us pointedly—"a foreigner gets in through the gates." He had made himself clear. We were not to ask too many questions. Fine.

We followed him belowstairs. Were in a barrel-vaulted room lit dimly by electric lights, bare bulbs strung on wires. The room was quite empty; the walls were rough. "Follow me."

It was a maze. There were tables full of illuminated manuscripts, charts, diagrams, room after room of them branching off in every direction. After the first few chambers, the electric lights became more sparse, more widely separated. Some of the rooms were in almost complete blackness. Giovanni walked briskly through it all; whistled a discordant tune.

I was unsettled and fascinated at the same time. "Are these part of the catacombs?"

"They are catacombs, yes."

I was catching on to his style. "But not the part the world knows about."

"What good is a sphinx without a secret?" He looked back over his shoulder and smiled at me in the half-light.

"I had thought," I could not resist prodding him, "that the Resurrection had made sphinxes redundant."

"Just so, Clare. Just so."

"You're a bit of a sphinx yourself, Giovanni, you know that?"

"Yes. It is the secret of my eternal youth."

I looked back at Marty. He had not spoken since we entered the catacombs. His eyes were wide; his face was wet with perspiration. He was walking quite close behind me.

"Are you all right?"

"No, Clare, I don't think so. I'm claustrophobic."

"Oh." I looked at him more closely. The expression in his eyes was near to panic. "Is there anything I can do?"

"Hold my hand."

"Marty."

"Please. It'll make me feel better."

I took a firm grip on his hand, and he moved even closer to me. "I wasn't expecting anything like this. I was expecting a library."

Some of the corridors were no wider than our shoulders. There were spiderwebs in the doorways between them. Now and then I thought I could hear things moving. Giovanni walked steadily, quickly; was obviously used to it.

Finally we emerged into a broad, high chamber, so high the light did not reach the ceiling. Just inside the door something moved at me. I screamed, tightened my grip on Marty's hand.

"It is only me, Miss Markham." Monsignor Pontecorvo was standing there, cloaked in gloom, glaring at us.

"Oh. Monsignor." I tried to calm myself; could not.

"But you seemed so eager to come here." He smiled a smile that could only be called malevolent.

"I—we—were expecting something more like a usual library. This—this is—" I looked around. Scrolls, loose pages, thousands of them, were scattered on ill-lit tabletops; hundreds of huge bound volumes thick with dust were piled on the stone floor. I sighed deeply. "We should get to work. Is there any possibility of getting more light in here?"

"Alas, no, signorina." He smiled to show the fact pleased him. "Now, if you will excuse me . . ." He made a mock bow; turned; vanished into the next room. Almost at once the sound of his footsteps disappeared.

Giovanni hopped casually up onto the edge of a table. I turned to him. "There are other ways in and out of here."

He brushed it aside. "What you need, you should find here."

"And if we don't?"

"This is the only place you may search. The pertinent books would be here. You will have to make do with what you discover here."

I was about to make an issue of it, but Marty cut me off. "Of course, Giovanni. You have us completely in your power down here."

"On the contrary." He leaned back. His elbow crushed some scrolls. "We are entirely at your mercy. We must trust you not to reveal what you learn here. And not to misuse it. The consequences could be . . . embarrassing." His last word was too carefully chosen. It was a threat. We were to behave ourselves.

Marty looked at me. Was still on edge. I could see how much; hoped the priest could not. "Well, you're the scholar. What can I do to help you?"

Once more I looked around the vault. There were so many

things to read. Thousands of them. There would only be time to skim them. I think I was grateful there would be only this one room of them. "I don't know. Just help me keep track of what I've read and what I haven't, I suppose." I crossed to the nearest table. The manuscripts on it were piled a foot thick. Just as I reached for the first of them, the light bulb above it flickered and went out. "Evidently the church does not accept the idea that light is knowledge."

We worked for hours. At midday the monsignor, followed by a nun who looked as old as the catacombs, brought us a simple lunch, bread, soup, cheese, wine. He relieved Giovanni; watched us at our research. Then after a few hours the younger man came back to preside over us.

This became the pattern of our work. We were never alone, never assisted. At times I had the feeling it was a game to them, or that we were somehow specimens, to be observed with scientific detachment. It was no use trying to engage them in conversation. I read book after book; Marty kept a record of what we covered. It was exasperating to a librarian used to order, to system. "Do you mean," I asked Giovanni, "that none of this at all is indexed or cross-referenced?"

"Alas, no."

"You should do it, then."

"Clare, I don't have the time."

"You have all the time in the world to watch us."

"There would be no point to indexing our books. Most of the pleasure of working among them is to browse. To discover."

When our wine was brought to us each day, Marty drank heavily. I think it helped him deal with his claustrophobia.

The monsignor came to watch us now and then, and Giovanni went off somewhere. Marty enjoyed needling the old man. "We're really not thieves, you know. You could leave us here on our own."

"You might wander off and get lost in the labyrinth."

"If we gave you our word we'd stay here . . . ?"

"The Vatican learned its lessons about human nature a thousand years ago." He smiled cryptically, like the mandarin he knew himself to be.

"Giovanni." I flirted with our younger watchdog. "Why do you go by your first name? Why isn't it Father Pinello?"

He smiled that adolescent smile of his. "I have my reasons."

"Has Rome's worldliness taken root in your soul?"

"You are a beautiful woman, Clare." The smile became wider. He moved his eyes, not his head, to look across the room at Marty. "And Marty is a beautiful man."

Neither of us wanted to hear this.

Our fifth day in Rome the sun came out again. It hardly mattered to us; we worked in our subterranean gloom. Some of the manuscripts were so faded they were near impossible to read. I had headaches. Each night we were exhausted. Then finally I found something. A reference to glass of St. James the Lesser. At Chutreaux, in the French countryside. I stared at the manuscript. "Chutreaux. Is that one of the ones that were ruined in the war?"

"Chutreaux." Giovanni sifted his memory. "Chutreaux. I think a German airplane crashed into it." The customary smile left his face. "Glass of St. James. What can it mean?"

"We can't know till we go there."

"And you will tell me—us—here at the Vatican when you find it?"

"Of course."

"You can't possibly think us that naive."

Marty was on edge after all that time closed in. He decided to be blunt. Looked up from the table where he was working. "Why let us work here at all if you don't trust us?"

Giovanni smiled. "You might find something of value."

"What if we find it and don't tell you?"

"We'll know."

"How would Cardinal Hayes feel if he knew you were treating us like this? Like thieves."

"Cardinal Hayes knows exactly what is going on. And so do we. The blood glass is the property of the church. It will come into our hands, one way or another. We can afford to wait. We are not called the catholic—the universal—church for nothing."

We were more in their hands than either of us had realized.

There was one more reference in the scrolls. To glass from the blood of St. John the Evangelist, at Mount Niphates in Asia Minor. At "the Monastery Scriptorium of St. John." It was all we could find. In ten days we had exhausted our supply of books. Were worn out, as much from the oppressive presence of the priests as from our work. Went back to the Venezia Palace for a long night's rest. The next afternoon we would leave for France.

I posted a letter to Mr. Tiffany telling him what we had found, where we were heading.

It began to rain again that evening, a slow drizzle this time. Alone in my room, I took out the blood glass; had not seen it since we were still aboard the *Thornhill*. The Roman twilight was dark grey, but the glass glowed in its light. Felt warm in my hand.

Marty's room was next to mine. I thought I heard voices coming from it. He must have ordered from room service. I watched, felt the glass in my hand. Its surface was hard; should have been cool; was not.

There was a knock at my door. "Yes?"

"Clare. Let me in." It was Giovanni.

I walked to the door, opened it. He was soaking wet. "I forgot to bring an umbrella."

I held the door with my hand; made no move to invite him in.

"I'm chilly, Clare."

There was a loud noise; something struck the wall in Marty's room. I turned my head toward it. "What's going on there?"

"Nothing, Clare. He's just having a fit of temper. Can I come in?"

"You were in his room?"

"For a brief moment, yes."

"I'm afraid I've got packing to do."

"Only for a moment. I . . . I want to make love to you, you see." He grinned like a bashful schoolboy.

"You want—!" I could not have been more shocked. "After the cold way you've treated us, you want that?"

"Yes. I am a handsome man. All the women say so. I will be tender." He smiled; worked at looking boyish.

"I think you ought to leave."

"I want you."

The earnestness in his voice was so corny. I looked him up and down. He was dripping wet; looked absurd. He smiled that grin of his at me. I was almost tempted. "Please go."

"You are ours, Clare. You belong to the church. There's no escaping from it. Give in now, while it can still give you some pleasure."

I had no idea what this threat could mean. Did not like the sound of it. "Marty!"

"No, Clare." He reached out and touched my right breast.

"Don't touch me! Marty!"

In a moment he was in the hall. Rushed to my door. Glared at the priest. "What are you doing here?"

"I just wanted to say goodbye to Signorina Markham." He lied with a sober face.

"The way you wanted to say goodbye to me?" So it was Giovanni's voice I had heard in Marty's room. Marty turned to me. "Father Pinello asked me to copulate with him."

"We must be equally attractive, then." I smiled, pointedly, at Giovanni.

But he was not fazed by it. "You are. I want both of you." There was a moment's hesitation. We both watched him. "Perhaps, now, the three of us could . . ." He made a vague gesture, intertwined his fingers.

"The three of us most certainly could not." I tried to sound firm; found myself laughing at him instead.

But Marty was still angry. Grabbed Giovanni by the back of his clerical collar, escorted him to the top of the staircase. "I'd suggest you get out of here before I manufacture you into a few new relics. Or does the church still want martyrs?"

Marty was a head taller than the priest. Giovanni turned wonderfully pale, started to perspire, ran down the steps. It was the last we saw of him.

"I have a bottle of wine in my room. Chianti." I could see that Marty was still upset. I wanted to calm him down. "Why don't we drink to the end of our stay in Rome?"

"Hm?" He had not heard me. I repeated. "Oh. Oh, sure."

We went in, sat on the bed, filled two glasses. "A toast." I held my goblet out to him. "To the last of Father Pinello."

"And to the last of this city. I should have killed the little bastard."

"Marty, it's over with. Calm down."

"Shit." He stood up; started pacing. "The smug little bastard. I should have killed him."

"Don't you think that would have been a bit excessive?"

He crossed the room with long strides. Punched violently the wall. It was the sound I had heard earlier. "Marty, for God's sake, get a grip on yourself."

"Bastard!" He punched the wall again. I was not certain now whether he meant the priest or myself.

"Marty. Here, have some more wine."

He took a few long, deep breaths; they seemed to quiet him. "I'm sorry, Clare. When he propositioned me, I just . . ."

"You're a handsome man. Surely it's not the first time."

"It's the first time I've had it come from a priest. If he hadn't been a priest . . . He's been so callous with us. How could he think that I'd . . . ?"

"The male ego, darling, has performed wonders even greater than that."

"Huh?"

"Never mind."

The rain picked up. We heard it beating against the windows. The light in the room seemed artificially bright; unreal. I switched off the lamps, walked to the window. Everything was the dark grey of charcoal. On the table next to the window, where I had left it, was the blood glass. I had never seen the angry, violent side of Marty before. What had the priest said to him, to make him rage the way he'd done? I looked at him. He drained his glass, poured more wine for himself. Seemed to have forgotten I was in the room. "Marty."

"Hm?"

"Don't drink too much. Tomorrow is a traveling day."

He swallowed all the wine in his glass. Held the bottle out to me. "Here. Come and join me."

"Marty."

"I need to be drunk."

"You've had enough. Don't you think?"

"I need to get drunk."

I watched him from the window, watched the red of the glass, watched the grey rain.

9

There was rain, too, in Paris. Slow, heavy drizzle. To this day when I think of Paris I see rain. Notre Dame looked ominous in it, the famous stained glass there looked washed out to us.

It was a two-hour bus ride to Chutreaux. Rolling hills, vineyards, chateaus. A fairy tale land, I thought. The town was quaint, the kind of place a landscape painter would be drawn to. The Eure flowed quietly past. Two stone bridges spanned it, looked ancient; could have been built by the Romans. Over all of it towered the cathedral's remains, skeleton of a building, black and empty. We arrived at dusk, carried our bags from the bus depot. Just then the clouds parted and shafts of the sun's dying light lit the town, the ruins. We were crossing the bridge into town. I stopped walking, set my bags on the ground, took in the scene. "The sun doesn't help, does it?"

"Hm?" Marty was weighed down more heavily than I; seemed grateful for the chance to stop.

"The ruins look even blacker with the sun shining on them."

"You're right." He looked around. "But look at everything else. I've never seen a place so green." There were vineyards, fields waiting for the harvest; the banks of the river were dense with trees and flowering shrubs.

"Let's go."

The town was not large; we found the inn in a few moments. A plump man with a thick mustache greeted us. "Americans? It is a pleasure to have you here. I am Monsieur Cambris."

"Hello." I put down my things, helped Marty with his.

"You wish a room?"

"No, monsieur, we wish two rooms."

"You are in France, mademoiselle. You should take my counsel and make love to your young man."

"Two rooms, please." I was too tired for local color.

"*Oui, mademoiselle.*" He looked glum. "You are sight-seeing? This is the most romantic place in Europe."

"We've come to see the ruins, yes." I filled out the registration cards.

"The ruins. Yes. Our cathedral. It is what is called a tourist attraction now; it brings us money and visitors. But it is no longer a church for us. We go to Mass in the next town; there is no priest in Chutreaux. It is a pity you could not have seen it before the *boches* destroyed it. It was one of the grandest in the world."

No priest. I was half tempted to tell him how lucky I thought Chutreaux.

"What exactly happened?" Marty seemed to be warming up to the man.

"What do you call them, flying aces. There was a dogfight in the air over Chutreaux. Machine guns in the air above us, fire and thunder, like the battle between St. Michael and Satan. And when Satan fell, he made an inferno for us."

"The shell of the building is still standing." Marty leaned on the reception desk; liked Monsieur Cambris. "Couldn't you restore it?"

"Alas, monsieur, the skills of our ancestors are lost to us. There are no stonemasons, no carpenters, no glassmakers who could do the job. This is a melancholy age." He glanced at our cards. "Mademoiselle Markham and Monsieur Kampinski. Welcome to Chutreaux."

"Thank you." I was brisk. "May we see our rooms now?"

"*Oui, mademoiselle.*" He led us up a flight of wooden steps, along a wide corridor. The rooms were huge, filled with hand-made furniture; warm, heavy curtains to keep out the damp night air; each had an enormous overstuffed bed. I looked at mine longingly; wanted nothing in the world more than to be in it, asleep.

"Thank you, Monsieur Cambris. This will do perfectly."

Marty was equally pleased with his. We said our good nights. I undressed, fell asleep in what seemed an instant.

And awoke. Nightmares. Giovanni Pinello moving in them.

Threatening us. A labyrinth with no end, with no outlet, a maze as long as sin. "You are ours, Clare, we own you." What if his threats were not as ridiculous as they sounded?

I could not get back to sleep. Tossed, turned. It was no use. I got up, climbed into my robe. "Marty?" I knocked softly at his door. No answer. "Marty?"

There were voices downstairs. I went and looked. Marty and the inkeeper, talking, drinking, laughing. I could still hear him telling me, "I need to get drunk." The priest—or both of them, or the whole Vatican—had gotten to both of us.

"Marty." I called down the steps.

"Clare? What's wrong?" He crossed the room, stood where I could see him.

"Nothing, really. I just can't sleep."

"Come down and have a drink with us. Gerard—Monsieur Cambris—has been telling me about the cathedral. About the glass in it."

"No, a drink would only wake me up more."

"Then—?"

"I need company. I need to talk."

"Sure. Just let me finish my drink and say good night to Gerard." His French pronunciation was abominable.

I went back to my room; dressed. A moment after I was done Marty came. Knocked lightly on the door. "What's wrong?"

"Oh, nothing, really. I've been dreaming."

"About the priest." It was not a question. "He looks so angelic and he's so vile. It doesn't seem possible."

"It's possible. I can still feel his hand on my breast. Look, why don't we go outside and take a walk? The air will do us both good."

"What's it like outside?"

I walked to the window, pulled back the curtains. It was a landscape from another world. There was a large, bright moon and it lit the river, the town, the ruins. I had to be out in it. We both got sweaters, told the innkeeper where we were going; pulled the inn's wooden door heavily shut behind us.

There were frogs croaking along the river, and crickets chirped energetically despite the cool night. We strolled the bank, listened to the water's roll. The moon turned everything silver, the trees, the flowers, the river, us. The scent of chrysanthemums came to us.

"So it's nightmares." Marty watched the river, not me.

"I can't stand to think what he might have done to me if you hadn't heard me call out."

"I don't think he was very strong. You could probably have thrown him out yourself."

"No." The thought of touching the man repulsed me. "No, I don't think so."

"Anyway, it didn't get too bad, and now it's over."

"Except inside me."

Marty said nothing. An owl hooted half a dozen times, then stopped. It was chilly; I pulled my sweater around myself.

We were a good mile from the town. The river cascaded over some rocks, then returned to its lazy pace. I walked closer to Marty, to feel the warmth of him.

"Clare."

"Hm?"

"Do you think Mr. Tiffany knows that Cardinal Hayes told the Vatican what we're after?"

"I don't know." There was a wooden footbridge; we walked out onto it. "Maybe he couldn't get us permission to do our research unless they knew."

"Do you think he knows the kind of men who run the place?"

"Most likely. Marty, I'm cold. Will you hold me?"

Wordlessly he put an arm around me. Then, "Are you sure this is something you want?"

I pressed myself against him. Watched the long shadows the moon gave us. Felt him press his lips to my hair. I reached up and put a hand on his chest.

There was a scream, a bloodcurdling scream from behind us. We both jumped.

"Good Jesus." Marty let go of me, then took hold of me again, tighter.

Someone was standing at the end of the bridge, ten feet from us. A girl, ghostly white in the moonlight. She shrieked again, shouted something unintelligible.

"Christ, she's crazy. Let's get out of here."

We made it back to the inn quickly. Behind us as we walked we could still hear the girl, laughing, talking to herself, crying out.

She was following, but at a distance. We pushed open the front door, slammed it firmly behind us.

Monsieur Cambris came out from a back room, alarmed. "Good Lord, what is wrong?"

Marty described what had happened.

"La Prêtresse. She is from the next village. She is mad." He scowled. I wondered whether it was the lunacy or the geography that he disapproved of. "She goes all the time to play in the ruins. I wish I had warned you not to walk that way."

"Doesn't her family take care of her?" Marty still had an arm around me. "I mean, it's awfully chilly for her to be running around out there."

"She has no family." His features became stone.

"Then . . . ?"

"She has no family." He said it louder, as if that might settle it.

"Do you have anything warm to drink?" I was shivering.

"I will have Madame Cambris make you tea, if you like. Or coffee."

"Tea, please." I had not realized there was a Madame Cambris. We left our sweaters in our rooms, went downstairs again, drank. She was a large woman, plumper than her husband.

"That girl we saw. La Prêtresse, your husband called her."

"*Oui, mademoiselle?*"

"Why is she called that?"

"Called what?" She busied herself cleaning tables, straightening chairs.

"La Prêtresse. Doesn't it mean priestess?"

"*Je ne comprends pas, mademoiselle.*"

"A priestess. A female priest." I took a deep drink of hot tea.

"There is a legend, mademoiselle, a rumor. They say she is the daughter of the priest who died when the cathedral was burned."

"Do priests have daughters?" Marty smiled lecherously.

"*Non, monsieur.*" She went about her business; gave the impression she wanted to be in bed, not talking to tourists. We drank our tea, chatted, let the inn's warmth touch us.

Then it was time to retire again; it was nearly midnight. We climbed the steps. Stopped outside my door. "Marty."

"Hm?"

"I don't want to be alone tonight."

"You—" He stared at me. "You're not making fun of me? You mean that?"

"Yes. I don't want to have more nightmares. If I have them, I want someone beside me."

"Someone." He sounded hurt.

"You."

"Can I kiss you?"

I hesitated; nodded.

Monsieur Cambris appeared just then with a tray for one of the other guests. "You Americans. A French couple would simply have asked for one room. Why be so evasive?"

He tried to push his way past us, but I planted myself in his way. Took Marty by the hand; stared straight into the old man's eyes; led my beau into my boudoir.

In bed we kissed, cuddled, kept each other warm; that was all. But I dreamed, of Giovanni and of La Prêtresse.

Marty slept late the next morning, but I was up early. Had a full breakfast. Madame Cambris fussed over me, overfed me; seemed to approve of me now that I was not asking prying questions about the locals. Then I walked outside, strolled along the bank of the Eure. By sunlight it was beautiful, idyllic; the previous night's scare seemed just one more of my nightmares. This, I told myself, not New York, is the kind of place God meant us to live in. This is Eden.

When I got back to the inn Marty was up; was dressing. "You're missing a lovely morning."

He yawned, crawled into his trousers, ignored me.

"And delicious food. Madame Cambris's cooking is angelic."

"You know I never eat breakfast." He looked around for his shoes. "I can't see how people face new days with full stomachs."

"The morning's beautiful."

He muttered something into his undershirt as he pulled it over his head. I watched him. Watched his beautiful body.

An hour later we were at the ruins of the Cathedral of Chutreaux, were standing where its main door had been. A somber place even on such a beautiful day. Half of the walls were gone; lay in piles, enormous heaps of rubble. Other walls were intact, standing tall with nothing to support; the fire had made them black. Some of the flying buttresses still soared heavenward;

of others there was no sign. Here and there bits of the roof still hung above us, seemingly unsupported, seemingly free of gravity, of everything. And one of the two bell towers was still erect, standing as if nothing in the world had happened. There were occasional clouds now, huge cumulus clouds; sunlight alternated with black shadow.

"It must have been splendid." I looked around us again and again, taking it all in, trying to visualize it as it had been when it was entire. "It must have been taller and wider than Notre Dame."

"Your artist's eye must be sharper than mine." Marty seemed to be studying, not appreciating. "How can you tell that?"

"The bell tower. Its proportions. It must have been grand."

He walked into the ruin, walked slowly the length of the nave. "It's too big."

"Marty, it was famous. Its design and proportions were famous."

"I mean too big for us." He was halfway along the nave; had to raise his voice to talk to me. "How will we ever find what we want in all this?"

"Oh." Somber thought; it deflated me. I walked to the bottom of the bell tower. Pressed my hand flat against the stone. It was cold. I craned my head back, looked up to the top. A gargoyle stared down at me.

"Clare, come here." Marty had reached the transept. He was staring, fascinated, at the floor beneath him.

"What is it?"

"Come and look."

I walked to meet him. There were piles of stone everywhere. Some of it was obviously carved, obviously part of the building; much of it was just stone. Here and there among it could be seen fragments of glass. I stopped, picked up a brilliant blue piece, blue as the sky. Held it up to the light. "Marty, this is beautiful."

He was still standing at the cross-place. Studying, for reasons not apparent, the floor.

"Marty, have you looked at any of the glass?"

"No."

"Well—"

"Come and look at this, Clare."

I looked from the glass in my hand to Marty. Reluctantly let the piece fall where I had found it. "What have you found?"

"Look. Look at what they did here."

The floor was made of alternating rows of dark and light stone. "Yes. What of it?"

"Can't you see?"

"Yes. They used two kinds of stone here. So what?" I looked around the ruin, anxious to start searching for the blood glass. A huge cloud passed over the sun; we were in twilight.

"Clare, this is a maze. Follow the colored stone with your eyes. They built a huge maze into the floor of the cathedral. A labyrinth."

I looked around. Now that he had pointed it out to me, I could see it. "A maze."

"A tangible symbol of the soul's journey. Do you think that's what they had in mind?"

Yes, I thought so. "Maybe they just liked games."

He got down on his knees, pressed his hands flat on the maze's surface. Looked up with a bit of wonder showing in his face; scanned the ruin.

"Marty, I think we ought to climb the bell tower."

"Hm?" He was lost inside himself. "Why?"

"It'll give us a better sense of the geography, the layout. We might be able to guess where the St. James was."

He got quickly up. "You're right. But I wonder if it's safe."

"There's only one way to find out."

The entrance to the bell tower was boarded up. But there was room enough for us to squeeze, with difficulty, between the planks. I scraped my left forearm on a rough piece of wood. Inside, it was like night. We waited a few moments, let our eyes adjust to it. Brushed the dust of rotten wood off our clothes. Marty walked to the foot of the staircase. "I wish we'd thought to bring a flashlight."

From above us there came sounds; something—someone— moving. I stiffened. "It's that girl. La Prêtresse. She's up there."

"No." He looked up the black stairwell. "I think it's just birds or something."

"Marty, let's get out of here. It's dangerous."

"Try to be brave. Like a man."

"You read too much Hemingway."

"I don't read any at all. Let's go upstairs."

He led the way; took my hand and pulled me, unwilling, behind

him. The steps were worn by the centuries, were littered with
debris; the footing was not good. We reached the first landing.
And suddenly a stone came hurtling down the steps from above
us. A huge one, the head of a gargoyle. It careered past, barely
missed Marty. "Jesus." He pressed himself against the wall,
looked down where the stone had rolled.

"She's up there, Marty."

Another stone flew out of the darkness above. We sidestepped
it. The girl was on the next landing above us, we could hear her,
she was talking unintelligibly to herself, laughing. Then she
screamed, the same ear-piercing scream we had heard the night
before. A shower of glass fragments came flying down at us. We
were both cut. Bled heavily. "Jesus Christ!"

"Marty, we've got to get out of here."

Frantic, bleeding, we rushed down the steps, pushed our way
between the planks and were outside. We could still hear La
Prêtresse laughing, squawking.

"Christ." Marty was pale, was out of breath. His right cheek
was bleeding steadily. I got a handkerchief and mopped the blood.
He could not take his eyes off the bell tower; gaped at it. Then
finally looked at me. "You're bleeding, too, Clare. Here, let me
see to it."

It took a while for us both to calm down; for the blood to stop.
The sky was still overcast. We sat on a pair of large stones,
scanned the ruins.

"Gerard." Marty touched his cheek gingerly. It stung him.
"Gerard told me that the most lovely window in the cathedral was
in the apse, just to the right of the altar. An old saint, he said. He
did not remember which one. We should look there."

"Are you all right?"

"Yes." He looked at the tower. Halfway up was a small
window; in it faintly we could see the outline of La Prêtresse.
"Are you?"

"I think so. Let's try the apse, then."

We crossed the stone maze at the transept, headed for where the
altar had been. The damage was worse here; it must have been
where the airplane actually struck. All the stone was charred. We
sifted among it, worked there for hours. Kept an eye on the tower,
lest the mad girl come out; once we got used to the idea that she
was in there, we felt safe from her.

Near noon the sky cleared once again. The day became hot. "Marty."

"Hm?"

"We're not doing this right. We're missing something."

"What do you mean?" He was beginning to perspire; unbuttoned his shirt.

"In this light the glass will only look red."

He stared at me.

"We should come here at night. That's when we'll find it."

"But—"

"It will glow. It will lead us to itself."

"But the girl—"

"I know. But we want the glass." I looked around the cathedral; looked at Marty. "Don't we?"

His eyes were on the bell tower.

"Marty." I moved next to him. Put my hand on his chest. "Marty."

He looked at me. Kissed me. "If it's here, we'll find it, Clare."

"Despite the girl." I kissed him back. "If it's here."

From the bell tower there came a scream. La Prêtresse was leaning out the window, gaping at us, laughing at us, shouting obscene things. "*Baise-la*," she cried, "*baise-la*."

Marty froze. Glared at the girl. "What does it mean?"

"It's filth." I could not say the words.

"*Baise-la, baise-la, baise-la*." It was a grotesque singsong.

"Stop it!" He was furious. Bellowed at the girl. "Stop watching us! Stop talking to us like that!"

She laughed. "*Baise-la, baise-la, baise-la*."

"Stop it!"

"Marty, ignore her."

He let go of me, ran across the ruin to the tower, began to pound furiously on the boards. The girl laughed, yelled her obscenities. "Stop it, God damn you!" He punched the boards, roared at her. Then I saw her take a stone in her hands, poise it over him.

"Marty, for God's sake, look out!"

She let it fall. It hit him on the shoulder. I ran to his side, pulled him out of her range. She still laughed at us.

"Here, let me look at it." His shoulder was bruised badly, abraded, but there was no bleeding. "Can you move it?"

Slowly, with obvious pain, he swung his arm. "I think it'll be all right." He was red with anger; kept looking up at La Prêtresse.

"We should get back to the inn. You can soak in a hot tub for a while. That'll help."

"You little fiend!" He shouted at her; stood and raised his good arm. "I'll kill you! You hear me, bitch, I'll kill you!"

The girl laughed. *"Baise-la, baise-la."*

"Bitch! Foul-mouthed little bitch!"

"Marty! She's mad, she can't help the way she's behaving. Come on. We can come back later. This isn't accomplishing a thing."

I had to pull him away from the church. He wanted to stay, fight with the girl. It took half the afternoon to get him calmed down. The bath helped, and a filling lunch of Madame Cambris's country food. I made sure he drank plenty of wine, and when he was relaxed I put him to bed.

"Have you ever seen *The Hunchback of Notre Dame*?"

"Get some sleep, Marty."

"It was like that. The end of the movie, with Lon Chaney showering things down on the people. It was like that."

It was not something I wanted to hear. Not then, not Lon again. "Marty, go to sleep. We can talk later."

The innkeeper was curious about his injured shoulder, and I invented something about him stumbling among the rubble. Then I tried to get some sleep myself, but it wasn't possible. Marty's temper. I felt as if he were a different man, not the one I'd known for two and a half years. How was it possible for him to have changed so?

Evening. Still warm; no breeze to dispel the day's heat. The moon was just past full. It hung low above the horizon; dark clouds streaked its countenance. Frogs, crickets, night birds sang. Marty and I left the inn, amid much concern from the host and his wife.

"After last evening," Monsieur Cambris sat, drank a mug of wine, "you are going out again?"

"We love the countryside." I tried to sound offhand.

"But, mademoiselle, La Prêtresse alarmed you so last night." His wife drank, too.

"She's only a girl." Marty talked like a hero. His hurt arm was in a sling. "She can't really hurt us."

They took long swallows of their wine; said good night to us; clearly thought us eccentric, at best.

The moon was behind the ruins; we saw it through the church's bones. Bats circled noisily the bell tower. I watched them, not the stones. "Maybe she's afraid of the bats. Maybe she doesn't come here at night." I did not believe it.

"She was down by the footbridge last night." Reassuring thought. "We're ready for her tonight. There's nothing else she can do to us."

Aside from the bats, there was no movement in the tower, no sign of life. Marty walked to the boarded-up entrance, pounded on the planks. Everything inside remained quiet. "La Prétresse," he shouted. "Bitch!" Nothing. he looked at me and smiled halfheartedly. "No sign of her."

"Good." I did not believe she wasn't there. Scanned the ruins, the trees around them. "Let's go up to the apse and look for the glass."

The cathedral's columns towered above us in the night like black giants; made stark shadows in the moon's light. Something, some small animal, scuttled away as we walked through the church. There was a quick gust of breeze, then it died again. There was no talk between us; we watched all around us, for the girl, for the glass. Reached the rubble where the altar had been. There was no sign of the glow, of the glass we were after. In an hour or more of looking we found nothing.

I sat, tired, on the low stump of a column. Marty kept looking. Took off his shirt; the night was that warm. I saw sweat glistening on his chest, on his back. Wanted to touch him, wanted us to be back at the inn, in bed. "Marty."

"Hm?" He was turning over rocks, tossing them aside.

"If the airplane crashed into the nave, wouldn't most of the glass have blown outward?"

He stopped. Looked at me. "You're right."

"Let's make a circuit of the outside."

Marty picked up his shirt, wiped his forehead with it. "Come on."

"It'll be quicker if we separate. I'll go this way." I moved off to my right.

"What about the girl?"

"She's not here." I had stopped thinking about her. "Go on. I'll

make a circuit clockwise. You go the other way." We parted.
"Oh, but be careful of the devil." I shouted it over my shoulder.

"What do you mean?"

"Haven't you ever heard? If you go counterclockwise around a church, you meet the devil."

Marty laughed, walked off. I examined the ground as I made my way. Finally, just at the rear of the church, I saw the glow of the blood glass. Two large fragments of it, that was all. I bent, picked one up. Everything else was covered with dirt, but the red glass was clean, clear. I held it up, watched the moon through it.

Then Marty was there. "You've found it."

"Mm-hmm." I was pleased with myself.

"That's terrific." He took me in his arms, kissed me. My hands felt the sweat on his back.

And there, suddenly, was the girl. Laughing, shrieking, shouting foul things.

Marty nearly exploded again. But I caught his hand, held on to him. "Come on, Marty, we've got what we want. Let her rave at the moon."

He wanted to stay and fight with her, but I pulled him behind me. The mad girl followed us a few yards, then lost interest and vanished into the trees. Just before we reached the inn I put the two fragments into my bag; there was no telling how the local people would feel about us taking away part of their church, of their tourist attraction.

The moon lit our room. I played with the glass, pushed it through my skin. Compared it with the piece we already had; they matched, same color, same texture. Wrapped one piece of it for shipment, along with a letter, to Mr. Tiffany. The other would stay with us; I laid it carefully on the night table. We would return to Paris in the morning, then travel to Germany, to see if there was more glass to be found at Obergurgl.

Then to bed, with Marty once again at my side. We kissed, cuddled, fondled. Slept deeply and with satisfaction.

Early the next morning there was commotion. I awoke much earlier than I would have liked. Marty slept through it.

I dressed, went downstairs. Monsieur Cambris was excited, upset. "There has been a murder in Chutreaux, Mademoiselle Markham."

"A—" The town seemed so quiet.

"The girl you encountered. La Prêtresse. Someone killed her and threw her body into the river."

"The poor girl."

"*Oui, mademoiselle*. The church should have put her in a hospital years ago. But . . ." He shrugged.

"Have they found the killer?"

"No, mademoiselle. The authorities were just here, inquiring about our guests."

"But surely . . . surely we can't be suspects?"

"Please, there is no need to worry. We assured the officers that no one left the inn all night."

"We were planning to go back to Paris this afternoon. Will there be any problem, do you think?"

"No, mademoiselle. You are free to go when you like. You are not under suspicion."

My relief must have been obvious to him. He served me an extra-hearty breakfast.

After eating I went upstairs to pack. Marty was just waking up. He yawned, could not seem to shake off the night. I kissed him good morning, went on packing our things, left him to rouse himself.

The blood glass was not on the table where I had left it. I looked around. It was sitting on top of Marty's clothes. I could have sworn it had been on the table. I wrapped it, packed it away.

Downstairs, Marty had tea. Asked about the killing. Monsieur Cambris seemed unwilling to talk about it, but Marty pressed him for details.

"It was most horrible, monsieur. Her throat was slashed. It was cut so many times, her head was almost severed from her body. But even worse than that is what the killer did to her eyes. The poor girl's eyes were cut, too. Slashed so badly there was nothing left of them but jelly. It is terrible, monsieur. Chutreaux has never seen a thing like this."

The blood glass. Marty had been so angry at the girl.

The blood glass should not cut. But it had cut Michael, on the *Thornhill*. I was suddenly afraid of the glass, afraid to be carrying it. I did not want to think the thing I was thinking.

10

From Paris we took the night train to Berlin. It rained briefly, heavily; ferocious thunder, lightning covering the whole sky. Then, abruptly, it ended and there was a clear sky. Bright moon, bright planets. But in the wake of it everything was humid. The inside of the passenger compartments was unbearably hot.

The train's motion, the rhythm of the tracks put me to sleep early despite the awful humidity. I switched off the light in my drawing room, lay on the hard mattress, closed my eyes. Now and then passing lights shined in my window, disturbed my rest. Once the train whistled, and I woke with a start. Then mysteriously, inexplicably, we stopped dead. No sound, no movement. I got up and looked out the window. We were nowhere. No city, no depot. Fields surrounded us.

Marty's compartment was next to mine. I tapped on the connecting door. Called softly his name. There was no answer. I opened the door. "Marty?"

The compartment was empty. I looked back into my own. What could be wrong? In one of my bags were the two pieces of blood glass. I checked to make certain they were still there. They glowed; were undisturbed. Then I got dressed, walked out into the corridor.

The pullman porter was asleep at his post. I thought the train's stopping would have wakened him, but he dozed, snored. There was no one else in sight. I walked past him and entered the next car. Again there was no one. The car beyond that was the club car; there would be people there.

Two waiters leaned against tables. A handful of late diners ate sandwiches. At the far end of the saloon was Marty, arm still in its sling, talking to a young man. "Clare! Come and join us."

They were drinking. From their look and from the smell in the air, I would say they had been at it for some while. I joined them, kissed Marty, let him play host. "Clare Markham, I'd like you to meet Dieter von Schattenburg. Dieter, Clare." We shook hands, exchanged small talk. Dieter was tall, slender, dark, with enormous green eyes; more like Marty than like the stereotypical German. The way his clothes hung on him made him look quite muscular, quite athletic. "Dieter lives in Berlin. He's offered to show us the city."

"How nice of you." I smiled at Dieter; liked the look of him.

"But you must be prepared, Fräulein Markham." He smiled back. "Berlin tends to shock visitors."

"Shock? How do you mean?" I wanted him to shock me.

"There is no kind of vice you cannot purchase in Berlin, Fräulein."

"Please, call me Clare. I'm afraid that isn't very shocking, Dieter. In New York, all the best vice is free."

We all laughed at my little joke. I was not certain what to make of our new acquaintance. But he was all charm. "Will you permit me to buy you a drink?"

"Just a brandy, please." Dieter headed off toward the bar, and I turned to Marty. "Do you have any idea why the train's stopped?"

"Not a clue. Maybe there's a cow on the tracks."

"The Grand Hotel is only holding our reservation till noon."

"We'll be there in plenty of time. I asked the barman."

"Let's hope so. Otherwise we'll end up sleeping in an alley behind the Reichstag."

"Nonsense." He giggled.

"Exactly how much have you had to drink?"

"I'm not counting." He giggled again. "Dieter is wonderful company."

"So I gathered." He was back with my brandy. "Thank you, Dieter." I sipped it; it was expensive, and I paid it the appropriate compliment. "So. You are a Berliner."

"*Ja, gnädige Fräulein.*"

"We were just wondering what's holding up the train."

"Probably the border police." He was airy. "Since the kaiser fell, nothing has run well. We should be more like the Italians. Their trains run like clockwork."

"Are we at the border, then?" I looked out the nearest window.

"More or less." His tone was quite casual. "Germany's borders keep shifting."

So despite his heartiness, he thought of us as members of the conquering race. I caught Marty's eye, but he seemed not to have understood.

A moment later a contingent of German police entered the car, ordered us all to return to our compartments for our papers. It took them nearly an hour to check all of us. By then my weariness had caught up with me again. I said good night to Marty and Dieter; went back to my drawing room, back to sleep.

And woke to voices. Laughter. Marty and Dieter, in Marty's compartment. Loud; drunk. "No, honest to God, it won't cut. Let me show you."

There was a knock at the connecting door. "Clare?"

I was uncertain whether to answer; did not like the sound of what they had been saying.

"Clare? It's me. Marty." As if I couldn't tell. "Dieter wants to see the glass."

I got sleepily up, pulled on a robe, opened the door. Stared coldly at the pair of them. Dieter's shirt was unbuttoned to the waist. In the sternest tones I could manage, I said, "What glass?"

Marty grinned a drunken grin. "Why, the—" He caught himself. Realized he had been indiscreet. He looked shamefaced, like a guilty little boy. "Oh."

"Yes. Oh." I was hard as marble. I looked past him. "You'll have to forgive Marty, Dieter. He really shouldn't drink."

"I see." He was suddenly erect, stiff, Prussian. "Then perhaps I should say good night. Clare. Marty." He bowed to each of us in turn, buttoned his shirt, picked up his jacket, went.

"Really, Marty. How could you tell him what we're here after?"

"I—I—" He shrugged; giggled.

"You sound like a perfect idiot. Go to bed and sleep it off."

"*Jawohl, Fräulein.*" He tried to kiss me, but I closed the door in his face.

Late. The train rolling, swaying. Everything was black. I awoke once more. "Marty?"

There was no sound on the train, no movement. I could have

been alone, I could have been . . . "Marty?" I don't think I had been dreaming again. If I had, I don't remember it. But something woke me, and when I woke, I woke disturbed. "Marty?" I wanted him to hear me, wanted him to come into my compartment and hold me. I got up, pulled on my robe. We passed something, I don't know what, and for a brief moment light came in, filled the room, blinded me. It seemed to take forever for my eyes to readjust to the darkness. I sat on the bed and waited.

The blood glass. That was it. It had been moved from where I put it, that night in Chutreaux. The possibility that . . . It could not be. I opened my bag, pulled out the second piece, the one we had found there. It was bright red in the black room. I took it, touched it to my forearm. Warm; it was warm. I pressed. Felt it go beneath my skin. Pushed. The tip raised the skin on the back side of my arm; came through. No pain, no blood.

"Marty." I knocked on the door. Opened it. He was asleep; he was still dressed. "Marty, wake up. You'll ruin your clothes."

"Hm?" He stirred, did not open his eyes.

"Marty."

He awoke. "What's wrong?" Yawned. "Are we there? Jesus, it's still dark out."

"I can't sleep."

He yawned again. Stared at me.

"Here." I held out the glass to him. "Take this."

"Hm?" He could barely keep his eyes open.

"Take this glass."

He reached out, puzzled, and took it from me.

"Now cut me with it."

"What?"

"Cut me. Take the glass and cut me."

"But it— You know—"

"Please. I need to prove something to myself."

He yawned again; gaped at me. "Couldn't you prove it in the morning?"

"Marty, please, take the glass and cut me."

"I don't want to cut you. I love you."

"Goddammit, Marty. Cut me with the goddamned glass."

He looked from me to the fragment and back. Extended his arm. Touched the point of it to my hand. Pushed. It went through; did not hurt me.

"There. Are you happy now?"

I was confused; I had expected pain and blood. "No."

"I need to get some more sleep."

"All right. Good night, darling." I went back to my compartment, and pulled the door shut. Put the glass on top of my bag and watched its red glow. The color of blood. There was something about it—or about myself, or about Marty and me, or about God knew what—that I needed to know, that I did not understand. Marty could not have killed La Prêtresse with it; it would not cut; but it had cut van Boeven. There was no more sleep for me that night. I sat on my bed and watched the glass's light and thought that it looked not divine but malevolent.

Berlin. Bright sunshine, cool winds. The sun gleamed on the canals. Marty's school German was sufficient to get us a taxicab. Along the route here and there were piles of debris, street after street of ruins from the war. The black rubble made sharp contrast with the beauty of the day.

Then we were at the Grand Hotel. Crowded, busy. Elaborately decorated in the latest Art Deco style. Beautiful, elegant people. Seeing it all, it would have been easy to think there had never been a war. It was a world inside itself. But then I saw a man sitting in a corner of the lobby. An older man, stiff, erect. One side of his face was horribly disfigured. I presumed he had been hurt in the war. He looked lonely, or perhaps merely bored.

We checked in, left our things in our rooms. For once our rooms did not adjoin. Then we met in the bar, had sandwiches, planned our visit over the house specialty, a cloyingly sweet drink called, for whatever mysterious reason, a Louisiana flip.

Marty looked impatiently at his watch. "Dieter said he'd meet us here at noon."

"Oh." I was too tired to conceal my disappointment.

"You don't like him." It was an accusation.

"No, he seems perfectly fine. He's certainly handsome enough." I watched with pleasure the flicker of jealousy that crossed Marty's face. "No, I just wish you hadn't told him about the blood glass, that's all."

"Did I do that?" He blushed.

"Maybe you should go easy on the Louisiana flips."

"I need them. I have a hangover. You don't think Dieter's trustworthy?"

"Who knows? The stuff is certainly valuable, if only as a curiosity. And this is a conquered city. A poor city. You saw what it's like out there."

Just then Dieter appeared and pushed his way quickly through the crowd to our table. "Good morning to both of you."

"Good morning." I did not want Dieter to be there.

"The sausages here are famous. You should try them."

"Oh. Do you come here often, then?"

"It is the most elegant place in Berlin."

I decided to ignore this evasion. "There's an old man out in the lobby. He must have been disfigured in the war. Everyone seems to be ignoring him. Does Germany have no more regard than that for her war heroes?"

And Dieter ignored me; turned eagerly to Marty. "I have made plans for us this evening. First the Philharmonic. And then to a wonderful night place I know. You both have evening clothes?"

"We'll be sure to get them." Marty was charmed by him once again.

"Good. I want your first night out in Berlin to be memorable."

Dieter had lunch with us, made light conversation; then told us he had to leave "on business."

I decided to be rude to him. "But Dieter, you promised to show us the city."

"And so I shall, *gnädige Fräulein,* but not today. Until seven-thirty, then." He smiled stiffly, bowed to us, left.

I looked at Marty, amused. "So much for our tour."

"Well, we'll se him tonight."

" 'Business.' I'll bet you he sells narcotic baby food."

"Clare. He's a nice man. He's being friendly to two strangers, that's all." He looked at the entrance, as if Dieter might reappear there. "Why have you taken such a dislike to him?"

I really didn't know. "I'll give him this. He's an extraordinarily handsome man."

Marty's face darkened; I had scored.

"Come on." He drank, too swiftly, the rest of his Louisiana flip; made a sour face, as if to counter its sweetness. "Let's see if the front desk can make the arrangements for our excursion to Obergurgl."

The clerk at the front desk was completely accommodating; arranged a car for us, and overnight reservations at an inn. "But . . ." He was hesitant, discreet.

"Yes?"

"Are you certain you wish to go there? There is nothing of interest."

"Quite certain, thank you."

He looked at us as if he were afraid we might be escaped lunatics. "Obergurgl. Yes, sir. I shall make all the arrangements at once."

This was the first place we'd visited where I did not speak the language. Marty had to keep translating for me. It gave me an odd feeling. I did not quite belong in Berlin.

We spent the balance of the afternoon strolling about the city. In the Friedrichstrasse we shopped for our evening clothes. Marty bought his tuxedo quickly; disliked waiting while I tried on gowns, but I needed him to translate. I bought a sleek gown in peach silk, like one I had seen Louise Brooks wear in a film. I was not sure I liked it, but Marty's eyes lit up when he saw me in it. "You look gorgeous, Clare."

That settled it. If I was going to have to compete with Dieter for Marty's attention, this would give me an edge.

Then we walked hand in hand along the Kurfürstendamm and Unter den Linden. The linden trees there filled the air with a beautiful aroma.

Dieter had not mentioned dinner. We dined in the hotel restaurant, had delicious sauerbraten. Marty looked quite uncomfortable in his evening things; kept pulling at the starched collar. Then at half past seven Dieter appeared in the lobby. Very formal, very continental. At his neck, instead of a black tie, he wore a military order of some kind. I prodded Marty. "Ask him what he earned it for."

"Stop it." He whispered; was flustered. "He's our host tonight. Try to be civil."

"Yes, dear."

The concert was wonderful. Furtwängler conducting Rossini's *Thieving Magpie Overture*, Respighi's *Gli Uccelli* and the Beethoven *Pastoral Symphony*. Dieter had somehow gotten a private box for us. I began to think I might be wrong about him; no mere lounge lizard could have afforded it.

"And now." He paused to build a bit of suspense; rubbed his hands together. "We are going to the Club Broadway."

"An American club?" I was disappointed.

"Not at all, Fräulein. It is very much part of Berlin."

It was only a few blocks to the club, but we took a taxicab. Dieter was working hard to impress us, or at least to impress Marty. The club itself was awash in neon, lit as brightly as anything on the street that gave it its name. The maître d' knew Dieter; we were ushered inside amid considerable fuss and given a table close to the dancing. Despite myself, I was beginning to be a bit impressed by Dieter.

Everyone looked affluent, everyone was dressed formally. Women in elegant gowns and dressed hair; men in tails. Military orders not ties were the rule for neckwear. The dance music was jazzy, discordant. "I hope the music is to your taste." Dieter browsed the menu. "It is from Kurt Weill's *Mahagonny-Songspiel*. It is all the rage."

"The music is fine, Dieter." Like him, Marty read the menu.

But I could not take my eyes off the dance floor. It was crowded with couples. Men were dancing with men, women with women. Dancing intimately. I had heard of such places, never dreamed I'd find myself in one. Not a yard away from me, two young men kissed. I focused my attention on the club's streamlined decor; was determined not to let Dieter see my astonishment.

There was champagne. We drank and toasted the night and the city. Marty finally noticed the dance floor; turned a bright shade of red; said nothing. A waiter came, took our orders.

The band switched to Gershwin. "Would you like to dance?" Dieter addressed Marty, not me.

"Who? Me?" Marty looked around us; he obviously had no idea what to say. "I—uh—"

"Marty isn't much of a dancer." I smiled; enjoyed Marty's discomfort. "Are you, darling?"

"Then perhaps, Clare, you would do me the honor." Dieter smiled, stood. "It will create a bit of a flutter, but then I always enjoy being talked about." I was charmed, not by him but by the situation; and we danced.

When we got back to the table the champagne was half gone. Marty was giggling again. He grinned at our host. "Now me."

"But of course." Dieter smiled more widely than I would have thought possible and escorted Marty out to the dance floor. I sipped the wine; told myself, at least you know he isn't after the blood glass.

It was impossible not to watch them. Marty kept laughing, giggling; I don't believe it was quite the reaction Dieter was hoping for. He kept trying to hold Marty more closely, and Marty kept backing away and laughing. Dieter's face was a study in frustration. Despite it all, I found the sight of them in each other's arms exciting; two such handsome men.

By the time they got back to the table, the champagne seemed to be wearing off. Marty was silent. Dieter ordered another bottle of it. Our salads came. Just as we finished with them, the band struck up the Charleston. "Dieter," Marty chuckled, "I just love the Charleston. Let's dance again." And they left me alone at the table once more.

"Good evening, Fräulein. You are an American?"

Standing behind me was a woman of about my own age. She was beautifully dressed; wore emeralds. Smiled at me.

I smiled back. "Yes, I am."

"Welcome to Berlin."

"Thank you. I must say the city lives up to its reputation."

The woman laughed. She was tall; had red hair. "After you've been here a week, it will look like home to you. Your gentlemen friends seem to have deserted you. My name is Greta Schillinglein."

I introduced myself.

"Do you dance the Charleston, Clare?"

I glanced at Marty and Dieter. They were dancing like men gone mad. "In my hometown of Zelienople, Pennsylvania, I used to win contests."

"Zelie—?"

"Never mind. Let's dance."

The music was energetic and so were Greta and I. We made, in all modesty, a bit of a sensation; everyone watched us. Everyone but Marty, that is; he was too engrossed in his own dancing—or perhaps too drunk—to notice us. When he finally did, his eyes widened with astonishment. "Clare. What are you doing?"

"Why, dancing, of course."

"But—but she's a—"

"When in Rome, Marty darling." I grinned at him; poured even more zest into my dance.

We were the only two couples left on the floor. No one else could compete with us. When the music finally ended the crowd applauded loudly. Our main courses were waiting for us back at the table. I invited Greta to join us.

"No, I couldn't think of interfering."

"Please. I like your company."

"I'm afraid I'm here with a friend. I couldn't possibly—"

"Well, have her join us, too." I looked across the table. Marty and Dieter both looked glum. "You don't mind, do you, gentlemen?"

So Greta brought her friend to our table, introduced her. A girl of perhaps twenty. "This is Annemarie Schmitt." They took their seats, lit cigarettes, settled in.

"Dieter darling." I was being outrageous, and loving it. "We need more champagne."

He smoldered; ordered the wine. Talked softly with Marty.

"Where are you staying, Clare?" Annemarie had deep blue eyes, blue like the sea; had skin like porcelain; was beautiful.

"We're at the Grand Hotel."

"Oh, but that is lovely. We have a flat in the Grunewaldstrasse, not two blocks from there. You must all come to visit us."

Dieter was stiff. Looked longingly at Marty. "I'm afraid that does not fit with our plans."

"Oh?" I smiled broadly at him, showed him my teeth. "What are our plans?"

"I was hoping that we might . . . that is, that Marty and I might . . ."

"Nonsense!" Greta had caught on to my little game, joined cheerfully in. "We insist that you must come and visit us."

Marty looked helplessly around the table. "But this is Dieter's city. And he wants so much to be our host."

"But Marty"—she blew smoke in Dieter's direction—"Berlin is our city, too."

"Yes, I know, but—"

"Good, well, it is settled then."

The band began a tango. Annemarie took my hand, asked me to

dance it with her. In a moment we were on the floor. Dieter and Marty followed us; held each other closely; made a show of it. The music, the rhythm was deep, passionate; there was heat in it. I could feel Annemarie's cheek against mine, could smell her perfume; was grateful she and Greta had appeared. Greta sat at the table, sampled everyone's food, smiled at the pair of us. When the number ended and we rejoined her, she settled the bill—over Dieter's flustered protests—and had a taxicab ordered for us.

It was a dark night. There were brilliant stars but no moon. In the back seat of the taxi our bodies pressed against each other. Marty and I sat side by side. The touch of him, the thought of him in Dieter's arms excited me. Greta and Annemarie smoked cigarettes. There was not much talk.

Then we were in the Grunewaldstrasse. Greta permitted Dieter to settle the taxi fare and we followed them up the steep stairs to their garret. Annemarie took our coats, Greta switched on the lights. The furnishings were a beautiful mixture of Art Nouveau and Art Deco, sinuous curves intersecting with airy geometries. There was an enormous skylight through which the stars shone and, directly below it, an oversized bed. And to my delight there was a Tiffany lampshade, an elaborate green and pink cherry tree. "It's wonderful. Marty and I work for the Tiffany Studios."

"It must be splendid fun there." Annemarie put a bottle of liebfraumilch on ice; rolled it between her palms in the bucket. "To make such beautiful things. Industrial art—mechanically reproduced art—stained glass and moving pictures—that is art for the twentieth century. I do sketches myself, and I feel old-fashioned, like an extinct creature. Like a fossil."

"You shouldn't. All of us at Tiffany's paint or draw as well. I'd like to see your work sometime."

"She is a wonderful artist." Greta put an arm around her waist. "Everyone says so. But she does not have the courage to try to sell her work. We are going to make love now, Clare. We should like you to join us."

"To—"

"You dislike the idea." She sounded hurt.

"I'm afraid it isn't what I'm used to."

She kissed Annemarie on the lips, with remarkable force. And in a moment they were in their own world. Fondling, caressing, kissing again and again. They they were on the bed. Undressed.

They made love as if there were nothing in the world but each other. I had never seen such passion. I watched them closely, intently, as if they might give me some of their fire. The graceful lines of the decor complemented perfectly the sleek lines of their bodies.

Like me Marty watched them, could not take his eyes away from them. Dieter seemed bored; lit a cigar and blew smoke rings.

Every now and then I could see Greta watching me from the corner of her eye, as if she were saying, Come and join us, come join in our love. But I only watched.

When they were finished, when they were exhausted, they climbed into silk dressing gowns. Greta opened the wine and we drank. Annemarie pulled a sketchpad out of a closet and began to draw. In a few moments she was done; presented solemnly the sketch to me. It was a red-pen portrait of me, in a style like that of George Grosz; I was dressed in a man's evening clothes and my hair was short, like Marty's. To my astonishment, I looked beautiful that way. Her art had made me beautiful. "Thank you, Annemarie. I can't tell you how much I like it."

Marty looked over my shoulder at it. "You look like a man."

"Yes." I did an imitation of his giggle. "Isn't it attractive?"

He scowled, did not answer me.

Greta sat on the arm of a chair. "There is a new play opening tomorrow night. Max Reinhardt's production of *Twelfth Night,* with Elisabeth Bergner. Will you come as our guests?"

"I'm afraid we'll be out of town for a day or two. Suppose I contact you when we get back?"

"Fine."

It had been a long evening, longer than I'd anticipated. We said our good nights, left Dieter to find himself a taxi and walked the two blocks back to the hotel. Marty saw me to my room; took me in his arms and kissed me. "Good night, Clare. I love you."

"But"—I couldn't help teasing him—"you danced with Dieter."

"He's a striking man." He blushed.

"It's been a striking night."

I sat up for a while, studying Annemarie's drawing of me; finally slept.

Late the next morning I was awakened by Marty knocking at

my door. "Clare, get up. Our car will be here at noon." I rolled over, tried to stay asleep. "Clare, are you in there?"

"Yes."

"It's time to get up."

"Can't we go there tomorrow?" I did not want to go; I wanted to be with Annemarie and Greta.

"Clare, get up. I'll meet you in the restaurant for breakfast."

I yawned; glared at the door.

"Clare?"

"Oh, all right."

After breakfast Marty checked at the front desk. Our car was due soon. We just had time to pack.

The drive to Obergurgl was a long one, more than three hours. Marty and the driver chatted in German. Once again I found myself on the outside of things. We passed south through Germany's fertile plains; beautiful rolling farm country and quaint houses, like pictures out of Watteau. Then the landscape began to darken. Low hills, then mountains, all of them covered with dark pines. I nudged Marty. "Is this the Black Forest?"

"No, that's miles to the west."

"The trees look black. Everything looks black. How can people live here?"

He looked around. "I don't know. I guess the trees give them plenty of raw material for their cuckoo clocks."

"Very amusing. Where exactly are we?"

"In the mountains called the Erzgebirge."

"You're no help at all."

He laughed. "I thought you were the scholar of the party." I glared at him; he ignored it and went on. "We're passing about midway between Dresden and Leipzig right now. Off to the southeast"—he pointed to our left—"is the Czech border. Bohemia." He put on a rakish tone. I watched the passing land.

The mountains held, or more accurately hid, village after village. Picturesque places, but as we drove past we got nothing but unfriendly looks. The road slowly deteriorated; after two and a half hours it was not much more than a wide track. The black pines grew taller, blocked the light of the sun. Then things leveled off, a central plateau. For a long time there were no towns. And then we reached Obergurgl.

It was like all the other villages we had passed. Small, ancient, quaint. The driver took us to an inn, settled our things in our room; would be back for us in two days. Marty conversed briefly with the innkeeper, a thin old woman dressed, like the pines, in black. He introduced us. "This is Frau Eckstein."

I said hello in halting German and she greeted me with a rapid flow of talk. Marty translated. "She says you should be Frau Kampinski."

"What's the German for 'mind your own business'?"

"Clare. Will seven o'clock be all right for supper?"

"Fine."

"Frau Eckstein says we're her only guests. I think she means to mother us."

I looked at the woman. Harsh, craggy face, pallid skin; she had not smiled at us once. "Splendid."

We settled in; walked around the town; were regarded with suspicion. Ate Frau Eckstein's dinner; everything tasted sour, and the bread—a bitter egg bread filled with caraway—must have been three days old. But for some reason Marty seemed to be enjoying it all. I half suspected he was just putting on a show to annoy me, a little revenge for my ruining his night with Dieter. But then for all I knew the crone might actually have reminded him of his mother.

Then it was dusk. Time for us to work. Marty asked our hostess where we could find the cathedral. It took her forever to answer. Much guttural cackling, much waving of arms. "The cathedral's remains are off in the woods. We mustn't go there at night. There are bears and wolves. Obergurgl was a major mining town in the Middle Ages, gold, silver, copper, even some diamonds. *Eckstein* is German for diamond, you know. Her ancestors were the local lords."

"That's wonderful. We can stay here and listen to her or go out and take our chances with the bears. I vote for the bears."

"Why are you being so irritable?"

"I want to find the glass and get on with our trip. The sooner we collect it all, the sooner we get home."

"You seemed fine in Berlin last night with Greta and what's her name."

"Annemarie. And what have they got to do with it?"

He sighed. "Nothing. I just said— Let's forget it. I'll ask her if there's anywhere we can get a gun."

"Don't let it get into my hands."

"There. Now tell me you're not in a foul mood. Really, Clare."

"I'm sorry." I was not sorry at all. He was starting to know my moods better than I did myself. "Let's get going."

"No gun?"

"Marty, come on."

We strolled southward from the village. The ruins were in the forest, overgrown by the pines. Once we left the last houses behind, there was no light. Occasional stars flickered among the branches; the sky was moonless. There was mist rising from the forest floor; the air was damp with it. It was quite impossible to see. If we hadn't held hands we could have become separated. The blackness made me even moodier.

"Let's go back, Marty." We had not gone a quarter of a mile.

He stopped walking; put an arm around me. "Are you okay?"

I didn't answer.

"You're right." He looked around; sighed. "There's no point trying to find anything in this. We can get lights somewhere tomorrow, and come back at night. Or we could just try in daytime."

"We can try, but it's impossible when it's light out. With everything overgrown here, it'll be even worse. We'll just have to get lights."

He took me in his arms. We kissed for a long time. Went back to Frau Eckstein's. She had mulled some wine for us, and it was delicious; it took the dampness out of my bones.

The next morning we walked out again; went to the cathedral's ruins. There was not much to see. A few courses of stone standing, covered with moss, obscured by the undergrowth. A few arches still intact, rising among the trees, dwarfed by them, draped with vines. Everything in the forest was silent, no wind, no animal sounds. There was a brook not far away, but even it made no noise.

We stood in the middle of it all, tried to take it in, tried to see it as it had been in its day. It had been huge. Obergurgl had been important indeed to have such a church. Now look at them both.

Frau Eckstein fed us four times that day. Got for us, despite her clear disapproval of our plans, a pair of torches. And at night we went out again.

Bird noises; owls. The flapping of wings. Nothing else to be heard. We planted our torches in the ground, walked back and forth among the stones, combed the earth for our glass. Finally found it. Glowing, pulsing, three small pieces, no larger than the palms of my hands. I pushed one into my skin; it did not cut. We embraced by the torchlight, made love. There in the black-green cathedral Marty and I made love for the first time.

When we were finished, he would not stop kissing my throat. It made me giggle. "Marty, that's enough."

"I love you, Clare."

"Our things are soaked with the dew."

He came out of his frenzy; looked around. One of the torches had gone out. We dressed.

"Clare?"

"Yes, dear."

"I don't want you to see those women again."

I was dressed before him; stared at him as he pulled his trousers on. "Those women."

"Yes." He buttoned his shirt. "The two in Berlin. Annemarie and Greta. I don't want you to see them again."

"I see." I pulled the torch out of the ground. "And may I ask why not?"

"They're not good for you. They're not . . ." He fiddled with his zipper.

"And do I presume you are not going to see Dieter again, either?"

"That's different."

I could not believe I was hearing it. I glared at him in the torchlight. "It is."

"Yes. We're men."

"That fact had not escaped me."

"Anyway, I don't want you to see them again. All right?" He could not find his left shoe; scrambled about on the ground.

Without saying another word I turned and left.

"Clare!"

"The glass is on the ground beside you. Bring it." I moved quickly.

"Clare! Wait for me, goddammit! My shoes!"

At the inn Frau Eckstein watched me enter; asked me something in German, presumably where Marty was. I pretended not to know what she wanted. She cried out something else, waved a loaf of her stale bitter bread at me. I ignored her, went to my room and packed.

Marty came in ten minutes later. I heard him talking to her. Then he pounded at my door a few times; wanted to "talk things out."

"Please, Clare."

I left him in the hall. Frau Eckstein had never smiled once at us while we were in Obergurgl.

The next afternoon our driver picked us up for the journey back to Berlin. It seemed to take forever. I was still furious at Marty's arrogance; there was no talk between us on the drive. It was evening before we got back to the Grand Hotel. I went to my room and locked the door. I was exhausted. He knocked a few times; called my room on the telephone a few times. But I refused to answer. That night I slept long and deeply, the sleep of the angels.

And in the morning I woke bright and refreshed. I had breakfast alone, those succulent sausages Dieter had recommended, and delicious coffee.

Then I made for the Grunewaldstrasse. For Greta and Annemarie. I needed the company of women. The walk was not long, but I got lost; I had had too much champagne that first night. Finally I found the way, recognized the landmarks. And outside their building was a crowd. Two ambulances and a police car were parked in the street. I rushed to see what was happening. Asked one after another of the onlookers if he spoke English. Finally found one who could, a young blond man.

"The police are inside, Fräulein."

"Police? Why? What happened here?"

"Do you have friends who live here?"

"Please, tell me what happened." I kept staring at the entrance, at the steep stairs; was frightened of what might be inside.

The young man shrugged, craned his neck to see. "They say there were people killed here last night."

I ran to the door, looked up the stairs. The hallway was black. Two men in white uniforms were carrying a stretcher down out of the gloom. Light came from the door at the top, the door to Greta and Annemarie's garret. I looked around, half expected to see Marty in the crowd. The men with the stretcher descended rapidly, pushed their way past me. One of them said something in German; sounded irritated at me.

"Please, *mein Herr,* what happened here?"

He barked at me in German. They placed the stretcher in the back of one of the ambulances, crawled in after it, pulled shut the doors.

I looked up the stairs again. There was no one in sight. I scanned the crowd to see if there was anyone in charge, anyone who might object to my entering. There was no one. I had to go in.

The staircase was precipitous. I had to hold the railing to keep my balance. Climbed. The steps seemed to reach on forever, there were a thousand of them. I lost my breath, had to wait a moment; climbed again. Then I was at the door.

There was blood, the room was covered in it. Floor, walls, furniture. Two men in suits stood at the side of the bed; they were cool, were unaffected by it. On the bed before them was a dead woman. I could not tell which of them it was. Her eyes were gone, the top half of her face was gone; her throat was slit through. It was the killing in Chutreaux again. Marty. This time I knew he had the glass with him; I had left it for him. I turned, ran down the steps, pushed through the crowd. A man's voice called out behind me, in German, but I kept running.

The hotel. The desk clerk.

"Please. Is there someone on the hotel staff who speaks English?"

"*Bitte?*"

"English. I need someone who can speak English."

He found a clerk who could help.

"Herr Kampinski. My companion. I need to know if he left the hotel during the night."

"You are asking us to be most indiscreet, Fräulein."

"Please. It's terribly important."

He made inquiries among the staff. I sat on a sofa near the scarred old war veteran and waited. Then he came back to me. "According to the night porters, Fräulein, Herr Kampinski's friend arrived shortly before midnight, and the two of them did not leave all night."

I stared at him blankly. "His friend."

"Herr von Schattenburg."

"Oh." I looked around the lobby. "Oh. I see. You're quite certain they didn't go anywhere?"

"Quite certain, Fräulein."

I did not know what to feel. If the night staff were right, Marty could not have done the murders, could not have killed them. But he had spent the night with Dieter. I went to the bar and began drinking Louisiana flips; wondered how many of them it would take to bring oblivion.

11

We were to have left Berlin that afternoon, but I was in no condition. A porter helped me back up to my room and I locked myself in once again. I could not bear the thought of Marty. Room service brought me my meals; small ones, I did not have much appetite.

Marty knocked. "Clare? Are you packed? We have to leave soon."

"Not today."

"Are you all right?"

"No."

"I'll call the house physician."

"I've already seen him." I lied through the door. "I have stomach flu. I should be better tomorrow."

"I've written to Mr. Tiffany, Clare. Sent him two of the three pieces we found and told him where we're heading next."

I did not answer this.

"There was a letter from him downstairs. He's delighted with the news we've sent him so far. And he's arranged a line of credit with the American Express in Istanbul; they should be expecting us."

For a moment he was silent. Then, "Clare, what's wrong?"

"Go away. I told you, we'll leave tomorrow." I did not want to fight with him; I wanted to be dead.

The next day was somber; dark grey clouds. We took the day train to Prague, then on to Vienna; were to transfer to the *Orient Express,* but we had missed it. We spent the night in a small hotel near the railway station. Marty asked me to have dinner with him, but I pretended I was still unwell; avoided him.

Then we were on our way on the next day's Express. When we made our original booking, we had requested connecting rooms. Now that was the last thing I wanted. But it was too late to change. I feigned illness for two days; when that wore thin I just went to the club car and drank. "Do you know how to make a Louisiana flip?" "No, mademoiselle." "Then mix me a Gibson." Since Rome I had watched Marty get drunk day after day; now it was his turn to watch me. After a time he stopped bothering me; gave me the distance I needed.

The second night, we passed through Budapest. I was asleep; saw nothing of the city. The interruption of the train's movement did not wake me; too much gin.

All the next day we rode through the Balkans. Rolling hills, stark black mountains, farm villages. Late in the afternoon I went to the restaurant car; was horribly hung over. The bright sunlight outside hurt my eyes; I forced myself to watch it.

"Oui, mademoiselle?"

"Ham and eggs, please. And black coffee."

"I regret that it is too late for breakfast. Perhaps a light sandwich . . . ?"

"Just coffee."

"Oui, mademoiselle."

I sat, drank, looked out the window at the passing country.

"We're in Romania. Dracula's ancient homeland." Marty had entered behind me. Smiled tentatively.

I did not have the energy for any more conflict. But I did not want him to be there. "You're too immersed in that kind of thing. The real horrors in the world are the things we do to each other."

He started to say something; caught himself. He looked like a nervous little boy with a crush on his teacher. "You're having lunch?"

"Breakfast. At least, that was the idea. But it's too late in the day."

"Did you try bribing the waiter? The railroad personnel are notorious for their corruption." He smiled at me; the boy next door.

"I'm still not feeling very well."

"Oh." He dropped the smile. "Oh. Shall I go?"

"Have something to eat."

"No, I'm full."

The waiter brought my coffee. "Is Mademoiselle certain there will be nothing else?"

I stared out the window.

"Bring the lady some cheese." Marty took charge. "And some wine to go with it."

"We have some fine cabernet sauvignon, monsieur."

"Fine. Bring enough for two."

"*Oui, monsieur.*" He left discreetly.

"I hope you don't mind." I could hear it in his voice, he was terrified I'd send him away.

"No. No, Marty, I don't mind."

"I like taking care of you."

"Thank you." I'm sure it did not sound at all genuine.

"Clare." He looked, like me, at the passing Balkan landscape. Waited a long time to go on. "Why won't you tell me what's wrong?"

"There's not a thing wrong."

"Is it what I said about those lesbians?"

"I don't much like to be given orders. Do you?"

"It was for your own good."

For the first time I looked directly at him. "I'd be careful of that, if I were you."

"But—"

"I'm perfectly capable of deciding what is and what is not for my own good."

The waiter was back. Served us. Left.

"Look, I—" He was going to press it. But I glared at him, and he stopped short. "All right. I'm sorry. Is that what you want? I promise it won't happen again."

I tore off a piece of cheese with my fingers; ate.

"Clare. Say something."

"The cheese is delicious. Try it."

"Clare." He picked up the wine bottle; started to pour for himself; put it down again. "Look, I've told you again and again how much I love you. I can't keep on saying it forever."

The image of him and Dieter together, in each other's arms, came to me. Kissing, making love. I poured myself a glass of wine. Put on a casual tone. "Our relationship isn't exactly stacking up the way I'd imagined it would."

"What's that supposed to mean?" He poured his wine; drank.

"Why should you be allowed lovers on the side when I'm not?"

"I—" He stared at me; his eyes widened a bit; he realized that I knew what had happened. "Oh. Well. I didn't think . . . That is, I thought . . ."

"I still don't know if I love you, Kampinski." The use of his surname stung him. I could see it. "But if there's to be anything more between us, it will be on terms of equality. I won't play *Hausfrau* to a philandering male."

Marty sat back in his chair. Took a long drink of wine, drained the glass. "You should have spoken up yesterday. We were still in Bohemia then."

"We're artists, Marty. We're always in Bohemia." I smiled; the wine was relieving my headache.

For a long moment he said nothing. Then he laughed. "We make a fine pair. A sot and a debauchee. We were made for each other, Clare."

I watched him. His smile was so innocent. So good. He had slept with another man while professing to love me. He might have been the killer of my friends. But his smile was so good and so innocent.

He said it again. "Clare, I'm in love with you. Whether you want me or not—whether I want it or not—I'm in love with you."

"What do you mean, whether *you* want it or not?" I was amused; bit, pointedly, into a piece of cheese.

He poured more wine for each of us. Widened his grin. "You can be absolutely impossible. That's what I mean."

It was a dangerous joke to make, but I made it. Did not know if I meant it. "Then we may be a good match after all."

"Huh? What do you mean?"

"I mean that you, Martin, are thoroughly improbable."

Early that evening we passed through Bucharest. The city was full of light, like New York, like Paris. What I could see of it from the train station was beautiful. I wanted to get off, go and see more; but we did not have visas. Then, heavily, noisily, the train left the station, the city behind.

We were getting close to the sea; the air was turning humid. Marty opened the connecting door between us; opened all the windows in our drawing rooms. The flow of the air felt wonderful. I sat on my bed and watched him change clothes. His body. I could never take my eyes off his body. I remember thinking then, as I watched him, Perhaps you're being foolish, Clare, perhaps that's all love is. Perhaps you should simply take it and stop asking questions.

Marty still had his shirt off. "I still have the German glass in my bags. Why don't you take it and put it with the rest?"

"What did Mr. Tiffany say in his letter?"

"Oh, pretty much what you'd expect. He's delighted that we've found what we have, wishes us luck with the rest of our journey. Not much more than that."

"That's all?"

"Well . . ."

"Yes?"

"He did ask if we're married yet."

I sighed. "People say love makes the world go round. But obviously that's wrong. It's not love, it's marriage."

"Aren't they the same thing?"

"Don't kid yourself."

"Clare, what are you?"

I stopped short. Had no idea what he meant, what I could say.

"Are you . . . ?" He turned a deep red; lost his voice.

I stared at him.

"I said what I said about Annemarie and Greta because I don't want you to end up like them."

I went cold. *End up*, he had said; those were the words. I had no idea what to expect. I looked around the room. Reached for something, anything to say. Whispered weakly, "I don't know what you mean."

He sat down next to me. Put his hand on my arm. I pulled uneasily away from him. "Clare, I've wondered for two and a half years what there is between you and Agnes Northmon."

It was the last thing I expected to hear. "Between—"

"The two of you were always together, at work. Always sharing little jokes. Always laughing at me."

"A shared sense of humor, even a pointed one, hardly makes two women lovers, Marty. Agnes and I are friends, that's all."

"You always seemed to be laughing at me for the same reasons."

The shock had worn off. I felt myself smiling, just as I had always done back at the studio. "Maybe. What of it?"

"You went with Greta and Annemarie."

"Yes. And you went with Dieter."

He turned glum. Looked away from me. "I thought you loved me."

"You keep telling me, Marty darling, how much you love me. And yet there you were with Dieter."

He turned his back to me. I reached up, ran my fingers through his hair. "It's what I said before, Marty. Artists are all Bohemians. It's in our blood. Just think about that for a minute. Never mind the saints. Imagine the kind of glass you could make out of our blood."

"Clare, stop it."

"I can't help it. Isn't teasing a part of love?"

He looked at me, wide-eyed. We kissed. Slept together that night.

12

Istanbul. For the first time we were in a place where neither of us spoke the language. Crowds of people milled around us in the train depot, talked, shouted at each other, and we comprehended none of it. "How in the world will we find the American Express office?"

Marty played my protector. "We'll find someone who can understand us. Someone here has to speak English."

He stepped into the throng, tapped people's shoulders at random; was ignored by them. He kept it up for a good ten minutes while I stood by, half bored and half amused, and watched our things. The air in the station was thick with smoke from the trains and from what seemed a million cigarettes. Everyone smoked. After a while it began to get to me; my eyes watered and I felt a headache starting. "Marty."

"Hm?" He rushed back through the mob.

"I need some fresh air. Watch our things. I'll see if I can't find the stationmaster on my way."

All of the signs were in Turkish. There was no hope. But then, at the front door of the station, I saw the American Express office. It was directly across the street. We got our things; crossed to the office. The street was more crowded with people than the station had been. Then we were in *terra cognita*.

"Good morning." A thin man in late middle age greeted us from his desk. He had a southern accent; wore a white suit; like everyone else in the city smoked a foul-smelling Turkish cigarette. "I'm Arthur Presbitt."

We introduced ourselves. "Mr. Tiffany should have contacted you about us."

He rummaged through a file. "Yes, yes, here it is. Well, welcome to Istanbul." He stood up to shake our hands. Was tall and lanky, almost gaunt. "We've reserved a suite of rooms for you at the Hotel Constantine the Great. Your bedrooms overlook the Bosporus."

"That's fine."

"And what else can I do to be of service to you?"

"Well." I looked at Marty. "We want to see the city, of course. But our real purpose in Turkey is to visit Mount Niphates."

"Mount—?" He was baffled. "Where on earth is that?"

"We thought you'd know."

"Oh." He checked a huge map on the wall behind him. "Mount . . . ?"

He repeated it. Picked up a desk atlas and thumbed through it. "Niphates. Niphates. Ah. It's called Mount Nipotu now." He tossed the book aside. "Turkish nationalism. They're renaming everything. Mustafa Kemal has made it his mission to reform the entire country."

"Where is our mountain, Arthur?"

"You're sure you want to go there?"

"Quite. Where is it?"

"Here." He pointed to the right edge of the map. "It's right near the place where Turkey, Iran, Armenia and Russia all come together. A geographical no-man's land. An unpleasant part of the country, and it takes forever to travel there."

"But you can take us there." Marty stepped up to the map, studied it.

"Oh, certainly." From his tone it was plain that he wasn't looking forward to it. "I've been out that way any number of times. Mount Ararat is in that neighborhood. There are always . . . enthusiasts going there, looking for Noah's Ark." A sudden look of concern crossed his face: were we "enthusiasts"? had he spoken indiscreetly?

"We're collecting medieval artifacts for Mr. Tiffany." I smiled at him.

He relaxed; had said nothing unwise. "What exactly will be our destination?"

"We're going to the Monastery Scriptorium of St. John."

"'Monastery Scriptorium.' Strange way to put it. And what is your—our—object there?"

"They have some ancient glass Mr. Tiffany is interested in."

"I see. Well, why don't we get you over to the Constantine and settle you in, hm? I'll get moving on the travel arrangements." He found some boys to carry our things. "By the way, have you heard the news from home? Hoover beat Smith."

"No. We hadn't heard." We followed Arthur to the hotel.

Arthur showed us the city. The Blue Mosque; Hagia Sophia. We saw the state palaces where successive dynasties of emperors ruled, lived, died. Saw the Purple Room where children of the royal blood were born; where the Empress Irene had had her son Constantine's eyes pulled out. There was gold, there were precious jewels; icons and mosaics covered the walls. Marvelous places, places from the Arabian Nights.

All of the streets were full of people, shouting, arguing. The air was foul with smoke and soot. Arthur took us up to the roof of the Topkapi Palace and we surveyed the city. Domes, minarets stretched as far as the eye could see through the smoke; the city looked as if it might extend through the haze to infinity. Arthur took it all in; sighed a deep sigh. "In the days of the Crusaders," he told us, "all the buildings in the city were roofed with gold. Look at them now. The Crusaders stole the metal." He made a sour face; threw aside his cigarette, lit another. "Christians."

It was nearly sunset. We sat down on the roof, ate sandwiches he had brought. "Well. There are two ways of getting where you want to go. We can take the train overland through Ankara and out to the western border. Or we can take a steamer down to Beirut and then the train northward. Do you have a preference?"

"I've always wanted to see Beirut." I ate.

"That's the longer route." He produced a bottle of wine, uncorked it. "It takes nearly a month longer that way. Where are you heading after you leave Turkey?"

"Back home."

"Ah, well there's your answer, then. We can take the train out to the Armenian border. Then, when you're through at the Monastery Scriptorium, I'll book you a passage south through Syria and Lebanon. You'll see everything you want to and still save time."

Marty had been silent; poured himself a glass of wine. "Is there any sort of air service in this part of the world? I mean"—he looked at me—"you keep telling me how anxious you are to get home."

"Air service? This is Turkey." Arthur laughed. That was that. "Those mountains get pretty cold, by the way. Have you got heavy clothes with you?"

"No. I don't think it ever occurred to us."

"We'll have to get you outfitted, then."

We spent a few hours visiting shops; trying on heavy clothing; wondering what to expect.

The night was cool. Marty and I strolled hand in hand along the Golden Horn. Even after dark there was water traffic. The boats all carried lanterns. Boatmen shouted one to another, noisy as their brothers in the streets. Behind our hotel was a lush botanical garden. We sat on a stretch of lawn and watched, listened to it all.

"Would you swim the Hellespont for me, Marty?"

"Why?" He looked at me, puzzled. "We're on the same side."

"You don't exactly have the makings of a Byron, do you?"

"Huh?"

"Never mind. Kiss me."

There was a breeze off the water; starlight shone on the Bosporus. It was too romantic to resist. We made love there. When I was in his arms it was impossible for me to think unpleasant things about him. An hour or so before dawn a crescent moon rose in the east, over the water, a glistening sliver of light. We did not get back to our suite until after sunrise.

And found Arthur waiting for us there. "I've got all the arrangements made. We can leave anytime you like."

"You've done it all so soon?" I was astonished. "It's only been a day."

"We never sleep." He smiled; was proud of himself.

"Neither do we." I yawned. "Can we wait until tomorrow?"

"Whatever you like."

We slept most of the day; were up at dawn the next morning and packed our things. Posted a letter to Mr. Tiffany detailing our plans. Took the ferry to the Asian side of the city and boarded the train west. The train was filthy; smelled, like everything else in the country, of cigarette smoke. Arthur oversaw everything; fussed over us; was the compleat guide. For once—at last—we made no pretense of sleeping separately; we had one huge drawing room between us. Arthur beamed at it, fussed over us.

Half an hour out of Istanbul the train stopped. Marty looked out the window. Turned to Arthur. "What's wrong?"

"Nothing." He did not look up from the book he was reading.

"Why have we stopped so soon?"

"The *Orient Express* spoiled you."

"I'm afraid"—I lowered his book for him—"I don't follow you."

"This side of the Dardanelles," Arthur lit a Turkish cigarette, "there's no such thing as an express train. We'll be stopping at every vilayet we pass."

"But . . ." I was astonished. "But that'll take forever."

"I did warn you about that. The train ride to the western border takes ten days. At least."

"Ten days." We looked around the compartment. My eyes were already watering from the smoke. "Ten days." It was too awful to think about.

"At least. You're in the Middle East now. You can't expect it to be like Manhattan."

Marty took my hand. "Couldn't it at least be like the Bronx?"

"Everything will be fine. Just give yourself a day or two to get used to it."

"A day or two." I was glum. A year or two would not be enough. "I'm just grateful we've got you with us, Arthur. God knows what we'd do on our own."

"You can express your gratitude very nicely when I hand you your bill." He let out a long plume of smoke; whirled a finger through it.

Marty and I were in bed together, the first night out from Istanbul. We had made love; were covered with sweat. The train made another stop. I got up and opened our window. Leaned out into the night air; it was chilly. We were at a tiny vilayet, not more than a dozen buildings. Marty came, stood beside me. There were stars. "Are you getting tired of hearing that I love you?" He kissed my hair.

"No. Not at all." I leaned against him.

We could hear bleating. There were sheep, or goats, somewhere nearby.

"I keep thinking about the glass." I liked the feel of his warmth. "I keep wondering what exactly it is."

"I don't follow you."

"How did they make it? How did they get the blood?"

"I thought the whole thing sounded odd when Mr. Tiffany first told us about it." He leaned farther out the window; tried to see the animals, or their keepers. "But you and he just brushed it aside."

For a while I said nothing more. But I could not shake what I was thinking. "I mean, someone would have had to be there when the Apostles died. And collected their blood somehow. Let it drip into a pan, or . . . or . . ." I tried to visualize it. "It just doesn't make sense, does it?"

"Not much, no."

"Suppose the stuff isn't what we—and the glassmakers and cathedral builders—thought it was. Suppose . . ."

Marty shifted his weight. "But we've seen what it can do. It won't cut."

"It cut Michael van Boeven."

"Yes."

"We shouldn't be thinking these things, Marty. We should have faith."

"Faith in what?"

"Faith in . . ." It was the last question I wanted him to ask. "Faith in . . . us, I suppose."

For a long while neither of us said anything. Then Marty repeated it. "Faith in us."

I was suddenly restless; pushed away from him, paced around the compartment. "I wish this train had a club car. I need a drink."

"Me too."

"Maybe there's a tavern in the vilayet."

"Sure. You could have a Scotch and goat's milk."

"If I were to die, Marty, could you make glass out of my blood?"

"I don't think it would occur to me to try. Clare, you're letting these thoughts carry you away."

"I can't help it. That glass, the blood glass, isn't what we think it is. Or there's more to it than we know. Or . . . Christ, I don't know, Marty, I'm just afraid of it. Afraid of . . . us . . . handling it. I think about it all the time. We should send it all back to Mr. Tiffany."

"And if it gets lost or shattered?"

"So much the better."

"No, Clare, we agreed to find it and bring it back to him. He expects us to do it."

"We should keep it packed away. We should not get it out."

"Fine."

"Don't be condescending!" I screamed it at him.

"I'm sorry. Look, I just don't understand what put you into this mood, that's all. You're not yourself."

I looked at him. And for the first time, I said it. "Marty, I love you. Do you know that? I'm in love with you." Even as I spoke the words, I was not certain I meant them.

But Marty put his arms around me and kissed me, and for the second time that night we made love to each other. I wanted that. Needed it. But our sex then was not good. I was too preoccupied. Stopped. "You've never read *Paradise Lost,* have you, Marty?"

"What? No?"

"According to Milton, Mount Niphates was the place where Satan first set foot on the earth."

More vilayets, more stops. Izmit; Adapazarı; a dozen smaller places, towns without names.

Then we were at Ankara. The train climbed the steep plateau and we were there. There was a day's layover. Arthur showed me the place. Marty stayed on the train; said he'd already seen enough of Turkey.

Ankara was a strange place to see. A city in the making, Mustafa Kemal's capital-to-be. Everywhere were new buildings, half-erected towers, stadia, places for the government. But interspersed among it all were ruins. Greek theaters, Roman baths, Hittite temples, preserved intact amid the steel and glass. One could stroll from one age to the next without thinking.

"You and Marty are very much in love, aren't you?" Arthur smiled at me, pretending he was not prying.

"You seemed to approve. Do you?"

"You look good together."

"Thank you." I did not know how to take his interest in us. "Yes, I love him. Very much." I said it for myself, not for him. Hearing the words made it easier to believe.

"Love in my own life has always been a destructive force. I'm glad the two of you are happy."

"Arthur." It was the first time he'd said anything about himself; he had been the perfect professional.

"Hold on to him." He lit a cigarette; coughed.

"Yes, sir." I tried to sound sarcastic; could not quite bring it off.

Beyond Ankara the towns came less frequently. But we stopped at them all. Oddly named places, Kayseri, Elâziğ, Diyarbekr. The landscape changed; harsh black mountains, dead volcanoes. The air grew colder and colder; now and then there was snow. The monotony of the trip—short ride, stop, wait, ride again—began to wear on me.

We copulated often. But I took less and less pleasure from it. Marty put his arms around me from behind one morning. I pulled away from him. "I don't know how we're going to get the glass from the monks, Marty. I mean, everywhere we've been so far, it was lying on the ground, it was there for us to take."

"Mr. Tiffany will pay well for it. I'm sure he will."

"But if they don't want to sell . . . ? These are holy relics, after all."

"I thought you weren't sure about that."

I got up, walked to the window. "You know what I mean. If it comes down to it, I would be willing to steal the glass."

"Steal it."

"Yes. For Mr. Tiffany."

"Would he want that?"

"I want it, Marty. I want the glass."

"That stuff has really gotten under your skin, hasn't it?"

"That isn't funny."

"It wasn't meant to be. I thought you were afraid of it."

I hesitated. It was him I was afraid of. And it was myself. I had no idea why. "I am."

"Then—?"

"I want it."

The vilayets we passed through were black, made of the same stone as the mountains. The people were pallid, ashen. More and more often the sky was black-grey, like the land beneath it.

Our eleventh day there was water on the horizon to the south. A huge body of it. "Arthur, what is that?"

"Van Gölü."

"What?"

"Lake Van."

"It's enormous. Is this a place for the summer?"

"No, the lake is salt."

By afternoon we pulled into the vilayet of Van. It sat on a mud flat east of the lake. The houses were built of mud, the people were built of mud. This, for us, was the end of the line. Arthur found us an inn. There was snow in the air. We bundled against it. The lake was a foul grey.

All around the vilayet and the lake were mountains of black. Jagged, hideous places. But to the northeast there opened a broad plain. In the distance, in mist, were the two peaks of Mount Ararat. Just to the right of it, closer to us, was Niphates. Black crags, half covered in snow. Arthur found a pair of binoculars. "There. You can see the monastery. Midway up the south face." It too was black; it could have been part of the volcano.

"Will it erupt?" Marty gaped at it.

"No. It's quite extinct."

The food at the inn was cold. Wind penetrated the mud walls.

We rented horses, three for ourselves, two for supplies. Rode into the northeast. Left early in the morning. It was bitter cold, there was an acid wind off the lake. Snow squalled around us. At times it was so thick we lost sight of Niphates. Arthur led, we followed; there was nothing in the world but us and our horses.

"Do you know anything about the monks?" Arthur shouted above the wind.

"No. I assume they're Eastern Orthodox."

"Or Russian Orthodox, maybe."

Every few hours we paused, let the horses rest. They ate snow from the ground; there was no water. We had canned food. Then at midday the storm broke. The wind calmed. We were in a broad valley between mountain chains.

"What are these mountains called?" Marty pulled a scarf around his face.

"They're called all kinds of things. The Caucasus, the Taurus, the Anti-Taurus. The natives call them the Varak. There are half a dozen ranges in this part of the world, and no one's ever decided where one leaves off and the next starts. It's what I told you back in Istanbul: this is a no-man's-land; this is nowhere."

That night we slept in tents. Foraged for wood and lit fires to keep warm. There were breaks in the clouds; now and then stars showed through. Marty and I cuddled; did not have sex.

At dawn Arthur roused us. "Breakfast time. If we keep moving the way we did yesterday, we'll reach Niphates by sunset."

"Will we have to make camp there, too?"

"No. There is a vilayet at the foot of the mountain, called Çisluk. There'll be an inn of some kind, or at least people willing to put us up in exchange for food."

I looked ahead of us. "How could anyone live there?"

Arthur ignored me, saddled the horses.

Now that we were closer I could see the monastery clearly. It was a medieval fortress; tall, precipitous sides; soaring towers; all of it black as night. I kept thinking to myself, there are men there who you're going to rob.

It was late afternoon when we reached our destination. Niphates towered above us, above Çisluk. Blocked our view of Ararat, of God's holy mountain. Çisluk was not much of a village, or vilayet, a handful of small stone houses. But around it, on the lower slopes of Niphates, grew fields of poppies, flame red under the grey sky. The ground was covered with snow; the people were all out harvesting them. I compared them to my memories of Mr. Tiffany's poppy lamps. But Marty found the sight jarring. "Why don't they just let them die? Why freeze to death for flowers?"

"They are not just flowers." Arthur dismounted from his horse, looked around town for the inn. "They are a cash crop, the last of the season."

"A—?"

"You have heard of opium, haven't you?"

Marty stared at the fields, the flowers, the people, as if he could imagine nothing more evil. "Why do the monks permit it?"

Arthur did not answer him, helped me down. Took the packs off the horses.

Someone shouted at us in Turkish. We looked around. A large man in a silk shirt red as the poppies was coming down the town's single street, waving at us. He had a huge mustache. Wore nothing but his shirt against the cold. He shouted more.

"What is it, Arthur?"

"He's the innkeeper. He's saved us the trouble of hunting him out."

"Good. Let's go with him and get warm."

The inn was a half mile outside of town, toward the mountain, in the middle of yet another poppy field. There was a small barn surrounded by a stone enclosure; we left the horses there. The inn itself was a black stone building like the monastery above. But the stones were not dressed; there were chinks in the wall, and the wind whistled through them. A young boy, sixteen or so, worked there; deep olive skin, huge brown eyes. He took our packs, helped us to get settled in. He was quite striking; I saw Marty watching him, smiling at him.

"Our host is named Korvuç. His young helper is Izlik." Arthur set down his packs. "He'll tend to the horses for us. Korvuç wants to know how much opium we want."

"Tell him none." Marty glared at the man.

"Don't be hasty, darling." I climbed out of my heavy coat. "By the time we're through with the monks, we may need it."

"Tell him we don't want any!" He barked it.

"Yes, sir." Arthur was amused. Said something to Korvuç. The innkeeper laughed.

Outside, snow began to fall again. I watched it through a window; looked up the mountain. Above the poppy fields there were birches, bare, leafless. Then, just beyond the timberline, on barren ground, sat the monastery.

We had good hot food, the first since the train. Izlik waited on Marty, fussed over him. We slept. Korvuç insisted we each have a separate room, I presumed so he could charge us more.

Then in the middle of the night, something woke me. There was something, someone in my room. I reached for a match. It was Korvuç. He stood there, shirtless, smiling at me. Made a gesture to show me what he wanted. He was fat; his body, even his back, was covered with hair. I could not have touched him. "No!" I said it firmly, hoped he would understand the tone if not the word itself.

He took a step toward me.

"No!"

Another step. He smiled, tried to look harmless. Pulled a pipe out of his pocket, presumably full of opium.

"Stop it! Marty! Arthur!"

There was a commotion. I heard them moving outside. Arthur appeared, then Marty, then Izlik. They were climbing into their clothes. It took them only a moment to realize what was happening. Arthur entered into a spirited exchange with Korvuç; voices were raised. Finally the Turk left. "It'll be all right. He says you're beautiful. He has not been with a woman in a long time." He glanced at Izlik. "He insists that once you've smoked his opium you'll find him beautiful, too."

"Not likely. Is there any way to lock my door?"

"That would be an insult to his hospitality."

"Splendid."

"I could stay with you." Marty spoke for the first time.

I looked at Izlik standing behind him. Did not want him to be there. "Yes, Marty, sleep with me tonight."

Arthur left; Izlik left. We slept. Now and then in my sleep I reached out and touched him. Dreamed he was Korvuç. Woke, remembered where I was, who I was with; slept again. The night seemed endless.

The next morning it snowed heavily. We had a full hot breakfast, saddled the horses, set off up the side of the mountain. The wind gusted; the squalls blinded us. The horses seemed to think nothing of the weather; they were used to it.

Arthur led the way. "By the way." He pulled on an extra sweater. "Korvuç and Izlik both urged us against going up to the monastery."

"Why on earth not?"

"They say the monks guard one of the mouths of hell."

"Fine."

It was two hours before we reached the monastery gate. It was made of heavy beams of cedar with enormous iron rings for knockers. The building itself was made from blocks of stone that seemed impossibly large; dark, forbidding place. I found its appearance even colder than the wind and snow. "Look at it. If hell really has any entrances, they couldn't look any more appropriate than this."

It was midafternoon when we arrived. Arthur knocked. We waited. Then slowly, heavily, one of the gates swung open. A middle-aged man stared at us; was dressed in robes black as the stones; had a full beard and shoulder-length hair. He conversed with Arthur. Then finally he smiled and gestured us in. There was a courtyard; we left the horses tied to the gate and entered the building.

I was expecting more black inside. But the walls were white-washed; everything was blindingly lit by electric lights, bare bulbs strung on exposed black wires. Monks came and went, all of them bearded, all dressed in black; most of them were surprisingly young. A few of them stared at us curiously; most took no notice. Their black robes, black beards made stark contrast with the walls.

The air was thick with a sharp odor. Marty sniffed the air, made a face. "What on earth is that smell?"

"Don't ask." Arthur stuck close to our monk.

We followed him down a long bright corridor, were ushered into a white room. There was no furniture. The monk left, and we stood there staring at each other. Marty regarded the blank walls. "What did he say?"

"Not much." Arthur sat down on the floor, leaned against the wall. "There's apparently an English-speaking priest here. He went to get him. We are welcome, though."

"Did you tell him what we want?"

"No. Not yet."

The room, the building were warm. I climbed out of my heavy things. My eyes had not yet adjusted to the blinding whiteness.

"Welcome to the Monastery Scriptorium of St. John." In the doorway stood a monk identical to all the others. Young; covered in black. His English was thickly accented, not easy to understand. "I'm Father George."

We introduced ourselves and he shook our hands, repeated our names. "What a pleasure it is to grant you our hospitality. Not many people come to Mount Niphates."

We said the polite things.

"And what exactly is it that brings you here?"

Marty started. "We're looking for—"

But I cut him off. "We're on a pilgrimage, Father George. We're seeking out all the existing relics of the Apostles. To do them veneration."

"I see. And you came here for . . . ?" He asked with a straight face; was giving nothing away.

"We have read about the blood of St. John, miraculously preserved."

"You have read that." He was stony.

"We have letters of introduction from Patrick Cardinal Hayes, of New York." He said nothing to this. "I'm sure they will establish our good faith." He stood stiff. "The honesty of our intentions."

"A cardinal. A Roman. I'm afraid they don't carry much weight with us."

"He is a man of God. Surely—" I was getting testy.

Arthur had the sense to cut me off. "Exactly what sect do you belong to, Father, if we may ask?"

"We are a sect unto ourselves." He could have been announcing, I am a Plantagenet. "But let me see your letters. I shall show them to the abbot, and we shall see what he says."

We produced the letter His Eminence had written for us. The priest took it and went off. We were alone in the blank room once again. Marty started pacing. "I don't like this place. That stink in the air is making me sick. What is it, Arthur, some kind of incense?"

"Yes." He was lying.

A boy appeared with washbasins and towels for us. He put them on the floor and left without saying anything. He was clean-shaven; was a novice. We washed, and I at least was grateful for their thoughtfulness. Then the boy was back with black bread and red wine. We ate. Chatted. Marty was more and more on edge.

"Abbot Nearkos has chastised me." Father George reentered; bowed to us. "I have been most inhospitable to you. Please forgive the ill manners of a man who is a hermit at heart. As I told you, we seldom receive visitors. One forgets the graces. But that is no excuse. You are quite welcome here. I shall be happy to show you anything you wish to see. And the abbot wishes you to join him at table this evening."

"Thank you." I beamed at him; I would get what I had come for. "We are most honored."

"Let me show you to cells where you can change and refresh yourselves. Then, if you like, I shall escort you through the monastery and show you the relics you came to see."

"That's wonderful, Father."

We toured. The plan of the building was regular, geometric.

Most of it was taken up by a library. I had forgotten this was a "monastery scriptorium." Room after room, vault after vault were filled with manuscripts; monks busily made copies of many of them. But this was not like the collections at the Vatican. Here everything was neat, ordered, catalogued, indexed. The walls, as they were everywhere in the building, were a blank white. But the illuminated manuscripts made up for it. They were splendid, they were new, they were riotously colored. "Why, Father, this is marvelous. I was a librarian back home in the United States. To see a place like this, to see the care you give these old books, and the work you put into copying them . . . it's really quite a miracle."

Father George beamed. "We are proud of our scriptorium. We have books here that exist nowhere else in the world. Books other places, other people have long forgotten. And all of them are in perfect condition." His pride could not have been more apparent.

I picked up a manuscript at random from a nearby table. Read.

"You have Greek?" He disapproved.

"Yes, and Latin, and a smattering of Hebrew. I was taught by Russian nuns."

"Ah." That explained it, at least in his mind. "There are rare things here, Miss Markham. Please feel free to browse. Of course, a great many of our books are in Cyrillic. I don't suppose you . . . ?"

"No, I'm afraid not."

"A pity." He smiled; his masculine superiority was intact. "Let me show you the rest of the monastery."

We followed him. There was a treasury. Filled with gold, jewels, silver. Chalices, patens, ciboria. Silks and tapestries hung on the walls. The room was awash with color and texture, a beaming contrast with the stark white of the rest of the building. The prize of the room was an enormous golden monstrance, a forged sunburst nearly a yard in diameter. At the center of it, on ostentatious display, was a brilliant fragment of red glass. That would be it. I resisted the temptation to touch it. "This monstrance was given to the monastery by the Tsar Ivan the Great."

"It's magnificent." Arthur looked around, dazzled by it all. The room had no door; was empty of monks or novices. Anyone could go in.

"Yes." Marty, like me, eyed the glass. "Absolutely magnificent."

"This is it, isn't it?" I played dumb for the priest. "This is the relic we came to see."

Father George seemed disappointed that I'd caught on. "Yes, Miss Markham, that is the blood of our patron saint."

Without saying a word I went down on my knees, pretended to pray. Marty, a bit puzzled, followed my lead; and I was grateful for it. We continued our mock meditation for a few long moments. Then I stood, smiled at the priest, dusted off my knees.

We went on with our tour. Saw monks' cells, saw the chapel, saw all of it. But it was all white. And it left us exhausted. Marty yawned, covered it with his hand. "May we rest a bit before dinner?"

Father George took us back to our cells. Sleeping mats had been provided. Marty and Arthur took naps. But I was too excited.

The scriptorium. I went back. Pored over book after book. The fact that they were indexed by subject made my search more rapid. A few monks were working there; but they took no notice of me. I found verification of what they had: glass of St. John. And then there was more. I held the scroll in my hands, read it again and again. It was yellowed, it was crumbling; it could have fallen apart from my touch. But I could not put it down. What I wanted most was there. *Jesu Christi vitrum sanguinis*. It was there, in the scroll.

I rushed back to Arthur's cell. Shook him. "Arthur, wake up."

"Hm?" He opened his eyes, gaped at me. Yawned. "What's wrong?"

"Arthur, do you know where the Anti-Atlas is?"

Another yawn. "What?"

"The Anti-Atlas. Do you know the place? Can you take me there?"

"Just you?" He sat up. I was baffling him.

"Me and Marty. Do you know where it is?"

"Clare, what on earth has got hold of you?"

"They have it, Arthur. There's a nunnery in the Anti-Atlas that has glass made from Christ's own blood. We have to go there."

He was waking up. "The Anti-Atlas is a mountain range in the south of Morocco."

"Good. Can you take us there?"

"I've been there. My Arabic is a bit rusty. But then French is the official language."

"We have to go there. I want that glass."

He stared at me. "You want it for Mr. Tiffany. Isn't that right?"

I wanted it. I wanted it. "Yes. For him."

"The usual route into those mountains is through Marrakesh."

"Fine. We'll go there straight from here."

Another yawn came. "We can go back through Istanbul. That would be quickest."

"Yes, yes."

"Whatever you like, Clare. Can I get some more sleep before dinner?"

I glared at him. How could he not be excited by it? "Go ahead and sleep."

I rushed to Marty's room. Told him what I had found. Like Arthur, he was exhausted. "I thought you were afraid of the glass, Clare."

This stopped me. La Prêtresse. Annemarie. Greta. "I have to have it, Marty. I can't resist going for it."

"Mr. Tiffany will be overjoyed."

"Yes."

I returned to my own cell. Tried to sleep. Could not; was too excited. Glass made from Christ's blood. I had to have it. To touch it. To feel its miraculous warmth. I could think of nothing else. To sleep was not possible.

Dinner. The monks' refectory. A long, narrow, white room; benches ran the length of it. At a head table we sat with the abbot and some of his aides; had soup, bread, wine. None of them spoke English; Arthur translated the conversation. What other sites had we visited on our pilgrimage? Was there one Apostle to whom we were especially devoted? I invented freely. The nuns had taught me to sound properly pious. Arthur, turning my lies into Turkish, plainly disapproved. But I went ahead with it. I wanted them to trust us—to trust me.

To our surprise the meal ended with dessert. Ice cream. The abbot explained with some pride that it was homemade, that the monastery's cows gave milk rich in butterfat. After the austere meal, it was just fine. We ate, savored it. Then the abbot turned serious.

"We are invited," Arthur told us, "to attend a passion play."

"Now? It's December. Surely Lent would be the proper time."
I licked the last of the ice cream off my spoon.

"It seems that passion plays in Advent are a tradition here. The
abbot says this is one of their oldest rituals, one of the most
sacred, one of the most vital. He makes it sound quite something."

"But . . ." Marty had not eaten all of his dessert. I took it
from him. "But we won't be able to understand it."

"The abbot assures me it is all in dumbshow."

We followed them to the chapel. The altar had been stripped of
its ornaments. Besides the electric lights, hundreds of candles lit
the room. Monks dressed as Roman soldiers, as Jewish priests, as
peasants, formed a tableau; stood motionless before us. The
abbot, the rest of his monks and we took our seats. And then the
electric lights went off. The candlelight made the actors look
spectral. None of them moved.

Marty looked around. Whispered to me. "I've never seen a
passion play before. I'm not sure what to expect."

"You know the Gospel accounts of Christ's passion and death,
don't you?"

"Yes."

"It's that."

"Not the most pleasant subject matter. Agnes Northmon was
right about Catholics."

"These men aren't Catholics."

"I'm not certain"—Arthur kept his eyes on the actors—"that
I'd expect precisely that."

From somewhere behind us smoke, incense began to fill the air.
It was the stuff we had smelled earlier in the day, the stuff Marty
had so disliked. He coughed. "Good God, Arthur, what is that
stuff?"

"You really have no idea?"

"No." He coughed again.

"It's opium."

Marty's eyes widened. "No."

There had still been no movement. From behind a screen came
a hymn, a chant in some Eastern language. There were flutes,
oboes, harps accompanying it. I inhaled the smoke. Felt it
working on me.

Our eyes were adjusting to the dark. The candles made stark
shadows, emphasized the contours of the men's faces, bodies.
They were the youngest, the handsomest of the monks. I breathed
deeply; was beginning to feel the effect of the opium, and its effect
was erotic. I reached over, put a hand on Marty's leg.

He fidgeted. "I don't want to be here."

"You can't walk out on one of their most important rites."
Arthur's voice was hushed. He seemed to be enjoying the opium.
"They wouldn't understand."

"But—"

"Shh!" The abbot hushed us.

I leaned very close to Marty, whispered in his ear. "Look at the
men, darling. They're quite beautiful."

He shifted in his seat.

Then, abruptly, the music stopped. More smoke came, and
more; the candles lit it, made it seem to glow. A man appeared,
seemingly out of the smoke, out of nowhere. He was dressed in
only a white loincloth. Was Christ. His body was lean and hairy
and muscular. His body was beautiful. Like Marty's body. For a
long moment he was as still as the rest of them. Then he moved.
Walked among them; they were still frozen. He inspected them.
Scrutinized closely each face, each body. Touched one of them, a
Roman legionary, as if to make certain he was real; touched the
man's lips; inserted gently a finger into his mouth. The Roman
turned his head slowly; kissed the palm of the Lord's hand.

I looked at Marty, at Arthur. They watched. The abbot was
completely rapt.

By now the monk portraying Christ was sweating; his body
glistened with it. He made one more circuit among the frozen
men, then returned center stage. Produced—it seemed from
nowhere—a flagellum. Pulled it lovingly through his hand. The
opium smoke came thicker and thicker. I breathed it, felt divine.

He lashed! Christ took his flagellum and lashed the Roman
soldier. Whipped him again and again. Then the soldier next to
him. There was blood. The soldier moaned in ecstasy, kissed his
hand, his lash, implored him for more. He turned on the Jews.
Lashed them savagely. The tongue of the whip tore their robes,
exposed their bodies. Lean, dark, muscled men. I took hold of
Marty's hand; squeezed it. Was excited by it all. The monks

writhed, not in pain but in bliss. One after another they kissed their Lord.

It was the opium. There was no pain. There was divine pleasure. It was the opium. I breathed it in, inhaled as deeply as I could, again and again. I wanted to join them on the stage, wanted to feel the Lord's love and beneficence.

But with astonishing suddenness the lights came on again. I was blinded; covered my eyes. It seemed to take forever for them to adjust to the lights. Slowly, my eye sockets still filled with pain, I looked up. Everyone in the room was unconscious but me. Arthur, Marty, the abbot, the monks and novices, the actors, all of them were asleep. I could hear someone moving somewhere, presumably the monk who had turned on the lights. I looked around. There was no one.

I could not resist. I walked slowly up onto the altar. Looked around to make certain there was nobody to see me. Bent slowly and kissed the lips of the actor who had played Jesus Christ. There was more smoke, not in the air this time but in my head. I lay quietly down beside him, put my arms around him and went to sleep.

Awoke. I had no idea when. A few candles burned; most had gone out. Otherwise it was quite dark in the chapel. No one else was moving. I knew this was the time to do what I had come to do.

I took a candle. Found my way out of the chapel. It took a moment to get my bearings in the halls. Then I walked quickly to the treasury. Even by the light of my one candle the gold and jewels glowed brightly. But brighter still was the blood glass. I opened the monstrance, pulled out the fragment. Pressed it hard into my palm. There was blood. A steady flow of blood. I smiled. Licked it up. Its pungent taste was like the odor of opium on the air. I went back to my cell, put the glass safely into a bag.

There was someone moving in the halls. Not everyone was asleep. I looked. Caught a glimpse of someone rounding a corner. Followed quickly. It was the boy, the young novice who had served us earlier in the day. "Stop!" I cried.

He looked back at me.

"Stop." I walked up to him. Reached up slowly and touched his face. Pulled his lips to mine and kissed him. The boy's eyes widened. He ran. I tried to follow, but he disappeared somewhere.

I was alone. I went back to my cell, curled up on the sleeping mat; let sleep and the opium take me once again.

Morning. The monastery's population was subdued, including Arthur and Marty; including myself. I had expected the opium to leave a hangover but there was none; only a lethargy, a numbness. We breakfasted with them; packed our things. Thanked them for their hospitality, for the opportunity to venerate their holy relic.

Our horses were waiting for us in the courtyard, saddled and loaded with our packs. The sky was dark grey; there were snow flurries on a gusty wind. We mounted. The novice, the one I had wanted the night before, pulled open the gate; smiled a broad smile as we left.

The previous day's snow had left the path slippery, dangerous. Our descent was slow. The horses tired often. We had to stop and let them rest, let them eat snow, let them regenerate. It was nearly evening before we reached the inn. Korvuç was waiting for us, waving energetically. We left the horses in the corral for Izlik to put away. There was hot shish kebab waiting for us.

Korvuç was talkative through the meal. How did we like the monks? Had they shown us their mouth of hell? Marty was irritable; was still hung over. The third time Korvuç asked about the entry to hell, he barked, "Tell him yes, we found it."

After dinner, there was not much to do. Marty and I strolled through Çisluk just at dusk. The people were distant, but then we could not have talked to them anyway; Arthur was resting at the inn. Most but not all of the poppies had been harvested. As the sky turned dark we returned; we would need a good night's sleep for our return to Van.

At the inn the air smelled of it: opium. Arthur and the two Turks were smoking pipes. They smiled as we entered. "Come and join us."

Marty scowled. "No thank you. I'm surprised at you, Arthur."

"I thought you enjoyed last night."

"No." He headed for his room.

But I wanted to smoke. "I'll join you, Arthur."

He smiled; translated for Korvuç. The Turk got up, fished another pipe out of a drawer, filled it for me. Before I even inhaled, I found myself thinking of that novice. He was such a handsome boy.

"You're all turning degenerate." Marty registered sternly his disapproval.

It amused me. "If you can think of anything else for us to do here tonight, I'd be glad to hear about it."

He snorted, disappeared into his room.

As it had the previous night, the opium affected me strongly. Aroused me. I found myself watching Izlik. Beautiful boy. Marty had seen it. If Marty could, I could. Korvuç said something to me. I seemed almost to understand him. Smoke was building up in the room; made it all look unreal. Korvuç. I looked him up and down. Perhaps, perhaps . . . No, the thing was not possible. Not with him. But Izlik . . .

Arthur scrambled to his feet. Had had enough to smoke. Lurched off to his room; to sleep. I was left with the two of them. I wished Korvuç would fall asleep, so the boy and I could . . . would . . . might . . . I touched Izlik's shoulder and he looked at me; smiled at me. The room was dark now. All I could see were the buoyant flame of the opium and Izlik's large brown eyes.

There was a disturbance, something noisy and terrible. I woke in my room; it took a few moments for me to get my bearings. Noise . . . the horses. Something was riling them. I got up; was still in my clothes. Went out into the inn.

There was no one in sight. "Korvuç? Korvuç?" No answer. "Izlik?" Nothing. I went to Marty's room, looked in. He was asleep, snoring softly; was naked despite the inn's chilliness.

In his own room Arthur was unconscious from the opium. I looked around once more; called Korvuç and Izlik; no one, nothing. The horses were still unsettled. Someone had to see to them.

I went to the front door, opened it. It was snowing heavily. In the east the sky was just beginning to lighten. I went out, made for the corral. The horses were whinnying and snorting, were nearly in a frenzy. I stood at the fence, made soft noises, tried to calm them, but they were too worked up. Then it struck me as odd that they should be outside in the storm. The corral's gate was barred firmly; I climbed the fence, went to the barn.

The door swung open. The snow was red. Inside were their bodies. Izlik, beautiful Izlik; Korvuç. Their eyes were gone, their faces were gone, their heads were nearly severed from their bodies. Izlik must still have been alive; blood bubbled weakly from his sliced throat. The ground, the snow around him were soaked in blood, blood as bright and red as my glass. I shrieked. I screamed again and again.

Marty.

Marty was the only one who had not smoked. The only one who could have been awake.

Marty.

I did not know what to do. Could not stop myself screaming. Ran back to the inn.

"Arthur!" I shook him, tried violently to wake him. "Arthur, for God's sake, get up!"

He moaned, rolled over.

"Clare, what's wrong?" Marty stood there in the door to Arthur's room. He still wore no clothing. Yawned; covered his mouth with the back of his hand.

I did not know what to say or do. I was trembling all over; I felt a fool. "Marty," I sobbed.

"What's wrong?"

"I . . . I . . ." I was crying; could think of nothing to say to him. He could not have done it. It must have been Arthur, it must have been someone from Çisluk, it must have been . . . "Marty, for the love of God, Marty."

He walked toward me, put his arms around me. And I let him. I could not let myself believe he was their assassin. Let my head rest against his chest. "Marty."

He kissed gently my hair. I was terrified of him, but his warmth felt so good. I think that the opium must still have been in me. I kissed him. "Marty, I love you so much."

"I love you, Clare, but what's wrong?"

I took him out into the snow, showed him the corpses. When he saw them he registered nothing; not the least flutter of emotion crossed his face.

We finally roused Arthur. He paled at the sight of the dead men. Grew frightened. "We have to leave. Turkish law—the people of Çisluk—would deal harshly with Westerners involved in this." We loaded our horses, were gone before the sky was fully light. I don't think it ever occurred to Arthur that one of us—that

Marty—could have done the slaughter. Before us, at the far end of the great valley, the waters of Lake Van were black.

Marty. I could not let myself believe it. La Prêtresse, the women in Germany and now this. All victims of his anger, of his jealousy. I could not let myself believe that the love he felt so passionately for me could have engendered such heinous things. I rode beside him. Watched him. Touched him, held his hand. "Marty."

"Hm?"

"Let's get married now."

"What! Clare, do you mean it? That's terrific!" We stopped our horses, dismounted, embraced, kissed. He picked me up and carried me around in circles like a child.

When, the next day, we reached Van, we found an Orthodox priest who performed the service. Arthur gave me away.

13

It took only eight days for our return to Istanbul; the train made unaccustomed good time. Each night before going to bed with Marty I sought out Arthur; he had opium. Smoking it made it easier to face my husband, made it easier to make love to him. I believed that he was a murderer; did not want to face it.

We spent only a night in Istanbul. Arthur made hasty arrangements for our journey to Morocco. Booked us passage on a Greek steamer called the *Clytemnestra*.

We traveled south, steamed into the Aegean. Late the first afternoon we were on deck talking, drinking bitter Greek wine. "There." Arthur gestured to port. "That broad plain there. That is where the city of Troy stood."

"What of it?" Marty had no use for history.

"Brave people died there. Noble souls suffered."

"Nursery stories." He took a long drink of the wine; gagged on it.

But I was fascinated. "Why are there no ruins to be seen?"

"All dust." Arthur looked at me. "Only their souls still exist. Just barely." He was morose. The supply of our drug was nearly gone.

"Good Lord."

"Yes?"

"Mr. Tiffany. We sent him word we were returning to New York. He'll be expecting us."

"It should be possible to send a cablegram from on board."

So we cabled him:

LOUIS COMFORT TIFFANY
TIFFANY STUDIOS
NEW YORK NEW YORK

DO NOT REPEAT NOT EXPECT US NEW YORK ON
DATE PREVIOUSLY NOTIFIED. ON STEAMSHIP
CLYTEMNESTRA BOUND FOR MOROCCO. HAVE
FOUND LEAD TO VITRUM SANGUINIS JESU
CHRISTI MOROCCAN NUNNERY, DETAILS TO FOL-
LOW. ITINERARY: L'HÔTEL PARISIENNE TANGIER,
HOTEL AL-DAHABI CASABLANCA, L'HÔTEL
GRAND MARRAKESH.
                        KAMPINSKI AND KAMPINSKI

Our steamer hugged the coast, followed the ancient trade route.
We passed the melancholy ruins of Pergamum, sad black-grey
stones, on the Aegean coast. Steamed into the Mediterranean;
passed Rhodes. I tried to envision it as it had been in its day, the
great bronze Colossus bestriding the harbor. But it was no use; it
was gone, corroded, melted for scrap metal. The ship made port
at Beirut. I wanted to get off and see the city but we had no visas.
From there to Alexandria; to Cyrene; to Tripolitania. "Arthur."
All the ruins were making me blue. "This isn't right. We're two
thousand years backward."

"It's the Mediterranean. All that vanished glory, all that vain
achievement. It affects me that way, too." He leaned at the rail;
tossed a cigarette over the side. "The cradle of civilization, and
look at it."

To think about cradles—I could not do that; said nothing.

"Another two days, we'll be able to see where Carthage was;
where the Romans ripped it down and sowed the earth with salt.
They made the whole plain barren."

I thought of Marty. Of my nightly copulations with him.
"Lucky plain."

"Clare, stop it. That's no way for a new bride to be talking."

"Two more days. Won't that be Christmas?"

"Yes."

"Not the merriest place to spend it. But then I don't think I feel
very merry."

"We'll be in Tangier for New Year's Eve. It should be great fun."

"I don't want fun, Arthur. I want to be dead as the ruins."

"Clare."

We made friends with the crew. They had hashish. It was not the same as our opium but it helped.

I had avoided playing with the blood glass. Kept it packed securely away. That night in Turkey it had cut me. But I was too intoxicated then to realize the implications. Now I was terrified to touch it, to hold it; did not want it in my bags. But it was no use giving it to Marty; that would not make it better, that would make it worse. And I could hardly ask Arthur to take it; could not trust him with what, I kept telling myself, was the property of Mr. Tiffany.

Late one night a reply to our cablegram came from Mr. Tiffany. A deckhand brought it to our cabin:

KAMPINSKI AND KAMPINSKI
STEAMSHIP CLYTEMNESTRA
MEDITERRANEAN EN ROUTE MOROCCO

DELIGHTED TO HEAR YOU HAVE INCORPORATED.
CONGRATULATIONS! ALSO DELIGHTED TO HEAR
YOU ARE MOROCCO BOUND. L'HÔTEL GRAND,
MARRAKESH, HAS ORDERED TWO WINDOWS.
PLEASE SEE TO THEIR INSTALLATION WHILE YOU
ARE THERE. BEST REGARDS.

TIFFANY

"A busman's honeymoon." When I read the message to Marty we were in bed. "Does that please you?"

"After handling nothing but the blood glass all these months, it'll be a pleasure."

Yes, I thought, but it does not slice flesh so neatly.

Tangier. Bustling city, blinding white in the Moroccan sun. The hotel was crowded for the holiday; there was a mix-up about our reservations. Arthur fought with them for hours before we got rooms. A suite for the three of us.

New Year's Eve there was a party in the grand ballroom. An orchestra from the Continent. Balloons, horns, dancing the Charleston, beautiful people in elegant clothes. It was too much like the Club Broadway. Then just after midnight, after the embracing and the champagne, there was a surprise. I was too drunk to follow the French of the master of ceremonies, but it became clear. A screen was put up, a projector brought in, speakers put in place. We were privileged to witness the first talking picture ever to be shown in Morocco. It was a thriller, an Edgar Wallace horror piece called *The Terror*. There were not even credits to be read. The voice of an unseen actor told us who made the film, who acted in it. Cobwebs, thunderstorms, a mad fiend playing at an organ . . . I could think of nothing but Mr. Chaney, his throat full of cancer, unable to speak for the new monster, the microphone. It was too much for me. I lurched drunkenly from the room. Walked out into the night. Electric lights lit the street. There were clouds. It was warm.

"Clare." Marty followed me. "Are you all right?"

"I am too healthy."

"I—" He gaped at me. Was drunk, too. "What's the matter?"

"I have more blood than I want. That's what's the matter." I laughed at him.

"You— Look, I—" He was at a loss.

"It's too warm for New Year's." I walked in a circle around him. "It should be snowing."

"We're in Africa."

"We're in Africa." I parodied his damned naive style.

"Clare."

"Clare," I japed.

"Stop it!" He took hold of me, shook me. "Why are you acting like this?"

"Too much blood." I laughed, found his brutality hilarious.

"Will you tell me what you're talking about?"

I pulled free of him. Walked coquettishly around him once more. "I haven't lost too much blood lately."

He was at sea.

"I've missed two periods."

"What?"

"My menstrual flow." I puckered my lips as if I were going to kiss him; then backed off. "The discharge of blood from my vagina. It has stopped."

"Your—"

"But then you've been making enough blood flow for the two of us, don't you think?"

"Clare, do you mean you're—you're—going to have a baby?" He was always, even at his evillest, such a boy.

"Yes, I mean that."

"But—but—that's great! That's terrific!" He let out a war whoop, like an Indian.

"You sound like the juvenile in a bad play."

"I'm so happy! Clare, I'm—" He caught himself. Began finally to recognize my mood. "Clare. Darling. This should be a beautiful time for us." He belched from all the champagne. "This—we should be happy." He was stone sober now; looked directly into my eyes. "What's wrong? Tell me what's the matter."

There was nothing that I could say. There was no way I could say to him, I believe you have slain five people. I believe you to be unbalanced, I believe you to be a madman. I think you are so evil you have taken holy relics and made them into vile things. But then I did not have to say those things to him. Words between us were not necessary. I looked back into Marty's eyes. At the corners of them tears were coming. One rolled down his cheek, glistened in the light from the streetlamp. "Clare. My sweet Clare. I've loved you since the first time we met. I thought if we got married you'd be happy with me. But look at you. Look at us." He wept.

I put my arms around him. "Oh my God, Marty. I do love you. But I don't believe . . . I can't believe . . ." I could not say the words. He felt good in my arms, warm, strong, good the way he always felt. But what if the child in my belly should have his nature?

Behind us the hotel door opened. "Ah, there you are. I've been looking all over." Like us, Arthur had had too much to drink. He staggered. "I've been talking with some of the residents. They say we should arrange our transport here. None will be available in Marrakesh. So I've made a deal on a secondhand Mercedes truck. Is that all right?"

It finally dawned on him what was taking place between us.

"Oh. Oh. I'll, uh, I'll just— We can talk about this tomorrow. All right?" He turned heavily, lurched back into the hotel.

We were still in each other's arms. Marty was still crying, very softly. We went up to our room and he cried himself asleep. But I was awake all night.

We drove two days to Casablanca. Arthur packed the truck with camping supplies; overnight on the drive we slept in tents. After the desert sand the hotel's bed felt good. The city was white, busy, European like Tangier.

Then on to Marrakesh. Three days' journey. Insufferable heat, chill desert nights. L'Hôtel Grand was just barely finished. Built in the grand style, ornate molded plaster, gilded accents. The manager greeted us anxiously; he wanted his windows up. They were waiting in huge crates. Marty inspected them, supervised the workmen who put them in; Arthur translated among them all.

My mental state was more and more blue. I made friends with a hotel porter. Bought from him a supply of *kif* and a *sebsi* to smoke it in. Sat on the balcony of our room, watched the sunlit city, inhaled deeply the pungent smoke; was free. But the room was too confining. I had to be out in the city.

Arthur saw me passing through the lobby. "You shouldn't go out, Clare. The people here all speak Arabic or Moghrebi. You won't get by with your French."

"I'll get by. We share a language more beautiful than that." I grinned at him like a cat.

"Clare."

"Why don't you go and see if Marty needs you?"

He turned, looked at where the work was going on. Marty was waving to him. "Stay here, Clare, I'll be right back."

"Yes, darling."

He went. And I went. Ran. Out into the city. A completely foreign place, a place where no one knew me, where no one *could* know me. There was a huge marketplace. Vendors, food sellers, fakirs. I walked through it all. Loaded more *kif* into my pipe, smoked. Alien faces looked at me, saw what I was doing; smiled their recognition, their approval; then ignored me. I was in my own place, my own time.

The streets wound, convoluted, crossed themselves, a labyrinth for me, a new Ariadne but with no proper Theseus. And at the end of it I found a sacred grove, an orchard of orange trees growing at the desert's edge. Red sand, orange fruit, green foliage, sweet smells in the air. Children played there, but when they saw me they turned and ran away. There was a cooling breeze. I relit my *sebsi*, sat among the trees, let them shelter me from the sun.

"Clare. Your name is Clare."

The voice, I told myself, of the orchard's god.

"Are you Clare?"

"Hm?" I looked around. There was a man standing in front of me. A beggar, near to my own age, dressed in rags. Under his arm he carried a huge basket. He was eyeless. The sunlight made the empty sockets bright red. He looked directly at me.

"I am looking for a woman named Clare. I am expecting her."

"My name is Clare." I laughed. "What do you want with me? Are you to be my Theseus?"

"It pleases you to be cryptic." The basket under his arm shifted. There were live things in it. "I have a gift for you."

"A gift."

"Yes."

"Fine. I like gifts. Will you smoke some of my *kif*?"

He walked, unseeing, directly toward me; took the pipe out of my hand. Inhaled. Sat down next to me and put his basket on the ground. Three yards from us a scorpion crawled out of its hole and sped away into the desert. "*Kif*," said my blind companion, "is a gift of Allah."

"Allah be praised."

"You can laugh, woman, because you have not yet taken my gift."

"Let me have it. I want it."

He took the cover from his basket. Three cobras crawled out onto the ground; coiled serenely in his lap. "You know the myths. You know the stories, the legends. You know the gift my snakes have to give."

I knew it. "Yes." I watched the sun play on their scales; they could have been made of bronze. Took back the pipe and smoked.

"You wish to see the things they can show you? You wish to know what they can tell?"

"Yes." I reached into his lap, took hold of one of them. It stiffened, spread its hood; then relaxed and coiled playfully around my arm. I blew some smoke into its face and it froze in seeming astonishment. Then it crawled slowly upward, toward my face.

"Wait." My beggar, my Theseus froze.

"What's wrong?" The cobra was half a foot from my head. "What is it?"

"You are with child."

"Yes."

"The flesh remembers."

"I— What do you mean?"

"The flesh knows. If you cut it, there is a scar. Even ten years, fifty years later, when all the cut skin is gone to dust, the new flesh knows and scars itself. The flesh remembers."

I put a hand over my womb. "My child . . ."

"Human flesh. It is pliable; it bears always the imprint of what has gone before."

I looked once more at the snake. It advanced. It kissed my ear. It whispered things to me. Whispered, "You are death." The sun became brighter and brighter till it filled my eyes, made me see, made me see, made me see inside myself. And so I saw. La Prêtresse. I had taken the glass and slit open her eyes; had watched the humors pour down her uncomprehending face. Had pushed the splinters into her throat and let flow the captive blood. I had done it. Annemarie, Greta, I had made them sing as they bled, sing with the knowledge of their freedom now from sin. The Turkish boy, I had kissed him, had fondled him, had put my mouth on his body, had fornicated with him; had done the same with his master; had given them ecstasy and blood, had taken their sins away from them. Their blood had foamed on the floor of the stable and I watched it and I saw that it was good. I had been the Lord's instrument, I had struck out obscene things. Myself, not my husband. I had done it all.

Knowing what I had done, knowing that it had been good, feeling still the *kif*, I laughed to myself, softly, gently, for a long, long time. It had been me, I had been blind to the Lord but I had done his work nonetheless.

Then it passed; I could see the world again. The beggar and his snakes were gone. I felt the sun's warmth; it was still high in the sky. I had seen myself in its light; had seen the things that, just a short time before, I had not wanted to know. Now I knew. And to know seemed good. Marrakesh was no longer a maze to me; I knew exactly how to reach the hotel. But just as I got to my feet, just as I was stepping out of the orchard, I felt the child in my stomach kick. Once more I laughed. The beggar had told me. The flesh remembers. My daughter would have knowledge, too.

But that night, after the *kif* wore off, there were dreams. Nightmares of the things I had done, the people I had made dead. Their voices called to me not from their mouths but from their severed throats. "Clare, Clare, why have you done this to us?" The blood flowed, the tears flowed, I did not sleep. There was a Bible in the room. I found Ecclesiastes: "He that increaseth knowledge, increaseth sorrow." I had given my unborn daughter the gift of knowing; but to know is a curse.

It took Marty more than a week to get the two windows installed. I kept to myself. He was more and more concerned about me, about my state, about our child. I left the drugs alone; faced the nightmares.

When the work was done Arthur found us a guide who spoke Moghrebi and we departed to find the convent. Crossed first the Atlas, then the Anti-Atlas. Were regarded with suspicion and wonder by the dwellers there. Reached the Sahara.

The convent was cut into the stone of a cliff; overlooked a wide green valley. The nuns were tended by Bedouins. I requested an interview with the mother superior. Was raised up the cliff in a basket. The convent halls were lit with torches. "Good day. I am Mother Samuel." She helped me out of the lift; was old, lined, not merely grey but white with age. I told her my name. Told her what we had come for. Was prepared to steal once again, to get the glass. This was my opportunity for redemption for the things I had done; this was my chance to touch the Lord.

"Yes, there is an ancient church on the mountaintop." Her voice was gentle. "Ruined now but still standing. There is glass there."

"Glass."

"Yes. It is what you want. It is the Lord's glass."

"Deep red? Does it glow?"

"Yes. That is the glass."

"May we . . . may we take it?"

The old nun frowned. "Are you certain that you want it?"

"We've been all over the world looking for it."

"It is not possible to come that close to divinity without also finding Satan." I could say nothing to this; Mr. Tiffany had warned me of it. Her eyes penetrated me. "You have already come close to finding both, the sin and the ecstasy. Is that not correct?"

"How . . . why do you say that?"

"You are here. This is your destiny." She made a broad sweeping gesture; indicated the convent, the stone. "There are forty-nine of us."

I was off balance; could find nothing to say.

"You and your young man—"

"My husband."

"Yes." Mother Samuel scowled. "Your husband. You and he may go up to the high place if it is what you wish. But I should like you to wait three days. Pray about it. Make certain."

We waited. Each night lions roared in the mountains. We heard them playing, mating, hunting. My unborn child was restless. Then three days later, just at sunset, we sent her word that we wished to go up onto the mountaintop. The three of us were raised up in the basket. Ushered by Mother Samuel through the corridors. Blank white faces, the faces of women, stared at us out of the stone. There was an ascending passage, steps cut into the mountain. Arthur waited for us at the bottom. Marty and I climbed.

On the mountain there was a broad flat place surrounded by steep rocks. In the center of it was the old church. Rough, black stones, not dressed but piled crudely atop one another; it could have been prehistoric. There was no roof. The day's dying light came in. The altar had been made of three flat stones in the shape of the trilithons at Stonehenge. And there just beyond them was the glass. A large piece of it, still fitted into the lead channels.

I went to it. Forgot Marty, forgot everything, everyone; forgot myself. It glowed bright and red, brighter and redder than the other glass, brighter and redder than anything. In the twilight its brilliance seared my eyes. "Look at it. Like Moses' bush it burns but is not consumed."

I had to touch it. Pressed my hand flat against it. It was warm, almost hot; it was warm with the blood of the Lord. It tingled, was electric. I thought that I could feel its pulse. The leads were ancient, corroded. I pried them apart and pulled out the glass. Held it in my hands.

From behind me Marty put his arms around my waist; he embraced me tightly. "Clare."

"Take your hands off me."

"Clare!"

I pushed him away. Backed off from him. "Don't touch me again."

"Good Christ, Clare. Please, not now." He looked around. Was terrified of me, of my mood, of my mind and soul.

"You've always told me that you love me. But you don't love me enough. There is only one who loves me enough. I'm a sinner."

"Clare, for God's sake stop this. I do love you. I've told you so often enough. Shown you so time and again."

"You don't love me as much as I love myself. Don't you see it? That's where the sin is."

"Clare." He took a step toward me.

"Stop!" I slashed the air with the glass.

"Clare, stop it. Stop doing this."

"Stop!" I shrieked it. Lunged at him, but he sidestepped.

"Clare, Clare, let me hold you, let me help you remember our love. You've forgotten. You don't remember what love feels like."

"Yes." I stood still; let my arms fall to my sides. "Yes." Lowered my eyes. Felt the hot glass beat in my hand. My infant kicked at the walls that confined her. "Yes. Come and hold me."

He was five yards away. Came to me slowly, deliberately, with his arms held out, palms upward, as if to show he was unarmed. But I knew that he was unarmed. It was I who was armed. I held up the red glass and watched him through it. He was red, my hand was red, the world was red. Everything had fire in it. There was fire inside me, inside my head; there was fire outside of me. Everything was covered in flame. The stones around us turned to white-hot sulfur; incandescent lava; the mountains boiled. When Marty reached me I pushed the glass into his face, into his eyes. "Oh Clare, oh good Jesus, Clare!" He wailed, he flung his arms about trying to touch me. Blood cascaded from where his eyes had been, blood not as red as my glass. I stepped back away from him and watched him through the blood of the Lord. He fell. Cried. Whispered three times my name.

"Marty." I spoke to him softly. The worst was over for both of

us. I went to him, knelt beside him. "Marty. You mustn't talk."
I cut his throat and ended his struggles. Kissed him. His lips were
already cool. The fire that had enveloped us died down but did not
quite go away.

It was dark. The lions were still bellowing in the mountains
around me. Above, there were a million stars. Perhaps the lions
were speaking to me; I don't know. Marty was motionless, and I
cried over him.

In my womb the baby kicked. Kicked violently in its prison. I
could free it. I could use once again the glass. It lit me, lit Marty's
corpse. I lifted it, held it high, tried to find the resolve to plunge
it into my belly and cut out the child.

"Clare."

Arthur was there. Had come up the steps. Gaped at what he
saw.

"I heard screaming. Good Jesus in heaven, Clare, what
happened here?" He looked from Marty to me, then back at
Marty.

"A lion. It attacked him."

Arthur looked around. Looked back at poor Marty. "A lion."

"Yes. It was horrible."

He walked to the body, got down on a knee, tried to see it by
the starlight.

I walked up behind him. "You are my last link to the living
world, Arthur." I pulled the glass across his throat and he fell
beside Marty. That was the end. The fire was gone now.

The night was black. I wanted to stay in it. If the night had gone
on forever I could have sat there enfolded by it. But in time the
misery of dawn began to grow. It was too painful. I descended the
steps. Knelt at the feet of Mother Samuel. Made my confession to
her and let her absolve me. "There, there, child, it's over now.
Take the vows and join the sisterhood. Be dead to the world. You
have touched the Lord now, you have learned to understand him."

"No, Mother, I have touched the face of Satan himself."

"It comes to quite the same thing."

I held out the glass to her, but she would not take it. I had to
show her what it was, what it could do. Made to draw it across my
wrist. But she stopped me. "No, Clare, you don't have to show
me. I understand. I know."

My clothes were exchanged for plain grey things. I wrapped the blood glass fragments carefully in linen and stored them in my cell, kept them to remind me of the truth I had unearthed. Made confession to all my new sisters and received their forgiveness. I was part of the stone now; and it was what I had, really, always wanted.

From time to time news came from the world outside. Two years after I came here a caravan brought us a newspaper. In it was an obituary for Lon Chaney. He had, at last, made a talking picture; had spoken in multiple voices for it, for the multiple characters he portrayed. And then, not long afterward, he died of the cancer in his throat.

PART THREE

Shattered

Blood, though it sleep a time, yet never dies.

–Chapman, *The Widow's Tears*

1

Everything in the convent was still; dark. Only a few torches lit the corridors. The nuns were asleep.

In her cell, Sister Martin slept with Steve. They were both dressed; lay on her cot with their arms around each other. Nuzzled in their sleep; whispered things to each other unknowingly.

Then something woke Steve. He sat up, looked around the cell. Dim light outlined Martin's face, lit her hair. He kissed her cheek gently. Looked at his watch. It was after five, and he should be going. He kissed her again, lightly so as not to wake her. Left.

In the east the first touch of morning made the sky grey. Steve stood at the convent entrance, stared down at the valley, at the tents where Robert and Charlotte were sleeping; at the Bedouin village; at the desert, at sand visibly red even in the predawn light. Then looked back behind him, into the corridor. He wanted to be with Martin. But it was time to go. His cut hand was still bandaged. Slowly, carefully he climbed down the cliff face; made for camp.

Robert was still asleep, facedown on his cot. Steve came noisily in; plopped down on his own. Robert stirred, looked around. Wanted to be asleep.

"Did I wake you? Sorry."

"Go to sleep."

"I will."

"Good."

By now the sky was light. Robert buried his face in his arms, tried to ignore the world and sleep.

Steve pulled off his boots; dropped them, one at a time, on the floor.

"It's a good thing you got here when you did." Robert sat irritably up. "I was afraid I was going to have to sleep for a few more hours."

"I said I was sorry." He stripped off his clothes.

Robert glared at him. "How is your love life progressing?"

"Second base." Steve was all cheeriness.

"A nun."

"I keep telling you. You should see her." He leered.

"No thanks."

Sunlight was shining on the walls of the tent. There was no way Robert would get back to sleep. He looked around for his clothes. On the floor of the tent was Mother Joseph's manuscript. He stared at it; wished the wind could have taken it away during the night. He got up. Stretched. "This camping out isn't good for me. I think I'm developing arthritis."

"You should work out more."

Robert ignored him; climbed stiffly into a pair of cutoffs, picked up the manuscript and walked out into the morning.

"Charlotte." He tapped softly at the flap of her tent. "Charlotte, are you up yet?"

"Go away, dear, I'm reading."

"We have to talk."

"Well then give me a minute. I'm not decent." She poked her head out the tent flap; grinned at him. "Or is that why you wanted to see me?"

"I'll wait over by the jeep."

"Fine, darling."

The day was finally beginning. Birds sang; there was a hot wind off the desert. After a few moments Charlotte bounced out of her tent; breezed across to join him. "I feel like ham and eggs. Why don't you start a fire?"

"Charlotte, I think we ought to get out of here."

"Why, darling?" She rummaged through their provisions. Pulled out a tin of meat.

"We're not getting anywhere with your sister, and I don't believe we're going to. She's a lunatic."

"I could have told you that forty years ago, Robert. What about the will?"

"Do you really need more money?"

She flashed a smile at him. "You're getting more and more out of character, Robert dear. Keep repeating to yourself, 'I'm a lawyer, I'm a lawyer.' "

"Do you have any idea where your son has been?" He refused to be needled.

"Not a clue. Maybe the lions ate him."

"There haven't been any lately."

"Pity." She looked him up and down; decided she'd had enough fun with him. "Look, what exactly is bothering you?"

He turned away from her. "Nothing much."

"Robert."

"I just don't like it here, that's all. The nuns are crazy, the Bedouins are crazy. We stay here long enough, we'll end up just like them."

Charlotte smirked. "Maybe you should borrow my Jane Austen. You sound like you could use a dose of *Sense and Sensibility*. Damn it. The key for the canned bacon's broken." She dug into the supplies again; pulled out a frying pan. "Do you suppose the Bedouins would sell us some eggs?"

"Charlotte."

"Yes, Robert dear." She sighed.

"Steve has been climbing up the mountain every night. He's trying to lay one of the nuns."

She froze. Looked around, looked at everything but Robert. "How am I supposed to react to that?"

"Your sister wrote a memoir. While he was up there, he stole it and tossed it down to me. You should read it."

"And I thought Jane Austen would satisfy you." Her eyes twinkled.

"Charlotte, I'm serious. She's out of her mind. We'll never get her to respond reasonably to what we want."

"I don't know if I'd want to read Clare's memoir." Conflicting things showed in her face. "It wouldn't be right."

He held it out to her at arm's length, as if to touch it were unpleasant. Charlotte stared at it, unable to conceal her curiosity. She reached for it; hesitated. "Look, why don't you just give it back to her? This can't be right."

"Take it and read it. Here." He pushed it into her hands.

"Robert, I—"

"She's a lunatic. And Steve's going up there into her place every night."

"I— Oh." She looked at it once more. Unrolled it, read the first few sentences. "Does she . . . does she say much about our family?"

"Practically nothing."

"About me?"

"No."

"Oh. I— No, I shouldn't read it."

"Look, just take the damn thing and sit down with it, will you? You know you're aching to."

"But, Robert, I— Well—"

"I don't mean to be sharp with you. This place is getting to me. But I think you should read that. I think you should have some idea what we're dealing with here. She told me the Bedouins think they're all madwomen. That may be true."

Charlotte sighed. "Well, I've reread Jane once too often, anyway."

"Have you ever come across what Mark Twain wrote about Jane Austen?" Robert smiled at her for the first time.

"No, what did he say?"

"He said it was a great pity they let her die a natural death. I'll see you later, Charlotte." He turned and walked back to his tent.

He expected to find Steve asleep. But he was wide awake, doing push-ups on the tent floor. And he was covered with sweat. Robert watched for a moment; walked in. "I think cold showers work a lot better than that."

Steve was panting; was bright red. He did another half dozen push-ups, then let himself heavily down. He exhaled deeply. "Boy, when I finally get her, she's going to have a lot to answer for."

"Should you be doing push-ups on that?" He pointed at Steve's bandaged hand. "What happened to it?"

"Nothing. It's all right."

Robert picked up a canteen, took a long drink of water. "Here."

"No thanks."

"I think the girl might be your cousin. She has Clare's husband's name and she's fair like all of you."

"How did you guess?"

"You mean you know it? And you're still going to—"

Steve sat up; he had still not caught his breath. "She told me that. But I thought she had to be wrong."

"She may be. They may all be insane."

"She sees things, too. Or hears them. Or something. She blacks out and foams at the mouth."

Robert hesitated. The last thing he wanted was to learn that any part of Clare's story was true. "Sees things."

"Yeah." He took his shirt, wiped the sweat off his face with it. "Like visions. She says she knew I was coming here. Says she knows we're going to make it."

"I don't like being here." Robert stood up, walked to the door. Stared out at the red sand. "This isn't a good place to be."

"You said that before." Steve looked around. "It's an okay place."

"No, it isn't."

"And you think Martin's crazy."

Robert was tempted to walk away from the subject. Stopped himself from doing it. "Do you believe that places have their own special characters?"

"Huh?"

"My son the quarterback." He mimicked Charlotte. "Do you believe in God?"

"Of course I do."

"And do you believe that God is everywhere? That he's in everything and everyone?"

"Yeah, I guess so. That's what they always told us." Steve stood up, joined Robert at the door. Was still undressed.

"Put your pants on."

"There's nobody to see."

"You'll scandalize the natives."

Steve looked around; scowled.

"Do you find it pleasant to believe that, Steve?"

"Believe what?"

He sighed. "That God is in everything."

"Yes." Steve stepped out into the sunlight. "It means he's never far away."

"That's what I used to believe." He followed Steve outside. "But the more I think about it, the more the idea scares me."

There was a small lizard basking on the outside of the tent. Steve picked it off the canvas, let it crawl around on his arm. "You think too much."

"Probably. It only makes things worse. You don't know how I envy you."

"I don't think I follow you." He turned suspicious.

"That stone there. It has God in it?"

"Yes. It has to. God made it."

"And the grains of sand? And the cliffs?"

"Yes, Robert, they've all got God in them." It was beginning to bore him.

Robert fell silent. Stared up at the convent.

"So what about God? Why does that scare you?"

"It scares me because . . . I mean, look, Steve, how close do you feel to that lizard? How can you touch whatever soul it has inside it? Much less the stones and the sand. Whatever God there is in them might as well be at the other end of the universe. Take a good look around you. Look at yourself and your mother. Or at you and me. It's practically impossible to get to know another person well enough to see the God in him. But the God in everything . . . Jesus, Steve . . ." He sat down on the sand; looked out into the Sahara. "I can't touch anything."

Steve had tired of playing with his lizard; put it on the ground and watched it scuttle away.

"I don't want to be here, Steve. Every day we stay here, I feel a little bit colder inside. I'm turning to ice. There's too much God around me here and I can't touch any of it."

Steve walked back inside the tent; came out in a pair of shorts. "I think maybe I know what you mean."

"Really." Robert did not look at him.

"I'm in love with Martin. I mean, I think I'm really in love with her. But I think she's . . . like you said . . . not balanced. Not quite right in the head. I find myself thinking if I could just get her away from here, she'd be all right, she'd get better."

"I don't suppose you read much poetry, do you?"

Steve looked at him; did not have to answer.

"Ever come across Robinson Jeffers?"

"No."

"He's not much in fashion these days. But I've always liked him. I remember one of his poems about a haunted place, full of lonely self-watchful passion. No imaginable human presence there, he wrote, could do anything but increase that. That's what this place is like. It frightens me. And yet . . . and yet, I've never known a place like this before."

"Let me get Martin down out of the mountain, and I'll get you both out of here. I'll rescue you both." He looked at Robert, who was looking directly back into his eyes. It made him uncomfortable; he tried to make a joke of it. Bowed exaggeratedly. "Errol Flynn, at your service."

Robert watched him; stared at Steve as if he had never quite seen him before. From the mountain came faintly the sound of the nuns singing matins.

Sister Martin stood at the telescope. Looked down at the valley, at Robert and Steve talking. Steve wore no clothing. She studied his body, compared it point by point with her vision of it, her vision of their copulation. Then he disappeared into the tent; came out again wearing shorts. She found herself wishing she could hear their conversation.

Mother Joseph came in behind her. Watched her curiously for a moment. "Martin. You should be in chapel."

"Mother." She turned; blushed.

"What are you watching?"

"The Bedouins. The children. They're playing ball."

"Martin."

The young nun stood there, said nothing.

"You've been spending too much time alone in your cell." Joseph walked up to the window, gazed casually down at the valley. "I don't see any children."

"They ran away."

"As quickly as that."

"You know how lively they are."

"Martin, you've been missing services. Missing confession. You know how important confession is to us."

"I— My head. It's been aching every night. The pain has been terrible."

Joseph pushed her daughter away from the telescope's eyepiece. Looked, saw the two men talking by their tent. "Headaches."

"Yes, Mother."

"Which one of them is it?" She did not move from her place at the telescope.

"I don't know what you mean."

"Martin. Daughter." She did not take her eye away from the lens. "The things you are feeling are sinful. Satan sent those men here."

"I don't think I believe that, Mother. God created men, too, didn't he?"

"Don't confuse the issue. You are to remain in cloister. You are not to watch them anymore. Do you understand that? You are not to look at them."

Martin flushed. Wanted to say, Do you think I need a telescope to see the man I'm in love with? But she bowed her head and said softly, obediently, "Yes, Mother."

"Go and tend to your chores. And don't have any more headaches. You'll be expected at services tonight. You'll be expected to confess the lie you told."

"Lie? What lie?"

"That you were watching the children."

"I can't help the headaches." Martin was growing impatient with Joseph's orders. "You gave them to me. Isn't that what you always say? That my visions and my headaches are your doing?"

"Martin, go and work." She was rigid; she barked it.

"Yes, Mother." Martin glared at the telescope; turned and left the room.

Mother Joseph watched her go. Looked through the instrument once again. Robert was alone on the sand now; sat there wearing only shorts. She stared at him for a long time.

2

Sunset. Vespers being sung. Songs from the Bedouins. Charlotte sat on the hood of the jeep reading her sister's book. Robert was fast asleep in the tent; was covered with sweat. Steve slipped out and made for the base of the cliff. The handholds, toeholds were familiar to him by now; he made a rapid ascent. It grew too dark for his mother to read, and she went into her tent and lit a lantern. For the first time in several nights there were lions calling.

The convent's halls were lit as always by torches. The sweet music of the nightfall service filled the air. Steve went quickly to Martin's cell; was dismayed not to find her there. Looked around the candlelit room; wondered what to do until she appeared. Ran his fingers nervously around the lines of the fish carved into the lintel. He wanted her.

It was no use. He was too full of energy to sit and wait. He walked out into the corridor; looked both ways along it; headed left, toward the nuns' burial gallery. Faces in the wall, ghostly faces. He took a torch and went quickly along, tried not to think about the bones that surrounded him. Then there was the huge gallery where the blind fish lived. He stared at the water, at the torchlight reflected in its surface. Resisted the temptation to put a hand in and play with them. The corridor continued. He walked along; wanted to see where it went.

At the end there were steps carved into the rock, going up into perfect darkness. He held the torch out at arm's length, as high as he could manage, but the light only cut a few feet into the blackness there. He took a few steps upward, then realized that the nuns' music had stopped. He looked curiously up the steps, wanted to see what was at the top of them; but Martin would be back in her cell soon. Steve turned and went back to where he'd begun. Sat on the cell floor behind the door, where none of the others could see him and waited for his woman.

She entered, closing the door behind her; crossed to her cot; began to undress.

"Let me do that for you."

Martin jumped; whirled around. "Oh. Good heavens, I didn't know you were there."

"You didn't have a vision of me coming up here tonight?" He stood, dusted off the seat of his pants.

"Don't make fun of me. There's more to me than you know."

"Yeah, but I mean to find out about it."

"Don't talk that way. We're going to make love tonight, and I want it to be sweet, not ugly."

"Yeah. I—" He stopped short. "What did you say?"

"I said," she repeated slowly, "that you and I are going to make love tonight." She pulled off her wimple; let her blond hair flow. "Now is the time for it. Isn't that what you want?"

Steve stared at her; said nothing.

Martin shook her hair, ran a hand through it.

"You're beautiful, Martin. Have I told you that?"

"Be quiet. Come here and kiss me."

Steve did as ordered, kissed her, squeezed her. "Martin, I love you."

"I love you, too." She whispered. "Kiss me more."

He kissed her throat; opened her robe, kissed her shoulder.

"Wait a moment." She made to snuff out the candle.

"No. Leave it lit. I want to see you."

She was undressed. His lips touched her breasts. She pulled open the buttons of his shirt; undid his belt. They kissed again and again.

"Say you love me."

He said it again.

Then they both were naked; they lay on the cot. Steve kissed the flat of her stomach. They coupled. Steve felt a rising ecstasy. Then, in the middle of their lovemaking, Martin began to moan. It was not the moaning of pleasure; it was the moaning of her heavenly visions. But Steve was too involved himself to notice.

The room was hot. There was dampness all over them, they were covered with it. Martin moaned hysterically. Steve felt more and more wet. Then suddenly he realized that something was not right. He pulled back; looked at her. Realized the way she was responding to him.

"Oh, Jesus, Steve," she said, "please don't stop now."

Martin's body was rigid; trembled all over. Her limbs flailed. There was foam on her lips, and her eyes were rolled up into her head. And there was blood. Wounds opened, blood flowed from the palms of her hands, the soles of her feet; a long gash opened in her side. There were punctures around her head, and droplets of blood soaked her hair; made it deep red. The cot was drenched in it. Steve himself was smeared all over, was black-red in the candlelight.

He jumped away from her. "Christ!"

Martin's blood poured onto the floor; made pools.

"For Christ's sake, Martin!" He shook her, tried to bring her out of her trance. "Martin! For Christ's sake, don't do this to me again!"

Her body shook uncontrolled. The amount of blood pouring out of her was impossible.

"Martin! Martin, this can't be happening."

Commotion outside. Voices, movement. He ran into the hall. Had to hide before the others got there. Took up a torch and headed once again for the burial hall. In the cavern he stopped and washed the blood from his body; hoped it wouldn't hurt the fish. Then he made for the ascending stairs beyond. He hesitated for a moment; the blackness there was unnerving. But he wanted to see what was there. And so he went up.

In her cell Martin moaned. "Oh Steve, oh Steve." And her mother stood over her, watching, listening. Sister Peter took the crucifix down from the wall, forced the shaft of it into Martin's mouth to keep her from hurting herself. Joseph walked to the door; looked both ways along the hall. She had to search. She had to find him.

The chapter hall; the refectory; then finally she went to the chapel. In her mind she heard things all through the convent, voices, breathing. She looked around her; listened to the still rooms. It was no use. She turned slowly and went back to her daughter.

The convulsions slowed; the stigmata stopped their flow. Peter got cloths and mopped up the spilled blood. Covered the girl in a linen blanket. Martin slept, finally at peace, or what seemed to be peace.

The chapel was empty. A large candle burned in an enormous brass holder; the flame flickered in a draft. Joseph entered slowly; knelt at the rail. She covered her face with her hands and cried into them. "O God, let them go away, let them go away. O God, let them go away." She was there for hours crying, speaking to the Lord. The other nuns were long asleep.

Then finally, exhausted with prayer and worry, she got up and went somberly to her cell. A lamp burned there for her. The moon lit the stained glass window. She walked to it, pressed her hand flat against it, felt its coolness. Looked at her cot.

An impulse made her get down on her knees beside it. Made her reach under, for the blood glass. But it had been moved. She took the candle; looked. It had been moved. And her box, her manuscript were gone. "Oh no. O God, please God, let them go away."

3

"Every time I come here I'm astonished at the place." Robert faced Mother Joseph across her desk. He wore his suit, carried his briefcase. "Do you have any idea at all who built it?"

Joseph stared at him. The goblet of wine on the desk in front of her was untouched. "There is a reference in one of our earliest manuscripts to an Anglo-Saxon architect named Aelfdern. Not a flattering reference. Apparently he was a completely dissolute man. But he may have been the one who cut our halls."

"Aelfdern." He looked around, as if the stone might tell him something. "Aelfdern. Never heard of him."

"Neither, I gather, has anybody else."

She was being even less communicative than usual. Robert tried to put himself at ease; tried not to remember the things he had read; could not do it. Forced himself to go on. "Well. What is it you want to see me about today?"

"I just thought we might talk, that's all."

"Oh. I see." He waited for her to go on, but she only stared. "Uh, talk about what, exactly?"

"This and that. The price of tomatoes. Cabbages and kings."

Robert drank his claret. Tried to think of something to say.

"How is the wine, Robert darling?"

"Fine."

"Did you know that in legend claret represents Christ's blood?"

"Blood." He pulled the glass away from his lips.

"Deep, red, holy blood." She smiled.

"Uh, yes." He looked around again, hoped another topic of conversation would suggest itself. Nothing came. "I was, uh, wondering whether you've thought any more about the will."

"Whose will? Mine, yours, the Lord's?"

"Your father's." He was in no mood to humor her.

"My father's. No. I haven't."

"We really can't stay here indefinitely, you know. Charlotte is feeling impatient."

"Charlotte always did."

"Listen to me. There's a great deal of money at stake here. Half of it is yours. You can't be so naive as not to want it."

"Naiveté, darling, has nothing to do with it." She leaned back in her chair; looked him up and down. "I want to meet with Charlotte."

"You—" It could not have caught him more off guard.

"Perhaps you should take another drink." She laughed at him.

"You want to see your sister." His mind raced; what could she have in mind?

"Precisely."

"To discus the will?" He wanted to smile; could not quite make himself do it.

"Not at all. Just for old times' sake. As you have pointed out to me often enough, we're sisters."

"I— Yes." He sat upright. "Well. When shall I bring her?"

"Why not now?"

"I think she'll want to get herself ready."

"Tonight, then. I'll have a little supper for the four of us."

"Oh. Shall I bring Steve, too, then?"

"I can't tell you how anxious I am to meet him."

"Should we dress?"

"Come naked, if you please."

"No, I meant—"

"Dress as casually as you like, dear." She got up; was smiling fixedly now. "Eight o'clock?"

"Fine." Robert stood. Drained the last of his wine. "I can't wait to see how Charlotte enjoys the ride up here."

"She's been needling you?"

"Constantly."

"That's my big sister." She escorted him out into the corridor. An elderly nun walked past them; kept her eyes turned away from Robert. He waited for her to pass. "Joseph, tell me why you really want to meet with Charlotte." They started walking.

"Oh, just morbid curiosity, I suppose. I want to see if she's ended as badly as I've always thought she would."

They were at the entrance. The valley was green and sunlit. "I'm not sure she's ended at all. Not yet, anyway."

"Hasn't she?" Joseph smiled; was serious. "Oh, and Robert, there's one more thing."

"Yes?"

"I want my memoir back." Her grin widened even further.

Robert went cold. Had no idea what he could say. He tried not to look at her.

"You will all be here for dinner at eight o'clock, and you will bring me back my memoir." Her teeth showed yellow in the daylight. "Do you understand that?"

"Yes, Mother Joseph."

The Bedouins on the ground had pulled on their line. The basket ascended the cliff, swayed, bumped against the rocks; then stopped in front of them. Robert stepped into it. It swayed. He reached out impulsively and caught her hand.

"Robert darling, do be careful."

Charlotte and Aoud were at the jeep, conversing in French. Robert walked from the foot of the cliff directly to them. Said hello to Aoud. "Charlotte, we have been invited to dine with Mother Joseph this evening."

"Really? Good Lord." She gaped at him, startled. "Two days ago, I'd have jumped at the chance to see her. If only to see how badly she's aged. But now that I've read that little story of hers . . . It's Grand Guignol. You're right about her, Robert, she's insane."

"She's expecting us. It is not so much an invitation as a summons. The sort of thing an abbess in the Middle Ages might have issued."

"I don't think I follow you, darling." She looked from Robert to Aoud.

"She knows we've got her memoir."

"Oh."

"Yes." He loosened his necktie. "Oh."

Charlotte looked around the valley. She shaded her eyes and glanced at the sun. "Well, we've got plenty of time to brace ourselves."

"She wants Steve to come, too. I think she knows what he's been up to."

"I've been talking about the nuns with Aoud, Robert." She climbed into the back of the jeep and stretched out. "The Bedouins claim the nuns guard the entrance to hell. To judge from Clare's memoir, I'd say they're not far wrong."

"You can't believe that stuff."

"No, but I think she does. To think such things about yourself, to carry around inside that picture of yourself . . . if that isn't a good definition of hell, I don't know what is."

It was the last thing Robert wanted to hear. "I wish I could convince myself she's harmless. Where's Steve?"

"Sleeping, off in your tent. Tired from a night of whoring, I presume. Let me tell you something." She cupped a hand over her mouth, whispered in exaggerated tones. "I don't much like my family."

"The same blood runs in your veins." Robert unbuttoned his shirt. "And in Clare's for that matter."

"That's right, Robert. You're out here in the middle of the wilderness with a family of psychopaths."

"Look, this isn't really very funny." The day was stifling. He took off his jacket and shirt; was covered with sweat. "She knows we've stolen from her, and I think she knows what your son has been getting up to. We need to decide what to do tonight. I'm not at all sure it would be a good idea to go up there."

"We need her signature to settle the will."

"Yes." He scowled at the thought. "And there is another Markham heir now. The senator has a granddaughter."

Charlotte gaped at him. "One of the nuns? She didn't invent that mad pregnancy in her memoir?"

"No. And I think her daughter is the one Steve has been . . . romancing."

Her features froze. "Good God."

"Exactly, Charlotte. The question is, do you want the money badly enough to risk all of our lives for it?"

"You really think it's that bad?"

"I wish there were some way to know."

She turned to Aoud, translated—selectively—the things they'd been talking about. The guide smiled at them. "There is an ancient church on the top of the mountain. It is the gateway to hell. I have never seen it myself, of course, but the people here all say it is there. And the fifty nuns are all in league with Satan. Some say they are his wives, or his daughters. I would not go up there." He shrugged to show his ultimate indifference.

For a moment nobody spoke. Robert craned his neck, looked up the mountain. "There can't be a church up there. It's too steep. It'd be impossible. How could they have . . .?"

"What's this? Huddling without me?" Steve came out of his tent; was pulling on a pair of shorts.

"My son the quarterback." Charlotte looked at Aoud, not at Steve.

"What's the big discussion?"

Robert told him about Joseph's invitation. "The question is, do we go up there tonight or don't we?"

Steve looked up at the convent. "You ought to see the place, Mother. It's really something."

"So you have been up there every night?"

"Yeah." He looked up at it again. "I think I'm in love with one of the girls."

"Your cousin?" Charlotte scowled at him.

"We can't leave her there. Her mother's nuts."

"She's crazier than you think." Robert summarized the story in Joseph's memoir for him. "I don't believe half of it. Women's faces staring out of the stone walls. An ancient church up on the cliff. She has to be out of her mind."

"I've seen the faces." Steve seemed pleased to hear about it all. "And I've seen the church. And I've already told you about Martin's trances. But you didn't want to admit it."

"What you described to me are seizures. Seizures are not visions. The girl's epileptic, that's all."

"When we made love last night"—he avoided looking at his mother—"she started bleeding. Wounds like Jesus. I've never seen anything like it. It scared me."

"Stigmata. A serious psychological disorder." Charlotte frowned, turned to Robert. "Look, darling, she's a Markham. If we get her away from here, she'll get her mother's share of the money, won't she?"

"Not while her mother's alive. And not without proof. All we have to go on is Martin's own claim and Joseph's manuscript, and it never mentions Martin by name."

"But she has the same name as Joseph's—Clare's husband."

"There's no proof of the marriage."

"We have the manuscript." She started pacing. "I think we should try to get the girl out of there. We'd hold all the trumps then."

"Trumps? Charlotte, this isn't a game of bridge."

"Properly viewed, darling, everything is a game, if not necessarily of bridge. It would give me a lot of pleasure to get what I want out of Clare."

"We can handle a batty old nun." Steve seconded her enthusiastically.

"Yes. Yes, we can." Robert's mood was suddenly black. The church, the visions, the Bedouin legends. They were not things he wanted to face. "But what about a mountainful of crazy nuns?"

"Well, it's decided then." Charlotte breezily ignored him. "We go up the cliff tonight. And we leave the memoir down here, where it'll be safe."

"And"—Steve rubbed his hands together—"we try to find a way to get Martin out of there."

"Fine. Fine." Robert felt distant from them, distant from the whole valley and the people in it. Needed to be alone. He went to his tent, changed into a pair of shorts; headed up the valley to the spring. He dipped a hand in the water. It was frigid. He plunged into it, let it make his body numb. Climbed out, lay beside the pool, stared into the empty sky.

"Monsieur Semnarek."

"Aoud. Hello."

"May I join you?"

"Yes. Of course."

The guide sat down beside him. "It is not good for you to swim in such cold water."

"Steve does it all the time."

"My son the quarterback." Aoud did a perfect imitation of Charlotte.

Robert looked at him, astonished. "You have talents I've never suspected."

Aoud laughed. "You do not want to go up there tonight."

"No. I don't." He did not want to talk about it.

"It comes to what you and I discussed once before."

Robert sat up, looked at him. "I don't follow you."

"One should never be a servant to anyone but the Lord." He got quickly up and walked away without saying anything more.

"I am not a—" It was no use. Robert glared at his retreating back. Then he stood up and jumped again into the icy pool.

At sunset they were raised, one at a time, up the cliff face. To Robert's annoyance, Charlotte took it in her stride. She had dug into one of her trunks and found an evening gown; wore her hair up. Sister Peter met them, showed them to the refectory. The rock-cut halls did not faze Charlotte, either; she could have been born to them. There was music; Mozart's somber Quintet in C Minor in the version for oboe and strings. The oboe's sound reverberated eerily.

The abbess's table at the head of the room was lit brightly with candles; set for four. Silverware; linen; wine bottles. They sat, waited for their hostess. There was a silver bowl with black bread and another with fruit from the valley's orchards. Steve bit into a piece of bread; chewed. "This is like linoleum."

"I can't wait to taste the wine." Charlotte frowned; ran a finger across the tabletop to see if it was clean.

"It will be claret." Robert avoided looking at either of them. "And it will be delicious. It's been aging forever."

"Like Clare."

"Like all of us, Charlotte." Mother Joseph entered. Had on her usual grey habit. But on her head, covering her face, she wore a veil of navy blue lace. She gestured to it. "I hope this isn't too gaudy. We have a lot of time to ourselves here, and some of the sisters do such lovely needlework. How nice of you all to come."

Robert and Steve stood up. And so did Charlotte. "Clare darling. How could I resist the chance to see my big sister?"

The nun ignored her. "You must be Steve." She looked him up and down; nodded her approval. "I'm your aunt, about whom you have no doubt heard. I see all the things I've heard about you are correct."

"What have you heard, Aunt Cl—Joseph?"

"Nothing good, darling." She made it a joke. "Robert."

"Good evening, Joseph."

"Well. Why don't we all sit down and get to know each other?" Joseph took a seat facing her sister. She was the hostess, was instantly in charge; clapped her hands and a young nun appeared with a tureen of soup. The girl placed it in the center of the table and left. "We serve ourselves here, darlings. I hope you don't mind. There isn't room for much formality in our lives." She took a piece of bread; reached for the ladle.

But Charlotte beat her to it. "Why should we mind, Clare?" She filled her bowl to the brim.

"My name is Joseph now." She stared at the bread in her hand. "Mother Joseph. No one has called me Clare for a great number of years."

"In my mind you'll always be my big sister Clare. But if you prefer Joseph . . ." She gestured broadly with the ladle; passed it to Steve.

"I'm afraid it isn't a question of preference. My name is Joseph now. It is so simple. Perhaps if you concentrate, you can—"

"What kind of soup is this, Mother Joseph?" Robert was determined to keep between them.

"Lentil soup, dear. I hope you like it."

"It smells delicious."

"Joseph." Steve handed the ladle to Robert; looked at his aunt. "It sounds so odd. I mean, I can't call you Aunt Joseph, can I?"

She leaned back in her chair. Smiled. "Just Joseph will do." She turned back to Charlotte. "Robert tells me you married well."

"I married happily, if that's what you mean." She tasted her soup; made an unpleasant face. "Good Lord."

"We don't use seasonings. I'm afraid it takes some getting used to." She clapped once again. The girl returned and uncorked the wine; served them; left.

"I don't think I've seen her before." Robert watched her go. "What's her name?"

"She is Sister Andrew."

"All of you have men's names." Charlotte sniffed the wine; looked doubtful. "Why is that?"

"A tradition in the convent."

"Nothing more?"

"Please, Charlotte, stop it. You're making me remember things I don't want to."

Charlotte blew on her soup.

There was a break in the quintet; the players started the sad slow movement.

"This place . . . this is my home now, and the sisters are my . . . well, they're my sisters."

"Clare, you can't have forgotten me."

"I've forgotten everything I ever knew." She raised her veil. "I wanted that, it's why I stayed here. We get news of what's happening in the world. All the wars. The death camps. Fire bombings, atomic bombings. For thirty years those things never touched us, never penetrated here. The convent was impregnable, like the grave. And now here you are, and you've brought all of it in with you, and more besides. I can't tell you . . . I can't tell you how deeply I wish you'd never come here." Through all of this her eyes were on Robert.

"Really, Clare. You always had such morbid sensibilities." Charlotte chewed a piece of bread, punctuated her sentence with it. "And such a flare for drama."

"I still remember what you were like as a girl. You were a foot taller than I, and you never missed a chance to bully me."

"Your memory's playing tricks on you, Clare. You were the older sister."

"If I was older than you, Charlotte, then you must have been a pituitary giantess. On my tenth birthday you were two heads taller than I."

"On your tenth birthday I was still in the cradle."

Robert turned into a judge. "It is beginning to sound to me as if you are both still in the nursery." He stared from one of them to the other. "Surely we have more important things to do than bicker for precedence."

"Yes. Yes, of course, Robert." Duly chastened, Charlotte tasted her wine. Sipped more. "Why, this is delicious."

"Thank you. The Bedouins pride themselves on their viniculture."

"They made this?" Charlotte drank more of it. "It really is quite wonderful. Next time anyone asks me which wine goes with black bread, I'll know just what to tell them."

Joseph drank her own wine, took long slow tastes. Ignored her sister. Settled her gaze on Steve. "Why, darling, you've cut your hand. Whatever happened?"

He stared at her blankly.

Charlotte spoke for him. "An accident with your penknife. Didn't you say so, Steve?"

"Really? An accident with a knife? You should be more careful. I wouldn't like to see you meet with any harm while you're here." There was a silence. Joseph adjusted her veil. The candles flickered. She looked for the first time directly at Charlotte. "I could listen to you lie all night, sister. But as Robert said, we have more important things to talk about. Are you all ready for some cheese?"

"Please." Robert sighed softly; perhaps now it would be business at last.

The musicians broke again; began the quintet's mournful minuet. Sister Andrew came with the cheese; kept her eyes diverted from the guests. Had a brief whispered conversation with her mother superior. Went.

Aged cheddar, rich with a deep bite. It went perfectly with the claret. Everyone commented on it.

Joseph looked around the table; watched them make small talk. Decided she had had enough of them. "Well. To business, then. I want you all out of the valley. Tomorrow."

They looked at each other. Were taken off guard by her bluntness.

"Tomorrow." Robert ended the silence. "I'm not sure that's possible, Joseph. I mean, we have things to pack, plans to make. Our guide is visiting his relatives in the Bedouins' camp. We can't simply—"

"You can and you will. I want you gone."

"You want. You want." Charlotte laughed softly at her. "You always were a selfish girl. You left home because Daddy wouldn't drop everything to give you what you wanted. Spoiled, self-indulgent little . . ." She left it unfinished; grinned across the table.

"Nevertheless. You are in my valley, and I want you gone."

"Your valley."

"Mine. Yes."

"Robert darling, do something legal. Ask her to show you the deed or something."

Joseph poured another goblet of wine for herself. Drank. "You always did have a gift for mockery, Charlotte. Your single talent. When I heard Robert say your name, when I heard it spoken for the first time in thirty years, all I could think of was the way you used to bring me to my knees by laughing at me. Good Christ in heaven, how I still hate you."

No one moved, no one said a word. The two sisters watched each other. Robert wanted to make peace, or at least a truce between them; but he could think of nothing he might say. Finally Joseph looked at the doorway where Sister Andrew was waiting. "Let me have it now."

The young nun entered. She carried a silver tray. On it were the pages of Joseph's manuscript. "If it occurred to you that this might give you some sort of leverage against me, think again."

"How did you get that?" Steve gaped at it.

"How slow you are to catch on. Like your mother. I told you, this is my valley."

"But—"

"Do you think anything happens here that I don't learn about? Do you think I don't know about you bellying with my daughter?"

Steve turned deep crimson.

"You are more your mother's son than you know." She glared at Charlotte.

Robert and Charlotte looked at one another. Said nothing; it was hardly necessary.

Steve said to Joseph, "Have you asked your daughter, have you asked Martin, if she wants the money?"

Robert turned to her. "Her presence in the Markham family makes things even more tangled than they were. Surely you should give her the chance to decide for herself."

"My daughter has chosen. The Lord."

"I don't think she wants to be here." Steve slapped the table. "I think she hates it here. I think she'd want to leave with us."

"Think again. My daughter, nephew, would never leave this place and the protection it gives. The stone shelters her, just as it shelters all of us."

"Protection." Robert placed his elbows deliberately on the table; leaned forward. "Protects you from what, exactly?"

"I think that should be obvious. As a matter of fact, Martin has expressed to me—to the whole sisterhood, in confession—her wish that Steve remain here, with her, to share her life of devotion to God. Would you like to do that, Steve? I'm sure we could work out some accommodation." She smiled a benign smile.

"Wh!—No!"

"So. You won't give up your life. But you assume Martin is eager to give up hers. That girl has touched the face of God, and you expect her to give it up for a life in Johnstown, Pennsylvania."

"The face of god"—Charlotte leered at her—"is not all she has touched."

"We assume nothing, Joseph," Robert interjected; tried to keep his voice calm. "We have a legal mess to unravel, and we're anxious to do it."

"I want you gone tomorrow."

"But the will . . ."

"Tell them you found my tomb. Tell them I'm dead. It's half true, anyway."

"Joseph, what is it you think this place protects you from?"

"All of you." She stood up; the meal was ended. "I want you gone tomorrow. You will find the Bedouins eager to help you on your way. Goodbye." She turned and left.

A moment later Sister Peter returned and led them back to the lift. There was another pause in the quintet; the interval seemed to last forever. Then finally came the agitated strains of the final allegro. As they reached the valley floor, they could still hear the strains of the music reverberating above them.

They changed into their camp things. Steve lit a fire. The three of them sat, stared into it.

"And that," Charlotte said wearily, "is that. I only wish we could do something about the girl."

"Do something?" Robert inched near the flames; let them warm him. "What is there to do?"

"If she's being kept up there unwilling . . ."

"Charlotte, for Christ's sake, you've lost. You will never get one up on your sister, not this time. Joseph has the Bedouins. God only knows if they'd do violence for her, but I don't want to find out."

"I brought guns." Steve was proud of his cleverness. "We could take care of them."

"We did not come here for a massacre." Robert stretched out along the ground.

"No, we didn't. Would either of you like a brandy?" Charlotte got up and crossed to the jeep. "But we didn't come here for what we found, either."

"No, but we found it."

Charlotte handed them glasses, poured the brandy. "Why don't we ask Aoud how far the Bedouins will go for her?"

"How could we trust what he said?" Robert sniffed his brandy, put the glass down without tasting it. "There is such a thing as resigning yourself to your fate. Let's all be Stoics. Let's just accept it and go."

"No!" Steve shouted it. Jumped to his feet. "I'm going back up there."

"Steve."

"I mean it, Bob. I told you, I'm in love with Martin. I need to be with her. I can't just leave her in that mausoleum." He turned to go.

"Steve!" Charlotte walked after him. "Look, you haven't read Clare's memoir. You don't know what kind of woman she is."

"I know what kind Martin is. I'm going back up."

Robert ran to join them. "Well for Christ's sake, if you have to go be careful. Keep yourself hidden. Don't get in her way."

Steve took a step.

And Robert caught him by the arm. "Steve, did you hear me? If you have to go up there, be careful."

Steve pulled violently free form him. "Yes, Mother." Then he calmed down a bit. "I'm sorry. I'll—we'll be all right. I know a place up there where no one ever goes. That old church up on the mountain. Nobody's been there for a million years. We'll be safe up there." He walked off, left the two of them in the firelight. Neither of them quite knew what to say. They looked up at the convent, not at each other. There were still lights in all of the colored windows.

4

Early morning. The valley was covered with dew. There were cumulus clouds. From the mountain came the roar of a solitary lion.

Robert and Steve were asleep in their tent. Someone rapped at the post. "For Jesus' sake, Steve. Be quiet."

Another knock.

"Hm?" He looked up. A Bedouin boy stood there, staring at him.

"What do you want?"

The boy said nothing.

"What is it?" Robert sat up; reached for his cutoffs. Tried his question again in French.

The boy looked pointedly at his naked abdomen. Looked at Steve.

Robert stood up and walked over to him. "Look, we're not going to communicate. Why don't you just go away?"

Laughter. The boy held out a note. Robert took it; turned his back; read: "Robert. Come and see me today. Joseph." He looked at it for a long time; what could she want? Then he turned back to the boy; but he was gone. "Fine."

Charlotte was up; was packing. Slamming things around angrily. He did not want to confront her while she was in that mood. But there seemed no choice. "I have been summoned back into the presence."

"Why don't you take a knife with you and murder her?"

"Charlotte, stop it. I can't imagine what this is for." He held out the note to her.

"You don't suppose she's changed her mind about anything, do you?"

262

"Not likely." He glanced up the mountain. "Steve just got back down here half an hour ago."

"My son the fool."

"I wouldn't like to think she . . ."

She tried to force her Jane Austen into a backpack. It would not fit, and she slammed the book onto the ground. "Goddammit!"

There was no sense talking to her. Robert walked off toward the cliff. A pair of Bedouins waited there to raise him up.

Mother Joseph was standing at the entrance. "Robert. Thank you for coming."

"As you told us so pointedly, this is your valley." He made a vague gesture to show his fatalism.

"Yes." It was not the response she wanted. "I . . . You've never come up here before except in your business suit."

"I could go back and change if you like."

"No, no, I just wanted to chat."

"Get out of my valley, but first let's chat."

She looked at his chest; stared at it. "Please, don't be that way." She started to walk, expected him to follow. But he stood there on the edge of the landing. "Robert, please, come with me."

There was something not right. Robert looked around. "I don't hear the morning hymn."

"One of our sisters died last night. We are in mourning. It has made me . . . realize some things."

"Who died?"

"An elderly sister. You never met her. She had cancer for a long time."

"Why did you ask me up here?"

"I told you. To talk."

They passed the chapel. All of the nuns were there, praying silently. They went on walking.

"What will you do with her?"

"The beetles will clean her bones of their flesh. We will polish them and inter them."

"I meant Martin."

"Oh. There is nothing to do. Robert, she is a saint."

"A saint." He stared at her. They were at the door to her study.

"When she and her cousin . . . did what they did, she erupted in stigmata."

"Yes, Steve told us about it."

"It was a miracle. The amount of blood that flowed out of her wounds. You should have seen it. She is close to the Lord." She went in, stood at her desk.

"Or to Satan. Isn't that the point of your memoir?"

"Come in and have some wine."

"It's too early in the morning."

"Come in and sit, then."

"Clare, I—"

"Joseph."

He sat down. "Joseph. Sorry. Look, what happened to Martin is—" He stopped himself; there was no point to a discussion of abnormal psychology. He could not stop thinking about the memoir. Her mother's blood in her veins.

"You've read my memoir, then? I was afraid Charlotte had been the only one. She could never understand it. Understand me. But you . . ."

"Yes, I read it."

"And . . . ?"

"What can I say?"

"I haven't read it myself in years. Not since I finished it. I don't remember the details, only the horror."

Robert watched her; did not speak.

"Tell me, did I . . . Is there a description of Marty? Did I describe him?"

"Yes. But all of your most vivid description is reserved for the glass."

"Do you mind if I drink?"

"It's your valley." He smiled, waved a hand casually in the air.

"Please, Robert, don't."

"No." He dropped the smile. "Of course not."

She poured wine for herself. "You look like him. You could be his brother."

"I'm afraid you've lost me."

"Marty."

"Oh." He whispered it. Fell silent for a long time. Watched the nun. "Marty."

"Not," she said slowly, "that you have his personality. You have a mind. I'm afraid Marty never thought about anything too deeply. But physically—"

"I don't understand why you're telling me this."

"I . . : I don't . . . I don't think I know myself."

"Joseph, I think you do."

She drank her wine, drained the goblet; looked away from him. Stared at the stained glass window. The light coming through it dimmed slightly. "It must be clouding up. We might have more rain."

"Then I should be going. I still have to find our guide and tell him we're leaving today."

"He knows it."

"Oh."

"Robert, is there anything else here you'd like to see? Anything else in the convent?"

"Nothing I can think of, thank you. I have a long trip ahead of me." He made to stand up.

"You do understand, don't you, that it is you, it is your presence here, much more than Charlotte's, that has upset me?"

Robert looked directly at her. "You can't think that I knew that. How could I have known that?"

"Everyone knows everything."

"No, Joseph, some of us know nothing at all. And we prefer it that way. I really should be going now." He got up, moved to the door.

And she followed him. "Robert, I'm sorry."

"There is nothing to be sorry for,"

"I'm sorry for all the things I did years ago. And for all the things I've done since then. I'm sorry I thought that you . . ."

"Clare, I—Joseph, I don't know what you mean. You can't apologize for being human."

They stood in the doorway, looked at each other. Then Joseph reached out and put a hand on his side.

"Don't." He pulled back.

"I don't want you to leave the valley. Stay, and we'll talk. We'll negotiate. I'll let you talk to Martin."

"Joseph, there's no point."

"Then we'll find a way for you to endow the convent with the money."

"You're letting the world in. You don't want to do that."

"Robert, please."

"Goodbye, Mother Joseph. I won't ever forget you."

"Robert." Impulsively she put her arms around him. Kissed him. Then recoiled. "Oh my God. I'm sorry."

Robert walked off down the corridor; made straight for the entrance. There were heavy grey clouds over the valley. The Bedouins lowered him. He expected Joseph to follow him to the landing, to watch him go; but there was no sign of her.

He crossed back to camp. Charlotte was waiting. "Well?"

"Never mind."

"Robert, what happened?"

"She offered to negotiate the settlement of the will."

"You're joking. What changed her mind?"

"Christ knows. She's crazy, Charlotte. We should just go."

"Not if we can get the money, darling."

In her office Joseph took another long drink of wine. Went to the chapel, wanted to be alone and pray, but the nuns were still making their funeral prayers. She went instead to her kiln. Lit the fire, pumped the bellows. Made the little chamber into hell. On the mountain above, the fire vented, made the clouds glow red.

5

Early evening. There was a thin silver crescent moon. The sky was deep black; was pocked with stars. A desert breeze made the valley warm.

Robert and Charlotte sat out under the sky.

"This is a mistake. We should have gone." Robert watched the sinking moon.

"But you told me she might change her mind. Give us what we want."

"What *you* want."

"What whoever wants. We can win."

"No. I don't think I believe that. We've been here one night too many. No one can win anymore."

Unseen by either of them, Steve left his tent, made for the cliff. Climbed.

On the mountain a lion roared; moaned.

The lions were active, restless. The wind from the desert made them too hot. They prowled among the rocks. One of them, a female, was pregnant; was due to deliver. The cubs in her womb kicked again and again. It was this female that was moaning. She needed to deliver; needed to be alone. She walked uneasily across the mountain and came to the clearing where the ruined church sat. A stand of rocks sheltered her from the wind. She lay down, cushioned her head on a small stone and let her labor progress.

There were two cubs. She had to work, to force them out into the world, as if they had no real desire to come there. Then for a while she lay exhausted. The cubs mewled weakly. Their eyes were shut tight, they were blind, but they groped their way infallibly to their mother's breasts. Drank. When after a few moments she began to recover her strength, she gave them her attention. Licked them free of the blood that covered them; cleaned them of the thick, clinging waters of the womb.

Then something disturbed her. A bellowing sound, like a rush of air from somewhere, from nowhere. She inspected her cubs, made certain they were all right; then raised her head to see what it was.

From just beyond the ruin there came a light. Red light. Fire. It vented up through the mountain, billowed in the air, made the landscape crimson. The lioness, startled, watched it. It made her eyes glow. It mesmerized her.

Inside the mountain Mother Joseph pumped frantically her kiln, melted her glass; prayed as she worked. "Make them leave. O God, please make them leave." The glowing mass of glass pulsed on its blowpipe. She put her lips to the pipe; blew; rolled flat the glass. Then she took a small knife, made a cut across her left wrist, let the blood flow into the melted glass. The blood hissed, smoked, boiled. "Please, God, make them leave." She tore a strip of cloth from her habit and bound the cut with it. The cut throbbed, burned, but all her attention was on the melted glass. The fire billowed, roared; was hot enough, lively enough to keep burning even though she had stopped pumping it.

Steve climbed to the landing. Entered carefully. Everything was quiet. The nuns were still at their requiem vigil. He stole along the corridors to Martin's cell. She was on her pallet; stared at the door. "I knew you'd come."

"Didn't your mother tell you we were leaving today?"

"I knew better."

They kissed.

"Come with me. I want to go up to the old church."

"If Mother goes to the chapel, she'll miss me."

"I want you to come away with me."

"What? No one's ever left the convent."

"Be the first, then."

"Steve, I—"

"Sh. Not here." He looked around; looked out into the hall. "Please, let's go up and talk about it."

He took her hand and she followed. Along the burial corridor. At the far end there were new faces; masks of the dead nun. Then through the lightless chamber where the fish lived. Up the stairs

onto the mountaintop. There was the red glow from Joseph's fire.
It leapt twenty feet into the air; dissipated in a flow of sparks.

"What—?"

"Steve, there's no point to my going with you. We'll always be
together wherever we are."

"Don't be foolish."

"I mean it."

"You sound like a lover in a book."

"We were together before you ever came here."

"Stop it. We have to talk about this. I love you."

Mother Joseph felt weak. She had lost too much blood. She sat
down in a corner of the room and tried to recover herself. But it
was too hot; there was no air. She went to the observatory.
Breathed the fresh air from the valley. Saw the tents still there.
"No." She turned the telescope on them. She had to see them, had
to see Robert. But it was no use; she needed rest. She went to her
cell and lay down.

Midnight. The nuns in the chapel ended their praying. Returned
in silence to their cells. Joseph watched them as they filed past her
door. Martin. She wanted to see Martin, to talk with her, be with
her. She got up unsteadily; felt dizzy, but in a moment it passed.
Walked to Martin's cell. Saw it empty. "No! Oh my God, no!"

She went to the chapel, hoped the girl would still be there;
rushed back to her own cell. Got down on all fours. Reached
under her cot. The six pieces of glass were there. She unwrapped
them. Her fingers trembled as she handled them. Laid them out in
a row. Watched them glow. Then she took the largest of them, the
piece with Christ's blood in it, and went.

Martin's cell; still empty. The burial hall. The fish. The
ascending stairs.

The lioness watched them embrace. Her eyes glowed red.

"Martin!"

They were in each other's arms. They were half undressed.
They were making love. The flames from the mountain lit them,
made them electric.

"Martin!" She screamed her daughter's name. Held up the
blood glass.

"Oh my God!" Martin pulled free of Steve's arms. "No!"

Joseph advanced on her. "Martin, what have you done?"

"Mother, I'm sorry."

"You will never see evil again, Martin." She plunged the splinter of glass into the girl's eyes. Martin shrieked. Waved her arms. Fell.

"Good Christ!" Steve rushed on them, tried to catch hold of Joseph's arms. But she was too quick for him. The glass went into his throat. Blood sprayed the two women. Martin had not stopped wailing. Blind, in agony, she called out, "No! Not Steve!"

The lioness moved. Was hungry. She climbed onto a high rock and sprang. In an instant her jaws were at Steve's throat. She bit, crushed his windpipe. His struggles against her, against the pain, ended quickly. She took the body, dragged it back to her place in the rocks and began her first meal since giving birth. She would have nourishment for her cubs.

The fire died down. Sparks, tongues of flame licked the air, vanished. Mother Joseph watched the lioness go with her prey. Looked at Martin crying, sobbing on the ground. Froze. Felt the warm glass in her hand. "Sweet Jesus, no, not again." She saw the last glow of the fire disappear. Got down on her knees and touched her daughter's cheek. But Martin pushed her hand away; moaned hysterically.

Joseph stood and backed away from the scene. It was too horrible. She could not bear to see it. She held the blood glass out at arm's length; looked into its profound redness. That was the way. That was the way. She got down on her knees and whispered the Lord's name and pulled the glass across her own eyes, as she had across her daughter's. And mercifully, inevitably, the light went. The sound was all, Martin's crying and the soft mewling of the lion cubs.

The cries brought up the other nuns. Andrew, Peter, John came up out of the mountain's belly. They gaped at the scene. Peter went to Martin's side and knelt over her. She held out a hand but was uncertain whether to touch her.

"Please, Peter, hold me," Martin cried.

Peter took her in her arms. Kissed her. Held her. The others tended to Joseph.

6

There was only one tent pitched at the valley's mouth now. Robert slept. Dreamed. Tossed and turned on his cot.

Activity outside, noisy and insistent, woke him. He rubbed his eyes, sat up, yawned. Looked at his pillow. He wanted more sleep. But the commotion got worse. He got into his shorts, looked outside.

There was a caravan. Camels squawking, snorting, bellowing; there must have been a hundred of them. Their drivers dismounted; slapped the animals on their backsides. And one by one the camels, still carrying their loads, got clumsily to their feet and dashed up the valley to the watering place. They drank greedily. The drivers walked in a group to the Bedouin settlement, where, it seemed, they were known.

Robert followed them. He found Aoud among the crowd. "What's going on?"

"A caravan, Monsieur Semnarek."

"I can see that. What else do you know about them?"

"They are nomads. The caravan formed at Ifni, on the Atlantic coast."

"I see. Are they Bedouins?"

"No, monsieur."

Robert scowled at him. "Then who are they?"

"Desert nomads. Tefu, Tuareg, Moors . . . I do not really know much about them."

"I see. What language do they speak?"

"None that I am familiar with, monsieur. My cousins have told me what I know."

Robert looked at them. Their robes were black and heavy; they

271

seemed impossible for the desert. "Well." He could not quite decide what to make of the visitation. "Thank you, Aoud." He turned to go back to his tent.

"Monsieur Semnarek."

"Yes, Aoud?"

"We have been here for a long time now."

"Aoud, I know it."

"Madame Alderson has been staying in the convent for a long time now."

"Yes." He looked glumly up the mountain. "She won't come down."

"Has she given you any indication when she will wish to depart?"

"I'm afraid not. No."

"My family are in Marrakesh, as you know. I should not stay away from them for such a long time. They have no way of knowing where I am or what has become of me."

"I understand, Aoud. I am feeling . . . restless myself. I'll speak to Madame Alderson about it. I have asked repeatedly to meet with her, but she says she is too busy tending to her niece and her sister." Robert wanted to comment on the irony of it, but he restrained himself. "I'll send word again. Perhaps Mother Peter will have some influence with her."

"Thank you, monsieur."

One by one the camels came back down the valley and sought out their masters. They sat awkwardly down. The nomads relieved them of their packs and, despite the day's growing heat, the camels slept.

"Charlotte." He met her at the convent's entrance.

"Hello, Robert."

"How are you today?"

"Well, I suppose. And you?"

"Hot."

"You were made for Johnstown."

"No, I don't think so." He looked into the maze of corridors. "How are Joseph and Martin?"

"Still bandaged. Still in pain."

"You've been avoiding me."

"No."

"For a week now I've been sending word that I wanted to see you."

"I've been—"

"Charlotte, it's time for us to talk."

"Talk? What is there to talk about?"

"Please."

She sighed; did not want to do it. "Come to the observatory."

They walked.

"I still remember this place just after the rainfall." Robert watched the black-grey walls; kept a pace behind Charlotte. "There were flowers everywhere to relieve the gloom, the heaviness. The place seemed almost human then."

"It seems quite human to me the way it is."

"But it's so—" They were at the entrance to the observatory. They went in. A nun stood at the telescope. "Mother Peter. Good morning."

"Good morning, Robert." The nun smiled at him. "It looks like the valley has come alive."

"For a day or two, yes. I gather they won't be staying any longer than it takes for their camels to rest."

"Here, Charlotte." She moved away from the eyepiece. "Take a look."

She looked; turned quickly away from it.

"Well. Would the two of you like to be alone?"

"If you don't mind, please." Robert felt awkward. Watched her go. "Aoud is complaining, Charlotte."

"Let him."

"I'm not feeling exactly content myself."

"You're both being paid."

"It isn't a question of money. And please don't make one of your jokes about lawyers."

"No. Of course not." She was stiff. She looked down at the valley, at the camels.

"It's been more than a month, Charlotte. Aoud is worried about his family."

"And you?" She eyed him. "What are you worried about?"

"About . . . about you . . . and about . . ." He stammered. He rested a hand on the telescope's barrel. "You've had things to keep your mind busy. Nursing your sister and her daughter. But I . . ." He waved a hand in empty air; let the gesture speak for him.

"I've offered to lend you my Austen. It could occupy you for months."

"Since you moved up here I haven't even had anyone to talk to."

"Neither have I. To the nuns, I am an intruder in the cloister. My sister still flinches when I touch her. And Martin . . ."

"She raves like a madwoman. Yes, I know." He looked away from her; looked at the valley. "You can't possibly mean to stay here."

"We haven't settled the will."

"We're never going to. There are too many other wills in the way."

Charlotte walked close to the unglazed window; looked down as if she thought she might jump. "Whose wills exactly did you have in mind?"

He backed away from it. "I've offered time and again to go up and get Steve's bones for burial."

"It isn't that."

"Charlotte, I think it is. It is that, at least partly."

"No."

"You want to be here with him, where he died."

"No."

"Charlotte."

"All right then, yes, I want that. We were never close. You know that. We loved each other but we were never close. And it was my doing. I raised him to be arch and distant. My son the quarterback."

"You can't blame yourself for what he was."

She looked at him, astonished. "Of course I can. That's what death's for, to leave the survivors blaming themselves."

"The nuns can tend Martin and Joseph as well as you can."

"No, Robert, they can't. They don't have the blood for it."

"Living in these halls is getting to you. Affecting your mind."

"Joseph and Martin are the only family I have left. I always hoped Steve would give me grandchildren to love. But . . . but perhaps it is what you said. Perhaps there are too many other wills involved in life for any of us ever to be . . ." She looked around them, waved at the stone. "Here, I can simplify all that."

"You can't mean it."

"Robert, I can. I have already talked to Mother Peter about taking first vows."

There was nothing he could say to this. He sat down; looked at the floor.

"Did you ever know my husband?"

"No. I never did."

"He died of cancer. There was nothing for me to do but watch it. They gave him pills for the pain. The pills made him high, but pain still broke through. He was alternately giddy and in torment."

It was something he did not want to hear. "When did he die?"

"It's been years. And the senator went the same way. Perhaps cancer is in our blood, too, as well as madness."

"Hubert didn't have your blood."

"No. But I loved him. Perhaps it is in my love that the cancer comes."

"Stop it. Please."

"Joseph's bandages have to be changed every few hours. She seems unable to stop crying, and the bandages get soaked. God only knows how her eyes will heal." She stared at him; seemed uncertain what more to say. "I've handled the blood glass. Everything Joseph says about it in her memoir is true."

"No." Like her, he was on edge.

"Yes." She stepped back to the telescope, scanned the valley. "There are blue roses blooming. I've always loved blue roses. I have to stay here and tend my blood. Take the jeep and Aoud and go. I'll give you a power of attorney for my holdings, and you can do with them what you please."

"Charlotte—"

"Please, Robert, you can't dissuade me. Don't try."

"But—"

"Mother Peter asked me to ask you not to come back up here again. Joseph keeps asking for you. We want to tell her you've gone."

"Lie to her."

"Why, when we can make it true?"

Robert was disoriented. He walked to the edge of the room and looked straight down. Things spun, there was vertigo. He caught hold of the stone, steadied himself. Sat again. "Look, I can't just go back. There'll be questions. Inquiries. The law is too busy to simply . . . leave you here."

"Then let the law come get me, if it can."

"Charlotte, I want to bury Steve. Please. Let me go up to the church and find him."

"No."

"Please. I don't understand why you won't—"

"The lion got everything."

"There must be something left to bury."

"There's nothing. Not even a drop of blood."

"Christ, this is like *Antigone*."

"*Antigone*?" For the first time he had caught her off guard. "Why, on earth? Steve wasn't your brother. You're under no obligation to tend to his funeral."

"No. He wasn't. And I'm not. But . . . I . . ." He let his voice fall; there was no point to going on with it. He turned, moved to the door. "Never mind. Goodbye."

Charlotte walked him back to the lift. Neither of them spoke. Just as he was about to step into the basket he turned and looked at her. "What will be your name after you take your vows?"

"I don't know. I don't know. I haven't thought about it."

"I see. Well, goodbye then, Charlotte."

She took him by the shoulders, kissed his cheek. "Goodbye, Robert. I'll pray for you."

"Thank you." He whispered it. The basket began its descent. He looked up at her and said, at the bottom of his voice, "I would pray for you, too, if I could."

He sent a note that afternoon to Mother Peter. "Please give me your permission to visit the church on the mountaintop. I don't understand why you won't let Steve be buried. I want to bury him."

An hour later the reply came. "There is nothing to do. Please leave our valley as soon as you can. Peter."

Robert stared at the cliff, at the convent.

Nightfall. A bright quarter-moon lit the valley. Robert studied the cliff. He wished he had, after all, learned rock climbing with Steve. The cliff face was steep, jagged. It would be too dangerous. There had to be another way.

At the head of the valley the cliff was less high, less steep. He walked to the spring. Washed himself in its cool waters. Went past it to the point where the valley first separated from the mountains. It was a long walk. The moon went lower in the sky.

Then he was atop the cliff, walking along its rim. The moonlight made everything look unreal. A lion roared. But Robert had gone too far to turn back.

Another roar, from the other side of the valley. Robert walked. Reached at last the ruins. Looked around them by the ghostly light. The lioness, her cubs asleep at her bosom, watched him. The moon made her eyes into fiery gold. Robert stopped moving. Looked around. Saw her there, watching him. He did not move. Waited. But the lioness only watched.

There was a hollow sound, a faint echoing. Robert found the vent in the mountain where Joseph's fire emerged. It was pitch-black; looking down it made him dizzy in a way that looking down the cliff face had not. The cliff could kill him; this could swallow him up. He backed carefully away from it.

He looked around. There, by the altar. Part of a skull. Part of a rib cage. Clean; polished. The animals had done nature's work. Robert stooped and touched them. Picked the skull up. Asked himself, What if this is not Steve but Marty? Or one of the ones before him? He pressed the bone to his cheek, felt its smoothness. Scanned the ground. There were a few more fragments, a thighbone, part of a jaw. He gathered them up; took off his shirt and wrapped them in it; went back to the valley's head. As he walked past her place the lioness growled at him, a warning, and he quickened his step.

There at the head of the valley, among the begonias and the blue roses, he buried Steve's remains. Dug the moist earth with his hands. Interred the bones. Knelt and tried to pray, but the words would not come.

"Steve. I knew you'd come."

Martin lay on her pallet. Her eyes were heavily bandaged. To move her head was painful. But she saw Steve standing there in front of her, dressed as always in only his shorts.

"Come in."

"I wasn't sure I should come."

"You couldn't come until tonight, Steve. Do you . . . do you still love me?"

"What? Why shouldn't I?"

"What my mother did . . ."

"Martin, that was your mother."

"We have the same blood in us."

"Yes, I still love you." He crossed the room to her. Kissed gently her lips. "It's horrible to see you like this."

"The bandages will come off. The pain will pass."

"But your eyes . . ."

"I don't need eyes, Steve. I never did. You know that."

"But—"

"Sh. Kiss me."

Their lips met. He touched her breasts, rubbed his cheek on them.

"Not too hard, darling. I'm still sore."

"I'm sorry. I don't want to hurt you."

"It will pass. You and I will make love again soon, if it's what you want." She ran her hand along his side; touched his thigh.

"It's what I want." His hands stroked gently her breasts. For the third time in the black room, in the heart of the stone convent, he kissed her.

"Please, Steve, not tonight. It hurts too much."

"Can I come back again tomorrow night?"

"I'll be waiting."

"Don't tell anyone I was here. All right?"

"I couldn't tell them, Steven. They wouldn't understand."

And he was gone.

Martin smiled in the black room, knowing that she had once again seen the truth, had once more touched the face of God.

Sunrise. The camels bellowed. Their drivers loaded them, secured the packs. Robert watched them; looked from time to time out into the desert.

"Good morning, Monsieur Semnarek."

"Aoud." Robert did not take his eyes off the nomads. "Where are they going?"

"Into the desert." Aoud smiled; was pleased at his unhelpfulness.

"Where in the desert?" Robert refused to be annoyed. "What is their destination?"

"I do not know, monsieur. May I ask what was the outcome of your discussion with Madame Alderson?"

"There was none."

"No discussion? But I saw you—"

"No outcome."

"Oh." He became impassive, watched the caravan forming.

"You have cousins who can speak their language?"

"*Oui, monsieur.*"

"Have somebody ask them if I can go with them."

"I beg your pardon?" He did not try to conceal his astonishment.

"Why, Aoud, I've actually gotten a rise out of you."

"Monsieur Semnarek is joking."

"No. Monsieur Semnarek is perfectly serious. Have someone ask."

"But . . . but . . . but we have to take the jeep back to Marrakesh."

Robert reached into a pocket, tossed him the keys. "And you can have all of our cash. We won't be needing it anymore."

"But . . . but surely you must return to Johnstown, Pennsylvania."

"Why must I?"

"It is your home."

"Not anymore." Robert leaned casually against the jeep. "Will you please go and arrange for me to leave with these people?"

"Yes, monsieur." Puzzled, disapproving, Aoud went off to find his cousins. He vanished quickly amid the caravan's confusion.

Robert walked around the tent, around the jeep, looked at all the supplies, clothing, utensils. Poked among it all. In the jeep he found Charlotte's Jane Austen; he stuffed it into his own backpack. Not far from him a camel screamed, snapped at its owner. Robert looked; smiled at it. He wanted to find something of Steve's. There were his guns. But no. In one pack there was an uninflated football; but that was not really right, either. After a quarter hour of searching he had found nothing of Steve's that seemed appropriate for remembering him. Looked around the valley. Walked to the base of the cliff. It took a while to find them but there among some rocks were the shattered fragments of

Mother Joseph's leaded-glass box. Robert took a piece of the glass, wrapped it carefully in a strip of linen; packed it away next to the book.

"No one understands why you wish to do this, monsieur." Aoud's disapproval showed even more clearly. "The nomads think you are mad."

"They will not have me, then?" Robert frowned.

"On the contrary, monsieur. They can hardly refuse the request of a madman. It would be sacrilegious. But they do not really want you with them."

"That doesn't matter. They'll get used to me."

"You do not even speak their language."

"I can learn."

"But—"

"Aoud, I am going. I'll be taking only this one pack with me. Everything else is yours."

"The caravan is going into the Tanezrouft."

"The—?" He stopped; blinked; for the first time seemed unsure what to do. "What is that?"

"The Tanezrouft. 'The place of thirst.' It is the heart of the desert. It is the deadest place in the world."

Robert glanced at the green head of the valley. "That is what I want, then."

"But—" It was too much. "But what shall I tell people? What shall I tell the legal authorities?"

"I don't know. The law doesn't concern me much now. Surely out of all our money you can arrange a suitable baksheesh and have the whole thing forgotten."

"I see." He was deflated. "Well. I suppose I must say goodbye, then."

"Goodbye, Aoud." Robert extended his hand.

Aoud looked at it as if he were unsure whether to touch it; as if whatever Robert had might be contagious. Hesitantly took it; shook. "*Ma' as-salâma.*"

Out of the throng of people a nomad, dressed in desert black, came toward them, pulling behind him a reluctant camel. The man shouted something unintelligible at Robert; waved his hand excitedly.

"I take it this is my mount?"

Aoud shrugged. "*Inshallah.*"

The nomad made the camel sit and Robert climbed nervously onto its back. Then it stood with a rough jerk and Robert nearly fell off; he held frantically on to the saddle. Steadied himself. Aoud and the nomad watched with faces of granite. But he was too busy trying to keep his balance to notice.

The caravan started outward. The camels formed themselves into a single line, followed their leader, progressed into the ocean of sand. Robert was tempted to look back for a last glimpse of the valley; forced himself not to do it. "No, Robert, don't look. You'd turn into a pillar of salt."

A boy on a young camel rode past and shouted something at him. Robert smiled, waved at him, hoped it was the right thing to do. "Hello."

The boy laughed at him; rode on.

Hours passed. The desert opened out before them; the desert seemed to stretch to the end of the world. They climbed to the top of an enormous dune, and there before them was another one to climb. The camel's gait became regular, comfortable, reassuring. There was nothing in the world now but the caravan, the people with whom he could not speak. The sand was a profound red, red as blood. He watched the sun glisten on it; tried to convince himself that each grain of it was not a particle of God. To believe that would have spoiled everything.